The ...

"An entirely different look to the wonderful Twain mysteries . . . Peter Heck introduces readers to the Twain family . . . provid[ing] an incredible degree of freshness to the story line . . . pleasurable . . . an enjoyable historical mystery that will garner him new fans as well as receiving accolades from old readers too." —*Midwest Book Reviews*

The Prince and the Prosecutor

"Meaty fare for fans of the quasi-historical with nicely done period detail and atmosphere." —*Kirkus Reviews*

"Very entertaining." —*Library Journal*

A Connecticut Yankee in Criminal Court

"An enjoyable tour of 1890's New Orleans . . . Twain can take a bow for his performance. Heck takes a colorful city (New Orleans) and a colorful character (Mark Twain), adds a murder, a duel, some voodoo, and period detail, and conjures up an entertaining sequel to *Death on the Mississippi*." —*Publishers Weekly*

"A period charmer . . . Against the background of this famous city with its colorful mix of characters, cultures, food, music, and religion, the famous author and his loyal sidekick worm their way into the heart of a scandalous murder." —*Alfred Hitchcock's Mystery Magazine*

continued . . .   MYSTERY

"Packed with casual racists, unregenerate Civil War veterans, superstitious rationalists, and poseurs of every stripe—exactly the sort of colorful cast that brings its satiric hero's famous talent for unmasking pretension into brilliant relief."
—*Kirkus Reviews*

"This Crescent City mystery simmers."   —*Booklist*

Death on the Mississippi

"Lovers of historical mysteries should rush out for a copy of *Death on the Mississippi*, the delightfully droll debut of Wentworth Cabot, newly hired secretary to the celebrated author Mark Twain. Twain lights up the pages as he gives his lectures, mourns his impecunious state with disarming honesty, tells a fantastic tale of hidden gold to his young clerk, and generally suffers fools none too gladly. Cabot is alternately dismayed, baffled, and awestruck by his new boss's behavior as they set out on a riverboat lecture series in the company of a New York cop, and, most probably, the killer the cop seeks. There's a good plot, a bevy of suspects, lots of Twain lore, and even a travelogue of life on the Mississippi in the 1890's. *Death on the Mississippi* is thoroughly entertaining."
—*Alfred Hitchcock's Mystery Magazine*

"Adventurous . . . Replete with genuine tall tales from the great man himself."
—*Mostly Murder*

"Exciting . . . deftly dovetails flavorsome riverboat lore, unobtrusive period detail, and a hidden treasure with an intricate mystery—all to give peppery, lovable Sam Clemens a starring role in a case worthy of the old inimitable."
—*Kirkus Reviews*

"A well-done historical. This catchy adventure features a treasure hunt and showcases Clemens's knowledge of the river as well as his legendary gift of gab . . . Recommended."
—*Library Journal*

"A thoroughly enjoyable period mystery with Clemens and Cabot forming an uneasy alliance that possesses elements of Holmes and Watson as well as Wolfe and Archie. A very pleasant debut that will have readers eagerly awaiting the next entry."
—*Booklist*

The Mysterious Strangler

A Mark Twain Mystery

Peter J. Heck

BERKLEY PRIME CRIME, NEW YORK

THE MYSTERIOUS STRANGLER

A Berkley Prime Crime Book / published by arrangement with the author

PRINTING HISTORY
Berkley Prime Crime edition / October 2000

The Penguin Putnam Inc. World Wide Web site address is
http://www.penguinputnam.com

ISBN: 0-425-17704-1

Berkley Prime Crime Books are published
by The Berkley Publishing Group,
a division of Penguin Putnam Inc.,
375 Hudson Street, New York, New York 10014.
The name BERKLEY PRIME CRIME and the BERKLEY PRIME CRIME
design are trademarks belonging to Penguin Putnam Inc.

PRINTED IN THE UNITED STATES OF AMERICA

10 9 8 7 6 5 4 3 2 1

Acknowledgments and Historical Note

Mark Twain had a remarkably varied career, from steamboat pilot to silver miner to newspaperman to lecturer to publisher—to mention just a few of the highlights. But at no point did he set up as a detective. The events (and most of the people and many of the places) I describe in this book are created for the purpose of telling an entertaining story. Still, there is a kernel of historical fact behind my fabrications, and readers may desire a general notion of which is which.

Mark Twain's extensive travels took him to Florence more than once, beginning with his visit as one of the *Quaker City* pilgrims and culminating in stays there in the 1890's and early 1900's. I have housed the Clemens family in Villa Viviani, where they lived at about the time of this narrative, and where the author worked on *Joan of Arc* and *Pudd'nhead Wilson*. While I make use of several other authentic Florentine landmarks—Palazzo Pitti and the Protestant Cemetery—most of the specific locales of this story are invented, even Cafe Diabelli. And, except for Mr. Clemens and his family, all characters here are fictional— although a few (for instance the German maid) had real-life counterparts.

In the nineteenth century, as now, Florence was one of the centers of the trade in fine arts, including an extensive trade in forgeries and frauds. Raphael (1483–1520), who had a studio in Florence in the early sixteenth century, was especially admired by Victorian art critics and collectors— and therefore his work, more than any other artist's, was copied and counterfeited. Given Mr. Clemens's own strong (and often heretical) opinions on the old masters, and my narrator Wentworth's strong interest in the arts, a newly discovered Raphael seemed an appropriate subject around which to build a Florentine mystery.

As usual, I have taken the liberty of sprinkling the text with quips and anecdotes borrowed from Mark Twain's own writings and sayings; Twain aficionados will recognize many of them. I have also inserted a few playful allusions to the various incarnations of *The Mysterious Strangler*, one of Twain's last and most problematical works, from which I have borrowed the title of this one. I have stretched out my borrowings with my own inventions and pastiches, which I hope are in the proper spirit.

As always, my debts to Twain scholars are too numerous to list; the Mark Twain listserv has been an especially rich resource, for which anyone doing Twain research must be grateful. I have been steered toward useful bits of Twain-iana from time to time by various friends, among them Trina King and David Honigsberg—to whom my thanks. And from my recently rediscovered cousin, Cliff Jewell, a professional actor and acting teacher who does a fine Mark Twain impersonation, I cribbed a nice bit of stage business after seeing a tape of one of his performances. (There must be something to this heredity business, after all.)

Special thanks are due my wife, Jane Jewell, who has dedicated long hours to the reading and critiquing of this manuscript. I have benefited from her help at every turn. It should go without saying that any remaining errors of fact or other shortcomings of style or execution are strictly my own responsibility.

To Paul, Ken, Bob, Jack, Marco
—and in memory of Gerry:
fellow explorers of the 64-square microcosm.

1

Cafe Diabelli was the finest place in all of Florence—
or so it seemed on that sunny winter day in 189—,
when I first happened upon it.

I had come to Florence with my employer, Mr. Samuel
L. Clemens, after a lecture tour in England. He had declared
himself surfeited with rain and fog and cold, and almost
the instant he had spoken the final syllable of his last scheduled lecture, had begun to pack for a warmer climate. So
he and his family—and I, Wentworth Cabot, his secretary—
found ourselves in sunny Italy. After my first day in the
southern sun, I don't think John D. Rockefeller could have
paid me enough to go back to an English winter.

Mr. Clemens had found a villa in Settignano, about five
miles east of Florence. Fortresslike Villa Viviani had been
rebuilt and refurbished several times in its long life, but the
foundations were said to date back to the thirteenth century.
And its view of Florence and the hills to the west was
enthralling—set off by a sky so clear and blue that it made
me feel as if my eyesight had improved. No wonder this
country had nurtured so many eminent painters and sculp-
tors!

From the moment I heard we would be wintering near

Florence, I vowed to seize every opportunity to see the profusion of art that city offers. I spent many spare hours planning trips to the various galleries. I doubt any general laid more extensive plans for an invasion than I did for my stay in Florence—unless my Baedeker neglected to mention it, I doubt there was any part of the city I left out of my plans.

Knowing my interest in art, Mr. Clemens released me from my normal duties until the household was set up. "Go on and gawk at the pictures," he said. "You'll get your fill of 'em soon enough. I'll get plenty of writing done without you in the daytime, and you can catch up with your part of things after supper." That struck me as a fair proposition, and I took advantage of it without hesitation.

I had spent my first morning in the city dazzled by the sheer number of paintings that could be crammed into a single gallery—and I began to understand Mr. Clemens's offhand remark: "The best stuff is often hard to find." The curators seemed to have taken perverse delight in hanging the pictures one was most anxious to see in obscure and ill-lit crannies. So it was with a mixture of awe and frustration that I gave heed to the call of my stomach, and went looking for someplace to eat—and stumbled upon Cafe Diabelli.

Cafe Diabelli was unassuming from the outside, but the aroma of good food wafted out to the street and drew me in before I knew it. I went up a couple of steps to a double door, entered, and found myself in a large room full of laughter and animated conversation. In one corner, by a bay window, was a baldheaded fellow with a round belly, a full beard, and the sort of profile one sees on ancient coins. The table in front of him had a stack of manuscripts on it, and around him were gathered a group whose clothes bespoke a bohemian lifestyle. He was pontificating upon some point, jabbing the air with a finger, and heads around him nodded as if hearing grave words of wisdom.

Across the room was the chess players' corner. As I entered, two young Italians were carrying on a fierce battle, while a couple of spectators stared at the action. One player was a short and stout dark-haired fellow, his opponent tall and blond with a thin countenance—opposites in every physical particular, like the black and white pieces of their wooden armies. Even as I glanced over at the scene, the blond fellow made a move, capturing a pawn, and the watchers murmured as his opponent scowled at the new position.

Then my attention was drawn to the terrace, visible through a wide archway ahead of me. This seemed a pleasant place to sit and have a meal, and any indecision I may have had evaporated when I heard a voice with an accent that would not have raised an eyebrow in Back Bay. "Eddie, old man, isn't it about time you bought a round? A fellow could die of thirst waiting for you to finish that drink."

A burst of laughter followed this remark, and as I stepped out onto the terrace I saw them: a group of young men and women, mostly my age, sitting around two tables pushed together, sipping wine or coffee. While I was not so bold as to intrude upon a group of strangers (fellow Americans or not), the light and open air were enticing. I sat at a table a little distance away from them, with a good view of the street just below, with the river Arno down the hill.

After a brief wait, a short man with a fringe of curly dark hair around his balding pate and a large black mustache came over to my table. "*Ciao, signore,*" he said. "*Cosa prendete?*"

"*Buongiorno, signore,*" I said, pronouncing the words carefully. "*Non parlo Italiano.* Do you speak English?" Having nearly exhausted my stock of useful phrases in the local language, I hoped my last question would not be answered in the negative. I had been making efforts, with the help of a book aimed at travelers, to gain some useful knowledge of Italian, but Mr. Clemens's daughters were already far ahead of me. And, as I had by this time discovered, many Italians knew English, although by no means all of them.

"Yes, of course, *signore*," he said, with a broad smile. "I speak the very good English. What would you like today?" His accent was quite good, I thought, though a bit closer to the British than to the American. Working in a place with many English-speaking customers, he had both the opportunity and the incentive to improve his command of our language.

I ordered red wine and, at the waiter's suggestion, a plate of noodles with tomato sauce and sausage, all of which went by some much more exotic-sounding Italian names. Even in the few days we had been in Italy, I had learned to appreciate the local cooks' ability to create subtle and tasty variations among these basic ingredients. The waiter soon returned with the wine, in a quaint little straw-covered flask, and filled a glass for me. I tasted it—a tangy, somewhat acidic red—and nodded my approval. He smiled again and left to attend to his other tasks, while I turned to watch the street scene.

The American tourist may find his first sight of an Italian city street as strange and colorful as something out of the *Thousand and One Nights*. Nothing one sees in New York or even New Orleans could prepare him for the distinctions of dress and the extravagance of gesture one sees in an Italian city. Mr. Clemens used to declare that an Italian will say more with his hands in thirty seconds than a New Englander says with his voice in a couple of weeks. Perhaps he exaggerated—but not by much.

That was nothing compared to the contrast between American and Italian dress! Here, it looked as if everyone were going to a masquerade. Red, yellow, green, blue, violet—every color of the rainbow swirled through the streets. Only the black that seemed to be the prescribed color for old women and for the numerous stern-faced Catholic priests was in accord with my previous image (based wholly on history books) of Florence as a staid and sober city given to the pursuit of commerce and the arts—a sort of Italian Boston. Instead, every station in life seemed to have its distinctive uniform, from the respectable merchants right down to the outrageous ragamuffins who besieged every passerby with the incessant demand for alms.

Just as I was about to lose myself in the scene, a voice

nearby said, "You want to buy *fotografia, signore*?"

I turned to see a thin, greasy-haired fellow leering up at me from the street below, waving a print of Michelangelo's famous statue of David in one hand. It wasn't a bad picture, although it lacked the majesty of the original—which I had already inspected in person. "No, thank you," I said. "I am not interested."

"I have-a plenty more *fotografia, signore*," he said, with a thick accent. He held up several more samples, all of statuary or buildings—some of which I recognized, though many were of unfamiliar subjects. "Here, see! I give-a you very good price, *signore*."

"No, I am not interested," I insisted. "I have no money to buy photographs."

"Ah, you have-a the money to buy the wine, and that will be gone in an hour. These are very fine *fotografia, signore*," he said. "I take-a them all myself, and I give-a you my best-a price."

"His best price will be outright robbery," said another voice at my elbow, a voice with an American accent. I turned to see a smiling woman of about my own age standing by my little table, her hand resting on the other chair. "Don't buy anything from these rascals, unless you have money to throw away."

"*Signore . . .*" the photograph-vendor began, but the young woman cut him off.

"*Caro signore, sei noioso,*" she told him with considerable heat, and in what sounded to my ears like an excellent accent. "*Va a Napoli!*"

The fellow flushed, and I thought he was about to answer her, but then the waiter reappeared, carrying a tray. The photograph-seller contented himself with a scowl and a gesture—a flick of his thumb against his upper teeth—that even I could recognize as rude. I stood up, ready to make him apologize, but he beat a hasty retreat, no doubt to harass some other tourist. The waiter sent a long hard stare after him, then shrugged and placed my food on the table. I nodded my thanks to him and he departed; then I turned to my rescuer.

"Thank you, miss," I said. "That fellow was beginning to be a nuisance."

"Yes, that's more or less what I told him," she said, smiling. Her hair was strawberry-blond, and her eyes light blue—a color echoed in her dress. "These photographers are as thick as mosquitos," she continued, "and just as hungry. This place doesn't usually let them pester customers, though—you saw how he scurried off when Pietro came. He only tried to sell to you because he saw you were new here."

"And you are evidently not," I said, standing and removing my hat. "Thank you again, Miss . . . I'm afraid I don't know your name."

"Virginia Fleetwood, of Greenwich, Connecticut," she said, with a little laugh. "I suppose it is most improper for me to introduce myself to a strange man in a cafe, but the customs here aren't quite the same as at home. Besides, I couldn't let a fellow American be taken advantage of, so I suppose it's all right. And you are?"

"Wentworth Cabot," I said, bowing. "I'm a Connecticut man myself, from New London—and Yale College. So we are in a sense neighbors. A great pleasure to make your acquaintance—and again, I am in your debt, Miss Fleetwood."

"Think nothing of it, Mr. Cabot," she said, but she smiled as if pleased at my thanks. Her eyes met mine, and she asked, "Have you been in Florence very long?"

"Not at all," I said. "My employer and I arrived a little while ago, but he means to spend the winter here, he and his family."

"Ah, then perhaps we shall see each other again," she said. "My sister and I—and her husband, Mr. Stephens—expect to be here for some time to come. But I am keeping you from your luncheon. A pleasure meeting you, Mr. Cabot!"

"Very much my pleasure," I replied, making another little bow to her. She smiled again, looking back over her shoulder at me as she returned to her friends. For myself, I tackled my luncheon, which was excellent—during my travels with Mr. Clemens I had come to appreciate spicier cooking than I'd gotten at home. The sausage was a special treat—the best I'd had since leaving America (especially compared to what passed for sausage in British kitchens). As I ate, I couldn't help but overhear conversation from the nearby table occupied by Miss Fleetwood and her friends. Several of them apparently were art students, and the man with the Boston accent (whom I took to be the brother-in-law she had mentioned) seemed to be an art dealer. After a while, the group got up and left in a body, Miss Fleetwood turning and waving cheerily to me as she went.

The waiter came by again, noticing my clean platter and half-empty wineglass. "*Signore*, do you need anything more? The wine, is it good?"

"Yes, *grazie*, Pietro, it is very good," I said. I was glad Miss Fleetwood had mentioned the waiter's name—I had discovered from watching my employer that learning and using the names of people one meets is a quick way to make friends when one is visiting a place for the first time. I looked at the empty flask, considered a moment, and said, "I think I will have a coffee—and the reckoning, please."

"*Si, signore,*" said the waiter. He cleared the table and bustled off. A short while later he was back with the coffee.

"Ah, thank you, Pietro," I said. Then, curious about the establishment I found myself in, I added, "This is a very nice cafe to be named after Old Scratch."

He looked puzzled. "Scratch, *signore*? I do not know the name."

"Oh, that's our name for him in New England," I said, remembering that our American slang might not be current here in Italy. "The devil, I mean—that is what *Cafe Diabelli* means, is it not?"

"Oh, no, no," he said, laughing. "We call the evil one *diavolo*, not diabelli. This place takes its name for the man who start it, long time ago—*Signore* Diabelli, a very nice man. He wanted to make this a place where artists and scholars and musicians come to eat and talk. And so you see—your English friends here, all artists. Inside, full of poets, critics, chess players. Best place in town for talk and argument."

"Well, the food is first-rate, too," I said, patting my belly. "And this coffee is excellent. Give *Signore* Diabelli my compliments."

"Thank you," said Pietro, nodding, "but *Signore* Diabelli sell the place, oh, maybe fifteen years ago. *Signore* Negri, the new owner, he keep the old name because everybody knows it. Any artist or writer, anywhere in Europa, they come to Firenze, they come to Cafe Diabelli."

"Well, I will come again myself," I said. "The food is very fine, and I like the people I've met. Tell *Signore* Negri that he has a fine establishment, and I mean to tell my employer to stop here when he comes into town."

"Ah, your employer is the artist?" said Pietro.

"No, a writer," I said. "He is well known in America, but I don't know if his works have been translated into Italian yet. He writes under the name Mark Twain."

Pietro's smile remained on his face, but there was a harder expression around his eyes. "Yes, we have heard of your Mark Twain in Firenze—everybody here knows about his book. I am surprised he has come back."

"Well, he has come back," I said, somewhat on my guard now. I did not know what Mr. Clemens had said about Florence in his books, but the waiter's reaction gave me the impression that it had not been favorable. Mr. Clemens was rarely diplomatic in expressing his opinions. So I smiled at Pietro and said, "I will tell him about the food in Cafe Diabelli—I have no doubt he will like it, and the atmosphere, a great deal. It is one of the best places I have found in my travels."

I meant every word of it. I later had ample opportunity to wonder whether I'd have been happier if I'd walked right past Cafe Diabelli and never set foot inside the place. It probably would not have changed what happened afterwards, but perhaps it would not have changed me quite so much, either.

2

Mr. Clemens did not express great enthusiasm about visiting Cafe Diabelli. This reaction should not have surprised me. "Well, I'm glad you found a place you enjoy," he told me, after I had described the cafe to him at the dinner table. "I suppose I'll find the time to stick my nose in there, sooner or later—but my guess is it'll be later. I've got a couple of books going great guns, and plenty of other work to keep me here." He said this in a tone that reminded me that I, too, was in Florence to work—and that my days in the city would have to be paid for by evenings with my nose to the grindstone, tending to my employer's accumulated paperwork.

"I thought it would be an interesting place for you to meet the local writers, who I understand make it a regular meeting place," I said, between bites of dinner—an excellent chicken baked in a spicy tomato sauce and served with rice, made by our Italian chef, who was beginning to prove himself a treasure.

"It might be, if I were a young fellow just making my way in the world," said Mr. Clemens, wiping the sauce off his mustache with a napkin. "Nowadays, if I walk into a place like that, everybody knows it within three minutes, and I've got about as much chance of a normal conversation as I do of flying to the moon. Less, in fact—if you believe Jules Verne, I have some chance of getting to the moon, if I don't mind being shot out of a cannon." He leaned back in his chair and took another sip of wine.

"I'm sure there are lots of people who'd like to see you shot out of a cannon," said his daughter Clara. "Especially some of the other writers." Clara was somewhat younger than I, and would be the last person on earth to show proper deference to her father's fame and accomplishments.

"You see what I mean, Wentworth?" said Mr. Clemens, with a lugubrious expression. I think he took as much pleasure in pretending to be injured by his daughter's "sass" as she did in inventing gibes. "I can't get any respect from my own flesh and blood. What kind of treatment can I expect from a pack of hungry writers in some local cafe? Odds are, the minute I step through the door, they'll all start trying to prove they're quicker-witted than the famous foreigner, and kill everybody in the place with boredom. The most humane thing I can do is to stay home, so as not to expose them to the temptation." Both the younger girls giggled at this comeback, and my employer reached for a second—or was it a third?—helping of chicken.

"It also spares you facing the possibility that someone there might be wittier than you are," said Clara, after a moment. "Let alone the effort of learning Italian, so as to meet them on equal ground." Jean, at age fourteen the youngest sister, gasped at this audacious reply, and elbowed Clara, who smirked at having gotten off this sally at their famous father.

"Young Miss Sass-pot, I'll have you know I speak Italian perfectly," said Mr. Clemens—a statement I found incredible, not having heard him get through even one sentence in that language without resorting to English or German—or wild gesticulations—to supply his deficiency in vocabulary.

All three of his children were taken aback by this bald assertion, but it was little Jean who took up the challenge, saying, *"Scommetto que tu no capisce que dico."*

Mr. Clemens would not rise to such obvious bait. "Now, there you go, trying to catch me out," he said, rolling his eyes. "You'd lose that bet, young lady. Shame on you, not trusting your poor old father. Why, I'll have you know I visited Italy before you were born—before I even met your dear mother . . ."

"I remember when you came back from that trip, Youth, and I don't believe you've changed one bit," said Mrs. Clemens, smiling fondly at her husband and addressing him by his pet name. Then, before he could spot her twinkling eyes and guess her intention, she added, "You didn't speak a word of Italian back then, and you still don't." She winked at her three daughters, who erupted in gales of laughter.

Mr. Clemens had just taken a sip of wine, and it says a great deal for his self-control that, while his face turned red, he managed to swallow that wine without a single sputter. At last, he looked around the table and said, "I can see I'm outnumbered." He pushed his chair back and rose from the table. "Livy, by your leave." His wife nodded cordially, still smiling, as he folded his napkin and placed it by his plate. Then he turned to me and said, "Wentworth, let's go up to the office and get some work done. At least I can hope you haven't been studying up your Italian on purpose to make your boss look bad."

"Sir, I fear that languages are not my strong suit," I replied, quite truthfully, as I pushed back my own chair. "One could best characterize my command of Italian as rudimentary." I smiled ruefully. The two younger children giggled again, and nodded their heads. They had tried to help me with my lessons, and knew too well that I was speaking the truth.

"Well, don't let it prey on your mind," said Mr. Clemens. "Just watch out for the grammar—that's the very devil of this language business, in my experience. Just when you think you've got your mind wrapped around a sentence, the grammar up and runs away from you, and then you find yourself holding just an empty clause or two, with a few useless words scattered nearby. But Italian's not so bad—

not compared to German. Between you and me, maybe we can knock it down and make it say Uncle."

"I hope so, sir," I said, conscious of the three Clemens girls' superior grins. I was nowhere near as confident as he.

As usual while traveling, I had made arrangements to have Mr. Clemens's mail forwarded, but as yet deliveries had not begun. Until they did, there would be less work than usual for me. We spent an hour or so after dinner on a few letters to his publishers in New York and London, and on other business matters. Then my employer sat down to write a long letter about our new domicile to friends in Elmira, New York, where he had once lived. I finished up my own paperwork, and went to bed at a sensible hour. The next morning, I was up early, and after a light breakfast, on my way into Florence for another visit to the museums—and Cafe Diabelli.

Villa Viviani was perhaps five miles from Florence itself, not a difficult walk in good weather, but far enough to stretch the legs. The Baedeker mentioned a tramway somewhere in our suburb, with cars into town every half-hour or so, but I hadn't yet found the stop. I didn't think it necessary to enlist Mr. Clemens's driver to take me into town; he would be needed if Mrs. Clemens (whose heart was weak) needed to go someplace. I was young and healthy, and had the time to spare—even though I would rather have had extra time to spend in the Uffizi galleries, my destination today, than to wear out my shoe leather between Settignano and the city.

These ideas were swirling through my head when I stepped into the mouth of a narrow side street and was nearly bowled over by a bicycle rushing out between the buildings. I leapt back with a shout, but the cyclist pedaled onward, waving a fist with two fingers extended and bawling something I probably could not have understood even had it been in English. I could guess the overall thrust of it, though. My first reaction was fury; then I thought to myself, *There's the perfect way to get around town.* I would have to find out what bicycles cost here in Florence . . .

These thoughts occupied me until my feet brought me to Palazzo degli Uffizi, where I spent an enthralled morning sampling the treasures of Florentine art. But my attention was drawn away from the masterpieces of Fra Angelico and Botticelli by mounting hunger—in my haste to get into town and view the galleries, I had taken only a light breakfast. So when I became apprehensive that the growls of my stomach might distract my fellow art lovers from enjoying the paintings, I made my way outside and went looking for luncheon.

At first I intended to try a new place, but during my hours indoors, the sky had clouded over and it had begun to drizzle. Thus, when the rain began to fall harder just as I found myself passing the open door of Cafe Diabelli, I said to myself *Why not?* and stepped inside again.

The rain had driven indoors those patrons who normally frequented the terrace, and the glass doors leading outside were closed. This made the place seem smaller, noisier, and more crowded—although in fact, there were no more customers than on my previous visit. But the overall effect was to make it more attractive, not less—the smell of good food and coffee was more concentrated, as was the buzz of conversation.

I paused just inside the door to scan the room for an empty table. There was another chess match underway at the tables to my left; this time the fair-haired player I had seen on my previous visit was an onlooker as his former opponent sat opposite a man in round-rimmed glasses who frowned owlishly at the position on the board. In another corner, the large bearded man again held court, with his stack of manuscripts and his circle of disciples. And at a table—rather, two tables pushed together—just inside the terrace doors, sat the young woman I had met yesterday, Virginia Fleetwood, with a group of companions.

Miss Fleetwood glanced my way and smiled, then leaned over and said something to the man sitting next to her. He looked up at me, then rose from his seat and approached me. "Hello, my name's Frank Stephens," he said in an accent that marked him as a Bostonian. He was a good-looking fellow, with smooth dark hair and an aristocratic profile—slim and energetic at perhaps thirty-five years old. I could imagine him on a tennis court, or sculling down the Charles.

I told him my name and we shook hands. He gestured toward his table and continued: "There's a whole crowd of Americans over here, and my sister-in-law, Miss Fleetwood, thought you'd like to join us for lunch. We've just ordered, so if you come on over and tell Pietro what you want, we can all eat together."

"Thank you," I said. "If it won't be an imposition on you or your friends, I would be delighted," I added, bowing again. Here was a stroke of luck—a group of Americans wintering in Florence. As much as I enjoyed spending time with Mr. Clemens and his family, he and his wife were of an older generation, and had more in common with my parents than with myself. I found it hard to relax in their presence. Even with his daughters, who were near to my own age, I felt an inevitable distance—as one ought to with the family of one's employer.

I followed Stephens back to the table. Virginia Fleetwood I had already met, of course. "Hello, Mr. Cabot," she said. "How pleasant to see you here again. I hope you're enjoying your stay in Florence."

"Very much so far, thank you," I said. "I'm doing my best to see the city before I have to go to work, which I fear will be soon enough. My employer has just moved into Villa Viviani, east of town, and he's given me a bit of free time until he gets settled in."

"Ah, that's always the way of things, isn't it?" said Stephens with a wry grin, pointing to a vacant chair at the next table. I appropriated it and sat down as he continued: "I'm here as much on business as pleasure myself, though I can't say my work is all that oppressive—buying art and antiques for a few clients back home. At least, when I walk around the galleries, I can tell myself I'm earning my keep. But here comes Pietro—why don't you tell him what you want?"

I ordered luncheon, a soup with chicken and rice that the

waiter recommended. Then Frank Stephens introduced me to the rest of the party. Bob Danvers and Eddie Freeman were Americans, two big fellows who could have been football players gone to seed, both somewhat tipsy despite the early hour. Jonathan Wilson was an Englishman, perhaps forty years old, and an avid art collector. There were two Englishwomen, as well: Penelope Atwater, the middle-aged widow of a British Army officer, and her boarder, Sarah Woods, a plump young woman with a comically serious expression. Miss Woods and Eddie Freeman were both art students, and their easels and paint boxes were stacked against the wall next to the table. Danvers appeared to have no fixed occupation—I sized him up for the vagabond son of a well-to-do family, a sort I'd seen before. Indeed, I reflected, except for my employment with Mr. Clemens, there were some who might with justification apply that description to me.

I started to order some wine for myself, but Stephens said, "Don't be silly, old fellow—have some of ours. There's plenty here, and you can buy the next bottle, if you want." He picked up a large, straight-sided bottle from the table—it looked like a claret bottle—and filled my glass.

I saluted him with the glass, and ventured a sip, then nodded in appreciation. "This is the same sort of wine I had yesterday, but quite a bit better," I said.

"Yes, I'd think so," said Stephens. "They don't put the good stuff in those straw *fiascos* I saw on your table—those are all right for picnics, where you can wet the straw in a stream and keep the bottle cool, but Chianti *classico* comes in these regular bottles. Pietro wouldn't have brought you that other stuff if he'd thought you could tell the difference."

"I suppose that's the disadvantage of being a tourist," I said. "I'm lucky to have fallen in with your crowd, I guess. Yesterday, Miss Fleetwood saved me from the picture huckster, and now you've shown me how to spot the good wine from the ordinary stuff. I suppose I'd have sorted it all out for myself by springtime, but you've saved me a winter's trouble." I grinned at the group and at my luck at finding good company and good food. It might be a very pleasant winter, after all.

"You'll save yourself even more trouble if you can learn to speak the lingo," said Bob Danvers, filling his own glass. "If you tell one of these fellows, *sei cafone bandito*, he'll know he can't cheat you."

"*Cafone bandito . . .*" I repeated. "What does it mean?"

"It means that someone is a vulgar thief," said Mrs. Atwater with a disapproving expression. "Perhaps Mr. Danvers finds it useful to go about insulting people, but if I were you I might choose a more refined instructor in the language. To begin with, his accent is deplorable."

Everyone laughed, and Danvers shrugged. "I'm never going to get work as an Italian tutor like you, but I know how to get what I want, and that's all that matters to me."

"Bob has a point, but so does Mrs. Atwater," said Frank Stephens. "Speaking even a little bit of Italian is fine—the locals always like that—but it's even better if you speak it with the right accent. Then you can go anywhere and say anything."

"I fear I'll never reach that state," I admitted. "They don't understand me when I tell them I *can't* speak their language, which you'd think would be the next thing to self-explanatory."

"What you want is a good instructor," said Mrs. Atwater, with an air of confidence. "It makes a world of difference, hearing someone pronounce things correctly, and repeating them until you learn them."

"I suppose it does," I agreed, twirling my wineglass. Mrs. Atwater had leaned forward, fixing me with an eager gaze, perhaps expecting me to engage her services as a tutor. I hastened to add, "Mr. Clemens has gotten someone to help his daughters with the language, and they seem to be coming along quite well. But I fear my work will take up too much time to let me get much practice."

"Mr. Clemens . . ." mused Virginia Fleetwood. "Would that be Mr. Samuel Clemens, the author who writes as Mark Twain? I saw in the papers that he was coming here."

"Yes, it is Mr. Clemens the author," I said. "I am his secretary."

"Why, there's a sensation in the making," said Frank Stephens. "Mark Twain back in Florence! I wonder if he's changed his opinions since he lampooned the city in that book of his, just after the war." I smiled; this confirmed my suspicion that Mr. Clemens had not endeared himself to the local populace with his previous comments on their city. Seeing my smile, Stephens put his hand on my shoulder and continued: "You'll have to bring him here and introduce him around. Everybody interesting in Florence comes to Diabelli's, so of course he'll want to see it as much as we'd like seeing him."

"I doubt he'll come here any time soon," I replied, remembering his lack of enthusiasm when I'd told him about the place. "He's still preoccupied with getting the family moved into our new quarters. Perhaps he'll come when his affairs are in better order."

"I should hope so," said Mrs. Atwater, with a stern expression. "We could show him a few things he missed his last time here. He doesn't appear to have seen the *real* Florence."

I found this line of conversation troublesome, not being familiar with Mr. Clemens's earlier book on Florence. It struck me now that I should have read it before coming here as part of his establishment, to be able to speak up for my employer in his absence. But just then, Pietro arrived carrying our food, and by the time the orders were sorted out and all the dishes set on the table, the group had turned its collective mind to other subjects. But by now it was clear that Mr. Clemens had made himself a figure of some controversy in this city. This was no surprise; his views were often controversial, and he did not hesitate to express them. I would not let it bother me. I was here to enjoy myself, and I had found a very enjoyable situation.

Mr. Stephens seemed to be the center of this little group, and he played the host very smoothly, refilling everyone's glasses when they got low, and leading the conversation when it slowed. Since I was a newcomer, he made an effort to "bring me out," and before long I found myself telling of my adventures with Mr. Clemens, from New York to the mouth of the Mississippi River, across the Atlantic, and in London. I rather enjoyed recounting some of the lurid incidents to which I had been a witness, making myself perhaps more the center of attention than some might find proper. But I did my best not to monopolize the conversation, or to exaggerate my own role in the events I had been part of.

At last, Miss Fleetwood said, "My goodness, Mr. Cabot! You can't complain that your time since college has been dull! I hope you haven't come to Florence in hopes of being shot at, or attacked by bullies in the street! The town has been quite peaceful up until now, and I hope your presence won't change it." There was a twinkle in her eye, and I answered in the same spirit.

"I can assure you I have no intention of looking for anyone to shoot at me," I said. "In fact, I would consider the afternoon a ringing success if I could find someone to sell me a bicycle. That would be adventure enough for me, today."

"That shouldn't be hard to find," said Frank Stephens. "Bob, you bought your bike here in Florence, didn't you?"

"Yes, and paid double what it's worth," said Bob Danvers, grumpily. "That was before I knew enough to keep from being robbed. The minute the rascal heard me speaking English, his eyes lit up. Worse, I was fool enough to take it for the price he asked instead of bargaining him down."

"Well, I'm afraid I'll be a fool myself," I said. "I don't speak enough Italian to find the bicycle salesman, let alone bargain with him."

"What you need to do is go bicycle-shopping with someone who speaks good Italian," said Mrs. Atwater. "If you can put off your purchase till tomorrow morning, I'd be happy to come along. But I'm afraid I don't know the first thing about bicycles, or what the prices ought to be."

"Well, I can tell you this much," said Bob Danvers. "If you go to the *cafone bandito* I got mine from, the first price he wants you to pay is bound to be twice what the thing is worth, if not triple." He chuckled, low in his throat, and knocked back the rest of his wine.

"Of course it is," said Frank Stephens. "The whole country runs that way. As long as you know that's how it works, there's no real harm in it. It's just when Americans or Englishmen come here and don't know they're supposed to haggle the price down. Believe me, it's the same thing when I go to buy a painting. But in the end, all that matters is that you and the other fellow are both happy with the price."

"I don't mind bargaining, as long as there's someone along to help with the language," I said. "But I don't know much about bicycles, other than how to ride one. Are they all pretty much the same, or are there different types?"

"The new ones are better, but more expensive," said Bob Danvers. "That's what comes of living in the age of progress. Isn't it grand?"

"I suppose so," I said, not quite convinced. Then a thought struck me. "I say—why don't you come along tomorrow? You may be the only fellow here who's actually bought one."

"Yes, and the worse luck is I never use the blasted thing," said Danvers. "I'd sell it, except that having paid so much for it, I'd never get my money back. So it just sits around collecting rust, and reminding me what a fool I've been."

"That's a shame," I said. "I'd offer to take it off your hands, but it sounds like you don't want to sell."

"I'm not against it in principle, anyhow," Danvers agreed. "The problem is, I couldn't cheat somebody on the price if I knew I had to look him in the eye every day. That cuts out everybody here. I ought to put an advertisement in one of the English papers, and sell it to somebody who won't be in town long enough to become friends, but I'm too lazy even for that." He laughed again, and this time everyone joined in.

"There's the real truth," said somebody. "He's not too

honest to cheat us, just too lazy." Even Danvers laughed at that palpable hit.

A sudden inspiration struck me. "Would you consider renting it to me?" I said. "That way you'd get back part of what you paid for it, instead of letting it sit idle. And I wouldn't have to worry about disposing of it, or paying to ship it, when I leave."

"There's a fellow with a head on his shoulders," said Frank Stephens, slapping his hand on the table. "I'd take him up on that, Danvers."

"It does sound like a good idea," said Danvers, his eyes narrowing. "I'm not sure what I should charge, though. It's a good bike, so I won't give it away for nothing. How about a lira a day?"

I thought for a moment, calculating the price from the currency exchange tables I'd memorized. "That's six dollars a month," I said. "I could buy one in a couple of months, at that rate. How much do new ones cost, anyway?" I remembered my college friends paying something like ten dollars for a bicycle in New Haven . . . but had those been new or used? I wasn't sure.

"It's not a bad price," argued Danvers, warming to his subject. "You'd pay more than that if you rode the *tramvia* into town every day. And you won't have to walk to the *tramvia* stop, either."

"Yes, but I could sit and read on the tramway cars," I said, recognizing the word despite its Italian disguise. "Besides, I doubt I'd use it every day, once Mr. Clemens gets me back on my regular work schedule."

"There you go, haggling as if you'd both been doing it for years," said Miss Fleetwood, laughing. "Are you sure you're not both Italians masquerading as Americans? Make it half a lira a day, and be done with it—unless you want to entertain us with your justifications for robbing one another!"

"She's right, you know," said Danvers, breaking into a broad grin. "Half a lira—that's a dime a day. Let's shake on it, and when we've finished here, I'll take you to my place to get the bike."

"Done—as long as I like the way it rides," I said, and we shook hands.

I rode the bicycle back to Villa Viviani in time for supper that evening.

3 ~

If I expected Mr. Clemens to be impressed with my new acquisition, I learned better the second I brought it through the front gate into Villa Viviani. He took one look at the bicycle and snorted, "Jesus, Wentworth, make sure that thing has a muzzle on before you turn it loose in the house."

"It's not alive," I said, knowing even as I said it that my employer was under no such delusion.

"No, but it *is* dangerous," he said. "What did you want one of those things for, anyway? There must be a hundred better ways to get someplace—more comfortably and conveniently, and without doing all the work yourself."

"It's quicker than walking, and cheaper than the tramway," I said, trying to be calm and reasonable. "And I can go at my own leisure, rather than waiting for your driver to be free."

"Well, it's your neck," he said, with a trace of resignation in his voice. "Just don't come calling to me if the thing takes a nip out of you, or runs off when you forget to tie it up."

"I doubt I shall have to," I said brusquely. I thought perhaps he was trying to bait me into a comic argument, but this evening I was not in the mood for one of his "leg-pulls." Perhaps the ride out from the city had tired me.

He must have sensed my mood, because he said, "Well, good luck with it, anyhow. Come on inside—there's just time for a drink before supper." This offer had the desired effect; I leaned the bicycle inside the front gate, under a bit of an overhang, and joined him inside, and soon was in a far better mood.

I soon became quite used to the bicycle, and though (between my work and the occasional rainy spell) I did not use it every day, it became my preferred mode of transportation into Florence. It provided me a welcome degree of freedom, as it let me double the range I could travel on a given day. I congratulated myself on having made a good deal, and gladly paid Bob Danvers the agreed-upon rent every week when we met in the cafe. As often as not, he'd spend it on drinks that same day, but he seemed pleased with the bargain as well.

I also became a regular denizen of Cafe Diabelli, and the crowd I had first met there became my most frequent companions when I was away from my employer's villa. To tell the truth, my time was much more my own now than when we had been on the road, traveling about giving lectures. As long as the work got done, Mr. Clemens was content to let me finish it in the morning and have the balance of the day to myself. So, more days than not, noontime would find me riding down the winding road from Settignano, with glimpses of the river Arno off to my left, through the little village of Coverciano, swinging south of Campo di Marte toward Piazza Beccaria, then south to the river and along it toward the heart of town, where Frank Stephens and his group of friends would be gathering.

My first image of Florence had been as a center of the art world—and the city had lived up to its reputation in that regard. But before long, I began to acquire a taste for Italian food, especially that of Florence and the adjacent Tuscan region, which has its own characteristic dishes. I picked up a smattering of Italian—at least enough to ask directions as I made my way around the city, and to bargain with shopkeepers or street merchants. I found myself first watching, then playing, the occasional game of chess in the cafe. I had learned the game as a boy in school, and thought myself rather good at it until I met the habitués of Cafe Diabelli. But I won often enough to keep coming back, and even managed to make the two local champions—Garbarini and Gonnella—work a bit before they managed to checkmate me.

And, bit by bit, I found myself spending a great deal of time in the company of Virginia Fleetwood.

I had been at first somewhat hesitant to become too close to her—quite frankly, my luck with the fair sex had not been at all good. And so I felt it safer to hold myself back from too close a relationship. Odds were that either she or I would soon move on; in fact, my employer had scheduled a series of lectures in Germany once the warm weather came, and I would perforce accompany him—indeed, accompany him gladly, since my thirst for travel was still unslaked. So I felt it might be premature to treat this interesting young woman as more than a friend.

And yet, I began to feel that she *was* more than a friend, and I began to believe that she saw me in the same light as I saw her. Even at our first meeting, I had been impressed by her energetic rebuff of the importunate photograph-vendor, by her easy command of Italian, and by her ready smile. Talking to her at greater length, and on a wide variety of subjects, I learned that she could articulate her opinion with considerable grace and wit—yet without seeming a bluestocking. She was well read, and (as I soon learned) had quite a passable singing voice. She drew well, too, delineating the essentials of a scene or a person in a few deft strokes. And more than once, she made me laugh despite myself. I found myself almost regretting that Mr. Clemens would require my presence on his upcoming lecture tour.

These ideas had come to a head one morning in mid-February. Mr. Clemens and the family had gone for a day's excursion out to Fiesole, giving me the day free. I met

Virginia at Palazzo Pitti, the official residence of the King of Italy in Florence. Virginia was as avid as I about painting, and the Pitti gallery was rated as one of the gems of Florence—where old masters were as common as apples in an orchard. I hardly need say I was looking forward to seeing this collection.

At Virginia's suggestion, I met her at the Uffizi, whence we could take the long corridor over Ponte Vecchio to the Pitti, a passageway built by Vasari to allow the Medicis to pass unseen between their palaces. This corridor, lined with woodcuts, engravings, and portraits of the Medicis, popes and cardinals, and other notables, is a museum in its own right. Perhaps a busy Medici might have traversed it in ten minutes; it took us over half an hour, and we did not linger to see everything.

At the far end, we climbed two flights of stairs to the Pitti galleries. Here, it became apparent that Corridoio Vasari had been but an appetizer for the feast of fine art that awaited us. In the first of the rooms alone—the Saloon of the Iliad, named after the ceiling frescoes—were works by Titian, Rubens, Raphael, Giorgione, Veronese, and a pair of Virgins by del Sarto.

I could have spent the rest of the day in that first gallery, but after a while, Virginia smiled and said, "There's more, you know." She took my hand and led me to the Saloon of Saturn—where my mouth practically fell open to discover four Raphaels on the walls! And thus it went all day long. Room after room presented whole walls of old masters. Perhaps the Uffizi outdid it in sheer number of works displayed, but I doubt even that great gallery could match the Pitti in the overall splendor of its offerings. It was with some reluctance that we finally dragged ourselves out of the galleries and back across the river to Cafe Diabelli to eat.

The usual American crowd had yet to appear, and so we sat at a small table by ourselves. We spent a few moments deciding on our meals—I chose chicken, while Virginia took soup—and asked Pietro, the waiter, to bring us a small bottle of a local white wine, which I had come to appreciate as much as the red Chianti. He smiled and promised to bring us a good bottle, and left us to ourselves. Virginia watched him go, then leaned forward and said in a low voice, "I think Pietro suspects us of being lovers."

"Pietro would be better advised to tend to his customers," I said, with a chuckle. Then, reflecting on it, I asked, "Do these Italians never think of anything else? I'm sure we've done nothing to put any such idea in poor Pietro's feverish mind."

Virginia laughed. "I'm quite sure Pietro is capable of jumping to conclusions with no help whatsoever from us," she said. "To hear him talk, he is the greatest lover in all Florence, so he might be expected to imagine others to share his preoccupations."

"Why, I have never heard a word to that effect from him," I said, surprised,

"Silly Wentworth, that's because you don't understand enough Italian," she said, looking at me with an amused expression. "I assure you, he has almost no other subject of conversation when he speaks to his compatriots. It is quite droll."

I thought for a moment, then said, "I suppose we ought to disabuse him of this notion. It would be a shame to let him labor under such a misconception."

"It might not be such a shame," she said, looking into my eyes. "I think it would be diverting, Besides, it doesn't matter what we tell him—he won't believe anything that goes against his natural disposition. So we might as well make the most of it. Shhh! Here he comes with our wine." To my surprise, she reached over and gave my hand a little squeeze, then snatched her hand back as the waiter came closer.

Pietro was beaming as he reached the table. He made a production of pouring the wine, and (rather to my embarrassment) winked at me and said, "Enjoy, *signore*!" as he set the bottle down. There was no doubt he was referring to something more than just the wine.

"Do you see?" Virginia said, with a little giggle. "Now he will give us especially good service—and I think he has brought us a better wine than usual. Of course, you'll have to give him a good tip today—but he is a good waiter, after all."

I tasted the wine, which was indeed better than I usually got. "Goodness!" I remarked. "If this is what one gets for pretending to be a lover, perhaps I shall learn to keep up the pretense."

She put down her wineglass and wiped her lips with the napkin. "You needn't pretend for my sake," she said, with a smile that might have meant anything, It wasn't until later that day, when I was riding my bicycle up the hill to Villa Viviani, that I realized just how many things that smile might have meant.

I suddenly realized that my employer had been speaking to me for some little time, and that I had no idea what he said. "Excuse me, sir?" I said, looking up from the pages I had been proofreading—*had* been, until my thoughts had wandered off someplace else. We were sitting in the large upstairs room that Mr. Clemens had taken for his office— he at his desk, and I at a long table set at right angles to it so we could pass papers back and forth without rising from our chairs. The south-facing window behind him gave plenty of light to work by during the day.

"Damnation, Wentworth, what are you mooning about? If I didn't know better, I'd think you had a lady friend," said Mr. Clemens, leaning back in his chair and stretching his arms above his head. Then he straightened up and peered at me. "Hmmm—maybe I don't know as much as I thought. *Do* you have a lady friend?"

"She's a friend," I admitted. "I don't think that's what you're asking about, though."

"You know what I'm asking about," said Mr. Clemens, peering at me. His brows were arched, and there was a quizzical little smile around his mouth. "Now, is she just a friend, or could she be something a little bit more interesting?" He leaned back in his chair again, nodding.

My first impulse was to tell him it was none of his business. Then I recalled to whom I was speaking, and bit back my response. "A bit more interesting, perhaps," I said mildly, shuffling a few papers and trying to pretend I hadn't already looked at them.

"And it's none of my meddling business just how much more interesting. Am I right?"

It was as if he'd read my mind. I laughed and slid the papers back atop the pile and said, "I was about to tell you that, but now I guess I shan't. She's a young American woman staying in the city with her married sister. She's very bright, and very interested in art."

"And interested in you, I reckon," said Mr. Clemens, bending down to open one of the drawers in his desk—the one where he kept a jar of tobacco. "Just make sure not to tell her how little I pay you, or she might stop being interested."

"I suppose if it ever got to that point, I'd have to think about finding some more settled employment," I said, and then stopped, surprised at myself for being so blunt. I hadn't meant to say any such thing, but there it was. The question that had been in the back of my mind was now squarely on the table. And having said it, I began to wonder if it was true.

Mr. Clemens, to his credit, treated my statement seriously. "I reckon that's inevitable, sooner or later. I can't afford to pay a lot—well, I suppose I *could*, since Henry Rodgers is the one digging in his pockets for it—but this is a job created with somebody like you in mind: a young fellow who isn't tied down with a family, and who wants to see some of the world while he can. I need to be on the road, and so does my secretary. Livy's used to her husband's being away for months at a time, but I doubt there are many young ladies who'd see that as an attractive proposition."

"I don't think we've reached that point yet," I said. "Perhaps she'd be able to travel with me."

"Maybe, if she has money of her own," said Mr. Clemens. He'd picked up one of his corncob pipes and was stuffing it with tobacco. He concentrated on that task for a moment, then looked up and said, "Is this all *what-if* and *could-be,* or are you serious about her? Because if you are, I'd like to get a look at her with my own eyes. Again, you can tell me it's none of my damned business. But I reckon it is my business, if there's a chance it'll cost me a good secretary."

That gave me pause. I had come to enjoy my employment with Mr. Clemens. Indeed, I was very fortunate to have gotten the opportunity to travel across America and Europe with a man who attracted interesting people and remarkable events. It would come to an end at some point, but was I ready to abandon it just yet? I was not likely to find another situation so suited to my nature.

My employer must have sensed my confusion, because he said, "I'm sorry, Wentworth, I didn't mean to put you on the torture rack. I'll just ask you to let me know if I should start worrying about having to replace you. And if you decide you're getting serious about this young lady, I promise not to embarrass you too much if you bring her here to meet me. Now, what was it we were doing before we got off on this?"

"You'd asked me something, and I still don't know what it was," I admitted, blushing.

"Hell, we've barely got one working brain between the pair of us," he said. "I guess if we don't remember what it was, it can't have been worth the bother."

"I suppose it'll come to us," I agreed. I picked up the papers I'd been reading before he interrupted me, and tried to find my place. Mr. Clemens nodded, and began looking for a match, and we said no more on the subject that morning. But I was not so naive as to think it would not come up again.

In the meantime, I began to divide my days between work and sleep at Villa Viviani and recreation in Florence with Frank Stephens's group. The center of our pursuits was Cafe Diabelli, where we drank coffee and wine, watched the chess games and the passersby, and talked endlessly. Stephens had an easy way of bringing everyone into the conversation, and the knack of launching a subject that made ample fuel for discussion by the rest of us, whether the mood was serious or playful.

In particular, Stephens and his circle were great connoisseurs of art. This arose naturally from his business buying paintings for several clients back in America. But he also cultivated the company of young artists, several of whom were among our regular group. He seemed to know most of the artists working around Florence, as well—it was not unusual for one or two of them to come by our table during an afternoon at the cafe, paying their respects. He told me his clients would often ask for first-rate copies of famous old master paintings. He would commission a local artist to sit a few days in front of the original painting and produce a copy. "There's a science to knowing who to give that kind of work," he told me. "Now, if somebody wants a Botticelli, Luigi Battista is just the man for it— you'd think he'd studied under old Sandro. But he can't do Fra Angelico worth beans—for that, I'd use Guisetti, or even Eddie Freeman. Eddie's developing a nice touch for the quattrocento."

"Do you mean that?" said Eddie, walking in with his paint box and easel under his arm. "I'll have to raise my rates, then." He stowed his gear against the terrace wall and sank into a chair.

"Well, Cabot, you see what comes of being generous with your praise," said Stephens, with a little laugh. "Now poor Eddie will get a swelled head and I'll never get good work out of him again. If I'd known the rascal was listening, I'd have said he shouldn't be allowed to paint a barn."

"Now, Frank, that's not fair of you," said Eddie, with a frown. There was an edge to his voice as he continued: "You know how hard I've worked."

"Yes, you have, and I'll buy you a drink to prove I'm only joshing you," said Stephens, laughing. "How about you, Cabot? Are you ready?"

"I believe so," I said. As if on cue, Pietro, the waiter, came into view, and Stephens signaled to him. He came over to our table and we gave him drink orders. When he had left, I turned to the other two and said, "Tell me, is there really that much market for copies of the old masters? Can someone make a decent living at that sort of work?"

"Good enough to keep body and soul together while I work on my own things," said Eddie, with a shrug. "The market for paintings by a young American nobody's ever heard of is about as good as the market for sand in Araby. But I can go to the museums and do a couple of copies a week, and sell them for enough to cover room and board, and have time left over to work on my style. Of course, it's more fun to sit here and pass the time with good chaps from back home. If I were a little bit quicker, I could make a better living at it. But it takes me a while to get things just right. I'm lucky I made friends with Frank—between him and a couple of the local dealers, I've got a regular market for the stuff."

"When you find a good man for the job you've got, you're a fool not to use him," said Stephens, nodding. "And as it happens, the art market's booming back home, and so I can find work for someone like Eddie. For that matter, there'd be a lot for you, if you'd want to come on board."

I was taken aback by this statement. "You must be joking," I said. "I'm all but a novice at drawing, and I've never had a paintbrush in my hand in my life. There can't be any market for the kind of thing I'd turn out."

Stephens and Eddie both laughed. "Well, if we were selling modern French stuff, I think even you could turn out a marketable canvas in a day or two," said Stephens. "But that's not what I had in mind. You're a bright young fellow, Cabot. You went to a good school, and you come from the right kind of people. You have easy access to circles where not everybody would have entrée."

"I suppose that's true," I said. I had never thought of myself in those terms, but there was undoubtedly some advantage to being a Cabot—at least in New England. I had been reminded very forcefully of that point when my father tried to persuade me to abandon my position with Mr. Clemens and study for the bar. "What does that have to do with art?"

"Why, everything in the world," said Stephens. "It's just

the sort of people you know back home who are the customers for art. That's the way it's been all through history—the wealthy and the well-bred have always been the patrons of art. There's more fine art in Boston parlors than in half of Europe, and a man who can help the folks back home find what they want can live pretty well, let me tell you. I'm living proof of it."

"What do you have in mind?" I said.

"I need an agent who can look after the American end of things," said Stephens. "Somebody who can run my gallery in Boston. Of course that fellow wouldn't be just a shopkeeper—he'd be doing a fair amount of travel over here, and to London and Paris, too. He'd be the link between the European operation, where we find the paintings, and the market back home, where we find the people who want something to hang in the dining room. Virginia says she's been to the galleries with you and that you know your art pretty well. I've seen the same, and I think you'd be a good man for the job. What do you say?"

I thought for a moment before replying, "I don't know what to say. I'm flattered that you'd consider me for the position. But as you know, I already have a job with Mr. Clemens." I was somewhat flustered at this offer, which to me seemed to come out of the blue. Apparently Stephens and his sister-in-law, Virginia, had been talking about me for some time.

"Yes, I'm aware of that," said Stephens. "I can see how the association with somebody so well-known as Mark Twain would have its advantages for a young fellow. But if you don't mind my saying so, the position doesn't offer any great future prospects. You're not going to take over writing his books, once he's gone. In fact, from talk I've heard, Clemens is pretty much washed up now, just riding on his name."

There was a burst of noise from across the room, and I looked to see two men standing up, their fists raised as if to fight. Then somebody said something in Italian, and the two broke into laughter and threw their arms around one another. One of them called out for wine, and I saw Pietro hurrying toward the table. Stephens, who had been watching along with me, chuckled and took up his previous subject. "It's been quite a while since your boss has had a successful book, you know. The times have changed. Readers today are more in the mood for Henry James than a rough old fellow from the frontier, or so it seems to me."

"Perhaps," I said. "I think Mr. Clemens may have a few more arrows in his quiver, though." But as I said this, I was all too aware of the projects he was working on—a novel about Joan of Arc, and another about identical twins caught up in a murder trial. Neither seemed likely to rejuvenate his career. Still, Mr. Clemens had been very good to me, and despite our discussion about my leaving his employment, I was not in a great hurry to do so.

"Well, maybe he does," said Stephens. "But I think you'd be a good man for the opening I have, and I'm offering it to you. Why don't you take a few days and think it over? If you have any questions, don't hesitate to ask. Just to lay my cards on the table, I think you ought to know that the position pays two hundred dollars a month. There'd be a commission on what you sold, as well, but you can bank on the two hundred."

"Really?" I said, trying to be nonchalant. "That seems a very fair offer." It was more than twice what Mr. Clemens was paying me. All of a sudden, the notion of life as an art dealer in Boston began to look very attractive.

Just as I was beginning to absorb the possibilities, Mrs. Atwater arrived, arm in arm with Jonathan Wilson with news of a new opera opening that night. That, and the arrival of Pietro with our drinks, diverted the course of talk away from the offer Frank Stephens had made. But my mind kept turning it over, and finding it more and more attractive the more I considered it. Perhaps the time *had* come to take my leave of Mr. Clemens and make my own way in the world.

4 ⌒

Bicycling home from the cafe that evening, I found myself mulling over Frank Stephens's offer of a job managing his art business in Boston. It was an offer I had to take seriously—if only for the very respectable salary he had offered me. (And presumably, if I did well, commissions would increase the amount of my income.) While my main business would be in Boston, he had indicated that regular European travel was an important responsibility—a duty that I, for one, would find far from onerous. And, for that matter, Boston was far from an onerous place to be stationed. As Stephens had reminded me, I had family there.

The liability of the offer was the loss of my position with Mr. Clemens, which despite its low pay and irregular hours, I had come to enjoy. If I left his employment, I couldn't expect to find myself in quite so many colorful situations, or meeting such a heterogenous mixture of humanity as I had. Even more attractive was the prospect of traveling with him—always first class, always in interesting company, and always to the most enjoyable destinations imaginable. Would I get another opportunity to see so many distant lands at someone else's expense if I went back to Boston and settled into the art business?

That all depended on Mr. Clemens, though—and he was among the most unpredictable men in the world. He *was* in straitened financial circumstances, and if he lost the favor of his millionaire patron, Mr. Henry Rodgers, he might well find himself unable to afford my services. And my employment had led me into several unsavory, nay even dangerous, predicaments. Stephens's proffered job could hardly find me becoming quite so intimate with police detectives and murder victims as I had in Mr. Clemens's employment—or listening to bullets whizzing past my head. All things considered, that had to be counted in favor of accepting Stephens's offer.

All that tumbled through my head as I pedaled out of town, past Campo di Marte, through sleepy Coverciano, and up the hilly roads to Settignano. And yet, as I turned into the gateway of Villa Viviani, another factor kept intruding into my musings: Virginia Fleetwood. Would she be willing to give up Florence and follow me back to Boston if I accepted Stephens's offer? Alternately, would she be interested in a fellow whose career consisted in following an eccentric writer about, looking after his papers and his hotel reservations? Or was I deluding myself in imagining that she even thought of me in the same way that I found myself thinking of her? By the time I propped my bicycle up against the wall outside the villa door, I was still as far from arriving at a decision as I had been when Stephens made his offer.

And then, almost before I had the door closed behind me, there was Mr. Clemens, taking me by the elbow and saying, "Wentworth! I've been waiting for you all afternoon. I need to bounce a couple of ideas off that hard New England noggin of yours. Come set down and have a glass of whisky—while you're wetting your whistle, I'll tell you what I've cooked up, and then you tell me what you think of it."

"My head is at your disposal, sir," I said, and I followed him into the sitting room, where he poured two generous bumpers. I had already taken on a fair cargo of Italian wine at the cafe, so I made sure to add an even more liberal helping of soda water than usual—else I might find myself crawling off to sleep at far too early an hour. With the drink diluted to my liking, I plopped myself on a sofa facing the fireplace, and turned to face my employer, who was perched on the arm of the same piece of furniture.

"Here's my idea, Wentworth," he said. "I've been puttering around Europe and America for nigh on to twenty-five years, with a few stops in the Holy Land and Egypt for variety's sake. And I was out in the Sandwich Islands before that—they call 'em Hawaii, nowadays. But crossing the ocean with Kipling made me think. There's a whole world I've never laid eyes on. Africa! Australasia! In-ja!" (He pronounced this last in the same exaggerated way as Mr. Kipling had.)

"Now, I've always had a reputation for my travel writing, Wentworth," he continued. I nodded. Indeed, it had been my impression upon our first meeting that he had written little else. "The novels and the humorous sketches and the political pieces are all very well, but three-quarters of the time, when somebody I haven't met comes up to me and starts talking, they want to know where I've been lately and what I saw there. I've got high hopes for the two novels I'm working on, but something tells me it's time to get back to the travel books. And what better excuse to go someplace I've never been?"

"Africa, and India," I said.

"And Australasia," he added. "The best part is, they speak English in all those places, so I can give lectures while I'm seeing the country—I can combine fundraising and research. It's the perfect trick, Wentworth. What do you think?"

"It sounds like a daunting expedition, sir, but I think you're right—it's perfect for you."

"The thing is, I'd have to take Livy, too. She'd never let me forget it if I didn't, and she'd enjoy it every bit as much as I would. The question is, will Henry Rodgers spring for it?"

"I don't see why not, sir," I said. In truth, never having met Mr. Rodgers, I had but the vaguest idea what he might agree to sponsor. I had heard him spoken of by business-men in the terms a New England merchant captain might use for the Barbary pirates. So far I had not known him to flinch at any expense, including the raise in salary Mr. Clemens had given me a couple of months before in Eng-land. But paying for a round-the-world voyage might be a different story altogether.

Mr. Clemens was going on ahead of me, though. He jumped to his feet and began to pace around the room, thinking out loud. "The way to do it would be westward; that way I could start out in America, go out to California, and pick up the Sandwich Islands on the outward leg. That'd be a great way to start the book about the trip—going back to my old haunts after twenty-five years." He paused at the window and looked out; my gaze followed his. It was a clear night out, with stars twinkling over the distant hills.

"That should be a fine journey," I said. It was an under-statement; it would be a journey few men take in an entire lifetime. And to take it in the company of Mr. Clemens would be an experience to dine out on for the rest of my days. And my ticket would be paid by Henry Rodgers. Bet-ter yet, I would be earning a salary the whole time! All of a sudden, Mr. Stephens's offer of a well-paid job in Boston, with occasional business trips to Europe, seemed less al-luring.

What gave me pause was the question whether, after a journey that might take six months, I could return to Flor-ence and find Virginia Fleetwood waiting for me. The fact that I even considered this a possible objection to the plan was enough to make me hesitate. Just how much impres-sion had that young lady made on me that I was weighing her in the balance against a journey round the world?—although I had to admit that, whatever her charms, they were not quite enough to tilt the scales.

I had to force myself to concentrate again on Mr. Clemens, He was making plans about India, and I was already imagining myself riding an elephant . . .

While I was excited by the prospect of accompanying my employer on his projected world tour, I did not at once turn down Frank Stephens's offer of a job running his art gallery in Boston. A nagging voice in the back of my head kept telling me it was time to settle down and take a respectable sort of job. That solid New England common sense that Mr. Clemens seemed to believe I had between my ears doubted that his plans had any chance of coming to fruition. Traveling around the world and getting paid for the privilege was not an option in the sort of reality my New London upbringing and my Yale education had prepared me to inhabit.

But there was another reason, as well, for my not giving Mr. Stephens a frank "No, thank you," right away. I feared that he might take offense at my rejection of his offer, now that he had announced to everyone that he was "bringing me on board." To hear him talk, I would be an utter fool to pass up such a golden opportunity. And while I did not feel as if I owed it to him to accept, I did worry that a refusal would make me unwelcome in his circle—and that might mean I would be banished from the company of Virginia Fleetwood,

I continued to spend my afternoons at Cafe Diabelli, drinking and talking with the same crowd, and contriving ways to spend a few minutes in private with the young lady. The easiest way to accomplish this goal was for both of us to arrive at the cafe before our usual companions. Then we could sit out on the terrace, entirely proper, and talk about whatever we desired without worrying who was listening. And so we found ourselves together a few days after Frank Stephens's job offer.

I had arrived even earlier than usual and found none of the art crowd on hand yet. I started to take a table, when a voice called out, "Eh, Americano!" I turned to find Garbarini, one of the cafe's unofficial chess champions, beckoning to me. "Come play a game," he said, pointing to one of the boards. I hesitated, but he came across the room and grabbed me by the arm. "Don't worry, you won't miss your friends," he said, with a grin. And so I took a seat opposite him and we began a game.

He was a thin, intense fellow with a piercing gaze—one might have thought the chessboard had the winning moves printed on it in microscopic letters, and he was doing his best to read them with his bare eyes. In any case, he beat me almost every time we played. It was with some relief that, having lost a bishop and a knight, and with my castled king under attack, I became aware of someone standing to my side and looked up from the board to see Virginia Fleetwood watching the game.

"How are you doing?" she asked, laying her hand on my shoulder. She had long since confessed her entire ignorance of the game.

"I am hopeless," I admitted. "I ought to resign the game and give Garbarini a chance to play someone who can put up a better fight."

My opponent looked up from the board and shrugged, "You no play so bad," he said. Despite his broken, accented English, he was clearly a man of above-average intelligence. (I had heard that he was considered a poet of some promise in his own language.) He moved his hand in a chopping motion, like a cook cutting up vegetables, and continued: "You play-a too fast, and you think on other thing-a too much, but you don' play-a so bad."

I smiled, then reached out and tipped over my king. "Thank you for the compliment, but I'm afraid you have me beaten in this game," I said, doing my best to speak slowly and distinctly. I dug in my pocket and handed him the quarter-lira coin (the price of a small glass of wine) that was the customary stake for a game in Cafe Diabelli. "We will play again, and perhaps you will buy me the drink then."

"*Grazie*," he said, and we shook hands. "You come play again, maybe you win-a." He emphasized this statement with a broad gesture of invitation.

"I'll do that," I said, smiling. I had enjoyed the game

despite losing. I followed Virginia to our usual table on the terrace.

"You should be careful around that fellow, Wentworth," she said as we sat down. "Frank won't hire him because the *polizia* keep him under constant scrutiny."

"I don't follow you," I said. "I understood him to be a poet, not an artist. What work would Frank have for him, in any case?"

"He may scribble a few verses," she said. There was a little frown on her face, but I did not think it hurt her looks. "But he earns his living as a typesetter, doing odd jobs for various local printers. Frank's business gives him occasional need for all sorts of craftsmen, but he doesn't want to use someone in bad odor with the law. And it doesn't look good for you to associate with such a person."

"I suppose I can see the point," I said. "What sort of trouble is Garbarini supposed to be in? Is he a thief or something?"

"No, Frank says he's a Socialist—or some such breed of radical," she said, shaking her head. "So's that other man he plays with—the plump one, Gonnella."

"Well, neither has ever said a word to me about anything but chess," I told her. "They could be good solid Republicans for all I can tell."

"Politics over here isn't like home," Virginia said. Her voice was low and conspiratorial, and she glanced around as if to see who might be listening. "It's best to keep one's opinions quiet. They've got a kingdom nowadays, but that's not very old—the nation itself isn't very old, although of course the country is. So even calling yourself a Republican might be dangerous, here. My point is, you'd best keep your distance from those fellows."

"Well, of course you've been here longer than I, and speak the language better," I conceded, "but I can't see the harm in a friendly game of chess, even with an outright Red."

"You may not, but it's the police's opinion that counts," she said, reaching out to take my hand. "And Frank would be very upset if you ended up in trouble with the authorities. He has important plans for you, and I think he would have to think twice if you got yourself in trouble with the law."

"Oh, Virginia, that's not going to happen," I said, looking her in the eye. It felt good to sit holding her hand. But in the back of my head, I recalled a night spent in a New Orleans jail cell, on suspicion of murder. Perhaps that episode was best left unmentioned. Besides, I reminded myself, I might well refuse Mr. Stephens's offer, so my putative criminal past was of no consequence. But I didn't want to broach that subject to Virginia just yet . . .

The silence was about to grow awkward when Pietro came and took our orders. A few minutes later, Eddie Freeman and Bob Danvers came rollicking in and began telling us how they'd talked their Italian landlady's pretty daughter into posing for Eddie, who planned to sell the painting to raise money to pay their rent. The way they told it, everything possible had gone wrong, culminating in the mother's throwing the painting into the fireplace when she discovered that her daughter had posed in the nude, and Bob drunkenly trying to fish the canvas out of the flames before it was ruined. The story scandalized Virginia and made me nearly choke on my wine from laughing. Before they were done, the rest of our friends had sat down at our table, and the story had to be repeated—and any worry about my chess opponent's unsavory politics was forgotten, for the time being, at least.

Frank Stephens arrived later than usual, all smiles. "I want you all to drop any plans you have for Saturday evening," he said, standing at the head of the table as if addressing a board meeting. "I'm throwing a dinner party, and you're all invited."

There was a general round of cheering and excited laughter. "What's the occasion?" said Bob Danvers, after the applause died down a bit. "You know I'm never one to skip a party, but this is pretty short notice. Did your rich uncle die?" This caused more laughter and Bob stood up and took a bow. We were all in a merry mood by now.

"No, but the next best thing," said Stephens, with a broad

grin. "I've closed a deal that's been brewing for months, and now I'm the proud owner of three Raphaels—well, they're from his studio, at least. They've been hidden in some villa out in Fiesole for generations. The old bandit who had them decided that his continued comfort is worth more than portraits of his ancestors. It took some doing to come up with the price he was asking, but I think I've buyers for two of them. They'll be hanging on my wall for all of you to admire before dinner."

"Raphaels!" said Jonathan Wilson. "You rotter, you never told me you were going to get anything of that ilk. I'd have bid for those, you know. Damn me, if I like them enough, I'll outbid whoever you've sold them to."

"We can do better than that, Wilson," said Stephens. "I told you, one isn't yet spoken for—a charming contessa, the former owner's great-great-grandmother. I'll give you first shot at it, if you're in the mood to buy. But I warn you—the old *don* I got them from made me pay through the nose, and I'm not about to let this one go at a loss."

"For a Raphael, I'll empty out my pockets soon enough," said Wilson firmly. "Well, Stephens, I think you can count on *my* being at your party. Congratulations, sir!"

"Hear, hear!" said Penelope Atwater. "I shall never have the wherewithal to hang a Raphael in my parlor, but it would please me no end to sit and admire yours, Frank—even if they are being shipped off to Boston the next morning."

"You'll be more than welcome, my dear," said Stephens. Then he turned to me. "Cabot, I hope you'll extend an invitation to Mr. Clemens and his wife to join us for the occasion. I've been hoping to make his acquaintance ever since you told me he was in the neighborhood, and now I've got something for him to come see. Please let him know that Isabella and I will be most eager to have him at dinner."

"I shall extend the invitation this evening," I said. "And my congratulations upon your acquisition, as well."

"You'll be handling your share of old masters, too, when you come on board," he said, leaning over to speak to me in a low voice. "Maybe seeing these pieces will help you make up your mind."

"I do look forward to seeing them," I said, quite truthfully. I still hadn't decided what was the best way to tell him I was leaning toward declining his offer.

"Good, good," he said. "I know it's hard to contemplate leaving a position with such a famous man as Mark Twain, but this is a golden opportunity. I've been looking for a bright, trustworthy young fellow to fill this spot for some time now, and I think you're the man for it. Be sure to come talk to me if you still have any doubts or questions."

"I shall, sir," I said.

"Good, and don't forget to invite Mr. and Mrs. Clemens for Saturday. Isabella is dying to meet him, and so am I. Even if I am planning to hire you away from him." He laughed, and clapped me on the shoulder.

I joined in laughing with him, but it occurred to me that putting my current employer and a man who was trying to hire me away from him in the same room might not be comfortable for me. But of course, having promised to invite Mr. Clemens to the party, I had no choice but to do so. However, to see these newly discovered Raphaels, I could tolerate a good bit more discomfort than I expected to find at Frank Stephens's dinner table.

5 ⟍

I had at first felt a bit awkward about inviting my employer to meet my new friends in the city. After all, while I considered myself his social equal, we moved for the most part in different sets. When we found ourselves together on social occasions, it was often a reception where the famous author was dumped in with a jumbled group of local admirers, from whom he needed periodic rescuing—at which point I would step in to earn my keep. So it seemed a bit odd to relay an invitation from one of my friends to my employer and his wife.

But Mr. Clemens was enthusiastic. "I feel in the mood for something different," he said. "Livy and I have been cooped up here the whole season, it seems. Do us good, getting out to see some different faces. I guess I ought to be able to trust your taste in friends by now."

"I should hope so, Youth," said Mrs. Clemens dryly. "Considering the old friends you have introduced me to from time to time, I would be inclined to trust Wentworth's taste far more than yours."

"Now, Livy, you should be more charitable," drawled my employer. "Wentworth hasn't had all my advantages, you know. Give him a few more years, and I reckon he can hook up with a bunch of scoundrels every bit as crooked as my old pals off the River."

Mrs. Clemens smiled. "In any case, we shall have the opportunity to judge for ourselves. If nothing else, Mr. Stephens may have a good story to tell about finding these Raphaels he's going to show us. And if his taste in company matches his taste in painting, so much the better."

"Well, we'll find out on Saturday," said Mr. Clemens. As he walked over to the window facing westward toward Florence and looked out, my gaze followed him. The sun had already set, and the city's lights had begun to appear— warmer and more diffuse than the winter stars that shone through a few thin clouds above the western hills.

Mr. Clemens turned and saw where I was looking. "Lovely view, isn't it?" he said. "You'd never think, just to see it, that this city was built by some of the most ruthless and greedy men who ever lived. The worst man I ever met was a piker next to the Medicis. And these people damn near worship them."

"They left a legacy of beauty," I argued. "The evil they did was buried with them, but the good lives on."

He shook his head. "You can't write off the evil so cleanly, Wentworth," he said. "That's why I'm not impressed with a fellow who can hang a pack of Raphaels on his wall for a dinner party. First I want to know what he did to get 'em. But I guess I can find that out on Saturday, as well."

"Yes, and you will behave yourself, Youth," Mrs. Clemens said very firmly.

"Why of course," said my employer, a look of surprise on his face. "Whatever gave you the idea I might do anything else?"

Not surprisingly, the Cafe Diabelli group was excited at the news that Mr. Clemens would be among the dinner guests.

"That's the icing on the cake," said Bob Danvers. "I've seen loads of Raphaels before, in museums and galleries, better stuff than Frank's got. But shaking Mark Twain's hand isn't something a fellow gets to do every day."

"Well, I'm glad he's decided to come out of his shell," said Mrs. Atwater. She took a sip of her wine and soda water—she'd long since given up trying to teach the Italian cook at Diabelli's to brew tea to her specifications—and continued: "I can understand he's got books to write, but one would think he'd need human society, as well. A writer who loses contact with the world won't have much to write about."

"I don't think Mr. Clemens has lost contact with the world," I said. "He'd claim just the opposite."

"That the world's lost contact with him?" said Virginia, smiling. "That would be quite a problem, I'd think."

"Yes, especially if they stop buying his books," said Danvers. "Then you'd be out a job, old boy."

"Well, that'll be a moot point soon enough," said Eddie Freeman. "Cabot'll be back in Boston, overseeing the gallery . . . say, what's that fellow doing? Isn't that your bicycle, Bob?"

I followed his gaze to a spot across the street where I'd gotten in the habit of tying up the bicycle while in the Cafe Diabelli. It was in plain view of the terrace where our group gathered, and so I considered it safe. Sure enough, there was a little fellow with dark hair and a huge mustache leaning over the bicycle I was renting from Danvers. I stood up and shouted, "Leave that alone, you rascal."

"Hey, that's my bike!" said Danvers, rising to his feet at the same time. *"Ladro, ladro!"*

The fellow started as he heard the shouts, then bent to his task with renewed vigor. Cursing now, Danvers vaulted the low wall between us and the street; I was right behind him, but the thief had the bicycle loose and was already in the saddle. I put on a burst of speed to try to cut him off before the corner, but Danvers had taken the same line, and the next thing I knew, the two of us had fallen in a tangle in the street. I hopped up almost at once, but the thief was rounding the corner, his left hand raised in the two-fingered salute I had come to recognize as a signal of contempt.

"The bastard's gone," said Danvers, coming to a halt

beside me. "I'd have had him if you hadn't gotten in the way."

"You tripped *me*," I snapped. I had fallen hard, and skinned the palm of my left hand catching myself on the paving stones. At least I had managed not to tear my jacket or trousers.

"We'll never catch him," said Danvers, staring at the corner the thief had gone around. Then he turned to me with a scowl and said, "You owe me money, old man."

"Yes, of course," I said, staring down at my palm. "I'm bleeding, hang it all."

"To hell with that, I've lost my bike," said Danvers, with more hostility. "You should've left it someplace safer."

"Safer! It was in plain view, right across the street. I'd have caught him if you hadn't tripped me."

"You owe me a new bike," insisted Danvers. He struck a belligerent pose, as if he were ready to fight me.

"Here, here, both of you calm down," said Mrs. Atwater, who stood just inside the terrace wall. "The bike's gone, and you won't get it back by arguing with each other. Come on back here and we'll figure out what to do next."

Danvers nodded and dropped his fists, and we both turned back to the terrace. We climbed over the low wall and took our seats again. I looked at my injured hand; I would have to find some way to clean it. For now, I dabbed at it with a napkin, hoping to get most of the dirt off. "We should call the police," I said.

Eddie Freeman guffawed. "There's a waste of time," he said. "I doubt there's anything less interesting to an Italian policeman than the theft of a foreigner's property. Unless he stands to benefit personally from it, of course."

"I understand that they accept bribes," said Heinrich Muller, a German art student who was one of Frank Stephens's freelance copyists. He had a very earnest expression, emphasized by his high forehead and thick spectacles.

"They do, but that won't do much good with a stolen bike," said Eddie, shaking his head. "Even if the thief isn't the policeman's cousin, you'd have to pay more than the bike's worth to get them interested. You might as well go buy another—or go look around the flea markets and see if you can get this one back cheap. I guess the rascal will sell it for ten or twelve lira, enough for a few drinks. You may be able to get it back for twenty-five, if you're a sharp bargainer."

"That's not coming out of my pocket," said Bob Danvers, still hot under the collar. "Cabot owes me the money, and I want it without a lot of nonsense."

"I don't carry that much around with me," I said. "But how about letting me see if I can find a replacement? Then you'll get back a bike, I'll apply what I pay for it against the rent, and we'll both be no worse off than we were. If I give you the money, I'm still going to have to find a ride into town."

"You'd buy one, and give it to Danvers?" said Eddie Freeman. "Lord, I thought I'd seen everything in the world, but that's a topper."

"It's the fair thing to do," I said. "Or at least to try. If I can't find a decent bike for less than what I'd owe Bob, then I'll just give him the money and start riding the *tramvia*."

"What if you buy some piece of trash?" Danvers objected. "That wasn't a cheap bike, you know."

"Don't worry," I told him. "I'm the one that has to ride it, so it's my neck I'm risking if it breaks down."

"He's got a point, you know," said Eddie Freeman. "The worst that can happen is you get enough to buy a new bike—or pay the rent and buy meals for a couple of weeks. I'm still waiting to get paid for the work I'm doing, so one of us needs to bring in some money."

"All right," said Danvers grudgingly, "I'll give you until Monday next week—that ought to be long enough to find a bike. If you haven't got one by then, or if I don't like the one you get, you owe me what it costs to replace the stolen one."

"Done," I said. We shook hands on it, and the conversation turned to other subjects.

•   •   •

I intended to find a replacement bicycle immediately, but as it turned out, my time for the next few days was not my own. Mr. Clemens received a large package of galley proofs in the mail from England, and for a while everything else took second place to reading and correcting them. With no need to go into town, I had nothing to remind me of the stolen bicycle, and so of course by Saturday my bargain with Bob Danvers was still unfulfilled. I thought I would still have the weekend, and if I couldn't find a suitable replacement bicycle by then, Bob would have to understand. As far as I was concerned, my commitment to my employer overrode my private business.

Mrs. Clemens joined in the work—my employer always called her his most trustworthy editor—and despite her delicate health, worked well past her usual bedtime. This made the work go faster, and she proved her worth by catching a number of printer's errors that escaped both her husband and me. Alas, this dedication had a price—by Friday afternoon, she was beginning to look fatigued, and by Saturday, she had a nasty cough. It was evident she had come down with a full-blown winter cold. Nor was she alone in her affliction—little Jean, the youngest Clemens daughter, was in bed with the same illness.

When Mr. Clemens realized that his wife was ill, he began to talk of canceling the dinner engagement. "Well, Livy, we'll just have to let Wentworth describe the pictures to us," he said to his wife. "Nothing Raphael ever painted is worth taking you out to catch your death of pneumonia." His tone was jocular, but it was obvious he was concerned for her.

Mrs. Clemens would hear nothing of it. "We haven't seen a soul but each other since we came here," she said. "It'll be good for both of us to get out and meet some local people. And I do want to see the paintings. Besides, Youth, you need a break from work as much as I do. We can come home right after dinner, if it gets to be too much."

And so, my employer agreed to attend the party despite his better judgment—or so he claimed. I thought he was in fact as eager as his wife to be out and about, but he let concern for her health override his own preference. In any case, late Saturday afternoon, the three of us climbed into the carriage and set out for Florence, to dine with Frank Stephens and his other guests, and to admire his Raphaels.

There was a light mist, threatening to turn into a drizzle, as we left Villa Viviani, and so we traveled with the carriage's top up and the windows covered. While the weather was nowhere near as severe as what one would expect back home in New England this time of year, there was enough chill in the air for all of us to put on topcoats. I had heard that occasional light frost and even flurries of snow were not unknown in this part of Italy, but we had seen neither one to date—a damp chill was the worst Tuscany had shown us. Still, Mr. Clemens grumbled about the weather, saying, "If I'd known we were due for London fogs, I might as well have stayed in London." Remembering the climate there, I was not inclined to agree with him.

Our destination was in the Oltrarno—the section of Florence on the south bank of the Arno, and so our driver took us down from the plaza of Santa Croce to a road skirting the river embankment as far as Ponte Vecchio, where we crossed over to the south side. I got occasional glimpses of ancient buildings as we passed—there were few people on the streets this evening—and there were several gloomy vistas across the river, flat gray and showing nary a ripple today. Had I not seen it under far brighter skies, I might have drawn the conclusion that Florence was a dreary, forbidding city. And Mrs. Clemens's cold had acted as a wet blanket both on her spirits and on those of my employer. I hoped the atmosphere at the party would cheer them both up.

Frank Stephens's residence was a modest *palazzo* dating from the early eighteenth century—almost a modern structure, by Florentine standards. At a glance, the gardens were pleasantly laid out, but the weather gave us no leisure to inspect them; we hurried inside and delivered our coats to a tall, hawk-nosed servant, who spoke English with a trace of accent. "*Signore* Ste-*fans* expects you," he said, motioning us toward a broad stairway. Above, I could hear the sound of voices in animated conversation, and a warm light at the top of the stairs invited us to ascend and join in the merriment.

Halfway up the stairs, Mrs. Clemens (who was leaning on her husband's arm) stopped and began coughing. Her husband looked at her anxiously, and I paused to see if I might be of assistance to them. Hearing footsteps at the top of the stair, I turned to see Frank Stephens descending to meet us, a look of concern plain on his face. "Hello," he said. "Can I be of any help?"

Mrs. Clemens shook her head, but continued coughing. "She's got a bit of a cold," said Mr. Clemens. "I didn't want to bring her out, but she insisted . . ."

"Well, now that you're here, I hope you can come up-stairs," said Stephens, turning to Mrs. Clemens. "You can sit by the fire if you'd like, and I think we can get you something warm to drink—something good for that cough, anyhow."

"I'll be all right," said Mrs. Clemens, but her weak voice belied her. "Let me rest for just a moment. Are you Mr. Stephens? Thank you for the invitation."

"I'm honored to have you, Mrs. Clemens, and your il-lustrious husband," said Stephens. "I'd apologize for the weather, except I don't take any responsibility for it."

It took a few moments for Mrs. Clemens to regain enough strength to climb the rest of the way to the second floor and I could see how worried my employer was. His wife had a history of heart trouble, and while it normally did not interfere with her activities, the incipient cold had weakened her. After getting her settled in a seat by the fire, he turned to me and said in a low voice, "I don't know how long we'll be able to stay, Wentworth. I'd be a lot happier to get her home in bed."

"Just say the word, and I'll go have the carriage come around front," I said. "But I think she should regain her strength here by the fire for a little while—it can't be good to take her right back out into the damp again."

"You're right," he agreed, frowning. "But try to keep an eye on the weather—it's bad enough to take Livy out in the fog and drizzle, but a downright soaking would be even worse for her."

I nodded my agreement, then looked around and saw that we were in a large rectangular room paneled in light wood—oak, I thought, or maple. The ceiling was high, and a big crystal chandelier full of brightly burning candles gave the room a warm glow. At the opposite end from the fireplace, a group of musicians were setting up in a corner—a string quartet. Stephens had clearly made a considerable effort to impress his guests.

Along the walls, and on two or three movable screens at the end of the room away from the fire were hung an impressive selection of paintings, many by the Florentine masters of an earlier era. At first I was stunned at how much it must have cost Stephens to acquire such a treasury of art; then I recalled that buying and selling art was his stock in trade, and that many pieces were on temporary display, destined for some wealthy collector in America. Or perhaps Stephens hoped to entice some of his guests tonight to make an offer for them.

In the corner farthest from the stairway were the Raphaels. Stephens had set two large floor candelabra along the wall to shed additional light on the paintings, and several guests had gathered to examine them. Seeing that my employer and his wife were settled for the moment, I strolled over to take a look for myself. Two of the paintings were clearly a matched pair of portraits: a sharp-chinned gentleman and a rather plain lady in the formal dress of the early sixteenth century, both looking rather stern and ancestral. These two canvases were of modest size—perhaps two by two and a half feet—but the workmanship and the presence of a good quantity of gold in the costumes and ornaments indicated that the original owner had paid a good price for them. While I cannot pretend to be an expert, I thought that any museum would have been pleased to have either of them in its collection.

But it was the third painting that caught the eye, a young woman of exceptional beauty, a striking blonde in a light blue gown, her hair flowing free, and a touch of mischief in her eyes. The artist had captured her for the ages, I thought; and while the other two were undeniably the work of a master, this one lit up the room. One wanted to hear her speak, to hear her laugh—to spend an hour gazing into her brilliant blue eyes. I almost thought I knew her, she seemed so alive here—but she had no doubt gone to her grave three centuries before I was born. I wondered who she had been, and what her history was—perhaps Stephens had learned some of that from her former owner. I would have to be sure to ask him.

"Gorgeous, isn't she?" murmured Jonathan Wilson, noting my interest in the third painting. "That's the one Stephens says I can buy, if I've a mind to. I'm trying to decide how much the master did himself, and how much is apprentice work. The face and hands are his, of course. But the rest—I suppose I ought to get it looked at, but damn me if I'm not almost ready to buy it on the spot, before somebody else snatches it up."

"I envy you the opportunity," I said, keeping my own voice low—it felt as if we were in a museum rather than in someone's parlor. "If my budget could stretch that far, she'd be on my wall this evening."

"Yes, I quite agree. This is quite a discovery for Stephens, I must say—but he seems to have a nose for the old masters. Perhaps he'll let you in on the secret, and you can do as well."

"Perhaps he will," I said, somewhat uncomfortably. While I still had not refused Frank Stephens's offer of a position in his dealership, I had pretty much decided to remain with Mr. Clemens. I simply had not found an opportune moment to tell Stephens my decision. I would have to do so without much more delay, but tonight was not the proper time for it. Unwilling to pursue the subject, I excused myself and returned to Mr. and Mrs. Clemens, who were still seated by the fire.

Despite my employer's worries, the fire and a cup of hot tea with honey seemed to have revived Mrs. Clemens's spirits. The musicians had begun playing, too, a sprightly piece I thought might be by Haydn; it lightened the mood of the whole room. Mrs. Clemens's color had returned somewhat to her cheeks, and she smiled bravely at the other partygoers, several of whom had come to inquire about her—and, not at all incidentally, to introduce themselves to her husband.

Among the group was Virginia Fleetwood, very striking in a wasp-waisted dark green dress with a pearl choker. Her strawberry-blond hair was topped with an elaborate pearl-studded comb in a sort of Spanish style. Her eager glance and bright smile raised my spirits, which I now realized had been low, no doubt from a combination of overwork, bad weather, and anxiety over Mrs. Clemens's condition. But now I was beginning to feel in a mood for the party, and I was glad to see that my employer's wife was showing more energy.

After a few words to Mrs. Clemens, Virginia turned to my employer and said, "What a pleasure to meet you, Mr. Clemens! I have been enjoying your books since I was a little girl."

Mr. Clemens raised his eyebrows and said, "Why, that must be all of seven or eight years ago. You can't be more than fifteen, young lady."

Virginia laughed and blushed. "I am afraid it is a bit more than that, but I will claim a woman's prerogative regarding the exact figure. In any case, we are honored that you and your wife were able to join us. Mr. Cabot has told me so many interesting stories about you."

"Wentworth is a bright young fellow, and a great help to me," said Mr. Clemens, chuckling. "But I don't think a Yale education quite prepared him for the likes of me, and I'm afraid he's swallowed a few of my taller tales whole. I'll hope you've taken his remarks with a few grains of salt."

"Oh, he has not told me anything I would not believe of the author of *Innocents Abroad*," she said. "I hope you find Florence more to your taste now than you did then."

"I do," he said. He took a sip of his whisky and soda—Stephens had inquired as to my employer's taste in liquor, and on my advice made sure to lay in some good Scotch—

and continued: "Of course, I didn't have a villa back then, or a family, or any of a number of such conveniences. I hadn't even met this sweet lady here"—he put a hand on his wife's shoulder—"just her rascal of a brother, who did his best to lead me astray."

Mrs. Clemens looked up at her husband with a mock-indignant expression, saying, "Youth! I'll thank you not to blame my brother for your misdeeds. Pay my husband no mind, Miss Fleetwood. He is of ripe years, but far from mature. I have the greatest difficulty getting him to be serious in front of company."

"Why, that's what I pay Wentworth for," said Mr. Clemens, smiling. "It'd be silly of me to put my efforts into something I'm not suited for, when he's so natural and convincing at it."

"So I can see," said Virginia. "He really is a very earnest and capable young man. I'm sure that's why my brother-in-law was so anxious to hire him . . ."

"Virginia!" I said in a whisper that everyone in the room must have heard, but the horse was already out the barn door.

"I'm sure you'll miss him," she continued blithely. "But of course he has to look to his future. He'd be foolish to pass up a chance at a settled occupation just to keep rambling from one place to another and looking after your papers."

"I reckon he would," said Mr. Clemens, peering at me under raised eyebrows. His voice was almost expressionless. Luckily for me, he made no further comment—but I did not look forward to what he would say when we were back in private. If I could have melted into the cracks of the floorboard, I would have done so in an instant.

6

After the fire had sufficiently warmed her, Mrs. Clemens put down her teacup and expressed a desire to see the Raphaels. We went over to the wall where they were hung, and stood in silence for a moment while my employer and his wife examined the three portraits. At last, Mr. Clemens said, "Well, they're mighty good. You don't often see old masters where they aren't swamped by five hundred other paintings. A fellow can really *see* them here."

"Yes, even an old master benefits from a good hanging," said our host, who had come to join us when he saw my employer looking at the paintings.

"A lot of 'em should've gotten a good hanging," growled Mr. Clemens. "A fellow who could draw those blood-stained Medicis lounging around Heaven with the Virgin and a pack of saints was no better than the thieves who paid him. At least, these aren't Medicis—though for all I know, they were just as rotten."

"Oh, I beg to differ," said Isabella Stephens, who stood by her husband's side. "An artist in those days had no recourse but to please the wealthy, or the Church. The common people could not support a Raphael. Even those among them who could appreciate what he had done could not buy his paintings."

Mr. Clemens was about to say something, but I saw his wife give his arm a pinch, and he paused before continuing: "Well, I've been supported by the common people most of my life, and they haven't done too bad by me. If I'm not a rich man, it's my own bad judgment that's to blame. But nobody alive can claim he's paid me to bite my tongue, or to whitewash an outrage. Raphael could paint a fine picture—that pretty blonde is as good as I've seen—but I wouldn't trade my conscience for his, not on a bet." I could tell from the set of my employer's jaw that this wasn't just an attempt to draw his host into a humorous dispute. If anything, Mr. Clemens was more serious than usual.

"All three paintings are very fine," said Mrs. Clemens, who gave her husband's arm another pinch. "But my husband has suggested an interesting question. Tell me, Mr. Stephens—do you have any information on who the artist's subjects were?"

"The old *don* who sold them to me said they were his ancestors," Stephens replied. "The man was his several-times-great-grandfather, a prosperous vintner, I believe. The dark-haired woman was his wife, and the blonde was their daughter, as I recall it. There must be family records to supply the names, but I don't know how helpful the seller would be in such research."

"These are very well preserved," said Mr. Clemens, peering at the paintings from close range.

"You have a good eye," Stephens commented. "These are in remarkable condition—the previous owner told me they were kept in a cool, dry storeroom, where there was no lamp- or wood-smoke to build up on the surface. He thought they might have been there since his grandfather's time before he found them and put them on the market. They may never have to be cleaned now, if they're hung someplace with electric lights and modern heating. I can't tell you how many times I've seen a painting ruined by cleaning."

"Well, they're mighty good," said Mr. Clemens again.

"If there were more old masters like that blonde, I might revise my opinion of the Renaissance."

"Perhaps you ought to consider adding that one to your collection," said Stephens.

"Collection? I don't have a collection," said Mr. Clemens. "But if you'd like to take one up for me, I'll accept it. I can't afford to let too many such opportunities pass."

Everyone laughed, and just then the butler came to inform Mr. Stephens that dinner was served. We followed our host into the dining room, and proceeded to enjoy some of the best food I had had since arriving in Italy—with the added pleasure of the string quartet, which played between courses. The meal began with little fried dumplings stuffed with salty fish, followed by a soup containing chicken liver and flat noodles. Both these, I was told, were traditional Florentine dishes.

The main course was one I had eaten in several local restaurants, broiled chicken parts on the bone, with a hint of lemon. This was accompanied by stuffed artichokes—a delicacy I had not tasted before—and a dish of white beans, baked with olive oil and sage. I remarked how different this was from the New England style of baked beans, and Mrs. Atwater laughed. "The Italians were making this dish when there was nobody in America except Red Indians," she said.

Frank Stephens picked up the subject Mr. Clemens had hinted at before we were called to dinner, saying, "It surprises me that you haven't made any investment in art, Mr. Clemens. Believe me, it gives a fellow far more pleasure than stocks and bonds. If the market collapses, you've got something pleasant to look at—assuming you've done the smart thing and bought something you like. It's a mistake to buy a piece one doesn't like just on the theory it'll increase in value."

"Yes, I know what it's like to look at something you paid thousands of dollars for and can't get rid of at any price," said Mr. Clemens. "There's a typesetting machine back in Hartford that ate up more than a whole museum full of art would have—and believe me, it's the least enjoyable thing to look at you ever saw."

"It's never too late," said Isabella Stephens, smiling. She was a very attractive woman with lively features and a quick wit, an older version of her sister, Virginia, I thought. "Frank will give you a very fair price on one of the Raphaels, or on something else, if they're not to your taste."

"I reckon I'll pass," said Mr. Clemens, chuckling. "Every time I see an old master, there's two or three students out in front of it making copies, and the copies always look better than the original. Why shouldn't I buy a copy at a hundredth of the price? I'd be just as happy. Why, I'd be just as happy with a good chromo."

"That's the same game everybody else plays," Eddie Freeman blurted out, in a strained voice. He gulped, leaned forward and said, somewhat more calmly, "I'm one of those people out front making copies, and half the time I can't get a decent price for my stuff. What good's art if you can't pay the rent?"

"I am absolutely surrounded by Philistines," said Penelope Atwater, placing the back of her wrist to her forehead and pretending to feel faint. "Mr. Clemens, I had hoped experience of the world might have changed your opinions since your previous visit to Florence, but I see you remain content to jeer at the productions of genius." She shot a fierce stare at Mr. Clemens, challenging him to contradict her.

"No, ma'am, I'm a great admirer of genius," said Mr. Clemens. "I just don't think it was confined to the Renaissance, or the Silurian, or some other ancient period. Why, Tom Edison's as much a genius as Leonardo da Vinci ever was."

"I am not surprised that you would think so," said Mrs. Atwater, with a ladylike little snort. "You think mechanics and tinkerers have as much to contribute to mankind as the old masters."

"No, ma'am," Mr. Clemens said again. "I think Edison's done *more* than any of the old masters, and without kowtowing to the Medicis, or the Popes, or other such impostors. I don't deny myself the pleasure of looking at fine paintings, but, with apologies to our artist friend here"— he nodded to Eddie—"I know where they belong in the scale of human values." He smiled benignly, and took a bite of the chicken.

"Do you think Mr. Clemens will convert Mrs. Atwater to his position?" said Virginia Fleetwood, who was seated next to me, some distance from my employer and his wife. "Could you pass the butter, please?"

"No, nor will she convert him," I said, reaching for the butter plate. I was not as comfortable being seated next to her as I might have been. She had put me in a very awkward position by taking it for granted that I would be accepting Stephens's job offer—and by saying so to my current employer. But I couldn't upbraid her for her indiscretion in front of company. It would have to wait for later. Almost as if she had read my mind, Virginia said smugly, "If he is so blind to the value of great artists, you shan't regret leaving his employment. I hope you won't delay it much longer."

That was rubbing salt in the wound. "Perhaps you should let me make my own decisions," I said, a bit more hotly than might have been politic. Across the table, Sarah Woods raised an eyebrow, and I lowered my voice. "Even if I had made such a decision, I didn't ask you to announce it for me."

Virginia leaned close to my ear and whispered, "I am surprised at you, Wentworth. I hope Frank hasn't overheard you—he might change his mind about offering a job to someone so hesitant to accept it. But we ought to be discreet in front of company. After supper, we'll discuss this in private."

I was tempted to point out that it had been she who had first been indiscreet in front of company, but thought better of it. Starting a public argument would compound the offense. I bit back my rejoinder, nodded my agreement, and returned to my food. It had been mere moments since my previous mouthful, but somehow I seemed to have lost my appetite. Indeed, I had a hard time doing the rest of the dinner justice.

As dessert, we were offered chestnuts cooked in a sweet sauce and—a special surprise!—ice cream in the American style. Accompanying this was a sweet wine, not port or Madeira but another local product. Vino Santo, our host called it. I began to calculate how many pounds this meal was going to add to my weight, and how many hours of exercise—something I got far too little of these days—it would take to counteract it.

Although Mrs. Clemens had recovered some of her strength and her spirits at the Stephenses' fireside, during dinner it became clear that she was by no means over her illness. She had picked at her food, and had several coughing spells. One of these was so persistent that she left the table (assisted by her husband) for perhaps ten minutes to recover her breath. When she returned, I could see that the color had drained from her face, and I was frankly more worried about her condition than about what I was going to say to Frank Stephens—or to Virginia.

At last, Mr. Clemens leaned over to our host, and I could see that he was giving his regrets at having to retire early. I excused myself to my tablemates, and joined him. His nod was enough to signal his intention, and I went downstairs to call our carriage around front, and asked the butler to fetch our topcoats. Mrs. Clemens huddled in a chair in the hallway, shivering. Her husband's arm over her shoulder was all she had to warm her. Luckily, the mist outside had lifted, though the air was still chilly.

The wait was brief—we had warned the driver that he might be needed on short notice, and evidently he had taken the admonition to heart. I was all ready to leave with my employer and his wife, when Mr. Clemens looked at me and said, "You might as well stay here, Wentworth. There's nothing for you to do back at the villa tonight—you might as well enjoy the party with your new friends. I'll send the driver back, and you can come home when you're ready."

"If you're certain, sir," I said, and he nodded. I helped

them on with their coats, stepped outside long enough to assist Mrs. Clemens into the carriage, and watched them drive off. It was not until I turned to go back inside that I felt the delayed sting of the phrase he had used: "new friends."

Thinking about that phrase, I began to worry about my future with Mr. Clemens. It was not easy to dismiss the implication that choosing to stay with new friends might cost me my old ones. Or was I imagining it? I saw that I would need to clear the air with Mr. Clemens upon my return to Villa Viviani. It would be a disaster to discover that I had lost my employer's confidence just as I had resolved to cast my lot with him.

That put me in a delicate position with Frank Stephens. Only the impending party had kept me from informing him of my decision—I wouldn't be comfortable visiting his home after turning down his job offer. But after Virginia's plain statement that I was about to accept the job, announcing my real intentions was likely to create an even more awkward situation. I would have to speak frankly with her and (despite my original intention not to spoil the party by talking business) with my host. Resigned to a pair of unpleasant confrontations, I made my way back upstairs.

The ladies had already left the table and were gathered by the fireplace in the room at the head of the stairs. While I wanted to talk with Virginia, I thought it proper first to spend a short while with my host and the other men. I took my old seat, responded to inquiries as to Mrs. Clemens's health, and let Stephens pour me a glass of brandy. Then Jonathan Wilson, who had been speaking when I came in, resumed what turned out to be a long and confusing story (at least to me, who had missed the beginning). I sipped my brandy, trying to sort out the characters, and the odd situation they seemed to have gotten themselves into. At this I had little success—perhaps in part because my mind was distracted by what I meant to say to Virginia. So when Wilson's story ended with a round of boisterous laughter, I hadn't the slightest idea what everyone else found so humorous.

Stephens, noting my abstraction, leaned over to me and said, "You're looking a bit glum, Cabot. Here, this'll fix you up," and topped up my brandy. I was surprised that I had drunk so much of it, and resolved to nurse the rest of my glass, not wanting to get too tipsy before going home. Besides, I needed my wits about me before I spoke with Virginia.

My chain of thought was broken by Bob Danvers, who leaned over to me and said, "Any luck finding a new bike, Cabot?"

"I'm afraid not," I told him. "Mr. Clemens has had me working like a Trojan all week, and I've had no chance to get into town before this evening."

"Well, damn it, you said you'd have it before Monday," said Danvers, a bit louder than I thought tactful. I realized he was drunk. "Nobody'll be selling them on Sunday, you know. You might as well just give me the money for it now."

"I'm sorry," I said, quite sincerely. "I meant to get the matter settled before now, but I couldn't leave Mr. Clemens in the lurch. Can I have till Wednesday?"

"You'll be leaving Clemens in the lurch soon enough," said Danvers, more belligerently. "Besides, we agreed on Monday, and I need the money for my landlady—the old witch won't listen to sense. Why don't you just hand it over?"

I could see there was no arguing with him. "Very well, I don't want to cheat you. How much is it again?"

"I paid seventy-five lira for it," Danvers said. "Since it was used, let's make it sixty."

"Sixty?" I said, frowning. "You already told me you paid too much for it—why, I bet I could get as good a bike as the stolen one for no more than fifty. Besides, I've paid you over thirty in rental. That ought to count for something."

Eddie Freeman snickered and said, "No wonder Stephens wants you to run his art gallery. If that's the way you're going to squeeze the customers, you'll bring in a fortune. Old man Battista could take lessons from you."

The others at the table laughed, although I saw nothing humorous in it. I thought Stephens's expression was a bit strained, as well. Nor was Danvers amused at his friend's quip. He pounded a fist on the table. "I should've known you'd try to worm out of the deal," he said. "I want sixty lira, and that's the last I'm going to say about it."

I was surprised at how adamant he was. Sixty lira was far too much for the bicycle. For that price, I could have bought a fine new one in America. "I'll give you fifty right now, and that's my last offer," I said. "You're lucky I have that much on me, to tell the truth."

Danvers half rose out of his seat. "Damn you, I'll take the other ten out of your hide," he said. He made a step toward me, and I tried to decide whether to stand and defend myself, or keep my seat and try to reason with him.

Stephens saved me the trouble. "Bob, stop being foolish and sit down," he said. "Cabot's been working for Clemens, so sixty lira seems like a lot to him. I'll pay you the whole thing now and Cabot can pay me back when he's working for me. I won't have my friends arguing over money at my table."

"That's a very generous offer," I said to Stephens, taking out my wallet. "But I pay my own debts. Let's get it over with, Bob. Will you take fifty now and the balance Monday afternoon?"

"Fair enough," growled Danvers. "I guess you're square, after all, Cabot." He took the money and we shook hands, but beyond paying his ten lira, I had already made up my mind to have no more to do with him. That would be easy, once I told Stephens that I was refusing his job offer. It would probably mean my being dropped by the entire American group at Cafe Diabelli.

All this I was ready to accept. I would find friends in other cafes—and in other cities—in due time. For all their wit and sophistication, I was not entirely comfortable with the group I had fallen in with here. But even if I was about to sever my relations with them, I still hoped to salvage something of my relationship with Virginia Fleetwood.

Stephens steered the conversation back onto safe subjects, but I thought the spirit had gone out of the evening. Freeman and Danvers drank more than they talked, and the argument had made me reluctant to put myself forward. The host and Jonathan Wilson did most of the talking; but accustomed as I was to Mr. Clemens's table talk, their repartee seemed rather lifeless. When I judged that I had sat with the other men long enough to satisfy convention, I excused myself, and went looking for Virginia.

I found her with a group of women, sitting by the fire in the main room, just outside the dining room door. Virginia sat reading a magazine, while several others in the group were debating the relative merits of modern French painters. This was a subject on which I knew less than I wished—the names of Degas, Monet, Renoir, and others, were familiar to me, but I had still seen very few examples of their work.

I stood for a moment at the fringe of the circle, hoping to catch Virginia's eye, but she seemed absorbed in her reading, and the others babbled on without paying me the least notice. At last, feeling uncomfortable, I said in a quiet voice, "Excuse me, Virginia."

To my chagrin, everyone's conversation came to a halt and all the women turned to stare at me as Virginia looked up and said, "Yes, Mr. Cabot?"

I soldiered on. "Pardon the interruption, but I need to speak to you. Is there someplace where we won't disturb these ladies?"

She raised her brows. "Mr. Cabot, don't you think we should have a chaperon?" she said crisply. This comment brought several ill-muffled giggles from the other women around the fire.

"I suppose I cannot object if you feel you need one," I said, trying not to react. "I don't think it will be necessary, though."

"Really, Mr. Cabot, I would think that association with Mark Twain would have taught you to recognize a joke," she said, rising to her feet. She smiled and winked at me, but her words had left a sting. She turned to the other ladies. "If you will excuse me? I do not expect to be long."

This statement was greeted with a few more giggles, but I did my best to keep my rising anger from showing as I followed her away from the group.

She led me to a small, very tastefully appointed reading room just down a short hall from the gallery. There were bookshelves behind her, with a bottom row of oversized art books, and a large table with one open to a color lithograph of Raphael's "Madonna del Granduca," which I remembered from the Pitti. Virginia sat in a cane-backed chair, next to a dictionary stand, and looked expectantly up at me—I found myself more comfortable on my feet, "Now, Mr. Cabot, what did you wish to say to me?" she asked.

I realized I was not prepared to say what was upmost in my mind. Instead, I paced for a moment, then stopped and turned to her. "I don't appreciate your putting pressure on me to accept your brother-in-law's offer of a position."

"Why, I did no such thing," she said, tossing her head. "The last time we discussed the subject, it seemed clear you were going to take the job. You acted as if it were merely a matter of finding the right moment to give notice to Mr. Clemens."

"Perhaps; even so, you should not have spoken of it in front of Mr. Clemens until you knew I had made the break. You put me in a very awkward position."

"Pshaw," she said, with a negligent wave of the hand. "Of course it's awkward. Leaving a position is always awkward, but one gets over it soon enough."

"Being made to appear as if I intend to leave, when in fact I don't, is even more awkward. Now I have to go to Mr. Clemens and convince him I want to stay with him."

"Why on earth would you want to stay?" she exclaimed. "His best days are behind him, and the pay is not congruent with your social position—at least, with the position you ought to have. With Frank, you would be on your way to earning a very substantial living. This is very foolish of you, Wentworth." She shook her head as if I had been speaking complete nonsense, then smoothed the long folds of her dress and looked up at me.

"If I cared about my social position, I would have stayed

home and joined my father's law practice," I said testily. This was a subject on which my mother had been eloquent—if mere persistence had been able to wear me down, she would doubtless have done it long before I had come to Europe with Mr. Clemens. "There are more things in life than social position," I added.

"There may be, but that's no reason to throw away what one already has," she persisted. "With your name and your family connections, you would be ideal for the Boston position. Frank considers them your main qualifications."

"I'm sorry to hear that," I said. "It makes me wonder if the job is all I thought it to be."

"I am beginning to wonder if *you* are all I thought you to be," she retorted, her face now red, and her eyes staring. "In fact, I am beginning to wonder if you are not a fool."

"I see that I have been mistaken in my assessment of our relationship," I said, biting back my anger. "I suppose I should be glad to have learned this before I did make a fool of myself. I think we have said all we need to, Miss Fleetwood. My apologies for taking you away from your friends."

She turned a cold eye on me. "I have said everything I mean to, Mr. Cabot. Please be so kind as to leave me."

"Good evening," I said, with a bow, and turned on my heels and left the room.

I strode straight past the circle of women by the fire and to the stairway. They looked up as I marched by, but if any of them said anything, I didn't hear it. Downstairs, I called for my coat, determined not to stay any longer. I had nothing further to say to anyone there.

The butler brought my coat, and without another word to anyone, I stepped out the door and into the night.

The mist that had hovered along the river when we arrived at the party had lifted, although the air was still damp and chilly. But having made up my mind to leave before I had a ride home, I had given myself no choice but to set out on foot. Perhaps I would meet the carriage returning from Villa Viviani. If not, I was ready to walk the entire way. It would do me good.

I kept up a brisk pace so as to feel the cold as little as possible. Fortunately, I knew the way well. Getting myself lost, late at night in a foreign city, would not have been a pleasant prospect even on a fine summer night. But the best route home was along major streets, and there was a fair amount of traffic still about. I would have no trouble finding my way.

In fact, I found my way almost as accurately as a carriage driver whose horse knows the road by heart—and with almost as little attention to how I got there. Every now and then I would realize that I had reached a certain landmark or turning, without any memory of passing through the streets that brought me there. Instead, my mind kept returning to the confrontation with Virginia in that little reading room at the Stephenses. The scales had fallen from my eyes, and now the world looked different to me.

I had been attracted to Virginia by her apparent independence of thought. Like my employer in many ways, she—and indeed, the whole group of Americans residing in Florence—had abandoned the conventional notions of common society at home. Their concern for art and beauty, for the creative spirit, set them apart—or so I had thought. Now I was not so certain. It was one thing to speak of art and literature, to lay claim to the republic of ideas and the life of the mind. But all that had been revealed as a façade.

Virginia had made it clear that Stephens's interest in me—and presumably her own—was only on account of my family connections. They looked upon me as a Cabot, as someone with entrée into the higher levels of American society that were closed to them. To them, I was a tool to get wealthy people to part with as much of their money as possible, with a minimum of actual effort. And if I wouldn't help them accomplish that, I was of no particular use to them.

Was I being foolish? I didn't object to earning a good living, not even to making a fortune for myself. But I wasn't about to be a pawn in someone else's cynical games.

Not even if that someone else was Virginia—or, I corrected myself, Miss Fleetwood—for now I realized that she and I were not, after all, suited. I felt a loss, even though we had never had any real understanding. Still, it must have been clear to everyone that we had been moving in that direction. Thank heaven I had not taken any irrevocable steps!

There was no longer any question of asking her to "wait for me" when I went traveling with Mr. Clemens, or of suggesting that her presence would be welcome if her travels should take her to the same distant city that my employer's itinerary had taken me. We could never be any more than friends now. Perhaps it was best so. She might well be as bitter about what she had learned of my character tonight as I was about my new insights into her. She must consider me naive, perhaps even stupid, for not wanting to be a part of Stephens's business. And, from her point of view, perhaps I was. But I was not about to change in that respect—not even for Virginia.

I realized that it might be awkward for her to see me again. Perhaps it might be best for me to absent myself from Cafe Diabelli for a few days—I might not be welcome in that tight-knit group, if they saw me as having toyed with Virginia's affections. I did not welcome the thought of losing that convivial company in addition to Virginia; but better that than making myself a possible cause of embarrassment and discomfort to all concerned.

I was so lost in these thoughts that I nearly missed the carriage coming back from Villa Viviani to fetch me home. But then the driver called out, "*Ciao, Signore* Cabot!" and I came to my senses. I climbed aboard, he turned his rig around, and we were home before I knew it.

7 ~

I awoke the next morning with a pounding in my head. This was a nuisance; while I had drunk a bit more than usual the night before, I had gone to bed clear-headed. Walking a third of the way home before meeting the carriage had burned off the drink, and much of the dinner as well. And my early departure from the party meant that I had gotten to bed at a quite respectable hour. So why did my head ache?

I shaved, bathed, dressed, and made my way downstairs, where the chef made me a plate of ham and eggs as good as one would find in the best American restaurant, with plenty of coffee to wash it down. By now, the headache was fading. I had not yet seen any sign of Mr. Clemens or his family, when the Clemens ladies' maid, Elsa—a young German girl who spoke almost nothing but her own tongue, with an occasional Italian or English word thrown in— came into the dining room and said, *"Kommen Sie bitte, Herr Ventvort, Polizei hier sind."*

I understood that well enough. "Police? What in heaven's name can they want?" I said to myself. Not wanting to disturb Mr. Clemens—who if awake, was probably still in bed, reading—I went to see what the matter was.

There were two men at the door, one tall, the other short, dressed in black frock coats with red facings and cocked hats. In other circumstances I might have found these uniforms comical, but the men's expressions were dead serious. "Good morning—how can I be of assistance?" I said in my still-rudimentary Italian.

The taller man replied with a volley of rapid-fire Italian of which I could make out close to nothing. My blank stare must have conveyed as much, because after an awkward silence the other fellow said, in good English, "We are here on police business, and we need to speak to some people here. Please, may we enter?"

"To whom do you need to speak?" I asked, standing in the doorway. "Has there been a crime?" It occurred to me that perhaps they had come to investigate the stolen bicycle. If so, I was ready to revise my opinion of Italian policemen—an opinion based entirely upon hearsay.

"Yes, *signore*, a very serious crime," said the short policeman, whose more elaborate uniform suggested a higher rank. "We must speak to *Signore* Clemens, and to *Signore* Cabot."

"I am *Signore* Cabot," I said. The mention of Mr. Clemens, who of course had nothing to do with the bicycle, put to rest any notion that their business had to do with that. "Please come in, and I will call Mr. Clemens."

The two men followed me into the front room, where the German maid waited. "Elsa, bring Herr Clemens here," I said, and she nodded and went out—which I hoped meant she understood me. There was an uncomfortable interval while I stood with the two policemen, who looked with undisguised curiosity at the room and its furniture—and at me—but remained silent. Having nothing to volunteer in the way of conversation, I stood and waited with them. It seemed a long time.

At last, Mr. Clemens came down the stairs. He entered the room looking markedly grumpy (as he often did before breakfast), and turned to me. "What's the matter here, Wentworth?" he said. "Who are these fellows? I couldn't get a lick of sense out of that girl."

"You are *Signore* Clemens?" said the short man, stepping forward. He had silver-gray hair and a close-trimmed beard. A pair of silver-rimmed spectacles gave his face a serious cast, but his eyes looked as if they could twinkle when the occasion was right.

"If that's who you're looking for, I'm the one," said my employer. "And who am I talking to?"

"I am *Capitano* Rosalia of the *carabinieri*, and this is *Agente* Maggio, my assistant," said the gray-bearded policeman. He took a notebook and pencil out of his coat pocket. "We are informed that you and *Signore* Cabot attended a dinner at the home of *Signore* Frank Stephens last night—is that so?"

My employer shrugged. "Sure, we went to Stephens's— me and my wife and my secretary. What happened that you're interested in?"

Capitano Rosalia spread his hands. "Excuse me, *Signore* Clemens, it is the custom here for the police to ask the questions. When you were there did *Signore* Stephens show you some paintings?"

I could see that Mr. Clemens was annoyed at the policeman's insistence on setting the agenda, but he held his temper and said, "That's right. What about 'em?"

The captain persisted. "Did you notice in particular a portrait of a young woman, said to be by Raphael?"

"Sure," said Mr. Clemens. "The main reason we went there, besides eating dinner, was to see the Raphaels. Stephens was trying to sell me the one you asked about, but I don't have that kind of money."

"Not many of us can afford a Raphael," said the captain, nodding. "Did you happen to see if it was there when you left?"

"No, we came home right after dinner because my wife was ill. I wasn't paying attention to anything else," said Mr. Clemens. Then he raised and eyebrow and said, "What's happened to the painting?"

"That is what we would like to discover," said the police captain. "*Signore* Cabot, did you notice this painting?"

I thought for a moment. "Yes, of course. But as far as I know it was still there when I left."

"And when was that?"

"Some time after Mr. Clemens—two or three hours later, perhaps," I said. "It might have been around ten o'clock when I left, and it was almost eleven when I got home. I walked partway, and then our coachman met me and brought me home."

"Did anyone see you arrive here?" asked the captain.

"The coachman brought me to the door. I didn't talk to anyone inside, but perhaps one of the servants heard me come in."

"We will question the servants if we need to confirm that," said Rosalia, looking in his book. "We understand that you spent some time alone with *Signorina* Fleetwood before you left. Is that true?"

"Yes, but I don't see how that's your business," I said, somewhat more heatedly than I intended. Mr. Clemens's eyebrows rose even higher than before, and I caught a flicker of a smile around his lips, but he said nothing.

"It may become our business," said the captain, again shrugging. "Did *Signorina* Fleetwood say anything to you that indicated she was planning to leave the party?"

"No, nothing of the sort," I said. "What—"

Mr. Clemens broke in. "I see what the captain's getting at. That picture's missing, and so's the girl. And they think there's a connection."

"You have it precisely," agreed the captain, with a thin smile. "As far as we can learn, *Signore* Cabot was the last person to speak to *Signorina* Fleetwood. Nobody admits seeing her at all after he left. Is that not interesting?"

"Perhaps, but it has no particular significance," I said. "We didn't discuss the painting at all, and nothing she said to me indicated she was going to leave the party. That is where she lived. Mrs. Stephens is her sister."

"Yes, we know that," said *Capitano* Rosalia. "Mrs. Stephens told us that she expected her sister to stay there. She wondered if your talk changed her sister's mind."

"Of course not," I said. "What would I have said that might have made her leave?"

"I was hoping to learn that from you," said the captain, spreading his hands again. "Pardon me if I seem to be impolite, *Signore* Cabot, but it is the nature of my work that I sometimes find it necessary to ask impolite questions. I will tell you this: The other ladies, when they heard you ask to speak with her, thought you were going to propose marriage to her. Is that true?"

At this, Mr. Clemens had a coughing fit, which I did not think at all natural. For myself, I felt the heat rising to my cheeks. "I could have had something like that in mind a few days ago. After last night, I don't think I would be quite so ready to do so."

"Ahh," said *Capitano* Rosalia. "And would you please tell me what happened last night to change your mind?"

My first reaction was to tell him to mind his own business, but then I realized that he was doing just that. I outlined Frank Stephens's job offer, my decision not to accept it, and Virginia's embarrassing me in front of Mr. Clemens by assuming that I would be changing jobs. When I was done, I turned to Mr. Clemens. "I'm sorry not to have been more forthright with you, sir. But I just couldn't find an appropriate opportunity to refuse Mr. Stephens, and kept putting it off."

"Well, I know it's hard to say no to people," said my employer. "I've gotten in trouble that way myself. But I'm glad I won't have to find a new secretary. I doubt there are many good candidates on this side of the Atlantic."

Capitano Rosalia had jotted down my explanation of what had gone on between me and Virginia. He looked up from his notes and said, "So, you say that the ladies were mistaken. In that case, I assume you do not know where *Signorina* Fleetwood might have gone after you spoke? Do you know of a particular place she might have gone?"

"No, as I say, I didn't know she meant to go anywhere except back to her friends at the party. The only places I have ever seen her are the museums, and a cafe in town where Americans congregate."

"Oh, yes, Cafe Diabelli," said Rosalia. "That place often comes to our attention for one thing or another. The food is very good, too. We will ask there—perhaps she will appear, and the mystery will be solved."

"Except for the missing painting," said Mr. Clemens. "That's a story you don't hear every day—a painting stolen right from the middle of a party. Well, good luck finding it—it was a nice piece of work, if you like the old masters."

"Ah, I like them very much," said the captain, putting away his notebook. "But like you, I cannot afford to buy them. I thank you for your time, *signori*. I may have other questions later, but for now, a good morning to you." He beckoned to *Agente* Maggio, who had stood with a placid expression during the interview, giving the impression that he understood very little of what was being said, unless one noticed his eyes. The captain gave us a formal bow that I found somewhat incongruous, and the two policemen swept out the door.

"I'll be damned," said Mr. Clemens, staring at the door that closed behind them. "What do you make of that?"

"I haven't the slightest notion what to make of any of it," I confessed. "I'm surprised enough that Miss Fleetwood is missing, let alone the painting. I'm sure she couldn't have stolen it."

"Maybe not," said Mr. Clemens. "But if she didn't take it, who did? And why would she fly the coop if she hadn't—or at least unless she knew who had?"

"I'm as baffled as you are," I said. "But I expect the truth will come out. It probably *will* make a good story for you, when it does." I tried to keep my tone light and easy, but from Mr. Clemens' raised eyebrows, I knew I had not managed to hide my concern about Virginia. It was not like her to walk off without telling anyone. And it was worrisome that she had disappeared at the same time as the painting. I hoped she had not met with some misfortune. But Mr. Clemens did not press the subject, and I was just as glad to let it drop.

•   •   •

I did not expect to learn any more about the missing painting that day. Mrs. Clemens's cold had not gotten any better overnight, and so she stayed in bed, with her daughters bringing her meals and nursing her. Mr. Clemens went to his office and tried to work and read, but for the most part he fretted and paced, and wondered whether there was an American doctor to be found in Florence.

For my part, I was catching up with tasks I had fallen behind in. There were always plenty of these—Mr. Clemens's correspondence and his body of work in various stages of publication would have kept an entire squad of secretaries busy, had he insisted on complete efficiency in the management of his affairs. He was usually content with something less, and so I was under pressure only when some project needed to be pushed through quickly. But there was nothing urgent at the moment, and so I busied myself with odds and ends.

I was completing letters of inquiry to several German spas where my employer thought Mrs. Clemens might find some relief from her chronic illness, when I became aware that he had been staring at me—for how long I couldn't tell. I looked up to see that he had put down the book he'd been reading—some historical treatise on the Hundred Years' War—and met his gaze. "Yes, sir?" I said, sensing that he wanted to talk.

"I feel like stretching my legs," he said. "Come on, let's go out and grab a breath of fresh air while it's still light."

We got our coats and walked out to a cedar-lined path affording a view of the city to the west, and the Tuscan hills beyond. There was a bit of a breeze blowing, but today the air was dry, and the light blue sky was almost cloudless. One could sense that the winter was gradually loosening its grip.

A short distance from the villa, Mr. Clemens stopped and turned to me. "You know, Wentworth, you don't have to feel guilty," he said. "There's nothing wrong with getting offered another job, or about giving it serious consideration. That means you're worth something to somebody besides me, and that can be valuable ammunition if you ever start to think I'm taking advantage of you. I'm glad you decided to stay on, but I wouldn't have blamed you if you'd taken that job."

"Well, I won't be taking it," I told him.

"I gathered as much from what you told those silly-looking cops," he said, fishing his tobacco pouch out of his pocket. "I wonder if their uniforms are supposed to make the people they're chasing laugh so hard they can't run away."

"I wouldn't take them so lightly," I suggested, scuffling my feet on the gravel path. "That *Agente* Maggio didn't say much, but his eyes were taking in everything. I'll bet he could list every item in the room after they left."

"Oh, I'm not about to underestimate them," he said. "In fact, I'm mighty impressed. They were out here the next morning after a missing-person report—and they'd already talked to some of the other partygoers. That's fast work—not what I'd expect in this part of the world."

"The missing painting probably made them take notice," I speculated. "Art thieves at work in their jurisdiction might spur them to extraordinary efforts. I don't know much about Florence, not from the short time I've been here, but I do know that art is one thing this city takes very seriously."

"You're right about that," he agreed. "They've got more paintings than Missouri has corn—you'd think they wouldn't miss one little piece. But I guess it'd be bad for business if they couldn't recover a missing Raphael. Stephens must be tearing his hair out."

"Yes, that must be the main thing on his mind at the moment," I said, stuffing my hands into my coat pockets. "Well, that and Virginia's disappearing at the same time. He must be wondering the same as the police—whether there's any connection."

"Not whether there's any connection, but what the connection is, I'd think," said Mr. Clemens. He had his pipe packed by now, and was about to strike a match when his eyes lit up. "Say, Wentworth, you're in a perfect spot to find out about this whole mess. Did you say you hadn't given Stephens your answer on his job offer yet?"

"I'm afraid so. I had made up my mind to tell him right before he invited us to last night's dinner party, and then it seemed tactless to accept the dinner invitation at the same time I was refusing his job. I thought I would wait until after, if he didn't press me on the subject."

"Well, now it's after, isn't it?" said my employer. He looked at me intently, obviously expecting me to draw some conclusion from this bald statement.

After a moment, I said, "Do you want me to go over there this afternoon and decline his offer? I'd think it would be even less convenient now than it was before the party."

"There's never a convenient time to tell somebody something he doesn't want to hear," said Mr. Clemens, striking his match and sheltering it from the breeze with the other hand. "If you wait for that, you and Stephens will both be on your deathbeds, and still not ready to inconvenience one another. No, today's as good a time as any—*he* won't know you've found out about the painting and the girl both being gone. In fact, I reckon it'd be a perfect time for you to find out what there is to learn about the situation."

"You're going to play detective again," I accused him. "I thought you'd sworn it off after that business in London."

"Did I?" he asked. He looked up from the burning match with an innocent expression. "Well, maybe I said something to that effect at the time. But that was a murder case—this doesn't look that serious, does it? A stolen painting, a pretty young lady gone missing—those aren't anywhere near as nasty as murder, are they?"

"Why are you asking me?" I retorted. "It looks to me as if you've let your curiosity get the better of you. And you certainly have no personal stake in this affair." As I said those words, I realized that *I* had a personal stake in it. I worried that Virginia Fleetwood might somehow be involved. Even though our disagreement last night had made me think twice about our relationship, I still liked the young lady. I did not like to think that she was mixed up in something possibly . . . *criminal*. There was no other word for it.

My employer shook his head. "A cop comes to my door, routs me out of bed, and asks me questions while his partner takes inventory of my parlor, as if I'd be fool enough to go to somebody's house and hook a Raphael and then hang it on my own wall the next day. If that ain't personal, neither's a punch in the nose," he said. The match had burned down close to his fingers, and he shook it out and dropped it on the path before continuing. "Besides, you pointed out yourself that there's a story in it. If stories aren't my business, I don't know what is." He looked pleased with himself.

I wasn't convinced by this. "If you're so interested in the story, why aren't you going to get it yourself?"

"Because I trust you, Wentworth," he said. "Besides, you can go there without anybody paying you much attention. You have real business there. I can't walk across the street without somebody taking notice, and if I show up someplace where something suspicious has happened, half the city will know about it by nightfall. Besides, I can't leave Livy, sick as she is."

"I suspect your daughters can take care of her as well as you can—if not better," I noted. "But I suppose the rest of your argument holds. Very well, I'll go over there to assuage your curiosity. What do you want me to ask about?"

"The obvious things, I suppose," said Mr. Clemens, pointing the stem of the still-unlit pipe at me. "Who noticed the picture missing, and when they noticed it. Who found out the young lady was missing, and when. Who was still there at the time. Who'd left, and when."

"The police will already know those things," I pointed out.

"Sure, but they won't tell 'em to me," said Mr. Clemens. He dug in his pocket for another match. "You can get it straight from the horse's mouth—start off by telling Stephens that you've thought about his job offer and decided you can't take it—and then you can ask for Miss Fleetwood, and act surprised when they say she's gone. That'll give you an opening to get them talking about the rest."

"What if they don't want to talk? Stephens may be angry

when I turn down his offer, and order me out of the place."

"Maybe—that's a risk we'll take," Mr. Clemens said, turning his steps back toward the villa. "I don't see him as a fellow who loses his temper over nothing, though. Even if he does, we're no worse off than we are right now. Now, go ahead before it gets too late. The coachman will take you over there—I'm not going anywhere today."

Resigned to the confrontation I had put off for so long, I stopped to tell the driver to hitch up his team. I did not relish the idea of bringing Frank Stephens his third piece of bad news in less than twenty-four hours. Then again, I reasoned, my refusal of his job was probably the least disturbing item of business he had to deal with today.

Besides, I was every bit as curious as Mr. Clemens to learn more about the disappearance of Virginia Fleetwood and the painting. I found myself hoping that I might arrive there to discover that Virginia had returned home after all. That would ease my mind a good deal—even though seeing her would be awkward after our unpleasant parting the night before. Still, it would be good to know that she was safe. It might even be sufficient compensation for the fact that I was turning down a steady, respectable job, the likes of which I could not expect to be offered any time soon again.

≈ **8**

On the coach ride from Villa Viviani to Frank Stephens's residence, I had plenty of time to stare out the window at the afternoon sun on the Arno and ponder my errand. Having gone on similar missions for Mr. Clemens before, I was no novice at entering someone's home under false pretenses and tricking them into telling me things they might not have volunteered.

But somehow this felt different. Other times, I had been sent to get information from people with whom I had no particular connection. At most, I had met them socially a couple of times. But Frank Stephens had befriended me; had offered me a position in his business. I had sat at his table in Cafe Diabelli many times, and he had often told the rest of us to put our money away, that he was paying for our drinks. I was not quite comfortable spying on him— there was really no more complimentary term for it.

On the other hand, I did have legitimate business at his home: first to give him my answer regarding his job offer, and then to ask about his sister-in-law—a friend, almost more than a friend, about whom I had good reason to be concerned. I would not pry answers out of him. What Mr. Stephens told me of his own free will would have to suffice.

But I did hope to learn what had happened to the missing painting, as well as to Virginia.

That much I had resolved upon when I stepped out of Mr. Clemens's carriage and knocked on Stephens's door. The butler answered, and I asked if Mr. Stephens was at home. The fellow shook his head, and said, "No, *signore*, he is not," and all of a sudden I was at a loss. Of all the scenarios I had played out in my mind, the last thing I had expected was to find him away from home.

"Can you tell me when he is expected back?" I began, thinking that if it was not too long, I might take a little drive around this quarter of the city and return.

But hardly were the words out of my mouth than I heard a woman's voice within: "Who is there, Carlo? Do they have any word of my sister?" The butler turned his head to answer, and over his shoulder I saw Mrs. Stephens on the stairs, looking anxiously toward the door. "Mr. Cabot, is that you?" she said, coming down the stairs and toward me. "You must have heard the news—I am so worried about my sister," she said. The butler stepped aside, and the next thing I knew, I was in the door.

"I have heard the bare outlines," I admitted, now anxious myself. It was clear that Virginia had not yet turned up. I said, "To tell the truth, I was hoping to find your husband at home . . ."

"Yes, of course," she said. "Frank had to go over to Eddie Freeman's. Eddie's been making a copy of the Raphael, and Frank thought that if it was far enough along, he could give it to the police to help them find the stolen painting. He'd already given them a photograph, but of course it didn't begin to suggest the color of the original."

"No, I'd think not," I said, remembering the vibrant color of the painting I'd seen the night before. Then, almost without thinking, I began asking the questions Mr. Clemens wanted answers to. "Do you have any idea just when it disappeared?"

"All I know is that we noticed it gone sometime after you had left," said Mrs. Stephens. "The police think someone must have taken it while we were all at dinner, since that was the one time when it could have been done without being observed. Whoever took it had moved another painting of about the same size there, so we didn't notice it missing when we came out—not until someone went to look closely."

"Ah, that's a clever trick," I said, nodding. "I'm trying to remember whether it was there when Mr. and Mrs. Clemens left, and for the life of me I can't."

"Frank will be back soon, and perhaps he'll have heard something new from the police," she said. "Would you like to come sit while you wait for him? I'm sure he'd be disappointed to hear that he missed you."

"Yes, thank you, Mrs. Stephens," I said. "I was hoping for a chance to speak to him." I took a few steps into the foyer, and she closed the door behind me. The butler took my coat, and I followed my hostess upstairs. She led me to a seat near the fire and rang for the maid to bring us drinks. I found myself wanting to look at the place where the painting had hung; but I realized that another subject would be nearer the top of her mind, as it was near the top of my own. "What about your sister? Has there been any news of her?"

She leaned forward and looked pleadingly at me. "Nothing, Mr. Cabot, nothing at all. I wonder if Ginny might have said something to you last night. As far as anyone can determine, you were the last person who spoke to her."

"Really?" I remembered that the policeman had said that, but I hadn't taken it at face value; it had seemed more like a ploy to see how I would respond. "I can't remember her saying anything at all unusual—as far as I knew, she intended to go right back to the party and carry on as before."

"She didn't seem . . . upset?"

"No," I said. Then, after a moment's thought, I corrected myself: "Well, she was upset with me. We had a misunderstanding, and she and I needed to talk about it—that's why I asked to talk with her in private, away from the other ladies."

"I see," said Mrs. Stephens, looking at me with a curious expression. Just then the maid returned with our drinks—a decanter of pleasantly dry sherry—with a dish of salted nuts on the side. There was an extra glass on the tray, a silent reminder that Frank Stephens was expected soon. We sipped, said a few polite phrases in praise of the wine, and then she returned to the subject. "I apologize for questioning you so closely, Mr. Cabot, but I hope you will understand that I am anxious to learn where my sister has gone. This is not at all like Virginia, to disappear without telling anyone where she is going." Her face was pale, except for the dark circles beneath her eyes; I suspected she had slept poorly. My heart went out to her.

"I understand you," I said. "Believe me, I share your concern. Please, feel free to ask anything you think I might be able to help with." Somewhere in the back of my mind I was aware that Mr. Clemens had sent me here to ask questions, not to answer them. But perhaps by giving a few frank answers—after all, I had nothing to hide—I would get as many in return.

She sat holding her sherry glass directly in front of her, and raised her chin. I was struck with how much she resembled her sister. More mature, perhaps a bit less sophisticated, but very attractive in her own way. She looked up at me and asked, "Mr. Cabot, did you propose marriage to my sister last night?"

That was the second time that question had been asked, but I was still not quite prepared for it. I stammered for a moment, then said, "No, ma'am. Our conversation was on another subject entirely. I hope Virginia had no false expectations in that regard."

Mrs. Stephens inspected me for a moment, then took another sip of her sherry. "I don't know that she did," she said. "However, several of the ladies present last night firmly believed that you meant to propose to her—in fact, when you left the party so abruptly, and with such a long face, the general conclusion was that you *had* proposed and been rejected."

"No, ma'am," I repeated. "We had argued, and I felt our relationship had taken a step backward. But it had not reached the point of my proposing. I would be surprised if Virginia thought it had."

Mrs. Stephens shook her head. "Men are very often surprised to learn what women think," she said, with an enigmatic smile. "Ginny liked you a great deal, and she told me that she thought you felt the same about her. Sisters do talk about these things to one another, you know, even when one of them is an old married woman." Here she managed a little laugh.

"I would not characterize you thus, Mrs. Stephens," I said, managing a smile. "But perhaps I should ask you an impertinent question of my own. Did Virginia ever indicate to you that she expected me to propose to her?"

Mrs. Stephens's smile spread ever so slightly. "I don't think I shall answer that," she said, with a toss of her head. It was a mannerism I had seen in her sister. She leaned forward and continued in a low voice: "An unwritten law between sisters is not to reveal the things they talk about to one another. If Ginny wishes to answer that . . ."

"Well, I don't know if I have the courage to ask her," I admitted. "You say nobody saw her after I left. When did people realize that she was missing?"

"Not immediately," Mrs. Stephens said, her expression serious again. "The ladies began talking about what to make of your departure, and when Ginny didn't return, I thought she wanted time to herself—that rejecting the proposal affected her more than she expected. After a while, I went to see if she was still in Frank's library. When she wasn't there, I decided she must have gone to her room. Now I think I should have gone to check on her, but at the time I thought that she needed her privacy, and I decided not to intrude."

"That is all perfectly natural," I said. "So when did you realize she had disappeared?"

Mrs. Stephens was about to speak, when we heard the downstairs door open, and footsteps in the hall. "That may be Frank," she said, rising to her feet. "Perhaps he has news for us." She turned expectantly, facing the stairs. I set down my wineglass and stood, moving a few paces away from her. I remembered another occasion when a man had come home to find me sitting with his wife, and had drawn the wrong conclusion. I did not want to repeat that scene, or its aftermath.

Sure enough, after a few moments, Frank Stephens came up the stairs, looking tired and perhaps a bit discouraged. But when his wife said, "Frank, Mr. Cabot has come to see you," his expression became more animated, and he came over to shake my hand.

"Cabot! Good of you to come," he said. "I take it you've heard the news?"

"Some of it," I said, truthfully enough. "If this isn't a good time for me to be here, I can come back tomorrow."

Stephens waved a hand. "No, no, no need of that," he said. "We could use another good set of brains to help sort things out. You left the dining room before the rest of us—first with Clemens, then again when you went to talk with Ginny. Do you remember seeing the painting either of those times? The police think it must have been stolen during dinner."

"I don't remember noticing it, but I don't remember noticing it missing, either," I said. "When did you realize it was gone?"

Mr. Stephens was about to answer when his wife caught his eye. "Yes, Belle?" he said.

"I'm sorry to interrupt, Frank," she said. There was a tremor in her voice, and her gaze was averted; I wondered if she was afraid of him. But then she looked up and asked, "Is there any news at all about Ginny?"

"Nothing new," he said, shaking his head. Then, looking at me, he said, "The police think she might have absconded with the painting, but of course that's absurd. They don't know her, so they jump to the first conclusion they think of. She's more likely gone off to mope about something—if she's not back for supper tonight, it'll be time enough to start worrying."

"I certainly hope she comes back soon," I said earnestly. "I can see how upset your wife is." I did not mention that I was upset as well.

"Yes, well, we're all upset," he said, pacing back and forth. "That painting is worth a small fortune. Who would have thought it would be stolen right under my nose, with two dozen people here?"

"Is there any chance a guest might have taken it?"

"Well, the police are looking into that angle," he said. "I suppose a couple of people here last night would be capable of it, but I'm at a loss to figure out how any of them had the chance. The only time somebody could have taken the painting without being seen was when we were all at dinner, and I don't recall anyone leaving the dining room—at least, not until the Clemenses went home. If you didn't notice it missing, that's good enough for me."

"I wouldn't put too much weight on my not having seen it missing, because I wasn't looking for it," I said. "I was more concerned with getting Mr. and Mrs. Clemens safely off, and when they were gone, I came straight back up to the dining room."

"Yes, of course," said Stephens. He noticed the extra sherry glass, nodded, and poured a drink for himself. Then he looked back at me and said, "To answer your question, I don't think anybody noticed that the Raphael was missing until we'd finished with brandy and cigars in the dining room. A few people left after you did, but perhaps a third of us were still at the table. Jonathan Wilson decided to take another look at the painting—you must have heard him talking about wanting to buy it. Well, he went over to look at it and saw right away there was another painting hanging in its place. He came back and made some joke about my switching horses on him, and that's when I realized something was wrong."

"What did you do then?"

"I sent for the police right away," Stephens said. "They aren't very reliable in ordinary matters, but they don't dawdle when it comes to art theft. Captain Rosalia was over here at once."

"Yes, I met him," I said. "He was out at Villa Viviani this morning—so he's obviously a man who takes his job seriously."

"Rosalia and I are old allies," Stephens said, grinning. "There was a case four or five years ago where I was offered several pieces that I recognized as part of a collection I was familiar with. I suspected they'd been stolen, and I got word to Rosalia. That tip let him capture a very active gang of art thieves. I wouldn't be surprised if that little piece of timely information helped him get his promotion to captain. So in a sense, he's just repaying a favor." Stephens smiled complacently at the memory, obviously proud of his role.

"Well, I hope he can repay it by getting your Raphael back," I said. Then, noticing his wife's face, I hastily added, "And by bringing Miss Fleetwood home safely, too." Stephens seemed more worried about the missing painting than about his sister-in-law. But what if she had been abducted? Or perhaps she was lying somewhere ill, or injured. I tried to push such notions out of my mind, but without success.

"Yes, of course," Stephens agreed distractedly. He took a few salted nuts, popped them into his mouth, and washed them down with a sip of the sherry. Then he looked at me and said, "It was after the police got here—Rosalia and another man—that we realized Ginny was missing. He wanted to speak to everyone in the house, and so Belle went to Ginny's room to find her."

"There was no sign she'd been in there at all," said Mrs. Stephens. "The bed hadn't been slept in, and none of her clothes were missing. Except a winter cloak and hat, which of course you'd expect if she'd gone out into the night— but the butler hadn't seen her get them, and said he didn't see her leave. Captain Rosalia questioned him quite a bit on that point, or so I assume—they spoke in Italian, so I could only follow a little of it, but Frank translated for me."

I thought a moment, then said, "She must have left some time after I did, but I suppose it could have been almost anywhere between then and when you found her missing. Do you have any idea when it could have been?"

"No," said Stephens. "To tell you the truth, we thought she must have left directly after you did—in fact, we told Rosalia she might have run off to meet you somewhere.

I'm sorry, but it seemed an obvious possibility at the time."

"So that's why the police were out at Villa Viviani so early this morning!" I said, making the obvious connection. "I guess they must have been disappointed to find me there."

"*Disappointed* might be an overstatement," said Mr. Stephens, toying with his wineglass. "But I think Rosalia had more hopes for that line of investigation than I did—he didn't quite understand that two young Americans might not be as impulsive as two Italians of the same age."

"Well, once I told him what Virginia and I had been talking about, I think he understood that it was unlikely we'd run off together," I said. "In fact, we had something of an argument, and it wasn't entirely patched up when I left."

"Really? I'm sorry to hear that," Stephens said, frowning. "I don't want to intrude, but is there any chance the argument had something to do with her leaving?"

"I've thought about that, and can't see how it would," I said. I paused to take a deep breath and collect my courage, then plunged ahead. "She had been taking it for granted that I would accept the position you offered me, and said as much in front of Mr. Clemens. Naturally, that put me very much on the wrong footing with him."

Stephens held up a hand to stop me. "Do I understand you correctly? Do you mean to tell me you don't intend to accept the job?"

"I'm afraid so, sir," I said. "It's a fine opportunity for the right person, and I'm flattered that you would offer it to me. But after considering all my choices, I've decided to stay with Mr. Clemens. I—"

"I'd advise you to consider again," Stephens broke in. He set down his wineglass and rubbed his hands together. "I can understand the attraction of working with a famous man—why, even my butler was impressed, when I told him Mark Twain was on the guest list. When I was your age, I might have found the association with his fame hard to resist, too."

"Well, Frank, it's more than that—" I began, but he cut me off with a wave of his hand.

"I think you'll realize, if you look a little further ahead in life, that Clemens's fame isn't going to rub off on you. Once you leave him, nobody will much care who you used to work for. A well-known man can turn into a has-been quicker than you can imagine. When you get to my age, you'll have seen it a hundred times. And all you'll have to show for it is the skills and experience of a secretary— that's all you'll be qualified to do, in the eyes of any real businessman. Is that the kind of work you want to be doing when you're forty? Fifty?"

"Well, no—"

"I didn't think so," he said, cutting me off again. "You *do* have a head on your shoulders, Cabot. Now, what I'm offering you has a rock-solid future. Once you prove you can run a business, there's no place on Earth you can't go from there. What's more, you'll be meeting successful people from every walk of life. They're the ones who buy art, and if you make the right impression on them, you could be set for life. Suppose you want to start your own business after a few years—why, if you've made friends with the right sort of people, getting start-up capital is the easiest thing in the world. Somehow, I don't think the Boston Brahmins I've met would be quite as sanguine about putting their money in the hands of a fellow who's never done anything more demanding than keeping track of someone else's papers." He set his wineglass on the mantelpiece and hooked both thumbs in his lapels, throwing out his chest. His posture made it clear *he'd* never kept track of anyone else's papers.

"That's not quite a fair description of what I do for Mr. Clemens," I said, trying to get the reins back in my own hands.

"It doesn't matter if it's fair, if it's what people *think*," said Stephens, stepping forward to prod me with his forefinger. "Be honest, now—do your family and friends back home think you've made the right choice of a career? Would your professors at Yale endorse it? Or is this just a new way to sow your wild oats, gallivanting around Europe in the company of a humorous lecturer under the guise of having a job?"

That gave me a guilty twinge; my father had said something very like it when I told him of my decision to come to Europe with Mr. Clemens. But something—perhaps the prodding finger—made me stand my ground. "Sir, I have told you my decision. I suppose I should be flattered that you want to change my mind. I will not even take exception to your disparaging remarks about my work for Mr. Clemens, since you don't really know the extent of my responsibilities. But I think it ungentlemanly of you to denigrate my employer's character in an attempt to sway me."

"I see," said Stephens, his voice turning cold. "If this is the line you were taking with Ginny last night, I'm not surprised she was upset with you. Well, I guess I've learned my lesson. I didn't think you would turn out to be such an ingrate, or such a fool." This was turning out just as badly as I'd feared. I had held some hope he'd take my decision in stride, and move on. But it was not to be.

Still, I could try to bring things to as gracious a conclusion as possible. "Sir, I know that you have had your share of bad news today, and I am sorry to have added to it," I said, putting down my empty glass. "I appreciate the hospitality you've shown me, and I wish I could accept your offer to take me into your business. I am certain that upon reflection you will realize that I am still very much in your debt, and that I feel no animosity toward you."

"Perhaps," he said, with a resigned expression. "You're throwing away a golden opportunity, Cabot, and I think you'll regret this in years to come. But I've led the horse to water, and that's an end to it. I think we've said all we can say. I'll have the butler bring your coat and hat." He went over and touched the bell-pull.

I nodded. "Sir, before I leave, I want to reiterate my hopes for the speedy return both of your painting and of Miss Fleetwood."

"Thank you," he said, tight-lipped. "My wife and I share

those hopes. Now, I believe it would be best for you to go."

I saw no reason to contradict him on that point, and so I made my departure without further conversation.

U pon my return to Villa Viviani, I found Mr. Clemens in his office, cleaning one of his pipes—one with a large briar bowl and a curved amber stem. The rest of his "working" pipes sat on the desk in front of him, awaiting their turns. He looked up as I entered and said, "Well, what's the news, Cabot? Are the girl and the painting still among the missing, or did one or the other come back?"

I sat wearily down. "Neither's back, I'm sorry to say. And from what Frank Stephens says, the police thought I had something to do with her disappearance."

"Well, it's an obvious inference from their point of view," said Mr. Clemens, putting down his pipe tool and examining the bowl he'd been scraping out. "I'd have thought that myself, if I didn't know you as well as I do. Do they think she was the one who smouched the painting?"

"That's another obvious inference, but Mr. Stephens didn't place much stock in it—nor would I. On the other hand, his wife—Miss Fleetwood's sister—was present while we were talking, and maybe he didn't want to voice suspicions about her sister in front of an outsider."

"Good point, Wentworth," said Mr. Clemens, picking up
the tool to take another scrape at the pipe bowl. He shook
out the loosened residue, then looked up at me and said,
"Why don't you tell me the whole story, and we can both
sort through it to see whether there's anything useful."

I recounted the entire visit, while he fiddled with his
pipes, nodding at intervals and once or twice interrupting
me to ask a clarifying question. When I was finished he
said, "Well, that doesn't get us much farther, does it?
There's a long space—at least two hours, maybe more—
between the last time anybody saw the painting and the
first time anybody noticed it missing. And another long gap
between when you saw Miss Fleetwood and when they realized she wasn't there. It's a shame none of the ladies went
to talk to her after you left, or looked at the Raphael when
they came out from dinner. Then we might have a better
idea whether or not the girl and the painting vanished at
the same time."

"For that matter, she couldn't have come back into the
main room to take the painting without the other ladies
seeing her," I said. "She would have had to come right past
where they were sitting. In fact, they were probably looking
for her once they knew I'd left—if they were under the
impression that I had been proposing to her, they'd have
been dying of curiosity." I shook my head at the notion. I
had not thought that anyone suspected that I was interested
in Virginia. But now it seemed that everyone knew—from
her sister to her friends to, apparently, my own employer!

Mr. Clemens nodded. "You're right, she'd never have
gotten out of the room without answering a hundred questions. So even if she did have something to do with the
painting going off, she had to have done it before she talked
to you. It couldn't have been on the spur of the moment
afterward."

"What about the police's idea that someone took it while
everyone was in the dining room, eating?"

"Makes as much sense as anything, but it has its problems, too," he said, tapping his fingers on the desk. "It
allows the thief to work without the owner or guests seeing

him, but how did he avoid being spotted by the servants? They had to pass by there on the way from the kitchen to the dining room. They ought to have yelled their heads off if they saw somebody come in and take a painting off the wall."

"What if the servants were bribed?" I suggested. "If the painting's worth a small fortune—Mr. Stephens said as much—perhaps the thief could afford to buy off a whole household of servants."

"Could be," said Mr. Clemens. He rubbed his right forefinger against his lower lip. "I'll bet you a nickel that *Capitano* what's-his-name has thought of that, though—If he doesn't put the whole household to the inquisition, he ought to hand in that fancy uniform."

"*Capitano* Rosalia," I supplied. "Apparently he's investigated art thefts before—Stephens informed him when he was offered some stolen pieces a few years ago. So he may know some of the places stolen art turns up. There must be dealers who specialize in reselling it—I assume the thieves don't just steal paintings to hang over their own mantelpieces."

"Well, I've heard of a rascal in London who stole a Gainsborough to hang in his parlor," said Mr. Clemens, with a mischievous grin. "But I reckon you're right, for the most part—a painting ain't like cash, or jewelry, that you can pawn without a lot of fuss or attention. You have to find a collector willing to buy something he knows is stolen, and who doesn't care."

"That must be a strange breed of collector," I said. "Why, they could never dare display it where anyone honest might see it. It's as bad as if they stole it themselves."

"Well, if you get right down to it, things haven't changed that much since those no-account Medicis ran this town, you know," said Mr. Clemens, picking up another pipe to clean. "The kind of people who can afford to buy a Raphael probably didn't come by their money much more honestly than the average stickup artist or snake oil huckster. And most of their friends are no more honest than they are."

"Then I am glad to have turned down Frank Stephens's

job," I said. "After hearing your description of my likely customers, I shall consider myself fortunate not to have been robbed at gunpoint by a gang of Boston Brahmins."

Mr. Clemens looked up from the pipe and raised an eyebrow. "Wentworth, if I didn't know better, I'd think you were developing a sense of humor. Maybe you *have* been working for me too long." He winked playfully at me, but I pretended not to notice.

"Mr. Stephens was trying to persuade me of that very point," I said. "But I fear I've already refused his job offer, so you will have to keep me on a little while yet."

"Say, until after you've seen Africa and Australasia, hey? I reckon I could manage that . . ."

"That would do very nicely, sir," I said.

He shook his head as if to caution me. "Hold your horses, Wentworth—you didn't let me get to the *if*, and that may be bigger than you think. If it's all up to me, I'll take you along. But that's if I can go at all, and if I can convince Henry Rodgers, or whoever's footing the bills, that I need to take along a secretary. I can't undertake that kind of trip on my own say-so anymore, you know," he said in a more serious tone.

"I understand," I said. "I think my chances are good enough, thank you."

"Well, then, I'll keep you on—but if I catch you working up comic lectures on your own, I may have to let you go. This is a risky enough business without breeding my own competition." He set down the pipe he had been working on and reached for a jar of tobacco.

"I promise you, sir, I have no ambitions in that direction," I said. Then, after a moment's reflection, I added: "I won't make the same promise about writing, though. If I ever find the time to write up some of my notes, you may find me in competition with you in that department."

He looked up from the tobacco jar and smiled. "I knew you had to be in this for something besides the salary," he said. "Well, I'll take my chances, there. One thing I'll say: Finding the time—hell, *making* the time—is half the game. Everybody and his uncle thinks he could write, if only he could find the time. Most of 'em never do it. It's the doing that matters—and until you've got the words down on paper, I won't worry about you stealing my readers."

"I shall remember that," I said. It occurred to me that I might have been writing at almost any point during the months I had spent with him. But what had I to show so far? I should have to make better use of my free time . . .

These thoughts were interrupted by the appearance of Clara, Mr. Clemens's middle daughter. She stuck her head into the office and said, "Father, there's a fellow in a silly-looking uniform at the front door. He says he's a policeman, and he's come to see *Signore* Cabot. Shall I let him in?"

"So soon?" said Mr. Clemens. "They must have found something interesting if they're back here again. Sure, let him in—we'll talk to him downstairs." Then, after a moment, he said, "Wait—maybe I'm jumping the gun." He turned to me. "It's you he wants to see, not me—do you want to talk to him?"

"Why not?" I answered. "I haven't done anything I need to worry about the police finding out."

"Well, I believe you, mostly—but will the cop? I managed to talk you out of a jail cell once, but that was someplace where I knew the language. How about this?—I go talk to him, try to feel out just what he's looking for. You can listen from the next room and learn what this is all about. If it's nothing but routine, you can walk in and say you just got home. What do you say?" He winked at me again, but I recognized the serious import behind what he was suggesting—it wouldn't be the first time the police had arrested an innocent man to make it appear that they had solved a case.

"Well, perhaps it would be the prudent course," I said. "Still, I can't see what I have to worry about."

"Neither do I, but this isn't America, you know. There's no Bill of Rights here, no 'innocent until proven guilty'— hell, for all I know, the cops in this country still use the strappado when they aren't getting answers they like. Why don't we just find out the lay of the land before we let them have a chance to get their hooks in you?"

I was not sure what the strappado was, but the sound of it was sufficient to convince me I didn't want to learn about it firsthand. "Very well, we'll do it your way." I said, and we went downstairs together.

At the bottom, Mr. Clemens pointed to an armchair beside the parlor door. "You sit there and keep your ears open; I'll bring him into the parlor and leave the door ajar so you can hear. We'll see what's going on, and then decide what to do about it."

I nodded, and sat down in the chair. A minute or so passed; then I heard the other door to the parlor open, and footsteps going in. "Make yourself comfortable, *Capitano* Rosalia," said my employer's voice, identifying our visitor for me. "Now, can I get you a drink? A cigar?"

"No, *Signore* Clemens," said the captain. I heard the creak of upholstery springs—presumably he and my employer had taken seats. "Perhaps another time, but today I am here about important business. I came hoping to find *Signore* Wentworth Cabot. We are very curious to ask him the questions."

"Well, I'm sure sorry you missed him," said Mr. Clemens. "He went out earlier—said he was going into the city to see Frank Stephens, the fellow who gave that party last night. For all I know, he's still there. Maybe you ought to check."

"In fact, I have spoken to *Signore* Stephens since your man was there," said the police captain. "He believed *Signore* Cabot was on his way to Villa Viviani—but now you say he is not here. Do you know where he might have gone?"

"No," said Mr. Clemens. I heard the scrape of a match, followed by a brief pause that I guessed was Mr. Clemens lighting his pipe. The odor of sulfur, then of tobacco smoke, wafted faintly through the door. I smiled at my guess's being confirmed. Then my employer continued: "Cabot's a grown man. I don't make him account for where he goes or what he does, as long as he does his work to my satisfaction—which he does, I might add. There's a cafe in town he goes to sometimes, but I don't know if it's open on Sundays. Anyhow, he didn't give me an itinerary, so I guess I can't help you."

"Do you expect him back soon?" asked *Capitano* Rosalia. His voice was calm, cordial, exactly as if he were on an errand of no particular importance.

"I don't know," said Mr. Clemens. "As I said, he didn't tell me his plans. If you want to leave a message, I'll have him get in touch with you. We don't have a telephone here, but maybe he'd come to the police station if you need to see him. Was there something particular you wanted to talk to him about?"

"As you know, we are investigating the disappearance of a very valuable painting," said the policeman. "It is possible that *Signore* Cabot saw or heard something that might help us find the person who took the painting."

"I reckon it's possible," said Mr. Clemens, speaking slowly as usual. His Missouri drawl contrasted sharply with the Italian police captain's animated, almost singsong speech. "Cabot likes those old paintings, a lot more than I do, so he might have paid more attention to it than I did."

"I see," said the captain, his voice neutral. Hearing it, I was sorry that Mr. Clemens had mentioned my enjoyment of art. Well, there was no quick way to disprove any suspicions the captain might have, unless the Raphael showed up elsewhere. But even if Italian law differed from American in key respects, I found it hard to believe I was in danger of being arrested simply for having been at Stephens's home when the painting disappeared. If that were the case, then fifteen or twenty others stood in the same jeopardy . . .

I suddenly realized that I had gotten lost in my thoughts, and hadn't been listening; the captain was still talking to Mr. Clemens. ". . . know whether he owed anyone money?" he said, apparently referring to me. He must be looking for possible motives for the theft, and I realized that several people had overheard my argument about money with Eddie Freeman. Of course, the sum involved there was nothing like what the painting must be worth—I wondered how much a stolen Raphael would bring—but sometimes the police didn't see such things in proportion.

"Not that I know of," Mr. Clemens answered. "I pay him a fair salary, and give him a place to stay and three meals a day. He don't smoke, or gamble, or buy fancy clothes, at least as far as I've seen. Hell, if he needed a quick loan, I hope he'd know he could come to me."

"But he was considering leaving this job, was he not?" The captain persisted. "He might not feel he could come to you for money."

"That's all straightened out," said Mr. Clemens. "He's staying with me, I'm happy to say."

"So he says today," said *Capitano* Rosalia. "Are you sure he did not change his plan since yesterday?"

"Maybe you should ask him about that instead of me," said my employer. "Do you want me to send him over to see you when he gets home, or is tomorrow morning time enough?"

"I will wait for him a little time longer," said the captain genially. "It will save us all time, in the long run. And perhaps I will have something to drink, if you are still offering it."

"Sure, what's your poison?" I heard the creak of springs again, and surmised that Mr. Clemens must have stood up.

There was a brief silence, then *Capitano* Rosalia chuckled. "Ah, an *americano* joke. I forget you are the famous humorist—is that the word?—in your country. It is not very often that someone offers poison to a *capitano di carabinieri*—though I think I could name some people who would give it to me without asking if I wanted it! But a small glass of wine would be most welcome—without the poison, *per favore*." He chuckled again, amused at his own joke.

"Coming right up," said Mr. Clemens, and I heard him cross the room and ring for a servant. I heard another set of footsteps cross the room, as well, in heavier boots. It sounded as if Captain Rosalia had stood up and gone to look out a window—watching for me to return home? Neither man said anything for a moment while they waited for the servant.

It wasn't until I heard the door *behind* me opening that I realized the servant would have to come directly past me to get to the room where Mr. Clemens and the policeman were waiting. I turned partway around in my chair, finger to my lips, to urge silence—but too late. The butler stopped in front of my chair and asked, "*Signore* Cabot, you rang?"

It was not especially loud. Someone in the next room might not have heard it, had they been speaking with another person, or engrossed in a book. But *Capitano* Rosalia did not miss it; after all, he had come out to Settignano expressly to see me. I had barely time to jump up from my chair when I heard the captain's approaching footsteps and his voice. "*Signore* Cabot, what a pleasant surprise! Now I will not have to return here to talk to you."

"Oh, hello, *Capitano* Rosalia," I said, trying my best to appear surprised. "I just returned from a long walk. I was coming to see Mr. Clemens, but when I realized he had a visitor, I decided to wait here . . ." The story sounded contrived even as I said it.

The police captain did not bat an eye at the manifest falsehood. "Ah, then it is even more fortunate that I heard your name. Perhaps now you will join us for a drink—if *Signore* Clemens does not object?"

"Oh, not a bit," said my employer, who looked as embarrassed as I felt at having been caught in our little subterfuge. He somehow managed to smile and carry on: "Captain, you wanted wine, and I reckon I'll have a whisky and soda. What about you, Cabot?"

I ordered wine, then followed Mr. Clemens and the policeman into the parlor. I stood there for a moment wondering whether to talk or keep quiet, but then realized that I would have to answer the captain's questions eventually. Better to lead off with one of my own. "Have you had any success in finding the missing painting? Or Miss Fleetwood?"

"None at all with the painting," said the captain, with a

shrug that spoke volumes. "With *Signorina* Fleetwood—well, we have found her."

"Oh, good," I said. "That must be a great relief to her sister."

The captain's expression remained neutral, and he shook his head. "I am afraid it is not such good news as that, *Signore* Cabot."

"I don't follow you," I began, and then the implication of what he said hit home. "Good Lord, you don't mean to say . . ."

"*Signorina* Fleetwood has been murdered," he said, nodding. "We discovered her body just a short while ago. That is why I came to see you, *Signore* Cabot."

"Good Lord," I said again, sinking into a chair. "It can't be—that's not possible," I said, more to myself than to Rosalia. My knees felt weak, and my head was spinning. Virginia dead? I couldn't believe it. She had been so full of life, and it had been such a short while since I'd seen her—and suddenly I regretted that our last minutes together had been spent quarreling.

Then I looked up at the Italian police officer, hoping to find evidence in his face that this was a cruel ruse, meant to get me to blurt out a confession that I'd taken the painting. But *Capitano* Rosalia's eyes were fixed on my face, and suddenly I felt very cold. "Surely you don't suspect me?" I said, but I already knew the answer from those eyes.

The captain looked at me intently for a moment before he said, "*Signore* Cabot, as far as we can determine, you were the last person to see the *signorina* alive—and everyone says you argued with her that very night. What choice do I have but to make you my first suspect?"

ᔌ 10

The news of Virginia's death was a heavy blow to me.
I stared at *Capitano* Rosalia, seeking some refutation
of what he had just told me. But he looked me in the
eye and said, "*Signore* Cabot, I must ask you some questions."

Mr. Clemens was on his feet, interposing himself between me and the Italian policeman. "Give the boy a chance
to settle down, will you? Anybody can tell he's taking this
hard—he was very fond of the young lady. Do you need
another drink, Wentworth?" He pointed to the wine decanter, which the servant had left for us.

I waved away the offered drink. I had questions of my
own. "How was she murdered? Where did you find the
body?"

The captain shook his head. "I am sorry, but I do not
think I should tell you those details until we have spoken
a bit. If you consider, you will understand why."

"Yes, of course," I said. "You want to find out whether
I know things only the killer would know. Very well, ask
away—I don't have anything to hide. I hope you will do
me the courtesy of answering my questions once you know
I had nothing to do with this terrible crime."

"If I can," agreed *Capitano* Rosalia. "I do not wish to see an innocent man suffer, any more than I desire to see a guilty one go free."

"Of course not," said Mr. Clemens, sitting back down in his chair and picking up his glass. "But most cops I've seen would rather lock up the first suspect they find than let people think they're stumped by an important case. I don't know whether you've paid any attention to my doings the last year or so—I'm not quite a household name, here in Italy. But solving murder cases has turned into one of my sidelines. Maybe Cabot and I can give you more help than you'd expect."

Capitano Rosalia spread his hands and shrugged. "Signore Clemens, if you had been on the *carabinieri* as long as I have, you would expect no help at all with a case involving foreigners. If this affair follows the customary pattern, the American consul in Firenze will soon send me a message expressing grave concern, and insisting that the rights of Americans be protected, and making it clear that he expects me to arrest an Italian. So I tell you in all frankness, to carry on my investigation without such obstacles would make me very content, and to get any cooperation from the witnesses would be a small miracle. Actual help would be without precedent, and I am a realistic man. Now, *Signore* Cabot, are you ready for me to begin?"

"I think I'll have another glass of wine after all," I said, walking over to the decanter. "But please, *Capitano* Rosalia, go ahead with your questions." I filled my glass and turned to face my questioner, who had taken out a notebook and a pencil. "What can I tell you?"

"You were the last person who admits to have seen *Signorina* Fleetwood, living or dead. How long did you speak with her, would you say?"

"Half an hour, perhaps a little longer," I said. "It was a little before nine o'clock when she and I went off to talk."

"So you spoke with her until half-past nine, you think," said the Captain, turning over a page as if to cross-check my statement with something he had already written. "Did you spend the entire time in *Signore* Stephens's library?"

"Yes," I said. "She was the one who chose that room. I had never been in the house before."

"I see," he said, jotting something down. "Now, when you left, did you go straight downstairs to the door, or did you stop and speak to anyone?"

"I spoke to the butler downstairs," I said, "when he got me my coat. I went out through the main sitting room, where the other ladies were gathered. Mrs. Stephens said they talked about me after I left, so they can undoubtedly vouch for the time."

"I assume, from what you're asking, that you've established the time when Miss Fleetwood was killed," said Mr. Clemens, peering at Rosalia over the rim of his glass.

"Actually, we are still waiting for the doctor's opinion on that question," said the policeman. "Until we have that information, we assume it could have happened at any time between when she left the other ladies to speak with *Signore* Cabot and the discovery of her body."

Mr. Clemens took a sip of his drink and nodded. "If it turns out she was killed after Cabot left the place, he's off the hook, you know."

"Not so," said the captain. "He could have made an appointment to meet her outdoors, after he had left. Or he could have gone to meet her earlier today, when he returned to *Signore* Stephens's place to ask about her." I shook my head to deny this, but I was too stunned at everything that had happened to refute the captain's implication.

Mr. Clemens leapt to my defense. "And he could have folded up the painting and put it in his hat, frame and all," he said, dripping sarcasm. "That's about as likely as a pig singing opera, though."

"I would be very surprised if a pig sang opera," said *Capitano* Rosalia severely. Then his eyes twinkled, and he added, "Perhaps it could manage to sing Wagner . . ."

His face turned serious again, and he said, "*Signore* Clemens, all comedy aside, you know I must think about improbable things as well as probable ones. A young woman has been murdered, you know. And just for your information, we *have* found the frame of the painting—

empty, of course. So the idea of it being folded up, or at least rolled up, is not so impossible, after all."

"My God, it would be ruined!" I said, thinking of brittle centuries-old canvas and delicate pigments. As soon as I said it, I felt ashamed of myself for caring so much about the painting when a young woman had died.

"I hope not," said the captain quietly. "I would expect the thief to be very careful with this Raphael, so as to get a good price when he sells it. Although he may be willing to take a lower price, to get some money quickly. But he would still try to keep it in good condition, and so it may be when we recover it."

"Let me guess," said Mr. Clemens, setting down his glass. "You found the frame near the young lady's body, didn't you?"

"Yes, very close by," said the captain. "But again, you will excuse me if I don't say more—there are things only the guilty person would know, *capisce*?"

Mr. Clemens knit his brows. "I *capisce*. You're forgetting something, though—we're as anxious to catch this killer as you are. I only met Miss Fleetwood once, but anybody who'd murder a young girl deserves everything the law can do to him. Besides, Wentworth thought a lot of her, and his opinion counts for a lot with me."

"You appear to know your secretary well, *signore*," said the captain, rubbing his bearded chin. "I do not have that advantage, and so I cannot take his word at face value. I will tell you in all frankness, if he were not attached to someone so prominent, I would already have taken him into custody—foreigners associated with a crime often disappear before we can ask all our questions. And in fact, *Signore* Wentworth hid from me when I came to your door. That is not the way an innocent man acts." He looked at me with accusation plain on his face.

My heart sank. *Not the way an innocent man acts*—it *did* look that way! "What am I supposed to say?" I temporized. "I have answered all your questions, and I have told the truth."

"You have not said anything I *know* to be untrue," said *Capitano* Rosalia, nodding. "However . . ."

"However *what?*" Mr. Clemens growled. "If you think Cabot's lying about something, why don't you say so? At least give the man a chance to deny it."

The captain sat up straight and squared his shoulders. "*Signore* Clemens, my superiors are anxious to prove that our city holds no danger for foreign visitors. They want to show that we are making, ah, *diligent efforts* to solve the case. I have been given hints that it would be a good thing to arrest your secretary and let him prove his innocence afterward . . ."

"While the real murderer gets away!" exclaimed Mr. Clemens. "So that's what passes for police work in this city, is it?"

"It is what passes for police work in many cities," said the captain soberly. "As perhaps you may gather from my telling you all this, I sometimes disagree with my superiors."

"I'm glad to hear that, at least," said my employer. "I would hate to think I'd been wasting my time arguing with a damn fool who was going to do just what he was told to do, whether or not it made any sense."

"*Signore,* I am in accord with you—but on the other hand, I have to show proper subordination to my superiors, whatever I may think. They have made it very clear to me that we must make progress in the case."

"Does that mean what I think it does?" I said, making as if to stand up from my chair.

Mr. Clemens was more direct. "Damn it, if you're going to arrest the boy anyway . . ."

"No, no," said the captain, smiling and holding up his hand to stop our protests. "*Signori,* I know a way to make my superiors content without restricting the liberty of your secretary, whom I do not yet believe is the murderer. Listen now, and I will make everything clear. I am going to place Signore Cabot under the guard of *Agente* Maggio . . ."

"What?" I said. "Am I to be followed everywhere I go by a policeman?"

"This is not so bad," said the captain, with a shrug. "I do not limit where you may go as long as you remain near Firenze. Believe me, you will prefer this to being locked in a cell."

"Still, it's as good as announcing to the world that you consider me a criminal," I pointed out. "I can't imagine anyone wanting to associate with me."

"The *agente* will not sit by your side in the cafe, or lean over your shoulder to read your letters," said the captain smoothly. "I will instruct him to allow you to enter a private home without him—and trust you not to go out the back door while he is watching the front."

Mr. Clemens poked his finger at the captain's chest. "What about in here? I'll be damned if I'm going to have that big galoot sitting in my parlor, scaring the ladies and wearing out the furniture. It's against the Constitution."

The captain laughed. "I did not know your American Constitution was so concerned about the ladies. But I will put your mind to rest. I will instruct *Agente* Maggio to stand guard outside in the courtyard, and keep his distance from the ladies and the furniture, unless you invite him in. We will hope the weather remains dry for him. But, for your part, you must instruct *Signore* Cabot not to leave the villa by a secret way. If Maggio comes looking for him and he is not where he is supposed to be, there will be bad consequences."

Mr. Clemens nodded and said, "Well, it's not the answer I'd have chosen, but I take it you aren't going to give us any choice about it."

"The other choice is to let your secretary be locked up, as my superiors would prefer," said Rosalia. "*Signore* Clemens, I would not offer this if I did not understand you to be a man I can trust. I am extending that trust to your secretary. You realize I must take the responsibility for this myself. I will have to answer hard questions if I have misjudged."

Mr. Clemens shot an inquiring look at me, and I said, "I don't like being followed by a policeman, but I agree it's better than going to jail. How long do you intend to keep me under watch?"

"Who can tell? If we find the murderer today, then *Agente* Maggio can go home and all will be as it was. Perhaps it will take several days—perhaps even longer. One thing, though. As long as we have you under guard, the real killer may think he is safe. Then he may make a mistake—attempt to sell the painting, for example. But I cannot predict the future."

"And if you don't find the real killer?" asked Mr. Clemens. "I reckon you aren't going to pay for Maggio to go to Australasia if I decide to go there—and you'd better not ask me to leave Cabot behind."

"*Signore* Clemens, we will have to decide that when the time comes," said the captain, smiling. "It would not be the first time a trail has grown too cold for us to follow, but I hope it will not happen. This is a vicious crime, and I want to find the beast who did it. But for now, I think this is the best answer we have to our problems. Are we agreed? Do I have your word that your secretary will not run away?"

Mr. Clemens looked at me again. "Cabot, I can't promise for you, but I'll stand behind whatever you decide."

I tried to think of an alternative, but nothing came to mind. Well, if something did, perhaps the captain would accede to a modification in the plan. Until then, I could not see that I had any choice—unless I wanted to learn how an Italian jail compared with the New Orleans lockup where I had spent several long hours. Besides, how could I work to prove my innocence—or to find the real killer—if I was in jail? I sighed, thinking of poor Virginia, and said, "Very well, I accept."

Capitano Rosalia left a short while later, leaving *Agente* Maggio stationed outside the front door. He and Mr. Clemens had jousted with questions and answers a bit more, but neither had learned much of consequence from the other. This left the captain somewhat ahead of us, since he knew the details of Virginia's death and neither I nor my employer had any significant information except what he had told us. In truth, I was not anxious to learn how Virginia had died. What I really wanted was to see her still alive, but I had begun to understand that this was not possible.

I stared out the window as the captain gave *Agente* Maggio whatever final orders he needed, and remarked, "We'd best hope the police can find the murderer quickly. *Agente* Maggio may be a good fellow, but I don't look forward to having him trail me all over the city."

"Well, you could always stay at home and work," said Mr. Clemens, with a twinkle in his eye. "I'd think you'd have had your fill of museums and cathedrals by now, anyway."

"Very amusing," I snapped. "My point was that I won't be able to do anything useful in finding the murderer." I began to pace the floor. I still had a hard time believing what had happened. But I knew I had to do whatever I could to find the murderer. This was no abstract puzzle to be solved, no case of some stranger being killed. It was Virginia, and I meant to see her killer brought to justice.

"Sorry," Mr. Clemens said quietly. "I know how you must feel about that girl being killed—it's damned hard when somebody close to you dies. But you don't have to take the whole job on your shoulders, Wentworth. I suspect that captain's going after the case with all his resources."

"He may be, but I'm not used to sitting on the sidelines and letting the police do their job," I said. "To tell the truth, I have much less confidence in the police than I did before I became your secretary."

"I'm glad to hear you say that," said Mr. Clemens. He tucked his pipe into a pocket and retrieved his drink. "It's at least one particular in which I've improved upon your Yale education. But don't give up on our finding the murderer just yet. You may have a cop following you around, but there's none following *me*. We can go our separate ways, and I can do just as much as I've always done."

"I don't like that," I said. Before he could argue with me, I added, "It could be dangerous. What if you're talking with the killer and say the wrong thing—something that lets him know you're getting too close to him? If I were with you, you'd have some protection. Alone . . ."

Mr. Clemens scoffed. "You're turning into a mother hen, Wentworth," he said. "I've run into my share of dangerous varmints, and I'm still around to tell the tale. Maybe I can't knock 'em down and sit on 'em the way you can, but I can convince 'em I'm not dangerous. A joke or two at my own expense will usually do that,"

I persisted. "Whoever we're after killed a young woman in cold blood. What makes you think they'll stop short at killing an American humorist?"

He frowned. "For one thing, I won't give anybody reason to suspect that I'm investigating the murder," he said. "I don't have any official status, anyhow—that captain made it pretty clear he didn't think we could help him. And for that matter, maybe we can't. Hell, I don't even speak the lingo here."

"That is a formidable barrier," I agreed. I was beginning to think that Mr. Clemens had met a case that offered no opportunity for an amateur sleuth to solve it. Even I, who had been among the victim's circle of acquaintances, had no clear notion where to begin. It was hard just thinking of Virginia as "the victim"—I didn't want to delve into the details of her death. But if we were going to find her killer, and bring him to justice, we couldn't avoid facing those terrible facts. "Perhaps we *would* be better off letting the police do their job, this time," I said, reluctantly.

Mr. Clemens walked over to the window and looked out—*at* Agente *Maggio*, I thought. He shook his head and turned back. "In other circumstances, maybe I'd agree with you. For now, you have a certain degree of freedom, so your famous American boss won't squawk to the ambassador—but I'll guarantee you the cops would be all over you if you tried to get on a train headed out of town. What this plan really does is give Rosalia some breathing room—he can tell his boss he's keeping an eye on you, without making any other progress in the case. Sooner or later, though, he's going to have to show results. If he needs to make an arrest to keep him in good odor with his boss, he may decide to nab you. And once they've got a suspect in jail, what's to stop them from putting on some sort of sham trial and getting a fraudulent conviction? Unless we want to take a chance on that, we better take the bit in our own teeth."

"I see what you mean," I said. "Still, Rosalia seemed a decent enough fellow. He didn't have to allow me to stay free. What makes you think he'd change his mind?"

"Wentworth, this *is* Machiavelli's hometown," said Mr. Clemens. "That good old Florentine got all his ideas from watching his fellow-citizens stab each other in the back while pretending to be good neighbors, smiling and saying pious things. *Capitano* Rosalia is from the same town— except he's had the benefit of four hundred years of refinement on old Niccolo's so-called ethics. Maybe the captain's a decent fellow in spite of it all, but that ain't the way any smart man would bet."

I shook my head. Every time I thought I had become accustomed to Mr. Clemens's cynicism, he would surprise me. Still, for once, he appeared to have reason on his side. "Very well," I said. "I don't want to oppose any plan that could bring Miss Fleetwood's murderer to justice. Perhaps the danger to you isn't all that great."

"Of course it isn't," he said confidently. But, of course, he was wrong.

⫸11

The longer I thought about it, the angrier I became. Someone had killed Virginia. That someone would pay for his crime—I would make it my personal business to see to that. And nobody had better get in my way, including *Capitano* Rosalia and his officers. I wanted to rush right out and start searching for the killer—but as of that moment, I had no idea where to start.

"I want to find the brute who did this," I said. "I'd spring the trap on the gallows myself, if they'd let me."

"I think they go by Napoleonic code in Italy, so maybe they use the guillotine," said Mr. Clemens. "But I know just how you feel—any man who hasn't felt it sometime in his life is no man at all, in my book. We'll find the killer, all right—between you and me and the police, he won't get away with this."

"That would be all very well if the police didn't treat me as their main suspect," I said. "We'll have trouble finding the killer with all the impediments Rosalia's put in the way. A policeman with orders to follow me everywhere I go. A flat refusal to tell me how Virginia died. You'd think he'd rather see the case go unsolved than have anyone but himself solve it."

"Maybe he does feel that way," said Mr. Clemens. "Cops can get just as petty as anybody else, and they're often jealous of anybody butting in on their business. Remember, back in London, how stiff-necked that Chief Inspector Lestrade got about amateurs trying to compete with Scotland Yard? Rosalia may hide it better, but I wouldn't be surprised if he felt the same way."

"And while he salves his pride, the murderer may escape!" I slammed my fist into the open palm of my other hand and continued: "If only the police would be reasonable!"

"Don't bet on it," said Mr. Clemens, with a grimace. "If we're going to wait for the police to tell us what we need to know, it'll be next Christmas before we get started on the case. I think we'd better just light out on our own. I say we start by trying to find that stolen painting. I'll guarantee you, Wentworth: Whoever's got that Raphael, knows what happened to the young lady."

"Don't be so certain that the killer is the thief," I countered. "The Raphael could have been stolen hours before her death. I think we need to turn our efforts toward discovering the details of the murder. I'd particularly like to know where they found the body." I stopped abruptly, shocked at the words I had just said. *The body.* A short while ago, that would have been *Virginia*—the woman I had contemplated sharing my life with . . .

"Yes, it would be useful to know that," said Mr. Clemens, breaking into my thoughts. "I just don't see how we're going to find it out, if Rosalia isn't talking." He paused a moment, then looked up and said, "We could call your watchdog in and ask him." He gestured toward the window overlooking the courtyard, where *Agente* Maggio was waiting.

"I think not," I said. "I'm not in the mood for jokes, at the moment. You can pull his leg without my participation."

"Oh, I'm serious," said my employer. "*He* might not know he isn't supposed to tell us about the murder. If we

play our cards right, he might be a good deal of help to
us."

"I'd be surprised if he even speaks English," I said. "He
didn't look to be a very bright fellow, to me."

Mr. Clemens shook his head. "He can't be all that dense,
if the captain's set him to shadow a Yale man. As far as
English, I'd bet he knows as much as he needs to. He must
run into his share of Englishmen and Americans who've
been robbed. Go call him in and we'll find out if he knows
anything—or, even better, if he wants to talk about it."

"Very well," I said, starting for the door. "But please try
not to antagonize the fellow—after all, I'll have to spend
my time in his company, if I want to leave the villa."

"The last thing I want to do is antagonize the cops," said
Mr. Clemens, with a look of utter innocence. "In fact, I was
going to offer him a cigar and a drink."

I smiled in spite of myself. Mr. Clemens had an unde-
niable talent for making me smile when I least expected it.
"Why do you call the *carabinieri* 'cops'," I asked. "Isn't
'policeman' a more polite translation?"

Mr. Clemens chuckled. "That's an old writer's trick," he
said. "Never use a nine-letter word when there's a three-
letter one that means the same thing. If you're getting paid
by the word, you pay attention to things like that."

I laughed at his explanation, and started to go fetch
Agente Maggio. Then another thought crossed my mind. "I
hope the *cop* doesn't think we're trying to bribe him with
the cigar and drink," I said, suddenly apprehensive.

"Of course we're trying to bribe him," said Mr. Clemens.
"Do you take me for an infant? Now go get him, and let's
find out if he's a mind to help us."

"Very well," I said again, and headed for the courtyard.

Capitano Rosalia must have been very emphatic in ordering *Agente* Maggio not to follow me when I entered
someone's home, for it took all my meager stock of Italian
to get the *carabiniere* to come into the villa, even at my
express invitation. But after repeating *"Avanti in casa, per
favore, avanti in casa,"* and elaborating on these words

with broad gestures, I managed to convey my meaning. At last, *Agente* Maggio rolled his eyes, no doubt making some unspoken comment on the insanity of Americans, and followed me inside.

"Well, there you are," said Mr. Clemens, as the tall policeman came into the parlor. He gestured toward a chair next to the fireplace, and said, "Sit down, sit down and get comfortable."

Agente Maggio looked around the room with narrowed eyes, as if searching for something incriminating. In fact, I realized, he *was* looking for something incriminating. Despite *Capitano* Rosalia's denials that he considered me a prime suspect in the murder, I had no doubt he had instructed his subordinate to report anything that might prove me guilty after all. But after a moment, Maggio understood my employer's gesture, and took a seat in the chair Mr. Clemens had indicated.

"How about something to drink while we talk?" Mr. Clemens asked. He lifted his own glass and pantomimed filling it from a bottle, adding, "Nothing better to warm the blood on a chilly day."

"Grazie, signore," said *Agente* Maggio, nodding and pointing to my wineglass, which I had left on the mantelpiece. *"Un bicchiere di vino, per favore."*

Mr. Clemens raised his eyebrows. "What's he want? A pitcher of wine?"

"No, that means a glass of wine," I said. "I've heard people ordering in the cafe."

"That's a bit better," said my employer. He rang for the butler, then said, "I can see I need to learn some more Italian. If the grammar weren't so damned complicated . . ."

I refrained from pointing out that it was the vocabulary, not the grammar, that he had misunderstood, and said instead, "If we're having trouble with a sentence that commonplace, I don't know how much farther we can get with this fellow. I haven't learned the Italian for *murder victim*, let alone the other things we want to ask him about."

"You're right, Wentworth," said Mr. Clemens, looking at *Agente* Maggio, who sat waiting with a bland expression.

"Do you speak English?" asked my employer. "We have questions we'd like to ask you."

"*Non capisco, signore,*" said the policeman, shrugging and spreading his hands.

"I know what *that* means, at least," said my employer, scowling. "It stands to reason the rascal doesn't understand me when I want to ask him questions, but does just fine when I offer him a drink. That's a pretty convenient degree of ignorance."

"Don't judge him so harshly. You understood the Italian for *wine*, yourself," I pointed out.

"That's the mark of an experienced traveler," he said. "You learn how to communicate the important things. But here we've got important things to ask this fellow, and neither of us can understand the other. What are we going to do?"

I had no ready answer, but just then the butler arrived. Mr. Clemens turned to him and said, "Bring this fellow a glass of wine."

"*Si, signore,*" said the butler. "Does he wish the red or the white?"

Mr. Clemens frowned. "Damned if I know—why don't you ask him?"

"*Si, signore,*" said the butler, again, and turned to *Agente* Maggio. "*Per favore, agente, prende di vino rosso o blanco?*"

"*Di rosso, grazie,*" said the policeman, with a hint of a smile. Mr. Clemens and I asked for our own glasses to be refilled, and, after giving a little bow, the butler went to fill the orders.

"That was easy enough," I said when the butler had left. "I even understood most of it, once somebody else came up with the right words. What we need is an Italian interpreter."

"I suppose you're right," said Mr. Clemens. "I don't like having to rely on some stranger, though—not when we're dealing with a life-and-death problem here. It's got to be somebody we can trust."

"You don't have to rely on some stranger," came a voice

from the doorway. "I know enough Italian to do the job, and you know you can trust me."

Mr. Clemens and I turned to look, although we both already knew from the voice who the speaker was. Clara Clemens, my employer's second daughter, stood there with a little smile.

"You've been listening," said Mr. Clemens.

"Of course I have," said Clara, walking farther into the room to confront her father. "You're trying to solve another murder case, and now you need somebody to help you."

"Yes, but . . ." her father began, but she interrupted him.

"I can do it," she said, tossing her head. "I speak the best Italian of anyone in the family. Besides, we can't let them put poor Wentworth in jail." Standing straight, with confidence in her eye and voice, she seemed more like an eager lawyer than a pretty young girl.

Mr. Clemens shook his head. "No," he said. "I'm not going to have any of my daughters mixed up in a murder case. Even if you are almost twenty . . ."

"Susy was already mixed up in one, back in England," said Clara, sticking out her chin. "She was right there when the man was killed, and she told me and Jean all about it when she got home. It wasn't that bad."

Mr. Clemens walked over and patted his daughter on the head. "You may not think so, young lady, but I'm the judge of what's appropriate for my daughters, and I say no. Besides, your mother would kill me if I got you into trouble."

"There's no danger at all," insisted Clara. "All I'd be doing is helping you ask a policeman a few questions. Mama couldn't object to that. Besides, who else are you going to get to do it?"

"The butler speaks the lingo," said Mr. Clemens, without a great deal of conviction. Just as he spoke, the individual in question returned with the drinks, which he gave to each of us and then departed, without a word.

"Maybe the butler can translate, but you can't trust the butler to keep mum—you *don't* trust him. I can tell, because you all clammed up the minute he got here. But you *can* trust me," said Clara, when the servant had left. "Nobody outside the family would ever hear a word of what I heard."

"But everybody inside the family would hear all about it, and I'd have to listen to every syllable of it at every meal, and you'd all ask questions about what every detail meant, until I was sick of it," said my employer. This was true beyond much doubt. All three of the Clemens children were lively and intelligent, and interested in far more than the usual girlish subjects of conversation.

"You're going to have to listen to all that, anyway," said Clara. "Except this time, I won't be asking the questions, because I'll already know the answers I've helped you find. And the other girls will come ask me what I know, instead of pestering you. So we won't be anywhere near as bothersome as we were in England."

"And if I don't let you help me?" said Mr. Clemens warily.

"You already know the answer to that," said Clara. Her eyes twinkled. "I promise I'll ask enough questions to make you even more miserable than Jean and Susy put together. And you know I can do it." She arched her brow and smiled.

"She's got me over a barrel, Wentworth," said my employer, sighing. "All right, then, Miss Sass-pot, you've got the job. Let's see if you can get this fellow to tell us what we need to know."

Agente Maggio had observed the conversation between father and daughter with obvious curiosity. But his eyebrows rose when Clara walked over to him and said, *"Buon-giorno, agente,"* then followed it up with a stream of rapid-fire Italian that I had not the slightest chance of deciphering. The policeman replied in the same language, and my employer and I were left to stare at one another, wondering when we would be let in on the conversation.

At last Mr. Clemens's stock of patience ran out. "What the dickens are you two chattering about, Clara? Wentworth and I need to ask the man some questions."

"Really, Father, you ought to give me a few minutes to put the *agente* at his ease before you pepper him with questions," said Clara. "After all, he is a guest in our home."

Mr. Clemens's mouth fell open at this answer, and without saying another word he sat down in a chair across the fireplace from the policeman while Clara returned to her dialogue with *Agente* Maggio.

After a few more exchanges between the two, Clara turned to her father and said, with all the apparent innocence imaginable, "Now, Papa, what did you want to ask the *agente?*"

My employer hemmed and hawed for a moment, then said, "Captain Rosalia told us that Miss Fleetwood, a young American woman staying in the city, has been murdered. But he didn't tell us how the poor girl was killed, or where her body was found, or when they think it must have happened. If the *agente* can tell us any of those details, it would be a great help to us."

Clara spoke to the policeman, who frowned and replied in a sentence or two. She turned back to her father and said, "He says he doesn't know everything you've asked him, not yet—he expects to find most of it out from the captain before long. But he also wants to know why you're asking."

"Why, so I can help find the murderer," said Mr. Clemens. "Wentworth won't be able to leave the city until the police decide he's not guilty. I need to clear him if I'm going to be able to take him along on my travels, and I need to travel if I'm going to pay the bills. I need him along to handle all the arrangements; it'd be a nuisance to have to do it without him."

The policeman laughed when Clara relayed this information to him. He took a sip of his wine, then gave a brief answer, which Clara reported to her father: "He asks why protecting you from a nuisance is worth his getting into trouble with his captain."

Mr. Clemens bristled, but he leaned forward and said, "Tell him that protecting me from a nuisance isn't the point—it's protecting Wentworth from being thrown in jail when he didn't do anything to deserve it."

Clara spoke to the policeman again, and this time, they

exchanged several sentences. At last, she turned to her father again and said, "He apologizes for being so blunt, but he can't accept a stranger's word on such an important point. He has only your word that Wentworth isn't the murderer." She paused and raised her eyebrows. "And he says that Wentworth seems to be a nice person, but he has known other nice people who were bad criminals."

Mr. Clemens grimaced. "An honest cop! I was afraid we'd run into something like this. What are we going to do now?"

"You might try proving that you deserve his trust," said Clara. "He is very serious about his duty, but he doesn't seem to be inflexible about it—so you may be able to persuade him."

"Well, that's some hope," said Mr. Clemens, though his tone implied that it might not be enough. "Tell you what—since he's going to be out here as long as Wentworth is, why don't you tell him he can stay inside while the weather's nasty. That should dispose him a little better toward us."

"I'm surprised," I said. "I can't imagine working with a policeman looking over our shoulders. Are we to have him as a guest at meals, as well?"

"Don't be silly, Wentworth," said Mr. Clemens. "He doesn't have to come into the office with us, or sit at the table when we eat. He can stay in the kitchen, or the hallway, most of the time. But it ought to let him know we aren't going out of our way to hide anything from him, and that we're considerate enough not to leave him out in the rain and cold. Tell him that, Clara."

Clara spoke to the policeman again, and when she had finished he nodded toward my employer and said, "*Grazie, signore.* Zank you."

"You're welcome, you're welcome," said Mr. Clemens, waving a hand. Then he raised an eyebrow. "You *do* speak English."

"*Solo un po'*," the policeman said. "Hello, goodbye, zank you please, you un'er arres'." He laughed.

"I guess that's all you need," said my employer, chuck-

ling. "That's about as much as I can say in Italian. But if
the fellow can't tell us any more than that, we can let him
take his wine down to the kitchen and carry on our discussion in private. Tell him that, Clara."

She spoke briefly to *Agente* Maggio, who smiled, nodded
and rose to his feet. He followed Mr. Clemens's daughter
to the door, but just as he was about to leave, he turned
and said something else in Italian. Clara's face turned pale.

"What's that he says?" asked Mr. Clemens. *Agente* Maggio was standing by the door, his eyes fixed on me, and I
wondered if what he had said had some reference to myself.

Clara's voice was subdued as she said, "He says he
doesn't think the captain would mind his telling you how
the American lady was killed, since it will be all over town
by the evening. He says to tell you that she was strangled."
I realized that up until now the harsh fact that we were
dealing with a brutal murder had not struck home to her.
Nor to me. The notion of Virginia's death had still seemed
abstract and unreal. Now I had been slapped in the face
with the reality of it. My head reeled.

"Strangled, eh? Well, that's something for us to start
from," I heard Mr. Clemens say, as if at a distance. "Thank
the fellow again for us, and tell the cook to let him camp
in the kitchen and to give him something to eat."

"I will," said Clara, and she led *Agente* Maggio on out
of the room.

"*Strangled*," I said, sinking into a chair. "What a frightful
way for poor Virginia to die."

"Yes, I can't think of many worse," said Mr. Clemens,
with some vehemence. "All the more reason for us to find
the no-good skunk who did it and make sure he pays for
it."

I nodded. "Yes, he must be stopped from harming anyone else—ever again." Then my logical mind came into
play, and I said, "It's pretty certain it's a man we're looking
for, isn't it? No woman could have committed such a brutal
murder."

Mr. Clemens's face turned grave. "I've known a couple
who could have, not that I'm eager to remember them. But

yes, I think it's odds-on that a man killed poor Miss Fleet-wood. Now, let's start thinking about how we're going to find him—and prove to the police that he's the murderer. My guess is that it'll be one of the guests at that party last night."

"Not necessarily," I said. "Mr. Stephens has a large circle of acquaintances in Florence: artists, dealers, collectors, a lot of the resident foreigners. If Virginia's murder was somehow connected to that missing painting—and I'm be-ginning to think you're right that it is—any of those others could be involved."

"Good point," said Mr. Clemens. "We have to start somewhere, though, and I reckon the party guests will do as well as anybody else. Get some paper and let's see if we can put together a list of who was there. Once we have that, you can add on others you think we ought to be look-ing at."

I took out my pocket notebook and was searching for a blank page when Clara returned to the room. "He's in the kitchen," she said. "The cook was afraid he was going to eat everything in sight, but instead he sat down and pulled out a book and started to read. So I don't think he'll be much trouble."

"Good," said Mr. Clemens. "I'm afraid he won't be as much help as I'd hoped, but at least we got one useful fact out of him."

Clara stepped over to her father and lowered her voice. "There's one thing more you need to know about him," she said.

"What's that?" her father asked.

"He understands English much better than he let on," she said. "I figured that out when he answered one of your questions that I hadn't translated. I don't think he knows he let it slip, and maybe it's a good idea not to let him know you're aware of it."

"Hah! I should have known it!" said Mr. Clemens, slap-ping his thigh with his open hand. "That old fox Rosalia must have told Maggio to play dumb, in hopes we'd say something incriminating in front of him."

"It's just as well we have nothing to hide, then," I said.

"Don't be too sure of that," said Mr. Clemens. "A cop's whole job is to catch criminals, and that can make him see criminals everywhere he looks. Especially when he's listening to conversations in a foreign language, he could misinterpret something innocent. My advice is not to say anything in front of him that you couldn't tell to your Sunday school teachers, because I guarantee you Rosalia's going to hear it next."

"I'll remember that," I said.

"Good," said Mr. Clemens. "Now, let's see if we can remember all the people at that party. The sooner we catch the murderer, the sooner we can get that cop out of my kitchen."

≈ 12

Compiling the roster of party guests took only a few minutes; I knew the majority of them from Cafe Diabelli. But writing down the names was just the beginning. Our next step was to separate real suspects from those who simply happened to be Frank Stephens's guests the evening of the theft and murder. As we soon realized, for most of the guests, we had no idea to which category they belonged.

"Well, if we eliminate the ladies, we can cut the list in half," I said, staring at the paper.

"I could have figured out that much without even writing down the names," said my employer. "Come on, Wentworth, you've met these people before—you must have something more to put on the table. What can you tell me about Stephens, for example?"

"He's an affable fellow who seems a capable businessman," I said, shrugging. "I haven't seen any suspicious behavior from him. He was rather brusque when I turned down his job offer. Of course he had other problems on his mind at that point."

"You said he didn't seem worried about the girl's disappearance," said Mr. Clemens. "Was it that he thought she'd turn up safe after all, or was he more concerned with the stolen painting?"

"Both, I think," I said, trying to recall the conversation. It seemed strange that it had been only a few hours earlier. After the news of Virginia's murder, it seemed eons ago—almost as if it had been in another life. "He may have been trying to reassure his wife, of course. But he acted as if he expected Virginia to come walking in before dinner time."

"Well, maybe it *was* an act," said Mr. Clemens. "I wish you'd still been there when Rosalia came to deliver the news. It would have told us something to see Stephens's face when he was told the young lady'd been killed."

"I'm sure *Capitano* Rosalia has already learned whatever he could from Stephens's reaction, if there was anything unusual about it," I said. "Of course, we can't expect the captain to tell us all his conclusions."

"I reckon Stephens didn't give anything away, either, if Rosalia still considers you the main suspect," said my employer. "But then, Stephens is a salesman—a good poker face is a professional requirement."

"All of which brings us back around to the start," I said. "If Stephens had anything to do with Virginia's death, he wouldn't reveal it to me. I suppose we have to consider him a suspect on grounds of proximity to her, but I can't imagine what his motive could be."

Mr. Clemens wrinkled his nose and said, "I reckon I could imagine one, but that's all it'd be—just imagining. We'll keep our eyes and ears open, though. I ought to send you back over there to pay your respects to the bereaved—and to snoop a little, while you're at it. Would it bother you to spy on them?"

"I'm spending more time there than here," I said. "But I suppose it's all right, if it helps us find the killer. If nothing else, it would give me a chance to talk to anyone else who showed up—the others at the party were among her friends, so they'll want to pay their condolences. And they wouldn't be on their guard with me—they might tell me something they wouldn't tell the police."

"At least if Maggio doesn't hang over your shoulder listening," said Mr. Clemens. "Good, then, you'll go there tomorrow morning. Now, who else among that crowd strikes you as suspicious?"

I thought a second and then said, "Nobody, really. I had disagreements with one or two of them, but that doesn't make them murderers."

"Yes, you told me about that fellow you rented the bicycle from," said Mr. Clemens. "I thought that idea was a recipe for trouble all along, but I have to admit I'm prejudiced against the damned things. Have you got it settled?"

"I paid him most of what he wanted; I promised to give him the rest in Cafe Diabelli tomorrow," I said bitterly. "And then I'll say goodbye to the place. It was where I met Virginia—going there would just stir up memories."

"Wait a minute," said my employer, sitting up straight. "Now's when you *should* be going back there. You and she spent more time there than anywhere else, right?"

"I suppose so," I said.

"So if she was killed by an acquaintance, the odds are it'll be somebody else who spends his time there," said Mr. Clemens. He'd stood up and begun pacing, a sure sign that his brain was racing full speed ahead.

"We don't know that," I pointed out. "She could have been killed in the course of a robbery."

Mr. Clemens scoffed. "Then why's Rosalia putting a guard on you? I doubt you look any more like a common thief to him than you do to me, and I can spot larceny from ten miles off. He may not be telling us all the details of her death, but we can damn sure figure that one out for ourselves."

"I wasn't thinking about a purse-snatching," I said. "What if she stumbled upon someone in the process of stealing the Raphael, and they killed her to prevent her giving the alarm? Captain Rosalia said they did find the frame near her body."

"There's an angle we need to look at," said Mr. Clemens. "I see one problem with it, though. If she'd caught the thief in the act of stealing the painting, that would have happened right around Stephens's villa. The whole point of taking the painting out of its frame is to make it easier to carry away unnoticed—the thief wouldn't have taken it half a mile away, and then cut it out. By then, he's home free. So she must have been killed near home. But then they'd have found her body a lot quicker—in fact, the family or servants would have found it, instead of the cops. I doubt the thief would have taken time to hide her body if he was so anxious to get away."

"So, what does this mean, then?" I mused. "Her death does seem connected to the painting, but how?"

"What if she was a partner in the robbery, and got killed by the other robbers so they wouldn't have to split the take with her?"

"Impossible!" I protested. "Virginia wouldn't have been a part of any such scheme. It isn't the least bit like her."

"Are you sure?" Mr. Clemens said. He walked over and put a hand on my shoulder and continued in a lower voice. "Look, Wentworth, you were very fond of her, and I know her death must hit you hard. But you didn't know her all that long, or all that well. People can surprise you, even after years and years."

"Perhaps," I admitted. "But when I told her I wasn't taking the position with Mr. Stephens, she scolded me about missing such a sterling opportunity. That was why we parted on such unpleasant terms. I can't imagine her taking his part so vigorously one moment, then helping someone steal his painting the next."

"Well, that's even more of a puzzle, then," said Mr. Clemens. "There's got to be some connection between the theft and her murder, but damn me if I know what it is. There's something we're missing."

"If we can get Rosalia or Maggio to tell us the details they're withholding, perhaps it'll all make sense," I said.

"Yes, we're back to that, aren't we?" Mr. Clemens sighed. "Well, we can't bet on the cops being cooperative, so we'll have to find out whatever we can without their help. That's why you're going back to that cafe tomorrow—after all, you do have that debt to pay back. Come to think of it, this might be the time for me to go there with you, and see what I find out."

"I'll be interested in what you think of the place," I said, remembering his previous reluctance to visit it.

"Oh, I reckon I already know what I think of it," he said. "It's the people there I'm interested in, now. Because I think that, when we get right down to it, one of them is the killer."

"Do you think so?"

"Sure," he said. "If that's where all her friends spent their time, I say that's where we'll find her enemies, as well."

The rest of the afternoon passed quietly. Having set a course of action for the next day, neither Mr. Clemens nor I seemed to have the energy to do any more that day. The only thing I would think of doing, paying still another visit to Frank Stephens and his wife at their residence, could—and should—wait for the next day. I had been in their home twice in twenty-four hours, and both times had left on a sour note. Eager as I was to discover the killer and see him punished, I could not convince myself that appearing on that doorstep yet again—especially when I was under a cloud of suspicion—would produce anything useful.

Instead, I retired to my own room for a bout of pacing and inner raging. I could not yet put a face to Virginia's murderer, but that did not keep me from imagining driving my fist into it, again and again. I would find the killer—and then I would have my revenge.

At the same time, I was racked with recriminations. Again I thought that, if Virginia and I had not parted in acrimony, she might not have gone out to meet her doom. I could not believe Mr. Clemens's theory that she was involved with the disappearance of Stephens's Raphael. But how to explain the painting's being found near her body? I contrived and discarded a hundred theories, and when the German maid tapped on my door to announce that dinner was on the table, I was no closer to the answer than I had been before.

I had very little appetite—I had drunk a bit too much

wine in the afternoon, and now I felt tired and irritable. But I knew from previous experience that skipping the meal would make me feel worse later. More out of a sense of duty than actual hunger, I dragged myself downstairs for the Sunday meal.

To my relief, Mrs. Clemens had evidently decreed that the murder was an unacceptable topic for dinner conversation. I assumed the ban was for my benefit, and I was glad of it. I was in no mood to broach the subject, and so we spoke on general topics and I was able to forget my shock and anger for minutes at a time. Little Jean, the youngest Clemens daughter, cast an occasional speculative glance in my direction, as if she hoped I would open the door to the forbidden subject, but I resisted her unspoken invitation and so we got through the entire meal with no allusion to it.

After dinner, Mrs. Clemens said, "I think we should have some music. It has been a while since you played the piano for us, Clara—shall we all meet in the parlor?"

I had meant to return to my room after the meal, but the food must have revived my spirits somewhat, for I found myself in the mood for a bit of music and song. I followed the family into the parlor, where Clara leafed through several pieces of sheet music before choosing something by Mendelssohn. She took her place at the keyboard and began to play; she was an excellent pianist, and whether by accident or design, the music had a profound calming effect on me. I sat back and let myself be swept along by the tranquil flow of melody, nodding my head to the rhythm.

After a few minutes, the music came to an end, and I joined Clara's proud parents in applauding her performance. An unfamiliar voice came from behind me—"*Bella, signorina, bella! Encore, per favore!*" I turned to look, and there was *Agente* Maggio, grinning and applauding with undisguised enthusiasm. Clara smiled and blushed a bit, and nodded toward the uninvited audience member, then looked through her pile of sheet music and chose another piece. She set it on the music rack and with a sly smile, began to play.

This was a livelier selection, and *Agente* Maggio's face lit up with recognition. Clara nodded in his direction, and to my surprise, the policeman stepped over next to the piano and began to sing in his native tongue. Although I cannot count myself among the devotees of opera, even I recognized the melody: "La Donna Mobile," from Giuseppe Verdi's *Rigoletto*. He had a fine clear tenor voice, and his face assumed an animated expression as he delivered the aria.

The music ended, and we all broke into hearty applause for the singing *carabiniere*. As we clapped, Mr. Clemens leaned over to me and said, in a stage whisper, "He's a mighty fine singer, but I wonder if we can afford to put him up. He must have been eating damn near everything in the kitchen. Look at that sauce stain on his sleeve!"

I turned to look at the policeman, who lifted up both his arms to look at the sleeves. I could see no stains, and wondered what Mr. Clemens was talking about. Then *Agente* Maggio's face changed and he glared at my employer.

Mr. Clemens smiled and tucked his thumbs under his lapels. "Well, now we have that settled. You do understand English, don't you? By the way, I did like your singing."

With his own ironic smile, the Italian policeman directed a little bow toward my employer. "I should know not to get caught with such a trick," he said. "*Congratulazióne, signore.*"

"I had a pretty good idea already how much English you understood, thanks to my daughter," said Mr. Clemens. "But I thought we all should know what was going on here. You and I and Cabot ought to talk about it, a bit later. But for now, why don't you and Clara do another song? I do enjoy that stuff, even when I don't understand it."

"My pleasure, *signore*," said the policeman, and after a quick consultation with his pianist—reverting to Italian for the purpose—he launched into another aria, familiar even though I could not remember its composer. I guessed the title to be "Caro Mio Ben," but I knew too little Italian to make out the lyrics.

After this number, the policeman (at Mrs. Clemens's ges-

ture) took a seat and listened to Clara play another piano
solo, followed by her two sisters, neither of whom was
quite her match—although little Jean had the excuse of
many fewer years of study. Susy, while she seemed adequate technically, betrayed a lack of enthusiasm; perhaps
the slight imperfections were the result of this rather than
any lack of talent or practice.

After all three of his daughters had played, Mr. Clemens
said, "I wish I had my good old guitar here—I can't play
that piano near as well as the girls, and I reckon I'll make
a fool of myself after they've played. But I do think it's
time for some American music here." He sat down at the
piano and struck an experimental chord, then began to play
and sing an old Negro spiritual in quite authentic dialect.

While I had heard my employer sing several times before, *Agente* Maggio raised his brows—I doubt he had ever
heard such a performance in his life. But when the Clemens
daughters joined their father in the chorus, the policeman's
foot began to tap and his head to nod, and I could see that
he was enjoying himself despite the unfamiliar material and
style.

The impromptu songfest made me wish that I could contribute to the performance. But while I had always been an
enthusiastic singer, my training had progressed no farther
than learning the notes of the scale. As for my repertory,
it was limited to hymns and college drinking songs, none
quite appropriate to the occasion. I wondered how a local
policeman had become so conversant with Italian arias—
then I remembered that of course he was a native, and that
the songs were no more exotic to him than "Auld Lang
Syne" or "Old Folks at Home" to me and my companions.

Finally, Mr. Clemens started a more challenging selection. He hit several sour notes, stopped and tried to start
the piece again, and broke down in the same place, even
worse this time. Little Jean giggled, and her father turned
toward her with a frown. But before he could say anything,
Mrs. Clemens spoke up: "I think we have had a wonderful
evening of song and music, but I fear I am a bit fatigued,
and it is past Jean's bedtime. Thank you, young ladies, and

you too, Youth! And *Agente* Maggio, it is a pleasure to listen to such a voice."

"*Grazie, signora,*" said the policeman, smiling. He gave a deep bow as Mrs. Clemens and the three girls left the room.

Mr. Clemens and I also stood as the ladies left, and then my employer turned to the policeman. "Well, *agente*, I think you've sung well enough to earn a glass of wine. The three of us need to talk a bit, now that we all know we *can* talk, and maybe a drink'll make it go smoother."

"Yes, I drink a glass of wine with you," said Maggio. "And I think we talk *più candido*, all of us, now that I do not believe your servant is murderer."

"I'm glad to hear that," I said, not bothering to correct his misunderstanding of my position in Mr. Clemens's household. "How did you come to that conclusion?"

"When I tell your daughter that the poor American woman was strangled, I watch your face," said the policeman, looking me in the eye. "I don't think you play innocent—your surprise, your hurt, that was no acting. So I think you not the killer."

"I thought it was just a bit too casual, the way you fired off that parting shot," said Mr. Clemens, filling a glass from the decanter on the sideboard. He handed it to Maggio and said, "Well, maybe I paid you back in part for that trick, just now. Why don't we all stop playing games and see if we can do business together?"

"Do business?" *Agente* Maggio frowned, then nodded. "Ah—*capisco.* Yes, I think we can do some business—but there are things I no can do myself. *Capitano* Rosalia . . ."

"Yes, the captain," Mr. Clemens said. "I guess you have to tell him what's going on, unless you want to get into trouble. I don't object to that. But I want to make sure you don't do anything to stop us from helping find the killer—we've got a personal stake in that, you understand?"

"I understand," said Maggio. He took a sip of his wine, then allowed himself to sit down. "I think I can do that business with you."

"Good," said Mr. Clemens. He pulled a pipe from his

inside breast pocket, and started searching for his tobacco pouch, then stopped and looked at the policeman. He pointed with the pipe stem and asked, "Now, first of all, why don't you tell us where that young woman's body was found?"

Agente Maggio cupped his chin in his right hand, holding the wineglass in his left. "How well do you know Firenze?" he asked.

"A little better than most tourists, but not really well," said Mr. Clemens. "We've been living here maybe six weeks, and I get into town every now and then. Why?"

"Do you know—" He paused, looked at me, and continued. "You ever go to a place just outside the old city wall, at Porta di Pinti?"

"Sorry, I don't know Porta di Pinti," said my employer, and I confessed my own ignorance, as well.

"Ah, that is interesting," said *Agente* Maggio. "You see, they find her body in a place near there. And the *capitano* thinks first, who lives near that place? And when he learns who else saw her that night, he sees that it is halfway from *Signore* Stephens's home to Settignano."

"Aha!" said Mr. Clemens. "That's one of the reasons he suspected you, Wentworth—he thought she might have been coming here to see you."

"If it's on the way here, I suppose I must have passed it on my way into the city some time or another," I said. "But other than what the *agente* just said, I couldn't tell you where it is."

"Well, I am under orders to follow your man wherever he goes," said the policeman. "But I understand, you go some places with a *carabiniere* following you, nobody wants to see you. Here's an idea. Suppose instead of my uniform I wear regular clothes, and drive you wherever you go. Then nobody pays attention to me, and I can still follow my orders."

"That makes sense," said Mr. Clemens. "Our regular driver doesn't speak English worth a damn, anyhow—it'll be a relief to be able to tell you where I want to go without pointing and hollering and making faces."

"I will be your obedient servant, *signore*." said Maggio, with a comical bow. "But you understand, there will be times I am saying where we need to go. And tomorrow will be one of those times. We will go to the place where *Signorina* Fleetwood was murdered, so you can see it yourself. It is a place you ought to see, anyhow, since you are a visitor to Firenze. It is a very pretty place."

"Perhaps it is," I said, "but I doubt I shall ever be able to think of it except as the place where Virginia was killed."

"That'll be hard to forget," said Mr. Clemens, nodding. "But maybe it'll be worth the pain it causes you if we can find something that helps us catch the killer."

13 ✑

The next morning, Agente Maggio took us into Florence to show us where Virginia's body had been found. As we had planned, the policeman wore civilian clothing instead of his uniform, so as not to attract attention to his presence in our company. He drove us along a route I had taken into the city on several occasions, without ever stopping to see the sights along the way. Just outside the old city wall, we came to an oval plot of land, perhaps a little larger than a football field. The stone markers made it obvious that we had come to a cemetery. In fact, it was the Cimitero degli Inglesi, Florence's Protestant cemetery. Maggio stopped the carriage outside the entrance, and turned to look at me.

"Why are we stopping here?" I asked.

The policeman peered at us for a moment before saying, "This is where you said you wanted to come, *signori*."

My mouth fell open. "What? Was she murdered here?" Terrible as the murder had been, it somehow became more chilling to learn that Virginia had been killed in a graveyard.

But Maggio nodded solemnly. He pointed toward the entrance and asked, "You want to go in?"

"If this is where the body was found, I do," I said, looking in all directions for any clue to where the murder had occurred.

Maggio clucked to the horses and we turned into the gate. He looked at me again, as if to ask which way he should turn, but there was nothing to make me choose a direction—no reason to think that one spot inside was different from any other. The only thing that affected me was a monument nearby marking the last resting place of Elizabeth Barrett Browning—a poetess whose books my mother owned. Someone I had heard of was buried in this cemetery. For a brief moment, that had more impact on me than Maggio's word that Virginia had died here.

"You sure you've never been here before?" asked Maggio, looking closely at my face. I realized he was trying to see if I was familiar with the place—perhaps I would glance toward the spot where the body had been found, and betray my guilty knowledge.

"Never in my life," I said. "I've gone by it on my bicycle, but I didn't come inside. I noticed the stones, so I knew it was a graveyard, but beyond that it made no impression on me."

Apparently convinced that I was telling the truth, Maggio took us to a little grove of trees in the northern part of the oval plot. He told us that Virginia's body had been found there by gravediggers working nearby; one of them had stepped into the grove, and saw something glittering in the bushes. When he went to investigate, he found a gilded picture frame; nearby was the body. The police had later confirmed that the frame came from the stolen Raphael portrait.

The police had gone over the site with a fine-toothed comb, right after the crime was reported. I saw nothing that I could dignify with the name of a clue, unless there were significant inferences to be drawn from broken twigs and scuff marks on the ground. That sort of investigation was, frankly, beyond my capabilities, and—having heard Mr. Clemens sneer at fictional detectives who specialized in it—I doubted he was any better at it than I. In fact, I wondered whether coming here would have any effect other than throwing me into deep melancholy.

My employer must have read my mind. "This is a damned dreary place," he said, his breath misting in the cool morning air. "I know some people claim to like grave-yards, but I'm not one of 'em. Why would that young girl come all the way out here in the middle of the night? It makes no sense."

"We don't know that it was in the night," I said. "Or do we?" I looked at *Agente* Maggio, who had volunteered no information since conducting us hither and pointing out where the body and the empty picture frame had been found. He was still looking to catch me in a contradiction, I realized.

"We don't know for certain," said Maggio. "They find the body just before noon, so maybe it was there a few hours, maybe overnight. I don't think anybody killed her while the gravediggers were working so close."

"I don't think anybody would bring a valuable painting out here at night, either," said Mr. Clemens. "Not just be-cause of the weather, but because if they were delivering it to somebody else, the other party would have wanted to see what they were getting."

"There's no proof at all that she brought the painting here," I said. I realized that I didn't want to think of Vir-ginia as a criminal. "She may have followed the thief and surprised him in the act of delivering it to someone else."

"Maybe, maybe. Why did they bring the frame, though?" said Mr. Clemens. "If they took the picture out of it in Stephens's back yard, they'd have made things easier on themselves. Once they got it this far, I think they'd have left the picture in it instead of doing something that could damage it. Either these thieves are damned stupid, or I'm missing something important."

"Thieves are always stupid," said *Agente* Maggio, ex-uding confidence. "That is why we catch them."

"Well, you'd better hurry up and catch this bunch," said Mr. Clemens, scowling at the policeman. "They've already killed that girl, and that may just be the start of it. *Do* you have any theory why they brought the painting all the way out here?"

"Yes," said Maggio, pointing to the north. "Over there, on Piazza Donatello, are shops of artists and dealers. Some of them are not ashamed to sell the stolen paintings, or the—how you say? *falsi? forgiarri?*"

"Forgeries?" I suggested.

The policeman nodded vigorously. "Yes, *forgery*, is almost the same word. I don't think the poor woman come here to see you, *Signore* Cabot. I think maybe she come here to bring the Raphael to show someone who will buy it. Someone who has already seen it . . ."

"And instead, he killed her," said Mr. Clemens. "Well, it's a better motive than anything else we've got. It's still got more holes in it than a chicken coop, though. For one thing, Wentworth doesn't think the lady stole the painting, and I'm inclined to give his opinion some weight on that point."

"Me, I keep the mind open," said Maggio, making a large circle with his right hand. "I find out what the American lady does before she dies, maybe then I find out who kills her. If I say 'No, she never do anything like that,' the way her friends want me to do, maybe I don't look in the right places to find the answer. So I don't make the—how you say?—*supposizione*, because I want the answer more than I want to feel good about the lady. Nobody ought to die that way. *Capisce?*"

"That makes good sense," I said, surprised to find myself agreeing with the policeman's logic. "All right, then. Let's assume that she—or somebody she was following—came here to show the painting to a buyer. You say there are art dealers' shops near here. Why don't we go visit some of them, and see if we can find some answers?"

"A good idea, Wentworth," said my employer. Then he pointed at Maggio and added, "But don't you think they'll be suspicious if we walk in with a cop in tow?"

I started to protest, but Mr. Clemens held up his hand. "He may not be in uniform, but he's still got his face. Anybody who's running a crooked business is going to rec-

ognize the local cops, in uniform or out. Especially a cop
whose boss has an interest in the traffic in stolen art. What
do you say, Maggio? Are these birds going to know who
you are?"

Maggio laughed. "You're right," he said. "I work with
Capitano Rosalia all the time, so anybody who saw me with
him might remember I am *carabiniere*. It is no problem. I
don't worry about *Signore* Cabot running away, so I don't
need to follow him into shops. You go ask questions. I go
to a cafe near here and wait. You come get me when you
finish, and tell me everything you find out—*d'accordo?*"

"If that means what I think it does, we've got a deal,"
said Mr. Clemens extending his hand to the policeman, who
took it and shook it, smiling. When I had shaken hands
with Maggio in turn, my employer clapped my shoulder
and said, "OK, now we're really in business. Let's start
finding out who murdered that girl."

Piazza Donatello appeared to be the center of a thriving
artists' community, with several shops and studios in the
space of a city block. *Agente* Maggio dropped us off at the
entrance to the street, then drove off to wait in the nearby
cafe, leaving my employer and me to interrogate the art
dealers.

Having no reason to choose one establishment over another, we entered the first shop we saw, with a sign in the
shape of an artist's palette displaying the owner's name in
ornate letters: Arturo Nori, Esercente d'Arte. Through the
front windows we could see several framed paintings on
the walls, although there was nobody visible within. But a
bell rang as we opened the door, and that called forth a
stout gentleman with a bald pate fringed with thick dark
hair, a full beard, and thick spectacles over a hawkish nose.
"*Si, signori, cosa prendete?*"

I knew that phrase from restaurants—"What do you
want?" Neither Mr. Clemens nor I were fluent in Italian,
but having discovered that most Florentines who dealt with
foreigners had a fair command of English, we tried our luck
in our own language. "Are you the owner?" asked Mr.

Clemens. "We're interested in some old paintings."

"You come to the right place," said the man, rubbing his hands together. "Is nobody in Firenze can show you the more better art like Arturo Nori."

"I'm glad to hear it," said Mr. Clemens. "Normally I'd settle for the less worse art, but since I'm in Firenze, I reckon I'll do as the frenzied. I see you've got quite a few good-looking pieces here."

"*Si, si,*" said Nori, beaming. "You show me what you want, I give you the best price."

"Well, the price isn't as important as getting the right piece," said Mr. Clemens. He put his hands behind his back and walked over to inspect the paintings on display; I followed him, doing my best to appear interested in *Signore* Nori's offerings. Actually, that wasn't hard—I was always interested in art.

Mr. Clemens walked up to within a few inches of one painting—a large still life of flowers in an ornate vase—and pretended to examine the brushwork. "This is fine stuff," he said. "What do you think, Wentworth?"

"Very competent," I said. "I'm not sure it's what we're looking for, though." In fact, had I really been in the market for art, there were several things here that I would not have been ashamed to hang on my wall, although this particular piece seemed rather undistinguished. The artists' names were unfamiliar, of course. But I couldn't afford the works of any artist I *had* heard of—other than my few personal acquaintances who happened to be painters, and some of them were talented enough to command prices beyond the means of an impoverished writer's secretary.

"Oh, *signore*, this is but part of what I have," said Nori, stepping up beside me and bowing slightly, his hands clasped in a sort of prayerful gesture. "You tell me what you like to see, and I show you much more."

Mr. Clemens peered at another painting, this one a view of Florence from south of the Arno, with dramatic clouds gathering behind the Duomo. "Well, I don't know if you can show me what I want or not. This all looks like new stuff, to me. I'm after the old masters. Can you get that kind of goods?"

"Oh, yes, *signore*," said Nori, grinning broadly. "But *signore*—excuse me for saying so—you understand, the old masters cost a great deal. Now, if you wish to save the money, I know the artists who can make you very good copy . . ."

"Copies won't do," said Mr. Clemens, with a chopping motion of his hand. "If that was what I wanted, I could find an artist myself, and save even more money by not paying you your cut. But I've got the money, and I want the real thing. Can you deliver the goods?"

All this was of course a complete fabrication. Even if Mr. Clemens could have afforded a genuine old master, he had made it clear on any number of occasions that he had little use for the art of earlier periods. He was a firm believer in progress, and often said he'd trade all the Michelangelos in Italy for an equal number of colored lithographs. However, either *Signore* Nori did not recognize my employer, or, if he did, he had no notion of his true opinions. For my part, I did my best to keep my expression strictly neutral.

Nori shrugged and said, "The old masters, I do not keep them here in the gallery, you understand. But it is my business to know who has something, and who would sell it for a price. Are you interested in some particular artist? Or is it a certain subject you want—a madonna, a crucifixion? Or are you interested in drawings, perhaps? If I know these things, then I can see what there is to show you." Was it my imagination, or had his English improved when he realized we might be ready to spend more money than he had at first thought?

"I've got a mind to pick up a Raphael or two," said Mr. Clemens, jabbing a finger at the art dealer. "Do you have anything along that line?"

"A Raphael," said *Signore* Nori, wrinkling his brow. "This is most curious, do you know? There are not many Raphaels that come to sale in Firenze, and yet three have been offered here just in the few days. And it is even more curious that one of them was stolen just two nights ago. And now you come to my shop asking for a Raphael."

Well, there's the end of that ploy, I thought. My employer's too-direct approach must have aroused Nori's suspicion. Now, we'd be lucky to learn anything useful in our investigation.

Mr. Clemens wasn't about to let Nori off the hook. "Yes, I heard about those Raphaels coming on the market," he said. "In fact, that's what got me thinking. I'd seen plenty of Raphaels in museums, and liked 'em well enough. But I thought they were the kind of thing a private party couldn't get his hands on. Now I know better, and I've got a mind to have one for myself. I'm willing to pay the asking price if the piece is good enough. So, can you help me out, or do I go talk to somebody else?"

After a moment, the dealer nodded and said, "If the *signore* will leave his name and address, I will consult my sources. As I say, a Raphael does not become available every day. But if there is any to be bought in Tuscany, Arturo Nori can find it." He puffed himself up as he said this, his thick glasses and beaky nose making him look remarkably like an owl.

"Well, that's fair enough," said Mr. Clemens, reaching in his pocket and handing Nori a card. "The name is Cabot—W. W. Cabot. I'm staying in Villa Viviani out in Settignano, if you know where that is. But I'll warn you—I'll be talking to a few other dealers, too, and the first one to come up with the goods is the one who gets the sale. I'm not about to argue about the price. So if I were you I wouldn't drag my feet."

"I understand, *Signore* Cabot," said Nori, with a bow. "I will send to you as soon as I have any information."

Mr. Clemens thanked him, in an offhand sort of way, then beckoned to me, and we swept out of the shop together, as imperiously as if we had enough money to buy the dealer's entire stock.

Outside, after we were out of sight of Nori's shop, I said, "I understand your not wanting to give the fellow your own name, but what on earth possessed you to give him mine?

And where did you get a card with my name on it?"

"Well, I needed a name that'd turn up as real if he tried to verify it, and it made sense to give him the right address. Yours fit the bill on both particulars. As far as the card, I had some of my own printed up a few weeks ago, and decided to order some for you while I was at it. I'd forgotten about 'em until this morning, when I went looking for my own. I grabbed a handful of yours, and decided they might come in handy. I'll give you the rest of 'em when we get back." He smiled innocently and began to amble down the street. I could only shake my head and fall in behind him. It was hard to stay annoyed with Mr. Clemens—a good thing, since he so often did things to annoy me.

"I appreciate the thought," I said, pulling up beside him. "But next time, perhaps you'd better notify me in advance, or I may have difficulty concealing my surprise." I kept my voice just above a whisper, as we strolled along the street, stopping to peer at the treasures on display in the shop windows.

"Well, consider yourself notified," said Mr. Clemens. "We're going to perpetrate the same hoax on the other art dealers along the street. But I wasn't worried about surprising you. You kept a straight face pretty well, there. If you get a little more practice, I reckon you'll make a half-decent poker player." He chuckled.

"I'm not certain I ought to consider that a compliment," I said.

"Take it however you want," said Mr. Clemens, grinning. "Now, let's go see if the other art dealers think they can come up with a Raphael for me." He set off briskly toward the next gallery.

The next two art dealers also promised to look into the possibility of obtaining a Raphael for my employer, although they were similarly cautious about encouraging him to think they might be able to fill such an order. Again, he left my name and card, and gave them to understand that it was to their advantage to find something quickly. And without quite saying it in so many words, he left the distinct impression that he would not look closely into the piece's provenance. Whether anything would come of it, only time would tell.

In the fourth shop on the street, we were greeted by *Signore* Luigi Battista, a slim man with a hawkish face and full head of bushy gray hair, whose personality was so charismatic that it was with a jolt that I realized that he stood no taller than five foot three. His name seemed familiar—had Stephens mentioned him, perhaps? The walls of his shop were covered with what to the layman's eye might look like authentic old masters. But I was quite certain that the Uffizi gallery had not decided to divest itself of Botticelli's "Pallas and the Centaur" and Leonardo's "Adoration of the Magi," especially not through a small shop in Piazza Donatello. And while I did not recognize all the other paintings on display, it seemed to me that they were equally unlikely to be what they appeared to be at first glance.

Luigi Battista made no bones about the nature of his wares. "You come look," he said with obvious pride. "You no see what you like, you tell me, and I paint it for you. I paint Botticelli, I paint Leonardo, I paint Signorelli—you tell me, I paint it." His pride in his work was obvious, and—based on what I saw hanging on the walls of his shop—amply justified.

"Well, I'm looking for a Raphael," said Mr. Clemens, taken aback by the little man's extravagant display of counterfeits. "But I was looking for one where the paint's dry, if you know what I mean." He sniffed.

"Ah, Raphael," said Battista, nodding vigorously. "I don' do Raphael myself, but I can get you some. I know some artists do very good Raphael—best materials, very careful work. You tell me what painting you want, I get it for you."

"I don't think you understand Mr. Cl . . . *Cabot*," I said, correcting myself at the last moment. "He's not looking for a copy, no matter how good it is. He's willing to pay for the real thing."

"Maybe he pay for the real thing, but that don' mean he get the real thing," said Battista, spreading his hands apart, palms up. The gesture somehow made him seem bigger. "Raphael, he paint for maybe twenty year. But people been making the Raphael *pasticcios* almost four hundred year, now—some so good, Raphael can't tell the difference if he come back to see. You buy from me, you know what you get. You buy from somebody else, maybe you get the real thing, maybe not. Your money—you decide."

"By God, an honest art dealer," Mr. Clemens exclaimed, only half-ironically, I thought. He leaned forward and peered down at Battista as if to record the sight in his memory, then added, "I didn't know there was such a thing in Florence. Tell me this, then—your friends who do the very, very good Raphaels; are they as honest as you, or do they ever paint one and try to sell it as the real thing?"

"Maybe, but they don't tell me if they do," said Battista, with a wink. "Some things, a smart man don' tell his friends. But sometimes—this happen to me, not so many years ago—I sell a nice Botticelli *pasticcio* to a man, he give me a good price for it. Then a few years later, I go to a gallery I know, and I see my *pasticcio* there, with a much bigger price on it, a lot more than that man pay me. I feel proud to see my work with such a big price, even if I don't get any more money. But I feel bad to see people think they buy the *autentico*, when I know I made it just a few years ago. I don't paint it to cheat people."

"Why do you paint something like that, then?" said Mr. Clemens. "You must know that, if it's good enough, some people are going to think it's real. And other people are going to sell it to them for too much money."

Battista shrugged. "Because I like to make beautiful things," he said. "Life is better with beautiful things, no?"

"Sure, but if you're good enough to paint like this"— my employer's gesture took in the entire wall of paintings—"why not paint something of your own? Why copy Botticelli?"

"Is good question," said Battista, walking over and leaning on the counter at the back of his shop. "I got a good answer, though. Suppose you know a violinist, plays Mozart and Schubert very, very well. Do you complain because he don't make up his own melodies, or are you glad he chooses something good to play? If everybody has to make up his own music, maybe not so many people want to listen."

"Hmm—I guess I see your point," said Mr. Clemens. "Let me ask you another question. You say you know some artists who do Raphael very well. Have you heard that a dealer in town just got hold of a bunch of Raphaels nobody's ever seen before?"

"Sure, I heard about that," said the artist, raising an eyebrow. "Giuseppe Volponi saw them, and he calls them *autentico*. Me, I didn't see them, but Volponi has a good eye. Maybe not as good as he thinks, but good enough for most people. You go ask Volponi, he tell you what he thinks. He tell you about painting, music, poetry, politics— he talk all day long, you don't watch out." Battista grinned broadly, and slapped a hand on the counter as if to make sure we understood his joke, knocking a few papers to the floor.

"I take it you don't agree with him," I said. I remembered seeing Volponi in Cafe Diabelli, holding forth to a circle of admirers. My rudimentary understanding of Italian had prevented me from judging the quality of his opinions, but it was clear enough that he had plenty of them.

"I don't agree or disagree," said Battista, stooping to pick up the papers. "I don't judge paintings I don't see, is all. But I tell you again—you want a good Raphael *pasticcio*, you come ask me. You buy from me, you get what you pay for."

"That's about as fair a proposition as we're going to get," said Mr. Clemens. "I need to think about it a little, but I reckon we'll be back in touch with you. Many thanks for your help, *Signore* Battista."

"My pleasure, *Signore* Mark Twain," said the little artist, with a broad smile and a deep bow. "You come back to see me, I take good care of you."

For once, my employer was speechless.

14 ⌒

"There is no law against copying pictures," explained *Agente* Maggio, patiently. "It is how the students learn, as long as there have been painters. The only wrong thing is to sell the false pictures as if they were the authentic ones. Then the *polizia* pay very serious attention."

My employer took the cigar out of his mouth and knocked the ash over the side of the carriage. "So this fellow Battista can paint all the fake Botticellis and Leonardos he wants, and nobody cares?"

"Little Luigi can paint them, and as long as he tells the truth about them he can even sell them. There is no crime in that," said the policeman. Mr. Clemens had given him a cigar, and he was puffing away on it with obvious appreciation as he guided the horses through the streets of old Florence.

"I noticed that none of the paintings in Battista's shop bore the artist's signature," I said. "If he sells them to someone who then adds a forged signature, presumably that person would be guilty of fraud, rather than Battista?"

"That is true in theory," said *Agente* Maggio. "It can be hard to prove who did what. Luigi says he sells his *pasticcios* only to those who know what they are. But that does not answer if he knows whether those buyers plan to sell them again, to someone who thinks they are authentic. It is not easy to prove this in a court, *capisce?*"

"I *capisce* enough that I'm starting to wonder about Stephens's so-called Raphaels," said Mr. Clemens. "Everybody at the party took his word that they were the real thing, but what's his word worth?"

"It is worth much," said Maggio, with a sweeping gesture that sent ashes flying from his own cigar. "In fact, an art dealer who is known to sell forgeries, people will not trust him. His business rests on his word that what he sells is genuine. In fact, *Signore* Stephens has often worked with *Capitano* Rosalia to stop thieves, and to expose forgeries. So he has the reputation for being honest."

"I think I'll ask him about those Raphaels, anyway," said Mr. Clemens. Having inspected the place where Virginia's body had been found, and having interviewed the nearby art dealers, we were on our way to Stephens's residence to offer our condolences on the death of his sister-in-law. This visit would also give us an opportunity to ask a few questions in furtherance of our murder investigation—or so we hoped. I dreaded it, and yet I was anxious to begin.

Agente Maggio turned the carriage across Ponte Vecchio, with its rows of ancient goldsmiths' shops along the sides, and took us into the Oltrarno. The day had brightened up, and the temperature at midday was comfortable enough that we had left our coats unbuttoned, and put our gloves in our pockets. Our route took us by Palazzo Pitti and its lovely Boboli Gardens, which I had explored with Virginia in what now seemed like the remote past. It was a perfect reminder that, even in its northern provinces, Italy had a far more benign climate than England—or New England. I would have been tempted to relax and enjoy the fine, springlike weather, but with a murder to solve, my mind had no room for enjoyment. There was work to be done, and until it was finished, I was all business.

At last we reached the district where Frank Stephens lived, a residential street off Via Pisano, a short distance from the river. Again, *Agente* Maggio went off to await us somewhere nearby. A funeral wreath was on the door, and when the butler opened it to our knock, his livery seemed darker and more formal—although my imagination may have provided that detail. "We've come to pay our respects," said Mr. Clemens, and the butler nodded and showed us in, his face as dark and mournful as his garments. I wondered if the household staff felt Virginia's death as keenly as I did. As everyone who knew her must feel . . .

Except, of course, the monster who'd strangled her.

That monster might be here even now, feigning grief among the genuinely bereaved. I wondered if a discerning eye would be able to pick out the guilt behind the mask of sorrow. Or was the killer someone practiced at deceit, showing a benign face to the world while cherishing the secret of his evil? I promised myself that it would do him no good; eventually, inevitably, I would find him and bring him to justice.

The butler took our coats, then led us upstairs to the main room, where Mrs. Stephens sat on the sofa next to the fireplace. There was a clergyman sitting beside her and holding her hand—a Protestant minister, perhaps even an American, to judge from his clothing. Opposite her were two women I did not recognize, both dressed all in black. Mrs. Stephens looked up as we entered the room and said, "Mr. Clemens! How kind of you to come." Though her features were concealed behind a heavy veil, the quaver in her voice made it evident that she had been weeping.

"The news was a shock to us, ma'am," said Mr. Clemens, in a quiet voice. "I know this is a difficult time for you. If there's anything I or my secretary can do, I hope you won't hesitate to ask it."

"I thank you for the offer, Mr. Clemens," said Mrs. Stephens. "Alas, the one thing I most want, no mortal power can bestow."

"I understand," said my employer, nodding.

"I am also at your disposal," I said, stepping up next to Mr. Clemens. "I cannot begin to tell you how much this loss affects me, but I hope you understand that my lack of words doesn't mean any lack of feeling."

Mrs. Stephens turned her head toward me. Her veil made it difficult to see her expression, but her tone was measured as she said, "I hope that is true, Mr. Cabot. I would have thought your last two visits here would have made you hesitate to return so soon, but still I suppose I owe you thanks for your kind words."

"I . . . I . . ." I stammered, unprepared for such a reception.

Mrs. Stephens raised a hand to stop me. "Say no more, Mr. Cabot," she said. "I have no desire to dwell on unpleasantness. I hope that Virginia is in a better place."

"She surely is," said the minister, in a voice that managed to be silky despite a very distinct Bostonian accent. "We all trust that she is among the saints today."

"I would rather that she was still here with us," said Mrs. Stephens, turning away from me and leaning her head on the minister's shoulder. "But I cannot have that, and I do not know what to do." Her voice, previously under control, broke into sobbing.

"Poor Isabella," said one woman. "Trust in the Lord, and he will soothe your pain."

Mr. Clemens touched my elbow, and—aware of our intrusion at a painful moment—we turned to leave Mrs. Stephens to compose herself without our scrutiny.

Now I realized that there were several others present besides those sitting with Mrs. Stephens. In the center of the room were Bob Danvers and Eddie Freeman; behind them, near the long wall with the paintings, were Jonathan Wilson, the art collector, Sarah Woods, and Penelope Atwater. All were staring at me with unconcealed animosity. Suddenly I was sorry I had come.

There was an uncomfortable moment of silence, and then Bob Danvers came over and stood in front of me, hands on hips. He said in a low voice, "I don't suppose you have my money."

"As a matter of fact, I do," I said, meeting his glare as coolly as I could, and keeping my voice level. "I was going to come by the cafe later and give it to you. If you want, we'll go downstairs and I'll give it to you—this isn't the place to be haggling over ten lira."

"I'm surprised you have the brass to show your face at all," Danvers replied, still keeping his voice low—although anyone who wanted to could have heard every syllable we'd said. I could smell liquor on his breath. "But yes," he said. "I want my money now. Let's go downstairs and you can pay me."

I responded to this by gesturing toward the stairs, and the two of us walked down, saying nothing. I was uncomfortably aware of several pairs of eyes on my back as I descended. I *had* made a mistake coming here.

We reached the bottom of the stairs, and turned to face one another. "It's ten lira I owe you, right?" I said, reaching into my pocket. It seemed an absurdly small amount to be arguing over—a couple of dollars in American money, enough to pay his rent for a week or so.

"To hell with you and your money," he snarled, and threw a right-hand punch that landed square on my jaw. "That's for Ginny," he said, and drew his arm back to hit me again.

Caught by surprise, I reeled back, and Danvers followed me, aiming more punches at my face. Stunned, I grappled with him, trying to get hold of his arms to prevent him from putting any strength into his punches.

"What do you mean by that?" I said, ducking. His aim was erratic—the drink, no doubt—but there was enough power in the assault to make him dangerous.

"You know what I mean," he said, his voice rising. "If it weren't for you, Ginny would still be alive." And then he was sobbing uncontrollably, even as he continued to throw punches.

I suddenly understood his anger. He must have been in love with Virginia himself, and resented her attentions to me. Had he been her favorite before my arrival? That, more than the stolen bike, would explain his animosity to me; I even felt a twinge of sympathy, seeing the tears roll down his cheeks.

But then he landed a wild blow to my shoulder, and my temper flared. "Don't blame me for Virginia's death," I shouted, trying to ward off his fists. And yet I could not escape a sense of guilt—would she have gone out that fateful night if I had not argued with her? I might never know.

Danvers continued to flail at me. I finally got his arms pinned, but he kicked at my shins. Hoping to end it quickly, I threw my weight forward and took him to the floor. I landed on top of him, and the air went out of him with a *whoof*! By then there were others standing over us, saying "Get them apart," and I felt hands on my shoulders. I let myself be hauled off my opponent and stood upright facing Danvers. Eddie Freeman was behind him, holding his arms, and I could see Mr. Clemens and the butler hovering in the background.

"You should both be ashamed of yourselves," said Jonathan Wilson, who had his arms around my midsection. "This is no place for your quarrels."

"The stingy cur should know better than to stick his face in here," growled Danvers, still glaring at me. My jaw ached, and there was a salty taste in my mouth—blood, I supposed.

I bit back a harsh response, and said instead, "Danvers, I'll pay you your ten lira, and as far as I'm concerned, that'll be the last we have to do with one another. I don't go looking for trouble."

Danvers made a vulgar suggestion about the ten lira, and Mr. Wilson clucked his tongue. "I'll chalk that up to the liquor, Mr. Danvers. If you want my advice, you'll take Cabot's offer and call it quits. Mr. Cabot, I think you made a mistake coming here today."

"So it appears," I said. "I want no quarrel with anyone here. I'll give you Danvers' money, and leave. Maybe you should hold it till he sobers up. Mr. Clemens, if you want to stay longer, I'll go find our driver and come back with the carriage."

"A good idea," said my employer, nodding. "I don't think I'll be long."

Wilson let go my arms, and I fished a ten-lira *Banca di*

Toscana note out of my wallet and gave it to him. The butler already had my coat and hat, and I put them on and left. The butler told me where the drivers were accustomed to await their masters' summons, and so I set off on foot to find our carriage.

In good weather, the drivers gathered at a small park a short distance off, where there was a watering trough and shade for the horses. There were five or six rigs tied up, and a group of drivers was a short distance away, sitting on a low stone wall and talking animatedly. (I had by now come to the conclusion that no Italian was capable of talking in any other fashion.)

As I had hoped, *Agente* Maggio was in the midst of them, gesturing and taking part in the conversation just as if he were one of their fraternity instead of a disguised policeman. He looked up as I came into view, saw my disheveled clothing, and raised an eyebrow. "Ah, *signore*, what is wrong?" he asked, getting to his feet and coming toward me.

The other drivers, hearing Maggio speak in English, turned to look; one of them reached down and concealed a wine bottle that had been sitting on the wall next to him. I was at first offended that he thought he had to hide his drinking from me, but then I recalled that they had no idea who I was—only that I was a well-dressed foreigner, and consequently they must see me as one of the bosses rather than as a comrade.

"A misunderstanding," I said, and told him about the fight with Danvers. "My only regret is that I wasn't there long enough to learn anything really useful," I concluded.

"Perhaps the other *signore* will learn something," said Maggio, rubbing his chin. Then he continued in a lower voice as we walked toward the carriage. "But see, I learn something myself today. There is Paolo, the husband of my cousin Sophia." He nodded to indicate one of the drivers, a thin, dark-skinned man with a drooping black mustache and a weak chin. "Paolo is *cocchiere* for the English *Si-*

gnora Atwater, who attends the party the night the young lady and the Raphael both disappear."

"Yes, Mrs. Atwater's there today," I said. "The other night, she chided Mr. Clemens for not showing proper deference to the old masters."

"Paolo don't tell me about that," said Maggio. "But late that night, he's waiting for the *signora* to go home, and a man comes from the Stephens house asking if somebody wants to take an American lady up to the city. Paolo got to wait for *Signora* Atwater so he can't take the job, but another driver—a man he don't know—does the job."

"And you think that ride was for Miss Fleetwood," I said.

"I think so," said Maggio, nodding. "The other ladies, they have their own coaches, or ride with someone else. *Signorina* Fleetwood, she left alone—unless somebody tells lies. To know for sure, we got to find that other driver. I ask the other men, but so far nobody remembers who it is." By now we had reached the carriage, and Maggio untied the reins. He gestured to me to climb up next to him on the driver's seat so we could continue talking while he drove back to Stephens's house.

"Well, I wouldn't think it'd be too hard to find the driver we're looking for," I said. Most likely, the driver had been someone who worked regularly in this part of Florence. The drivers for the other guests at Stephens's party would have had the same problem as Paolo—if they were off on another errand when their employers called for them, they would find themselves in trouble.

"Maybe not as easy as you think," said Maggio, flicking the reins. "Most of these men, they all know each other, 'cause the foreigners they work for go the same places all the time, so the drivers see each other while they wait. Somebody they don't remember, maybe he isn't a regular driver at all."

"Do you mean he was an impostor?" I said, and then all sorts of horrors began to rush into my imagination. What if he had been the sort of beast who preys upon unprotected women, and who seized upon the opportunity to slake his unspeakable thirsts? Could Virginia's last minutes have been even more terrible than I had hitherto believed?

If *Agente* Maggio had any such sinister notions, he was not about to voice them. "Maybe," he said, shrugging. "More likely, just a substitute driver. Or maybe somebody new the other men don't know yet. But still, if nobody remembers him, he's not so easy to find."

"I suppose we shall have to find out if any of Stephens's guests have changed drivers recently," I said.

"When I tell this to the *capitano*, he will learn if that is so," said Maggio, matter-of-factly. "We in the police have ways of finding these things out. Don't you worry, *Signore* Cabot. If this is an important clue, we will know soon. We will catch the one who murders your lady friend."

"I wish I had your confidence," I said. "The more I find out, the more nebulous the entire case appears."

"Nebulous?" asked Maggio, then immediately said, "Ah, *nebuloso*, cloudy. I think your language, it takes many words from Italian. But remember, the clouds may be thick today, but always the light comes through."

"That is undeniably true," I said, and then my spirits sank again. "But I'm afraid that even the brightest light will do nothing to bring back Miss Fleetwood."

"This, alas, is true," said Maggio. Having conceded this much, he scratched the calf of one leg with the toe of his other boot. We rode in silence for the rest of the short trip back to Stephens's house.

It was just as well; I was in no mood for conversation. My mind went off on a dozen side tracks. What was Virginia doing visiting a cemetery at midnight? Who was the mysterious driver who took her there? How was she connected to the stolen painting? Just as we turned into Stephens's drive, I looked up and saw Mr. Clemens coming out the front door.

He waved to Maggio and me. "Come along, boys," he called. "I've got another clue to follow, halfway across town from here."

Maggio stopped the carriage, and Mr. Clemens climbed in. Next thing I knew, we were back on Ponte Vecchio, heading into the heart of Florence.

"I can't understand why, after ignoring the place for months, now you want to go to Cafe Diabelli," I said to Mr. Clemens. I had been surprised when he told *Agente* Maggio our destination. "I have no desire to see the place again," I added, "although I suppose I can go in without actual inconvenience as long as Bob Danvers isn't there."

"He was still at Stephens's when I left, still soaking up the free drinks," said my employer. "So you shouldn't worry about him showing up at the cafe. Anyway, you have as much right to go into the place as that rum-bum does, and don't let anybody tell you otherwise."

"That's easy enough to say," I said. "But if he thinks I was somehow responsible for Virginia's death, I'll feel uncomfortable around him even if he doesn't start another fight. And if he convinces others of it . . ."

"You're not responsible for that girl's death, and you damn well ought to know it," said Mr. Clemens. "Danvers is a worse skunk than I thought if he tries to make it look as if you are responsible. Maybe that fight between you two got broken up too soon. If he'd gone on long enough to get you really mad, I reckon you'd have taught him not to spread lies about you."

"I'm not in the business of teaching lessons," I said, slowly shaking my head. "If I never had to swing my fist at anyone again, I'd be just as happy."

"There are times you have to fight," said *Agente* Maggio, turning back to look at me. "That is one thing I learn young. Is best if you don't have to hurt somebody, but you don't always have choices."

"I understand that," I said. "But I don't have to like it." Then, after reflecting a moment, I returned to the subject I'd asked Mr. Clemens about earlier. "You still haven't told me what you expect to learn at Diabelli's."

"Well, all I've got is a rumor, to tell the truth," said Mr. Clemens, smoothing his mustache with a thumb and forefinger. "That Wilson fellow—the one that was angling to buy the painting before it disappeared—said he'd heard about a plot by anarchists to steal old masters and hold them for ransom, to raise money for the revolution. He thought that might have happened to the Raphael that Stephens lost. Of course, nobody's asked for ransom yet, so that's pure speculation. But I figured it couldn't hurt to find out whether it's got any chance of being true."

"I still don't see the connection," I said.

"Wentworth, you continue to amaze me," said Mr. Clemens. "Do you mean to say you've been going to Cafe Diabelli all this time and didn't know it was one of the main haunts in all Florence for Socialists, anarchists, and other political wild men?"

"Is true," said Maggio, turning his head again, to look at me with a sober expression, although I thought there was a hint of amusement around the corner of his eyes. "We watch that place very close. Mostly nothing happens but talk, talk, plenty talk. But if revolution ever happens in Firenze, I bet you good money that's where they plan it."

"I thought Italy already had its revolution," I said. "Wasn't that twenty-five or thirty years ago, when Garibaldi united the country?"

"The *Risorgimento* changes some things, but not everything," said Maggio quietly. "These revolutionaries don't think Garibaldi got to finish what he started. They want a country like America, with no kings, everybody rich."

I laughed bitterly. "Everybody rich? I'd like to show those people the New York slums. Then they'd sing a different tune about Americans being rich."

"Don't be so quick to judge them, Wentworth," Mr. Clemens said. "You may not think so, but *you're* a rich man compared to most people here in Italy. A farm worker here might go his whole life without tasting meat more than a few times."

"It is true," said Maggio again quietly. "But these are not the farm workers who talk so much in Cafe Diabelli. These anarchists get their ideas from books and newspapers. Maybe they think to steal a painting is good for the revolution. The workers, they think the revolution is to eat three meals a day."

"You don't talk like a cop," said Mr. Clemens, his eyebrows raised. "Cops back home will run you into jail for talking about the revolution."

"I don't know how American cops talk," said Maggio, shrugging. "I know about farmers that don't get enough to eat. I know about a *cocchiere* that don't have money to take his *bambina* to a doctor when she gets sick. These *borghesi stonati*"—I didn't understand the phrase, but the way he spat it out, I could guess it meant something like "stupid burghers." He went on: "If they steal a painting, it don't feed the farmers. If they kill an American *signorina*, it don't cure the *bambina*. Maybe they do these things, or maybe not. But that's their idea how to make the revolution, I say they're *bastardi* and nothing else." He clucked his tongue and guided the horses around a corner into the street where our destination lay.

"I don't know much Italian, but I know *that* word," said Mr. Clemens, nodding. He clapped the policeman on the shoulder. "Maggio, you're one of the damnedest cops I ever met up with. I don't know if there are any more like you, but I'm glad Captain Rosalia picked you to follow Cabot around."

"That's good, because I got to keep doing it until we find the murderer," said Maggio. He reined in the horses. "Here we are, *signori*—Cafe Diabelli."

I had barely stepped over the threshold of Cafe Diabelli when the waiter Pietro came over to me and said, "*Signore* Cabot, I was so sorry to learn about *Signorina* Fleetwood. We all liked her very much, and I know you must be very sad, too." His expression made it clear the condolence was heartfelt.

"Thank you, Pietro," I said, moved by his sincerity. "It was a great shock to everyone. I will be a long time getting over it."

"Would you like to sit at your regular table outside, *signore*?" asked Pietro. "It is a very warm day today, and some of your friends are already here."

"No, I think I'll sit inside today," I said. "How about that table over there?" I remembered that Viginia had warned me that my chess opponents were among the political radicals whom Maggio said made Cafe Diabelli a regular meeting place, and they preferred the indoor tables. Pietro showed no surprise at the request, but took us to the table I had indicated—one near the center of the room, a good vantage point to see and hear what was going on throughout the cafe.

Mr. Clemens and I took our seats, and asked Pietro what was being served for luncheon. After hearing the choices, we both ordered the beefsteak—an excellent local specialty—and decided to share a bottle of Chianti classico, the good red wine to which Frank Stephens had introduced me. After a few minutes, Pietro returned with our wine and poured us each a glass. Then, while waiting for our meal, we settled back to eavesdrop, hoping to overhear something that would lead us to the art thief—and thence to Virginia's murderer.

As on my previous visits to the cafe, I found myself immersed in an ocean of talk in an unfamiliar language. Over the weeks, my ear had learned to pick out the occasional phrase, but I had associated mainly with other

English-speakers, and so had not progressed as well as I might have. Now it occurred to me that the two men speaking so excitedly at the next table could be hatching a detailed plot to assassinate the King of Italy and to burn the Sistine Chapel to the ground without my understanding one word in twenty. And Mr. Clemens was no more conversant in Italian than I. How were we ever going to locate the radicals we had come here to find?

Mr. Clemens's mind seemed to be elsewhere. He took a final puff on his cigar, stubbed it out, and sat back in his chair. "You know, Wentworth," he began, "that Maggio fellow is full of surprises. First, he turns out to be a fine singer. Now, today, he showed me he has a damn sight more good sense than a lot of men in his job."

"What do you mean, sir?" I asked. Mr. Clemens was speaking more slowly than usual, and in a voice that must have carried to the far corners of the room. I recognized at once that he was playing to an audience, with me as a sort of interlocutor. This was a ploy we had engaged in before. My part in the ruse would be to speak just enough to give the illusion of a conversation, without actually saying anything that would interfere with his purpose—whatever that turned out to be.

"You can't have a real revolution and still have a king," he said. "All these Italians did was throw out one set of thieves and put in another. If they ever want to do something about the people's real problems, first thing they'll do is put the toes of their boots to that king's tail end."

My first instinct at hearing these sentiments was to agree with them; after all, I was as patriotic an American as any. My ancestors had fought against King George and his minions. I had little sympathy with royalty or hereditary titles. But here in a foreign kingdom, in a room full of its citizens, I thought it imprudent to say so. By the time Mr. Clemens finished speaking, the room was silent as a tomb—a simile I suddenly hoped was not too apt. Belatedly, the thought flashed through my mind: *More of these people understand English than I realized.*

"Aren't the Italians entitled to choose the form of government that suits them best?" I asked, looking around nervously. There were men at the nearby tables staring in our direction. Even at the far side of the room, where the chess players congregated, Gonnella—one of the best players in the cafe—had looked up from his game with his archrival Garbarini to peer in my employer's direction.

"It would serve 'em right if they chose it," said Mr. Clemens, "but I'd be surprised if they really did. No man who wasn't taking bribes ever chose of his own free will to live under a king. We got rid of ours in America, and a damn good thing. But as long as a country lets any bully with a crown tell them what to do, the only people who'll get a fair shake in that country are the king's own friends and family." Mr. Clemens put his glass down with just enough force to splash a little wine onto the tablecloth. It seemed an appropriate gesture for the words.

"You speak a great deal of things that are none of your business," said a heavily accented voice from behind me. "Why do you come to Italia if you disrespect our country?"

"I don't disrespect your country, just your king," said Mr. Clemens, leaning back in his chair. I turned to see the person he was talking to: a bald-headed man with a round belly, a full beard, and a scowl that would have done a stage villain proud. I remembered his name: Volponi. Battista had chacterized him as a pundit, ready to expostulate on any subject that came to hand. He was a regular at Diabelli's, sitting at his favorite table amid a crowd of acolytes, playing the literary lion.

"The king and the country, they are one," said the bearded man. He scowled more fiercely, then said, "I know you. You are Mark Twain. Your slanders of Italia do not surprise me now that I recognize you."

"Well, you have the advantage of me in that respect," said my employer, calmly sipping his wine before continuing. "Who are you, and what country do you normally slander?"

"I am Giuseppe Volponi," the man thundered, striking his chest with one fist. "And I slander no one! I tell the truth, and if the guilty take offense, it is themselves they should blame!"

"Now there's a man after my own heart," said Mr. Clemens, slapping his hand on the table. "Sit down and have a glass of this wine and let's try to figure out which one of us is telling the real truth. I reckon a good argument is just the thing to work up my appetite."

Volponi hesitated just a fraction of a second, but then the temptation of a free glass of wine overcame whatever reluctance he might have had to drink with a man who bore no respect for kings. He took a chair from a nearby table and sat down between me and my employer, leaning his elbows on the table. I caught Pietro's eye, and he brought another glass, which Mr. Clemens filled from our bottle of Chianti.

The silence that had followed Mr. Clemens's opening diatribe against kings had somewhat abated, as those in the dining room resumed eating and drinking. But we were no less the focus of attention; the group of hangers-on who sat at Volponi's table had turned to face us, and over at the chess tables, Garbarini (evidently having made his move) was looking over his shoulder at us while Gonnella studied the board. I knew that my employer had some purpose in baiting the crowd, but I wondered whether he had thought through the consequences.

Volponi sipped his wine, nodded in appreciation, then said, "You came here many years ago and wrote a book that all the world read, mocking our beautiful city and our glorious history. I thought that years might bring you wisdom, but I can see it is not so." While he had a heavy accent, his English was quite good, formed on the British model as was common with those Italians who spoke our language well.

"Changing your mind isn't wisdom, if you were right to start with," said Mr. Clemens, leaning back in his chair and putting his thumbs in the lapels of his white suit. "And let's get one thing straight—if I were such an enemy to Florence, I wouldn't have come here to live. I just don't pretend it's perfect, any more than I do back home. You ask the folks in Arkansas, or Washington, or Boston, or a few dozen other places, what I've said about them, and you might think Italy has got off pretty easy."

"You Americans do not respect history, because you have none of your own," said Volponi, shaking his head vigorously. "Italia has been glorious before, and she will be so again. As Vittorio Emanuele proclaimed, she must not only be respected; she must make herself feared. King Umberto understands this, and in Francesco Crispi he has a man who can make it so."

"Crispi's a crook," said Mr. Clemens. "But everybody's scared of the Socialists, so they forget about that. Crispi will probably send the army somewhere in Africa to shoot the natives and enslave the survivors. That's wrong when England does it, and it's wrong when Belgium does it, and when France and Germany do it, and it'll be damn well wrong when Italy does it. If there's any justice in the world, the natives will throw it all back in his face."

"You speak of the Socialists," said Volponi, scowling even more fiercely. "You Americans pay them to revolt in Sicily—Crispi has proof of it. America would like to destroy our nation. But Crispi will do what is needed. If we need to imprison every Socialist in Sicily—and in all of Italy for that matter—we will do it, to protect our glorious country. And the *fico* to America, if it does not like it." He made an abrupt gesture with his right hand.

"I guess a nation that's survived the Caesars and the Medicis and the Borgias won't be much bothered by a petty thief like Crispi," said Mr. Clemens. "He may think he can derail the Socialists—and maybe he has, for now—but they'll be around to dance at his funeral unless he solves the problems they're addressing. Hell, he *is* one of the problems they're addressing."

"You are no better than a Socialist yourself," said Volponi, in a deep rumbling voice. "I should report you to the police."

Abruptly, I became aware that the room was again silent, and that our table had become the center of a ring of spectators. So far, they had let Mr. Clemens and Volponi do all the talking. But now, from behind me, a voice growled, "You do so at your peril, Volponi. We know where you live."

I turned to see the speaker. It was Gonnella, the chess champion, who had left his game to watch the debate between my employer and the cafe's resident polymath.

Another voice answered Gonnella. "What kind of Italian defends a foreigner against one of his own?" The speaker was one of Volponi's hangers-on—a handsome youth wearing a colorful, artfully disheveled outfit, which on close inspection revealed expensive materials and workmanship. *A rich boy playing bohemian,* I thought.

Then another bystander said something harsh in Italian— or so I assumed, for the would-be bohemian youth responded by blurting out an epithet of his own, then lunging forward and taking a wild swing at Gonnella. Gonnella ducked under it and grappled with his assailant, and the next thing I knew, there were voices raised and fists flying all around us.

My first thought was to protect Mr. Clemens, who was (for all his talk of a rough-and-tumble youth), after all, a mature man of sedentary habits. But no sooner had I stood up from my seat than I was accosted by a wild-haired fellow wearing a corduroy suit and thick spectacles, who attempted to bludgeon me with a half-full wine bottle. I was perforce in my second fight of the day. I managed to grab his arm, spilling wine on both of us, and wrestle his weapon out of his grasp, only to find myself attacked from behind by someone who seemed intent on ripping off my jacket. Out of the corner of my eye I saw Mr. Clemens slip out of his chair and take shelter under the table, so I decided I could concentrate on defending myself.

The next few minutes were pure chaos. I don't know how many actual fights were going on, but it seemed as if the whole room had become a field of combat, with bottles flying, chairs and tables tipping over, and invective spewing forth in four or five languages. The waiters made an effort to break up the fighting, but after one was knocked senseless and another fell back with blood streaming from his nose, they abandoned the attempt. I saw Pietro dash out the door, no doubt to summon help before the entire place was destroyed.

Meanwhile, I had plenty to keep me occupied. I disposed of my first two assailants with a little effort, and turned again to look to Mr. Clemens's safety—the best plan seemed to be to get him out of the room, if that was possible. But right at that moment, another fellow decided I was of the enemy camp—I have no idea what side of the fight he thought I was on, or even how many sides there were—and came rushing at me like an enraged bull.

I picked up a chair to fend him off, but his bulk and his momentum carried me backward and I found myself pinned in a corner. Luckily, the chair kept him at sufficient distance that he couldn't land a blow, and I managed to keep him at bay until he decided to look for easier game. Again I turned to look for my employer, but I had lost track of which table he'd ducked under.

At that point someone shouted, "*Polizia!*" The door flew open and a half-dozen uniformed men poured through, brandishing clubs. There was a sudden exodus of combatants through the doors leading to the terrace, leaving a fair number of dazed and maimed on the field. At last free of my assailants, I cast my eye around for my employer, hoping to see him emerge unscathed. But Mr. Clemens was nowhere to be seen.

⤳ 16

"**D**on't worry about your *padrone*," said *Agente* Maggio. "He'll come back before you know it."

The *carabiniere* and I sat at a table on the terrace of Cafe Diabelli, while Pietro set the waiters and cleaning staff to repairing the damage. The police had rounded up everyone still inside the cafe, without bothering to ask who had done what. They were about to haul me off to the local clink, when Maggio—who'd seen a group of police going toward the cafe and followed them—showed his identification and vouched for me. Now we were trying to figure out what had happened to Mr. Clemens, who had been among the missing when the police arrived.

"It's easy for you to say that," I answered, taking a sip of wine. Pietro had replaced the bottle spilled at my table— very generously, in my opinion, since my employer had incited the melee that led to its spilling. I looked at the Italian policeman and continued: "But what if he's hurt and can't come back? I should have done more to protect him."

"He's a very smart man," said Maggio, wiping his chin with his coat sleeve. "I think he crawls out between people's legs while they fight. That's what a smart man does in a fight—go someplace else very fast. That way, when the *guardia* come, he don't get arrested. I bet *Signore* Clemens is home when you go there."

"I hope you're right," I said, remembering that my employer had a penchant for making snap decisions and telling me about them afterwards. I remembered the time he had impulsively gone off overnight into the Louisiana bayou country, leaving me to guess where he might be. Perhaps this was another of those times . . . but I had no confidence that it was so. And I did not relish the prospect of looking Mrs. Clemens in the eye and telling her I had no idea where her husband was . . . even though I suspected that she had heard similar reports more than once before.

This train of reflection was interrupted by the arrival of a uniformed policeman who came over to Maggio and spoke in rapid Italian. Maggio replied, and after a few brief exchanges, the other officer turned and left. "What did he say?" I asked, realizing even as I said it that it might well be none of my business.

"No sign of *Signore* Clemens," said Maggio, with a shrug. "They got seven or eight men in jail, and five more they take to the hospital to get patched up. And a few, they let go. I told them what your *padrone* looks like, and they say they didn't see him. I didn't expect them to, but you don't know before you ask."

"This doesn't make sense," I said. "He may have run off during the fight, but he should have come back after it was over, to see if I was all right or if I needed help. The only reason I can think of for that is that he *can't* come back."

"He isn't in jail," said Maggio. "He didn't go to the hospital. He didn't go to where I waited with the horses, and he didn't come back here." He counted off these points on his fingers as he made them, then spread his hands and shrugged. "So where else did he go? Best guess is back home, like I said. He can ride the *tramvia*, same as anybody else."

"He could have," I granted. "But that's not the kind of thing he'd do. He would avoid the fighting—he's not a young man anymore—but he'd have come back afterward. If he's not here, and not in jail, and not in the hospital, then something's happened to him. I'm afraid it's something serious." For what must have been the fifth time, I looked around the cafe, searching for a cabinet or other hiding place where my employer might be concealed. But there was nothing I had not seen on my previous visits. Indeed, only three tables were occupied. Usually, at this time of day, the place was full. I didn't like the inaction, but I could think of nothing better to do but wait here for him.

"Could be serious," said Maggio. "But right now, I don't know what it is. And the captain told me to watch you, not him. You want my best advice, you stay here and finish up your wine. If *Signore* Clemens don't come back by then, we go back to Settignano and wait for him. And if he don't come there, I tell the *capitano* and we let him decide what to do next."

Having no better suggestion to offer, I did as *Agente* Maggio suggested. But when the bottle was empty, Mr. Clemens had still not returned. And so, with great trepidation, I let Maggio drive me home to Villa Viviani. Along the way, my head was full of terrible possibilities—Mr. Clemens's body would be found floating in the Arno, or dumped at the end of an alley. Alternately, persuaded by Maggio's optimism, I found myself expecting to walk in the door to discover my employer sitting there, loading a pipe, and spinning some preposterous story of his escape and journey home.

But there was no news when we arrived, and even Maggio could no longer keep from frowning.

It had fallen to me to deliver to Mrs. Clemens the news of her husband's disappearance, and she had borne it well, considering that it came when she was fighting a severe cold on top of her usual frail health. She had taken affairs in hand, jotting down a list of officials for me to contact, and other steps to be taken. I had already seen evidence of her considerable presence of mind in such emergencies, and I set about following her instructions.

At the same time, *Agente* Maggio had sent for his superior, and *Capitano* Rosalia arrived with commendable haste. Now we were sitting with that officer in the front room, sipping coffee and awaiting the captain's advice.

"I regret to report that there is no sign of *Signore* Clemens anywhere in the quarter," said *Capitano* Rosalia gravely. "The police have searched with care."

"What do you think this means?" asked Mrs. Clemens. "If he had just gone off with a friend without informing me, that would be no great matter. But for him to disappear in the middle of a riot, and not to get in touch afterward—that is not at all in character. I fear he has met with some sort of accident."

"That was our first thought," said *Capitano* Rosalia, nodding. "But an *agente* went to the police stations and the hospitals, showing a picture of your husband—there was one in the newspaper after his arrival here—and we are certain that he is in none of those places." He paused and held out his cup, which Mrs. Clemens refilled for him. He thanked her, then sat in silence for an awkward moment as he added sugar and stirred his coffee.

Then he continued: "However, two men we arrested after the fight in the cafe did recall seeing him, and from what they have said . . ." He paused again, seeming to gather his thoughts, then leaned forward and said, "We are considering the possibility that he has been taken hostage."

"What?" Mrs. Clemens gasped, and her hand flew to her mouth. The lid to the sugar bowl fell to the floor—luckily it landed on the carpet, and escaped damage. She bent to pick it up, but her ashen face revealed her state of mind. I started to rise to go to her, but *Agente* Maggio was there before me. He took her arm and guided her to a chair and helped her into it. His face showed genuine concern, and I thought how lucky we were to have had him assigned to watch me. Few policemen in any country would be as sensitive.

The captain's face was full of concern, too. He cleared his throat and said, "*Signora* Clemens, it gives me no pleasure to bring such hard news, but we must face facts. The police will need your help."

At this request, Mrs. Clemens's composure returned. "Yes, of course," she said, nodding. "Please forgive me. I have not been well. And now this shock . . . But of course I will do anything I can to help. Tell me what you need, and if it is in my power, you shall have it."

She looked out the window for a moment, as if gathering her thoughts, then turned back to the captain and said, "Tell me everything. On what do you base your supposition that my husband is being held against his will?"

"Yes, I find that hard to credit," I said. "Whom do you suspect of holding him hostage?"

"We suspect the Socialists or the anarchists," said Rosalia. "Members of both those outlaw parties frequent Cafe Diabelli."

"I doubt either of those parties would consider him an enemy, after hearing the positions he espoused in his argument with Giuseppe Volponi—have you spoken to him, by the way?"

"Yes, of course," said Rosalia. "*Signore* Volponi is one of our main sources of information—alas, he is in the hospital with a broken arm. He reports that *Signore* Clemens was taken from the cafe by two men he knows to be revolutionary agitators."

"What? Who are these men?" I asked. "And why do you take Volponi's word for it?"

"Volponi is a loyal subject of King Umberto," said Rosalia, shifting uncomfortably. "He has given us information on radical activities in the past, and it has always turned out to be very accurate. As for the men he identifies, they are regular customers at Cafe Diabelli. In fact, we have reason to believe that you know them, *Signore* Cabot. Their names are Gonnella and Garbarini."

"What?" I exclaimed again. "That is impossible!" But even as I said it, I remembered Virginia's warning me against too close an association with the two chess players, on the grounds that the police were watching them. Now I learned that Volponi was a spy for the police. It began to seem as if everyone at Diabelli's were something more than they appeared! When my employer and I had gone to the cafe to research a possible political motive for Virginia's murder, it had all seemed a bit far-fetched to me. But now I realized it might well be true.

Mrs. Clemens evidently shared my doubts. "Grant, for a moment, that he left the cafe with these men," she said, holding up her hand. "Perhaps they were simply helping my husband escape the brawl. Why must there be some sinister motive attached to a good deed?"

My employer's wife had regained her normal aplomb. I admired her confidence even more than before. If I was worried about her husband's safety, how much more worried must she be? Yet neither of us was ready to accept that Mr. Clemens had been taken hostage. Ironically, my earlier imaginings of my employer being injured or worse had given way to a conviction that nothing so terrible could have happened—a conviction I shared with his wife. This might be just another of his escapades.

Capitano Rosalia sensed our resistance to his conjecture. He cleared his throat, then said, "*Signora*, we in the police consider these men dangerous. We do not know that they are holding your husband against his will, or that they mean to hurt him, but the anarchists have shown us that they are ready to take desperate measures—even robbery and assassination—to gain their ends. I do not advise you to trust them."

"I suppose I must take your word for it, then," said Mrs. Clemens, a worried look on her face. "What do you propose to do?"

"The city police are already working to arrest their known associates," said the captain. "They will also keep watch on their usual haunts. Perhaps someone will spot them. And on the chance that they have left the city, my *carabinieri* are gathering intelligence from a wider network—including the army, which is very active against these revolutionaries. We have eyes and ears in many places. *Signora* Clemens, your husband's disappearance makes this case very much more important than a simple theft and murder. The highest level of government has taken notice, and we are putting our fullest efforts into solving it."

"I am glad to hear that," said Mrs. Clemens. "I would be even gladder to hear my husband's voice, and to see him coming through the door."

"*Signora*, we trust that we will be able to provide you with those pleasures," said the captain, bowing.

"I also trust that you will, *Capitano* Rosalia," said Mrs. Clemens. "Can you tell me how soon you expect it to be?"

"With any luck, it will be very soon," he said, committing himself to very little. "But if the anarchists are responsible for taking your husband hostage, they may well be getting in touch with you to demand ransom. For that reason, we will leave *Agente* Maggio here to guard your family. As far as I am concerned, *Signore* Cabot is no longer under suspicion for the young lady's death."

"I am glad to be exonerated," I said dryly. "But I hope this new political conspiracy doesn't distract your men from investigating Miss Fleetwood's death."

Capitano Rosalia said, "*Signore* Cabot, I believe that when we unravel the anarchist conspiracy, we will lay our hands on the person responsible for the young lady's death. And now, if you will excuse me, *Signora* Clemens, I must go supervise the investigation. As soon as we have any news to report, I promise you will hear from me."

He stood, bowed, and took his leave. Maggio accompanied him, presumably to receive further orders.

"Capitano Rosalia is barking up the wrong tree," I said to Mrs. Clemens after the *carabiniere* captain and his *agente* had left the room. "The authorities are so anxious to crush the radicals that they see their handiwork everyplace that trouble flares up. I know the two fellows he was accusing, and they're as innocuous a pair as you could think of—away from the chessboard, at least."

"Please sit down and try to relax, Wentworth," said Mrs. Clemens, indicating the chair opposite her. "Your pacing makes me nervous—more nervous, I should say. I know that Samuel is capable of taking care of himself, of course.

Perhaps he went with these two men of his own will, hoping to find more evidence concerning the murder. But I am not quite as confident as you about these chess players being harmless. How well do you really know them? Have you ever had an extended conversation with either of them?"

I stopped and thought, still not sitting down. After a few moments, I said, "I suppose not—except to do a postmortem on a chess game. Still, if they were anarchists, I wouldn't think they'd come to a meeting place of their party and do nothing but play chess—or watch other people play. I've never even seen them in a long conversation with someone else while there's a game going on, which is almost always, when one of them is there."

"I see," said Mrs. Clemens, motioning again for me to take a seat opposite her. This time, I did as she requested, and then, after a brief pause, she said, "I wonder, though, whether your command of Italian is adequate for you to know what they were speaking of even if you were right next to them. I am not sure I could tell the difference between chess and revolution in a foreign language. Can you?"

"I should think so," I began, and then stopped myself. After a moment's reflection, I admitted, "Well, now that you raise the question, perhaps not. Someone talking about *an attack on the king* could be referring to assassinating the King of Italy or to a position on the chessboard."

"That is what I mean," said Mrs. Clemens. She reached out to touch my sleeve and looked into my eyes as she continued: "Playing a game with someone may shed light on that person's character, but not enough for you to know their deeper motives or concerns. If the captain has evidence that these two men are dangerous radicals, I would give his information due weight."

"We don't know whether it's evidence or hearsay—or plain lies," I said. "I'd guess that fellow Volponi is the one who accused them. He could be concocting his story out of whole cloth to ingratiate himself with the authorities."

Even as I made this statement, I found myself doubting

it. Gonnella and Garbarini might be anything at all when they were not playing chess. I had some vague memory of someone saying that one or the other was a poet, but I had no idea whether that was true—or about which of them I had heard it. Whatever its truth, it had no real bearing on the captain's accusations—any more than the dislike I had taken to Volponi for quarreling with my employer reflected on his veracity.

Mrs. Clemens seemed to sense my reservations. "My instinct is to trust *Capitano* Rosalia, unless we have some strong reason to doubt him," she said. "At least he has shown some concern for Samuel's safety. That is the most important consideration, at the moment." She sighed, and then began to cough, discreetly turning her head as she took her handkerchief from her sleeve. Her cold was better now than it had been, but I knew her health to be delicate. I hoped the added strain of her husband's being in danger would not bring on a relapse.

"I agree with you on Mr. Clemens's safety," I said. "But I still intend to find Miss Fleetwood's murderer and see him brought to justice. And I don't believe we ought to sit and wait for *Capitano* Rosalia to do something."

"I don't object to your taking independent action, as long as you don't endanger Samuel," said Mrs. Clemens. Then she frowned and continued: "But the captain believes that he has been captured by the people who killed Miss Fleetwood. If that is so, they may have no qualms about harming him, if they believe themselves to be in danger of exposure. I wonder if leaving the investigation to the police may not be our safest course, after all." She put her hand back on my arm, looking imploringly at me.

"I understand your feelings, Mrs. Clemens," I said, returning her gaze. "But one thing I have learned from your husband is that the police are not always right. I might accept the captain's theory that the anarchists stole Mr. Stephens's painting to finance their revolution. But that they lured a young American woman to a graveyard across the city, murdered her, and left the frame of the painting near her body is harder to believe. And the notion that they then swooped down on your husband in a cafe, where he was engaged in a political argument with one of their enemies, and spirited him away to hold him hostage, is beyond my ability to swallow."

I stood up and began pacing again, still talking. "Perhaps these revolutionaries *are* responsible for many of Italy's troubles," I said. "I have very little sympathy for their cause, in any case. But to blame this entire mystery on them is far too convenient for *Capitano* Rosalia. It lets him concentrate his energy on a target he already wants to hit, and never mind whether it's the right one. I don't think his approach is going to find Miss Fleetwood's murderer, and I don't think it's going to get your husband back home, either."

"And do you have an idea that *will* bring Samuel home?" asked Mrs. Clemens, in a quiet voice. She picked up her coffee—now long cold—and took a sip.

"Frankly, I don't know," I said, dropping back onto the couch next to her. "I'm going to try to think of something. One thing I can promise you, is that bringing your husband home safe is my highest priority."

"Don't forget finding Miss Fleetwood's murderer," said Mrs. Clemens firmly. "Samuel had undertaken to find the man who killed her, and I would not wish you to forget that. Very well, I give you my permission to continue trying." She paused again. "I think you would continue trying even without my permission, but that's all right." She smiled bravely, but I could sense her doubt.

"Thank you," I said. "I will do my best to justify your faith in me."

"Just do your best," she said, smiling. "That will be enough, I am sure."

I wasn't so sure, but I said no more. It was high time to turn my intentions into a concrete plan. And that looked like an all-night job.

It is one thing to find fault with another man's theory, but quite another thing to construct a better one. I was reminded of this when, in my own room, I began to mull over the facts available to me. These were sparse, but perhaps they would add up to something if I found the right way to look at them. *Agente* Maggio, who had returned to the kitchen after his talk with the captain, would call me if any news came.

To begin with, there was the manner and place of Virginia's death. There was also the remarkable circumstance that the frame of the stolen Raphael had been found near her body. This indicated that the theft and the murder were connected, but in what way?

I reluctantly concluded that, much as I would like to, I could not dismiss outright the idea that she had been bringing the painting to someone in that section of the city. We knew that there were several art dealers' shops near where the body had been found. Of course, the police knew this as well as I did.

Did this mean that Virginia had been in league with those who stole the painting—or worse yet, had stolen it herself? I still could not bring myself to believe it of her. Had she perhaps observed someone making off with it, and followed them? But she would not have had time to send for a carriage to take her into town had she been in hot pursuit of a thief—at least, assuming it had been she who sent for a carriage the night of the party, as *Agente* Maggio's informant had reported. Possibly she had overheard the thief tell his own driver his destination, and told her driver to take her there. But why would she pursue a thief herself, instead of informing the police or her brother-in-law?

None of this made sense, not even if one accepted *Capitano* Rosalia's theory that the theft and murder were the work of anarchists. Even those who wanted to abolish all governments and laws need not be irrational on other topics. But there was no reasonable explanation for the picture frame's being left near the body, with little attempt at concealment. Perhaps the killer had been surprised in his work, and fled before he could hide the body, or the frame—but then, the murder would have been reported earlier, would it not? And why had the whole business been conducted in a graveyard? Granted, it was a good place to meet if one were anxious to avoid being observed, but any private home would do as well—and would arouse far less suspicion.

If Mr. Clemens had been present to look at the evidence, I am sure he would have made a more coherent picture of it than I was able to. But he was off somewhere unknown, possibly being held prisoner. And while I had promised Mrs. Clemens to make every effort to bring about my employer's return, I had no more notion how to achieve that end than of how to penetrate the mysteries surrounding Virginia's death.

I must have dozed off, for I awoke to find myself slumped across the table, now littered with papers covered with my questions and speculation. The clock read half past three in the morning. I was no closer to the answer than I had been when I had sat down. Discouraged, I dragged myself to my bed and crawled in, hoping that daylight would bring some sort of insight.

I awoke in a cold sweat, after dreams of a fight with hideous masked men in a graveyard. In the distance I had seen Mr. Clemens being dragged away with a rope around his neck. Holding the other end of the rope was Bob Danvers. I shook my head to exorcise the phantom images. A glance at the window showed the sky still dark; I turned over and went back to sleep, but when I woke again, with light beginning to wash over the eastern sky, I was no better rested. With a yawn, I sat up on the edge of the bed. I had too many things to do to afford the luxury of sleeping late.

Unfortunately, I was not sure which things I needed to do first. I got out of bed and began dressing, anyway. It would be better to do something than to do nothing, and if I did enough things, perhaps one of them would work. It wasn't much of a plan, but it was the best one I had at the moment.

O
ver breakfast, I decided on a simple strategy. I had
last seen my employer at Cafe Diabelli. Therefore I
would return there. It was possible that a waiter, or
one of the customers, would know where Gonnella or Garbarini lived. If I pretended to be interested in finding them
for a game of chess, I might learn something that the police,
whom many people distrusted, had not been able to discover.

At the same time, I thought I would try to learn just how
early Virginia Fleetwood might have spoken to any of the
crowd at Diabelli's about Stephens's acquiring three Raphaels—an event that anyone interested in the arts would
have considered of high importance. She hadn't mentioned
them to me before Stephens announced his party, and that
struck me as curious. Had she herself not known of his
acquisition until he announced it? Or had she kept the news
a secret, so as not to spoil her brother-in-law's surprise?
And might she have told one of her other friends something
of interest about them after the announcement?

My mind was swirling with unanswered questions. There
was another question, too. What kind of danger was my
employer in? Had he just gone off on one of his whimsical

expeditions, or had he really been abducted by dangerous
radicals? Would there be another body in the Protestant
cemetery?

Just as I was getting ready to leave for the cafe, I remembered that I still hadn't found a replacement for the
stolen bicycle. I would now have to walk over to the *tramvia*, ride into town, and walk from the station at Plaza di
Giudici over to the cafe. More annoying, having repaid Bob
Danvers the money I owed him, I was now short of funds
myself. I had enough for the tram ride, but that would leave
me without much to spend in the cafe. This would ordi-
narily be but a minor nuisance; Pietro was not the sort to
push a regular customer to keep buying drinks every time
he walked past the table. But buying other people drinks
was a good way to get them to talk to me, and my shortage
of cash would limit my ability to buy. Had my employer
been at home, he would have advanced me sufficient funds.
But I did not feel I could make the same request of his
wife.

I threw on my coat and was on my way out the door
when I met *Agente* Maggio standing outside. He said,
"Where you go, Signore Cabot?"

"Back to Cafe Diabelli," I said. "I don't know if I can
find out anything useful there, but it's the best plan I can
think of."

Maggio nodded. "That's a good idea—maybe we find
something out," he said. "But no fights this time, *capisce*?
I don't like to owe those city police more favors for letting
you go."

"Wait a minute," I said. "You aren't coming along, are
you? The captain said you'd be staying here in case a message came from the anarchists."

"The *signora* is a very smart woman—she knows what
to do with messages," said the *carabiniere*, shrugging. "I
don't think she needs somebody to protect her. You the one
going out to look for trouble, so you the one I got to stay
with. Come on, help me get the horses hitched up."

That settled that. I followed Maggio to the carriage

house, and a short while later we were on our way into town.

This time, *Agente* Maggio came with me into the cafe, but he took a separate table so as not to give anyone reason to think we were together, just in case someone recognized him as a police officer. He ordered his coffee, then took out a pair of spectacles—which looked incongruous on such a robust man, but perhaps they would help disguise his appearance—and sat back to study *Il Sforzo*, a newspaper of some sort. Its name meant nothing to me, but of course I did not read the Italian papers.

That left me to decide where I wanted to begin my search. The American crowd, including Stephens's friends, were not at their usual table on the terrace. Belatedly, I remembered that this was the day that had been set for Virginia Fleetwood's funeral—they would all be there. While I felt a pang of guilt for missing that final chance to bid her farewell, I knew that my presence at the services would only create more awkwardness. So it might be just as well that I had more pressing business. The best memorial I could make to her was to bring her killer to justice. That thought made me feel better. Having a purpose was as healing as anything a minister could say over Virginia's remains.

With no other Americans present, I looked around at the Italian habitués of Cafe Diabelli to see who might know something of use to me. I was glad to see that Giuseppe Volponi and his clique were not yet present. But there was a chess game in progress, and (recalling that the men supposed to have abducted my employer were regulars at the chessboards) I made my way over to see who was playing and with what success.

The players (a German and an Italian, both of whom I knew by sight though not by name) had reached an endgame with rooks on both sides. The German was playing White; he was ahead by a bishop, and the player on the other side was struggling to promote an advanced pawn. It seemed to me that both sides had good chances, but after

a few more desperate moves, Black put his king and rook
on the same diagonal. White's bishop surged into action,
checking the king, and after it moved out of the way,
swooped down upon the undefended rook. Scowling, Black
tipped over his king and pulled a quarter-lira coin out of
his pocket. "*Danke schön,*" said his opponent, grinning.
Then he looked up at me and said, "*Möchten Sie spielen,
Freund?*"

I was no linguist, but I understood that much German.
"Yes, I think I will play a game," I said, sitting down in
the seat vacated by his opponent. The other player shook
up the pieces, and I drew Black. My opponent, who introduced himself as Herr Stenger, pushed his king's-pawn forward, and the battle was underway.

The initial moves were routine, but soon my opponent
moved a pawn to a square where I could capture it with
my bishop—not a blunder but a deliberate sacrifice my father had showed me when he taught me the game: Captain
Evans' Gambit, he had called it. I had heard it was a favorite master opening, but beyond the first few moves, I
didn't know it. I considered my response. Accepting the
sacrifice would give my opponent a fierce attack. Declining
to capture the pawn was safer in the short run, but it would
oblige me to defend a cramped position. After considering
the alternatives, I threw caution to the winds and took the
pawn: better to go down fighting than to back off and let
the other fellow box me in.

Half a dozen moves later, I had won another pawn, but
I was beginning to think I should have declined the gambit.
Still, if I could survive Stenger's attack, I thought I might
prevail in the end. That remained a very large *if*, however.
My opponent's replies came so quickly that it was obvious
he was playing by rote, while I was on unfamiliar ground.
He had both his queen and bishop aimed at my king, which
I had been unable to get castled. A small group of spectators had gathered round the table, no doubt waiting to see
who would get to challenge my opponent next. I heard
occasional whispered comments in Italian; it was probably
just as well I didn't understand the language well enough

to follow them. I had enough trouble trying not to lose the game.

That thought gave me a sort of mental jolt, and I realized that playing the game was good for me. I had been afraid that between the dull ache I felt whenever I thought of poor Virginia, and the nagging worry over my missing employer, I wouldn't be able to concentrate. Instead, the regular pattern of ranks and files and the unambiguous rules of play somehow cleared my mind. *Thank God for chess*, I thought. For a little while, at least, the tightness in my shoulders could dissolve while I worried about wooden pieces on a wooden board instead of precious human lives.

Herr Stenger moved a bishop to threaten the knight I had just stationed in front of my king. Retreating with the knight would leave me still unable to castle, but leaving it there for him to take left me vulnerable to an even more dangerous attack. I scanned the board with growing dismay; what could I do?

Then I realized that my opponent must expect me to move the knight. What if I launched a counterattack instead? If I put my queen's bishop *there* . . . but to do so, I would have to move my queens'-pawn, which would let him exchange it and increase the pressure on the knight . . . but then I would capture his pawn, and my bishop would be able to come out . . . Well, why not? The worst that could happen was that I would lose a game, and owe Stenger the price of a drink.

I made the pawn move. Now, for the first time, my opponent hesitated, frowning at the board. His memorized line of play must not have anticipated this defense. At last, he reached out and captured my pawn. I recaptured, and again he had to think. Two of my pawns were still vulnerable, but at least my queenside bishop was now free. The German captured the pawn I had just moved, and in response I brought my bishop out, attacking his queen. This would force him to move it, gaining me valuable time to get my king to safety. I waited for his response, calculating my next move.

My opponent looked the board over, then—instead of

protecting his queen—moved a knight off the back row, blocking my advanced pawn. He hadn't seen the threat! I studied the board again, trying to make sure I hadn't overlooked some simple trap. Convinced that the move was sound, I picked up my bishop and took his queen. My opponent's jaw fell as I removed the captured piece; then he slapped his hand on the table and exclaimed, "*Ich bin ein Blinder!*" I knew just how he felt; I had more than once fallen prey to that sort of blindness at the chessboard.

Herr Stenger stared at the position once more, and shook his head. With White's main weapon, the queen, off the board, his position was a shambles. I turned my attention back to the board, and saw that if I could force the exchange of a few more pieces, I would have a decisive advantage. My opponent wanted nothing of that; instead, he threw his army into a desperate attack, sacrificing a bishop and checking my king in an attempt to pry open my formation. But now I had sufficient means for the defense, and after a few more moves, I traded off his other bishop and seized the initiative for myself. Seeing that he had no more winning prospects, the German resigned and handed over the stakes. "*Bravo*," he said, then added in English, "You play a good game."

"Thank you," I said, shaking his hand. "I was lucky to win it. Who else wants to play?"

"I play you," said a familiar voice, and I looked up to see a slim, bearded man standing across the table from me. It was Garbarini—perhaps the best player at Cafe Diabelli. And, as I could not fail to be aware, one of the two reputed anarchists whom the police accused of abducting Mr. Clemens. I had never beaten him at chess. That record was likely to remain unbroken—I had a strong suspicion that I was going to have a hard time concentrating on this game. But I smiled and gestured toward the chair that Herr Stenger had vacated. Garbarini nodded and sat down.

Garbarini drew the Black pieces, so I had the initiative in the opening. I pushed a pawn ahead two spaces, and he responded symmetrically. Determined not to let him win too easily, I led the game into the tried-and-true Four

Knights opening, placing my pieces as advantageously as possible without exposing myself to attack. After fifteen minutes of cautious maneuvering, we were in a tangled position. It was Garbarini's move, and I waited while he studied the board. Several pieces on both sides were in jeopardy, but nothing had been captured—and, to my relief, I had so far avoided any outright blunders. Garbarini reached his hand out, hesitated—and made an innocuous-looking pawn move. He sat back with a sigh and I leaned forward to inspect the position.

I couldn't believe my eyes. The pawn move had removed the sole defender from his queen's knight, which was under attack from my bishop. Capturing the knight would check his king and at the same time the bishop would attack one of his rooks. Had he blundered, or was he setting a trap? Was I about to beat him, or was the little wooden horse a gift from the Greeks?

The more I examined the position, the simpler it seemed. Even his best defense left me a rook ahead. I made the play, said, "Check," and sat back to see how Garbarini would respond.

He stared at the board as if seeing it for the first time, and muttered something ugly-sounding under his breath. He turned his king on its side and reached out his hand. "Is a very good move," he said, as I accepted the congratulatory handshake. "I cannot win after such a stupid error." He reached in his pocket and handed me something—a quarter-lira coin. But as I took the coin, I realized there was also a folded-up scrap of paper with it. I nodded, put both items in my pocket, and—too stunned to say anything—watched him leave the table and the cafe. The game had already fled my mind, replaced by a burning curiosity about the paper—obviously a message—Garbarini had given me. It must be news of Mr. Clemens!

But before I could collect myself, another player sat down opposite me, and perforce I was in a third game. By this time, my concentration had evaporated, and I played like a beginner. He soon had me tied up in knots—down three pieces, with my king exposed to a merciless cross fire. The position was a dead loss even if I could have summoned all my wits to defend it. I sighed, turned over the king, and paid the forfeit. Another player took my place, and I walked over to the terrace doorway. Out there, I would be able to read the note away from prying eyes.

My path took me past *Agente* Maggio, who sat there with his newspaper. He was still wearing the spectacles. He looked up as I went past, and raised an eyebrow. I said nothing, but no sooner had I gone through the terrace doors than he was behind me. He pulled a small cheroot out of his pocket and lit it, giving himself an ostensible reason for coming outside. He had taken off the spectacles, too. I glanced around, and was relieved to notice there was no one else outside with us.

"Did you see what just happened?" I asked.

"You play with the anarchist," the *carabiniere* said in a low voice. "You must have played very good to beat him."

"I'm not sure—I think he might have lost on purpose," I said. "He gave me this." I took the piece of paper from my pocket, still folded, and showed it to him.

"What you waiting for?" asked Maggio, tapping the ash from his cigar. "Read it."

I opened the paper, wondering what sort of message Garbarini had slipped to me. Would it be a ransom note? A warning to keep my nose out of the anarchists' business? Would I even be able to read it? I had no idea what to expect. Thus, it was a genuine surprise and a great relief to see the familiar handwriting of my employer. The note read:

> Wentworth—
>   I'm all right. Go to No. 44 Via Tornabuoni and wait there for the man who gave you this. He'll bring you to me. Don't tell the cops.
>   —SLC

"It's nothing, after all," I said, "Just an IOU for the money he owes me for losing the game." I folded it up again and returned it to my pocket. I began to feel sorry I had told *Agente* Maggio about the note.

"Too bad," said Maggio, giving an exaggerated shrug. "I hope maybe it's a message from your *padrone*."

I feared he was going to ask me for the note, and I had no idea how to refuse a policeman such a request; but after a moment I realized he wasn't going to ask. I breathed a little easier. "Yes, I suppose that's what I was hoping for, too," I said, with a grimace that must have signaled my mendacity like a red flag. "Although I don't know why they'd think I'd be here to get a message, in the first place."

"Is right," said Maggio. He took a puff on the cheroot and looked out toward the street. "Maybe they send messages like that back to Villa Viviani. Maybe we should go there now."

"Well, I want to wait for the American crowd to arrive," I said, trying to appear nonchalant. "They gather at those tables on the terrace. I'd like to talk to a couple of Miss Fleetwood's friends. Maybe you should go back to the villa and wait to see if there's any news—I'll come back on the *tramvia* a little later."

"You sure you don't want to ride back with me?" asked Maggio, pointing inside the cafe, toward the exit. "Sometimes the *tramvia* is slow, and you got to walk at the other end."

"I appreciate the offer," I said blandly. "But thanks, I want to talk to the others who knew Virginia. I should be home by dinner time, I'm sure."

Maggio hesitated, and I thought he was going to insist on my returning home with him, but then he shrugged. "I see you then," he said. "*Ciao*."

"*Ciao*," I said. Causally, I took a seat at a terrace table and watched him go through the door back inside. The moment it closed behind him, I had my Baedeker out of my pocket, looking for the quickest way to Via Tornabuoni. As soon as I had a good idea which way I was going, I hopped the low terrace wall and began walking. I didn't know what awaited me at 44 Via Tornabuoni, but Mr. Clemens wanted me to go there. That was good enough for me.

18 ⌒

Via Tornabuoni was a short walk from Diabelli's, but I took my time getting there. I wasn't sure whether *Agente* Maggio had swallowed my story about the note's being unimportant. So I took a roundabout route, stopping several times to look at shop windows and once to step inside a church and leave it by a different door, in hopes of confusing the *carabiniere* if he had decided to follow me. At last, convinced that Maggio was not on my trail, I strode briskly over to Via Tornabuoni and began to search for number 44.

While I had passed through this neighborhood before, I had not had any particular business there. Now I saw that along the street were a variety of shops and restaurants, half a dozen interesting *palazzi*, the Hotel Londres, and the British and American consulates. The street was busy, with a considerable number of tourists. I heard English, French, and German—and at least one language I didn't recognize—in addition to Italian, as I scanned the numbers on the buildings I passed.

Number 44 sported a sign in English: D. Preswick, Chemist: the British term for what we Americans call a drugstore. I peeked through the window, past an array of bottles in various sizes, shapes, and colors, trying to decide whether I should wait inside or out. It wasn't a place one would drop into without specific business there, and I had no idea whether or not the proprietor would let me stay once he saw that I wasn't a customer. I doubted whether he knew anything of Mr. Clemens's whereabouts, unless he was in league with the anarchists—which seemed unlikely. On the other hand, if anyone had followed me here, I would be conspicuous waiting on the street. That decided me; I went inside.

A bell rang as I entered. Inside, the shop had the exotic blend of odors I had always associated with a pharmacy. There were shelves displaying various tonics, pills, and powders, only a few of which were familiar to me. Shaving brushes, razors, combs, soft soap, and the like occupied another rank of shelves, and to the rear of the store was a wooden counter, littered with bottles, vials, papers, and jars, beyond which was a curtain-covered doorway. "Be there in an instant," said a high-pitched, British-accented voice from behind the curtain. Then the speaker added in Italian "*Subito, signore, subito.*"

"Oh, take your time," I said. Indeed, I saw no reason at all why the shopkeeper should hurry out to attend to me, since I had no business with him. Embarrassed, I walked over to inspect a cabinet of shaving supplies. Perhaps I would pretend to be in the market for a new brush, or some shaving soap . . .

To my surprise, the person who emerged from behind the curtain was not the shopkeeper, but my chess opponent of a short while ago: Garbarini. Of course. He and his comrades must have some understanding with the proprietor. "Good, you come very quick," he said. "Does the *carabiniere* follow you?"

"I don't think so," I said. "He said he was going back to Settignano, and I did my best to lose anyone trying to track me here. Will you take me to Mr. Clemens?"

Garbarini put a finger to his lips. "Don't say names," he whispered, motioning toward the back room with a jerk of his head. I took that to mean that he didn't want the phar-

macist to know our business in any more detail than necessary. This made sense if he was not a member of their
conspiracy.

I nodded my assent, and he went on. "I take you there.
But we go out a back way, to make sure we don't be followed. Come."

I followed him through the curtain, and got a brief
glimpse of a rabbit-faced little man who pretended to concentrate on his bottles and potions, and to ignore the two
intruders leaving his shop through the back door. Then we
were out in the alley, and I forgot about him.

Garbarini looked in both directions and, seeing the way
clear, pointed to the left. We set off rapidly, leaving me no
time to wonder just what sort of trouble I had gotten myself
into.

Speaking as little as necessary, Garbarini led me along a
twisting route into a part of Florence I had never visited.
Much of the way was through backstreets and unmarked
alleys, with few other pedestrians, and I had little time to
take note of landmarks or compass directions. So while I
could make out the Duomo at a distance, I had no clear
idea in what quarter of town we were, and I am certain that
was as my guide intended. He had only my word for it that
a squadron of armed *carabinieri* was not dogging my steps,
and I myself could not have sworn I hadn't been followed
to our meeting place.

We went into the side-alley door of a nondescript building, near which two rough-looking men lounged, drinking
from a jug—ordinary loafers, to the casual eye. But their
alert stance and penetrating stare as I came into view, and
the way they relaxed after Garbarini nodded to them, told
me all I needed to know. They were guards, and he had
just told them I was no threat. Perhaps he thought so; for
myself, I reserved the right to prove otherwise, if Mr. Clemens had come to harm.

Inside, I found myself in a dimly lit room surrounded by
large bales of blank paper, with the smell of fresh ink in
the air and the muffled clank of machinery somewhere in

the building. We were in the storage room of what must be a printer's shop. I remembered someone—had it been Virginia?—telling me that Garbarini was a typesetter, or perhaps a printer's apprentice. This might well be his place of work, then. I filed the idea in the back of my mind, in case it became necessary to find the place again; it was a small clue at best, but with so few clues to rely on, I could not afford to ignore any of them.

Garbarini put his finger to his lips, and pointed to a ladder in the far corner, leading up to an open trapdoor in the ceiling. I nodded to indicate my understanding, crossed the room and climbed the ladder. At the top was a small garret room, with rough furniture—a low bed, a couple of wooden chairs, and a table along one wall beneath the single window. A shelf below the window held a selection of crockery, enough for one or two to dine—although there was no cooking equipment in view. At the table sat my employer, with pen and paper before him. He looked up as I came through the trapdoor and said, "Ah, it's good to see you, Wentworth. You didn't happen to bring along any of my Durham pipe tobacco, did you? This Italian stuff ain't worth the tinder to set it on fire."

"Quite frankly, sir, pipe tobacco was the last thing on my mind this morning," I said. I noted with relief that he looked hale and hearty, and most importantly, uninjured.

"Well, I can't say I'm surprised," said my employer, laying down his pen. For a fleeting instant there was a disappointed look on his face, then he pointed to Garbarini, who had followed me up the ladder, and was now standing, with folded arms, between me and the trapdoor. "Did this fellow tell you what's going on?" he asked, with a raised eyebrow.

"No," I said. "All I know is what you said in that note to me, which was hardly informative. When you didn't return, we had no idea where you might have gone."

"I didn't have a chance to tell you, at the time," said Mr. Clemens. "I would have given more particulars, but suppose Rosalia or Maggio had gotten ahold of it? You'd have been thigh-deep in cops, and no more chance of getting here than getting to the moon. That's the same reason I couldn't send a note home, with the cops watching the house. I just hope Livy isn't too worried about me."

"I fear she is," I said, trying my best to make him feel guilty. I had been worried myself. I continued: "*Capitano* Rosalia told us that you'd been kidnapped, and has been hinting that your life might be in danger."

"Well, the fellows who picked me up weren't acting very dangerous," said Mr. Clemens. "They were skedaddling just as fast as I was, even though they had a perfect chance to join in that bar fight and get a few licks at their enemies. That told me we had something in common: I mean common sense. And that was enough to convince me I was safe with 'em, unless the cops showed up with guns blazing. Do you think Rosalia or his boys followed you here?"

"I don't *think* so, but Maggio was at the cafe when I got the note, and he isn't stupid. I can't swear that he didn't guess what was going on."

"I reckon we'll find out soon enough if he did," said Mr. Clemens. "Meanwhile, why don't you sit down and I'll fill you in on the story. Garbarini, do you still have any of that wine you had last night? It'd come in handy right about now."

"You wait, I bring you wine," said Garbarini, nodding. He went over to the trapdoor, swung over and scurried down the ladder, and I heard him moving across the store-room downstairs. A door creaked below, no doubt Garbarini going outside or into another room for the wine.

"All right, he'll be gone long enough for us to talk," said Mr. Clemens. "He won't hurry back, because he figures those boys downstairs will stop us if we try to leave."

"I gathered as much," I said. "Are you being held against your will?"

"I don't think so," said my employer. "I haven't tried to leave yet, so nobody's tried to tell me I can't. I don't see much point in making a stink about it until I need to."

I didn't see the logic of that. "Need to leave? What do you mean? Of course you need to leave. Why are you staying with these people if you're not a prisoner?"

Mr. Clemens shrugged. "I'm not worried, as long as nobody's got a gun pointed at me. But to bring you up to date, when that donnybrook started back at the cafe, I decided it was the wrong place for a man who gets his daily exercise by loading his pipe. So I crawled under the tables, and ducked out the side door before anybody took a notion to hit me with anything. That's when Garbarini and Gonnella spotted me. From what they'd heard me saying before the fight broke out, they figured I was in sympathy with their side, whatever that is."

"You mean you don't know?" I asked, frowning. "Everyone seems convinced that they're anarchists . . . or did they say Socialists?"

"I reckon the distinction's important to them, and to the people they're trying to overthrow," said Mr. Clemens. "But I doubt it matters a nickel's worth, when you get to practical results. If they won an election, they'd throw out the king and the nobles, get rid of all the corrupt officials they could find, and put their own gang in power—and odds are, nobody outside the government would be able to tell much difference after six months."

"You surprise me," I said. "Just yesterday, you were talking about how getting rid of the king would cure all Italy's ills."

My employer waved a hand, dismissively. "Well, it would cure all the ills that are the king's fault, anyhow—and that's no small portion. I wasn't just blowing smoke yesterday, Wentworth. I call it a crime for any man to set himself up as a lord over others, whether it's a king and his subjects or a master and his slaves. Getting rid of all the kings in the world would go a fair way toward making it a better place. But would it turn Earth into Heaven? No, because the damned human race would think up some other nonsense to replace it with. The Socialists or anarchists don't have the real answer to humanity's problems—no more than the royalists or the capitalists or the Christian Scientists or the spiritualists do—because when you get down to brass tacks, you realize it's humanity itself that's the problem."

"I wouldn't deny that, sir," I said. "But how did you end up here? Did you come with Garbarini and Gonnella of your own free will?"

"Of course I did, Wentworth," said Mr. Clemens. "Remember, the cops were promoting the theory that these boys—or their political bedfellows—were responsible for stealing that painting and for killing the young lady when she caught them. I figured the best way for me to find out if they had anything to do with it was to come home with them and keep my eyes open."

"Perhaps," I said. "But why did you stay overnight? You must have known your wife would worry."

A cloud crossed my employer's face, and I knew he felt a twinge of guilt. "Well, after a bit, I realized the fellows I was talking to didn't know everything that was going on; I needed to talk to somebody higher up in their party. I said I'd come back in the morning—it's not too far from the cafe, so I could find it again. And then their faces got real hard, and I could see there was trouble. I knew right away what I'd said—letting them know I could find the place again made them worry I'd come back leading the cops. So then they said they could let me meet one of their bosses, but I had to stay overnight. I didn't like that, but they weren't going to give me any choice."

"Garbarini and Gonnella made you a prisoner?" I was suddenly angry at my two chess opponents.

"No, they were gone by then—it was a couple of other men, big fellows with guns in their pockets. I was worried that I'd gotten in over my head, to tell you the truth. But then another fellow showed up, somebody older—one of their leaders, I guess, if anarchists are allowed to have leaders. Anyhow, he apologized and told me they'd have to move their headquarters now that I knew where it was. And that would take long enough that I'd have to stay overnight. Nothing personal—but they couldn't risk my giving away their location, even accidentally. And that meant I couldn't even send a message home."

I was about to protest, but he raised a finger to his lips to silence me, at the same time pointing with his other forefinger to the floor. From below came the sound of foot-steps—Garbarini, returning with the wine. The steps came over to the ladder, and then we could hear Garbarini climbing. In a moment, he appeared, carrying a large earthen jug. He put the jug on the table and took down cups from the shelf above. "I bring the *vino*, like you ask," he said, smiling. "Now we drink a little, talk a little, see what bargain we can make."

"Bargain?" I asked. "What do we have to bargain over?"

"The usual horse-trade," said Mr. Clemens, reaching out to take a cup of the wine from Garbarini. "We're going to figure out what I can do for these fellows, and what they can do for me, and how much of the one is worth how much of the other."

"*Signore* Mark Twain is the famous writer, with great respect from everyone," said Garbarini as he handed me a cup. "He could do much to make our cause known to the people."

"I'm sure he could," I said. I took a sip of my wine; it was a robust red, earthy and full-bodied. Surprised, I raised my glass to Garbarini and nodded. "This is very good wine," I said. "Thank you."

"Zio Giovanni works in the vineyard," said Garbarini, with a grin. "He makes sure the owner don't send all the best to the *turista*. We Italians need good *vino* to drink, too."

"Well, this *turista* appreciates your saving some of the good stuff," said Mr. Clemens. "And I'm willing to write a few words for the cause of justice, by way of thanking you—but there is something else you and your boys could do for me. And if I understand the argument I've been given by certain policemen, it would work to your own benefit, as well."

"Ah, you mean *Capitano* Rosalia," said Garbarini. "He wants to blame us for the young American's death, not so?"

"That's what it looks like to me," said Mr. Clemens. "Now, I'm as anxious as he is to find out who's responsible, since she was a particular friend of Wentworth here."

"Yes," said Garbarini, with a somber expression. He

turned and put his hand on my shoulder, saying, "I see you with her in Cafe Diabelli. I am sorry she dies—I know you must be very sad."

"Sad, and very angry," I said. Looking Garbarini in the eyes, I couldn't believe that he was responsible for her death. But the rational part of my mind knew that he would have said the same words, even if he were guilty. "I want the killer brought to justice," I said. "If you and your friends can help me find him, I will be very much in your debt."

"So—we each have something the other wants, then," said Mr. Clemens, setting his cup on the table. "That's a starting place. But let's make sure we all know what we're asking for. You want Mark Twain to write something to tell the people about your cause. All right—I'm willing to undertake that. But don't expect me to parrot your party's platform. Because I can tell you, sight unseen, that I won't agree with it—I've never seen anybody's boilerplate I could swallow whole."

"Swallow boilerplate?" Garbarini looked puzzled for a moment, then laughed. "You would need the very good stomach indeed, *signore*. But I will promise you, we do not expect you to be the faithful parrot. Gonnella and I, we are poets—we know that the name means nothing if the heart does not come with it. You will write what you write, and we will trust you to be Mark Twain—the man who is not afraid to look Giuseppe Volponi in the face and tell him that the king is a thief."

"That's the only terms I'd write on," said my employer. "But let's find out about the other half of the bargain. You say you can help find out who killed the girl—and stole the painting, too. Why should I believe you can do this better than *Capitano* Rosalia? He seems to be a pretty good cop when he isn't looking after his own ambitions."

Garbarini shrugged. "We want to find the one who did it, because if we do not, Rosalia and his men will continue to say that we are the killers, and use that lie to hurt us every way they can. By finding the true murderer we can take the blame from ourselves."

Mr. Clemens put his hand on the table between himself and Garbarini and said, "I believe that part. But wanting to do something ain't the same as doing it—if it was, I reckon you'd already be running the country, or letting it run itself, if you mean what you say about getting rid of government. What I want to know is, what're your qualifications for catching this killer?"

Garbarini leaned his elbows on the table and looked my employer straight in the face. "*Signore* Clemens, I might also ask your qualifications for catching the killers you have caught—that news has come even to Italy. But here is my answer: The government has declared us criminals because of our politics—and by so doing, it has made us consort with thieves, counterfeiters, smugglers, and so forth. We understand their language, we know their meeting places, we travel in the same circles. If something is talked of by the criminals of Firenze, the anarchists will hear it. If someone has stolen a valuable painting and is trying to sell it, I think that we will learn of it before *Capitano* Rosalia and his *agentes*."

"Well, that makes more sense than most of what the police tell me," said my employer, rubbing his chin. "It doesn't answer one important question . . ."

"Whether we are the killers?" said Garbarini. He sipped his wine, then continued: "You have a big imagination, *Signore* Mark Twain—this is a compliment, if I say it of your writings, but perhaps it is not so good in this matter. *Capisce?* We draw attention to ourselves by coming forward to help—now you know who we are, and where one of our meeting places is. I do not think you will go home and tell *Capitano* Rosalia these things, but some of my comrades fear that you will."

"And I think you boys are smart enough to clear out of this meeting place and never use it again, once I'm gone," said Mr. Clemens. "That's how I'd play it if I were you. But I see your point. We have to trust each other not to renege on this deal, even though sticking to it might mean betraying somebody else we have to deal with—in my case, the captain, in yours the crooks you do business with."

"You summarize it well," said Garbarini, smiling. "We will trust you, and you will trust us. And we will do our best for each other. Because we both have something to gain as well as something to lose."

"I'm glad you see it that way," said Mr. Clemens, now leaning forward in his turn, to look Garbarini in the eye. "Now, when can I go back home to write that article I promised?"

For the first time, Garbarini failed to meet my employer's gaze straight on. "There is a small problem," he said.

"A small problem?" I echoed him. "I don't like the way you said that."

"Neither do I," said Mr. Clemens. "What's the catch?"

Garbarini spread his hands in front of him, palms up. "If it is for me to say, you both go home right now, as you please. But it is not for me alone."

"Wait a minute," snapped Mr. Clemens. He stood and pointed at Garbarini. "I thought I was doing business with honest men. Who says I can't go home?"

"*Signore* Clemens, nobody says that," said Garbarini. His lean face was impassive, but he sat back in his chair as if he feared that my employer might become violent. After a moment, he continued: "You can go home at once, if you wish. We have someone to take you to the *tramvia*, and from there you should have very little trouble."

"What?" Mr. Clemens peered at Garbarini as if he were examining some exotic creature. "Then what's the problem you were talking about?"

Garbarini's face took on an apologetic look. "*Signore* Clemens, you are free to go, but I am afraid that *Signore* Cabot must stay with us a little while longer."

At this revelation, I confess I was speechless. However, Mr. Clemens more than made up for my lack of words. In the end, though, it did neither of us any good.

≈ **19**

If you had told me, before I went to Italy, that I would spend most of a day with two Italian poets, eating, drinking, playing chess, and talking of whatever crossed our minds, I would have thought it a delightful prospect. Reality—waiting in a dingy garret while the anarchists finished moving their headquarters—was somewhat less attractive.

Garbarini had explained the situation to me and Mr. Clemens as best he could, considering that neither my employer nor I saw the necessity for my staying behind. Both of us were willing to promise to keep the location of the anarchists' headquarters secret until they had time to move, and to cover their trail. But from their point of view, the danger of exposure required more security; thus, my role was to act as collateral for Mr. Clemens's discretion. While neither of us liked the arrangement, we had no choice but to accept it. Since they had already held him overnight, they saw no reason why I should object to a few more hours.

To their credit, Bruno Gonnella and Giovanni Garbarini (I had learned their Christian names) did their best to make my captivity as comfortable as possible. One or the other of them stayed with me the entire time, keeping me well supplied with food and drink—and chess and conversation. And after a while, I was able to relax and enjoy my enforced idleness, and the chance to play chess against two expert players. After a dozen or so games, I had managed to defeat Gonnella twice, to stalemate Garbarini once, and to a draw by perpetual check once against each opponent. This, considering my previous record against these same players, could be taken as progress. Or it may have meant no more than that they had partaken more liberally than I of the wine.

I tried not to indulge too freely in the wine, knowing that my situation might change without warning. If my captors had more sinister intentions than they had so far shown, or if their superiors had a change of heart, I would need to have my wits about me. And so, while Gonnella and Garbarini continued to refill my cup whenever they saw it empty, I was careful that it did not become empty too often.

As the light through the lone window faded to dusk, Gonnella went down the ladder and returned with a loaf of heavy dark bread and a round of cheese, which we shared among us. It was a frugal meal, but a good one—the cheese was excellent, in fact—and in any case, I was hungry enough not to complain. The three of us washed it down with more wine—with food, I felt I could drink a bit more freely—the two Italians talking at a great rate in their own language, with occasional laughter—I could understand just enough to decide that they were speaking of painting, and of Raphael in particular. Annoyed at being left out of a conversation that might relate to the stolen painting, and more importantly to Virginia's death, I frowned, and asked, "What's so amusing?"

"I am sorry," said Gonnella. "Is easy to forget you don't know our language so well. We talk about the stolen painting, and Giovanni tells me your *padrone Signore* Mark Twain says he wouldn't pay so much for a Raphael when he could buy a copy for much less."

"Yes, I've heard him say much the same," I said. "He doesn't put much stock in the old masters."

"*Signore* Twain has better reason than many connoisseurs," Garbarini said. "Many Raphaels that cost thousands of lira are the copies, or the counterfeits. There are many artists in Firenze, and all over Italy, who do such work, and many dealers who sell it to *Inglesi* or . . . to other foreigners."

"Yes, I met one such," I said, and told them of our visit, the day before, to the shop of Luigi Battista, after seeing where the frame of the painting—and Virginia's body—had been found.

"We know that street," said Gonnella, fingering one of the knights from the chess set, which we had pushed aside to make room for our dinner. Even in this cheap wooden set, the knights were hand-carved with an unusual attention to realistic detail. "Many artists live and work near Porta Pinti," he continued. "Maybe twenty, twenty-five years ago, three painters asked the city to let them build their studios on some empty land there. The city agreed, and now the streets there are named for great artists—Donatello, della Robbia, Masaccio, and others."

"The police think the painting was taken out there in search of an unscrupulous dealer willing to sell it," I said.

"*All* the dealers are without scruples," said Garbarini, with some vehemence. "They buy a painting for a little price, and sell to the *inglesi* for a big price. They take the artist's work to make themselves fat, and the artist goes hungry. It is no big step from that to selling stolen paintings, or even to stealing the paintings themselves. The police are right to look there for the stolen painting."

"Luigi Battista, at least, was honest enough to tell us that his paintings were copies," I said.

"Ahh, Battista is no better than the rest," said Garbarini, growing more heated. "My friend Hugo dealt with him— never again! He does very good drawings in the style of Leonardo—I know how good, because I see them myself. When he takes them to Battista, that robber tells him the market is very bad, and gives him a few lira for his work, saying he gives him more if it brings a good price. Then an English *milord* buys it for a hundred times what Hugo gets. One of Hugo's friends is in Battista's shop when the *milord*'s servant comes with the money, and so Hugo finds out the drawings are sold. But when he goes to ask for his money, Battista tells him the drawings didn't sell yet. Then Hugo tells him how he knows the drawings are sold, and Battista slaps his hand on his forehead." (Garbarini demonstrated the gesture as he described it, with a comical expression.) " 'My memory is so bad—I must be thinking of some other drawings,' says Battista, and he gives Hugo a few more lira so he will go away. Hugo needs the money bad, or he would throw it on the floor and walk out, but instead he takes it and swears he never lets Battista sell his work again. That is no honest man!"

"If the story is true, I would agree with you," I said. I realized that I might have stumbled on information that Mr. Clemens and I could use. Perhaps we needed to make another visit to the art dealer's shop.

"Of course it is true!" said Garbarini. "Hugo would never lie to me!"

"Oh, I'm sure your friend is telling the truth," I said. "It is just that Battista gave the impression that he was honest, perhaps to a fault. But I think he recognized my employer, and was afraid he might be exposed."

Garbarini seemed to accept my assertion, although I could see he was still not calm. He took another sip of his wine, emptying the cup, and reached out for the jug to refill it. For my part, my mind was turning over possibilities. Now that I thought of it, Battista *had* recognized Mr. Clemens—could he have been trying to charm the famous author, hoping to beguile him into buying some of his counterfeit artworks? The meeting with the art dealer now took on shades of meaning I hadn't suspected.

"You say there are many other art dealers in that neighborhood," I said, searching for more information. "Do you know of any that might be willing to find a buyer for a piece they knew to be stolen?"

"For enough money, most of them would run to Hell to find a buyer for their own mother," growled Garbarini. He stared at his cup for a moment, then added, "The ones that *had* mothers."

Gonnella laughed. "Now, be charitable, my friend," he said, reaching to fill his own mug from the bottle. "They all had mothers. It is the fathers that most of them are lacking." They both laughed, with ferocious grins.

I tried to turn the talk back to something relevant to my search for clues, but the two men continued to joke until, after a bit, Gonnella excused himself and went down the ladder to the storeroom below. Garbarini set up the chessboard again, and I found myself in another head-to-head struggle on a sixty-four-square battlefield.

My two guards—for, despite the lack of any overt duress, that is the role that Garbarini and Gonnella were performing—took turns playing chess with me. The one "off duty" would wander off downstairs, presumably to help with whatever the anarchists needed to remove from the premises now that they had decided to abandon this headquarters.

While I had no real way to keep track of time, it was clear that the hour was getting late. I was anxious to return to Villa Viviani and share what I had learned—as little as it was—with my employer. I didn't know whether I was going to have to stay here overnight, or to find my way home from a strange quarter of town at some ungodly hour. Neither prospect was attractive, but so far I had elicited no answer from my guards beyond "wait and see"—which was not very helpful. As much as I enjoyed chess, it was beginning to pall. How much longer could it take for them to remove whatever it was they kept in this building?

I was in the middle of still another losing chess game—I had won a rook for a knight and a pawn, but Gonnella had lured my pieces to one corner of the board and, now that they were entangled, was advancing his extra pawn on the other side. I was trying to decide if I could postpone defeat by giving back the rook, when Garbarini came rushing up the ladder and spoke hastily to Gonnella in Italian. From his harsh whisper and agitated tone, the message was urgent. Although it was his turn to move, Gonnella at once stood up from the board and started toward the ladder.

"What is it?" I asked, rising to my feet. I decided it was time to insist on learning their plans for me.

"Somebody watching this place," said Garbarini, gesturing me back toward the chair. His eyes were wide, and his face flushed, probably from climbing the ladder. "Maybe is police," he said. "You stay here—is safest for you."

"The police don't worry me," I said, realizing even as I said so that they might still consider me a suspect in the murder—and that they might take my consorting with political outlaws as confirmation of my guilt.

"You stay here," Garbarini repeated, waving me back again. He and Gonnella both dashed down the ladder and I heard their footsteps running off somewhere down below.

I went over to the trapdoor and leaned down to look through it. The room below had one small light. I could make out bales of paper, and the outline of the door out to the street, but nothing else. Nobody was visible in the shop below, not even the guards I had seen earlier in the day. Should I go down the ladder? Or would the anarchists take that as breaking the promise Mr. Clemens and I had made? Even if they did, was that any great price to pay for a chance at my freedom?

Before I could decide what to do, I became aware of voices somewhere outside, shouting something incomprehensible. Then I became aware of running footsteps, more frantic shouts, and a *pop! pop!* sound that I realized must be gunfire.

All at once, my situation had become much more perilous. The available choices all seemed bad. Descending the ladder would place me in the line of fire; on the other hand, staying where I was might mean being trapped. If the shooters were the police, I might be able to surrender to them and let Mr. Clemens bail me out—assuming they gave me the chance to surrender. If they were not the police—well, that might be very tricky.

As I tried to think the situation through, the decision was taken out of my hands. Down below, the light suddenly got brighter, and someone ran through the door carrying a torch. Before I could make out his features, he flung the torch into the bales of paper. Bright orange sparks flew in all directions, and the fire caught almost at once, spreading rapidly. Thick smoke billowed up to assault my eyes and nose even as I watched.

I swung down through the hatchway in an instant, and got to the floor almost without touching the ladder. The smoke was already filling the room, and I strained to find the way to the outside door. I ducked below the smoke, peered to make sure of the direction, and then dashed toward the opening. Ahead of me I heard another *pop! pop!* sound, but I paid it no heed. Bullets might hit or miss, but to stay in the fire was certain death.

Coughing, I burst into the open air and tried to clear my vision to see which way to turn. The crescent moon showed me a wooden fence, with a few heavy wooden crates piled at its base, at the rear of the alley I had come out into. At a quick glance, the fence looked low enough to vault. I had no idea what lay behind it, but the shooting seemed to be coming from the other direction. I might regret it if there was a watchdog in the neighbor's yard, but I could better outrun a dog than a bullet. I ducked low and began to run toward the fence.

Someone behind me shouted something in Italian, but I lengthened my stride and leapt to place my foot atop a crate at the foot of the fence. Here my luck gave out; the crate cracked and toppled, throwing me to the ground. I landed hard, knocking the wind out of myself, and another crate fell on my leg.

Before I could rise, there was a man standing over me, with a pistol pointed at my face. "*No muove,*" he said, and I did not need my Italian dictionary to know what he meant. I raised my hands alongside my head and lay there panting. For better or worse, I was a prisoner again. But at least I was alive, and in the open air.

It did not take me long to learn who my captors were. The uniforms of the *guardia*—the Florentine city police— were easily recognizable in the moonlight. They took me to a station not far from the place where I had been cap-

tured. There were no other prisoners from the radicals'
hideout—at least, neither Garbarini nor Gonnella, nor (as
far as I could tell) the men who had been outside the building when I had come there. Perhaps they had been brought
in separately, but if so, they were not put in the large common cell that I was taken to.

This was a noisome place, in comparison to which the
New Orleans lockup I had been in was a veritable bed of
roses. The entire floor was covered with filth, and there
must have been a dozen prisoners in a space smaller than
the garret I had just come from. There was a man lying in
one corner, his head covered in bandages, moaning as if he
were on his deathbed. Two large men sat on the floor—
there was no other place to sit—with their backs to the
wall, eyeing me as if they thought I had something worth
stealing, if only my clothing and shoes. One poor wretch
repeated some phrase over and over again, without the
slightest variation, in some language I did not recognize.
The others in the cell either stood by the bars, peering out
into the corridor, or paced back and forth, brushing past
one another in the narrow confines.

I did not get to sample the pleasures of this cell for more
than a few minutes, for not long after the door had closed
behind me, it opened again and two officers led me down
the corridor to a sort of office, where a thick-bodied man
in police uniform sat behind a desk. My guards held me by
both arms while he barked a question at me in Italian, to
which I responded, "*No capisco italiano, signore.* I am an
American citizen—do you speak English?"

"Do not think you will escape punishment by being a
foreigner," the interrogator replied, in good (albeit heavily
accented) English. "We have many foreigners in our pris-
ons. You will go there yourself if you don't cooperate with
us. Where are your accomplices?"

"I don't know who you're talking about," I said, trying
to keep my face impassive. I had already decided what my
story would be. "I was taking a shortcut through the alley,
and when I heard the shooting, and saw the fire, I tried to
get away." I hadn't had time to think about that, until now;

someone had tried to burn the place down *with me in it*. I shuddered to think what might have happened had I not seen the fire before it spread.

"You could not be so innocent, or you would not have run from the law," the man said, rubbing his heavy jowls with his hand. He pointed at me. "Perhaps you set the fire yourself, to destroy evidence. Arson is a very serious crime, *signore*."

"I did not set the fire," I said. "I wish to send a message to my employer, Mr. Samuel Clemens. He is staying in Villa Viviani, in Settignano."

"You will send no messages until you tell us the truth," said the interrogator, standing up behind his desk. "Where are your accomplices?"

"I don't know who you're talking about," I said again warily. I had heard very unpleasant hints of what could happen to those who fell afoul of the police here. I had thought that if the man didn't believe me—in fact, I *was* trying to deceive him—he would simply lock me up again. But while I wanted as little as possible to do with that Italian jail, I began to fear I would get in even worse trouble if I changed my story.

The interrogator confirmed my apprehension as he reached down to his desk and picked up a riding crop. He flicked it lightly against the desktop, and it gave out a flat *crack*—not very loud, but it had the effect he undoubtedly desired. My attention was riveted on him as he said, "Perhaps I can help you remember." He stepped around the desk, and the two policemen took tighter grips on my arms.

I don't know for certain what would have happened next, for the door behind me creaked open just then, and a familiar voice said, "Aha, *tenente*, I see you have found the man we have been searching for." I turned my head to look. It was *Capitano* Rosalia.

The interrogator put the riding crop down on the desktop and turned to face the captain. "*Capitano* Rosalia, I will remind you that this man is being held for questioning by the *guardia*. Your *carabinieri* have no claim on him," he said, folding his arms across his chest.

"On the contrary, *tenente*," said *Capitano* Rosalia. "It is a political matter in which he has been meddling, and that is very much our concern. We have been watching him for some time."

"He is suspected of arson," said the *tenente,* stubbornly. "That is in our jurisdiction, and I will not be cheated of my right to question the prisoner." He had picked up the riding crop again, and was flicking it against his desktop.

"You have a right to question him," said Rosalia, spreading his hands apart. "But I tell you, this fellow is only a dupe of the revolutionaries. He knows nothing of use to anyone. The anarchists have run away and burned the building they were in, and left the poor trusting foreigner behind to be caught and questioned about it. You would do better to rake the ashes for clues than to waste your time with him."

"So you say," said the tenente, sitting on his desktop with a scowl. "I say, give me an hour with him and you will find out that he knows more than you suspect. I have my ways with this sort."

"We know your ways, *tenente*," said Rosalia, nodding soberly. "They are sometimes useful, I admit. But this man is the servant of a very important American—you will regret it if he comes to any harm. Better to release him to my custody."

"The cursed foreigners are ruining this country," said the interrogator sourly. He stared at me, flicking his crop, then turned to the captain again. "To the devil with them, and with the *carabinieri*, too. Take him away. But don't let me catch him loose in my jurisdiction again—it will not go easy with him, I promise. Away with you both!"

Capitano Rosalia took a gentle grip on my right arm. "Come with me, *Signore* Cabot," he said quietly. "The *tenente* has decided to be reasonable, and we should take advantage of it while it lasts."

I felt numb. I had no idea what lay in store for me; I knew what I had just escaped. And that was not even taking into account my escape from the burning building. I nodded my assent, and followed *Capitano* Rosalia out of the room.

⤳ 20

"It is lucky that I learned so quickly that the *guardia* had captured your secretary," said *Capitano* Rosalia. We were sitting in Mr. Clemens's office; it was close to midnight, but there was still a great deal to discuss before any of us were ready for bed. The captain and my employer were smoking cigars, and all three of us drank coffee and brandy.

"Damn lucky, from what you two have told me," said Mr. Clemens, from the chair behind his desk. "Cops everywhere get rough with people they suspect of serious crimes—that doesn't surprise me. But this *tenente* sounds as if he enjoys beating his prisoners just for the hell of it. I don't like that, even when the prisoner isn't my secretary. I wouldn't like it if the son of a bitch treated a known killer that way."

"I agree with you in principle," said the captain, who occupied an armchair across the desk from my employer. "But you, *Signore* Clemens, must be able to put yourself in another man's place—to see the world through his eyes. Your secretary was fleeing the scene of a crime, a scene in which shots had been fired, and for all the *guardia* knew, they had caught the man who set the fire. You cannot expect them to treat him with kid gloves in such circumstances."

"I expect them to try to verify his story before they start working on him with the truncheons," growled my employer. He stuffed his cigar back in his mouth, took a puff, then added, "Don't get me wrong, Captain—I'm grateful you found him and brought him home, and it'll be a long while before I let him out on such a damn-fool errand again."

Capitano Rosalia leaned forward and cleared his throat. "Speaking of which," he said, "what errand was *Signore* Cabot on in that part of the city? It is not a quarter frequented by tourists—for reasons that must be obvious, considering what happened to him today."

"I can answer that," I said. I was getting tired of being spoken of as if I weren't present. "A friend invited me to his home to play chess. We played right through supper time, into the evening, and then I decided to walk home. I was taking a shortcut through that alley when the fire broke out, and then the police came after me, with their guns drawn. I was frightened, and I ran. I believe you know the rest." I tried my best to look as if I were being candid. After all, enough of the story was true that it might pass muster.

The captain looked at me with raised eyebrows. "That is a very interesting story," he said, tapping the ash off his cigar. "Perhaps you would be so kind as to provide me the name of this chess-playing friend, and the location of his home."

"His name is no problem," I said. "He is Giovanni Garbarini, whom I know from Cafe Diabelli. As to his address, I am afraid I don't know it. We met by chance on Via Tornabuoni and walked to his home together—I didn't notice the street name or number where he lived. But if you went to the cafe, perhaps you'd find him. He plays there almost every day, and I'm sure he'd give you his address if you asked." I was even more sure that Garbarini would avoid Diabelli's—or any other place where the police might look for him—until the hue and cry had abated.

"Garbarini is known to us," said *Capitano* Rosalia dryly. He put the cigar down and picked up his glass, then turned back to me and asked, "Are you aware that he is a notorious advocate of armed rebellion against the kingdom?"

I took a sip of my own drink, then shrugged. "I know him as a very strong chess player," I said. "He beats me more often than not, but I enjoy the game. I think I learn something every time we play."

"I used to know a fellow like that," said Mr. Clemens. "He was a Mississippi River pilot—George Ealer. I haven't thought of him in years. A good pilot. He played the flute, and he played chess—I don't think I ever beat him. Well, I'd have beaten him sometimes, except that every time I had him cornered, he'd take back his last move and find another way to win."

"That's not playing fair," I said, laughing. "I didn't know you played chess, though. We'll have to try conclusions over the board some time."

Capitano Rosalia sat up straight in his chair, with a sour expression. "*Signore* Clemens, I have a very distinct feeling that your old friend was not the only one not playing fair," he said. "You have not yet given me a satisfactory explanation of your whereabouts the last day and a half. You disappeared from Cafe Diabelli in the midst of a riot between radicals and patriots, and were rumored to have been taken hostage by anarchists. In fact, your wife was very worried about your absence. And yet this afternoon, *Agente* Maggio tells me that you came home on foot, claiming you had visited a friend overnight in the city."

"Yes, I believe that's what I told him," said Mr. Clemens, lounging back in his chair. "I ran across the fellow right after that fight in the cafe. He didn't have a telephone, so I couldn't call and tell Livy—of course, we don't have one here, either, so it wouldn't have done much good. But I sent a local boy with a written message. I didn't know until I got home that it hadn't gotten here. The little brat probably spent the lira I gave him on candy. I wish you hadn't told Livy that stuff about anarchists kidnapping me, though. The last thing I wanted was for her to worry about me."

"This friend of yours will corroborate your story?" *Capitano* Rosalia's smile had no trace of warmth to it. "You can direct us to his residence?"

"Oh, I'm afraid he's left town," said Mr. Clemens blandly. "That's why it was so important to visit him last night, you see. He wasn't going to be around much longer, so we stayed at his boardinghouse. I think he was on his way back to America."

The captain drained his drink—there wasn't much left—stood up, and stubbed out his cigar. "My friends, I suggest you think about today's events, and about who your real friends are. Tomorrow, when you have reflected, we will talk some more. I remind you, there are dangerous men abroad in Firenze, men who killed your Miss Fleetwood. Perhaps with this in mind you will wish to reconsider your answers."

"I haven't forgotten Miss Fleetwood," I said, "and I appreciate your good services to me today. But you're right; I'm in need of rest, after all that happened today. Thank you again, *Capitano* Rosalia. I'll talk to you in the morning."

"Good night, *signori*," said the captain, bowing to us. Mr. Clemens showed him to the door, and returned. He picked up his cigar, which had burned down to a short stub, gave it a regretful look, and took one last puff before extinguishing it in the oversized cut-glass ashtray where *Capitano* Rosalia's cigar butt already rested. Then he turned to face me.

"Well, Wentworth," he said, "you were telling the captain about eighty percent lies—I know, because I was there for a fair bit of it. What I don't know yet is why. I reckon you better give me the whole story."

"Yes, sir," I said. "I'm not certain of this, but I suspect that my 'rescue' from the police interrogator was prearranged, to make me more willing to talk to the captain. For one thing, they spoke English the whole time—on purpose, I think, to make me see Rosalia as a friend."

"Yes, and the timing was mighty convenient, wasn't it?" said Mr. Clemens, nodding. "I wonder if *Agente* Maggio didn't manage to trail you to the anarchists' hideout, after all. Or maybe the cops knew where it was all along, and just didn't have a handy excuse to raid it."

"I don't mind their raiding it," I said. "But to come in with guns blazing, and to set the place on fire—that was more than I can forgive. They might have killed me. Or Garbarini and Gonnella. Whatever their politics, they don't deserve to be shot . . ." I was going to go on about freedom of speech, but Mr. Clemens held up his hand to stop me.

"Wait a minute, Wentworth. You don't know it was the cops who torched the place," said Mr. Clemens. He leaned against the mantelpiece and shook a finger at me. "It makes just as much sense to think the radicals did it, to keep the cops from getting evidence there wasn't time to move away."

"Perhaps," I said, turning partway around to face him. "If it was the anarchists, I'm almost certain Gonnella or Garbarini didn't know about it."

My employer smoothed his mustache with his thumb and forefinger. "Why, just because they treated you all right up until then?"

"No, because they told me to wait there when they left," I said. "I think they'd have warned me to get out, if they knew their comrades were about to set the place afire. And one small thing, but it seems significant to me—I don't think they'd have left their chess set to be burned up. I know that doesn't sound like much, but those two are passionate about the game. I think they'd have grabbed the set if they knew there was going to be a fire."

"Hmmm—you may be right about that," said Mr. Clemens, pacing back and forth. "It's not absolute proof, but it rings true to human nature. But tell me this. Why would the cops try to burn the place down if they expected to find evidence there?"

"For all I know, they put out the fire as soon as I was out the door," I said, drumming my fingers on the arm of my chair. "Where they started the fire, there was nothing but bales of unused paper. I see the difficulty, though. The fire might have spread faster than they'd planned. Or I might have panicked, and then they'd have had to send somebody in to rescue me. So maybe it wasn't the police who set the fire. But I still don't think Gonnella or Garbarini had anything to do with it."

Mr. Clemens sat down opposite me and picked up his drink again. "Well, you were the man on the spot, so I've got to give your opinions due weight," he said. "Still, we've got to play ball with Rosalia on the murder investigation—even if his claim that the anarchists did it is pure moonshine. I feel the same as you about that—he's letting that idea color everything he sees. Maybe he's doing it because it's what his bosses have told him to do. I can't tell; he's smart enough to tell sense from nonsense, but you could say the same of many another man who's fallen for some swindle or another. I have a better feeling about that Maggio—I think he's more honest than Rosalia, at least as far as saying what he thinks and to hell with official policy."

"I like *Agente* Maggio, too," I said. "But I'm not sure we can trust him, either. He does have to follow orders, and those come from Rosalia—or Rosalia's superiors."

"Right again," said Mr. Clemens. "So we're back on our own, as far as finding the rat who killed that girl. We'll just have to find our own clues and figure out what they mean without help. Speaking of which, did you learn anything useful before the place went to blazes?"

"One thing, at least," I said, and I told him about the two men's distrust of the art dealers on Piazza Donatello. "That fellow Battista seems especially shady," I said. "They told me he often cheats both the artists and the customers on the same transaction. I wonder if he was candid with you because he recognized your face, and thought he could flatter you that way."

"It wouldn't surprise me," said my employer. "It's a good bet that the thief took the painting up to that neighborhood to fence it to one of the dealers, whether it was Battista or not. But we still don't know what the girl was doing there, unless she saw the thief taking the picture, and followed him up there. But why wouldn't she tell Stephens, instead of going out alone at night, to a strange part of town, to follow a criminal? I didn't get the sense she was the reckless type."

"Brave, but not reckless," I agreed. "More likely, the thief took her hostage to prevent her from exposing him, then went to an isolated place and murdered her."

"Maybe, maybe," said Mr. Clemens. He stood up and walked over to slosh some more brandy into his coffee cup, then turned to continue: "That makes more sense than the damn-fool anarchist plot the captain keeps trying to peddle, anyhow. Although I suppose we could be wrong about that, too."

"You saw Gonnella and Garbarini," I said. "Did they strike you as cold-blooded killers?"

"No, but you can't always tell that," said Mr. Clemens. "There was a fellow who'd killed twenty-six men by the time I met him—Slade, his name was, a division agent on the Overland Trail back in the sixties. It was worth your life to cross him, for he'd been known to shoot a man over a glass of whisky, and never give him a chance to defend himself. I knew his reputation. Hell, I was in mortal fear the whole time I was with him—but he was the most mild-mannered fellow I ever sat at a table with. He could've been a Quaker for all the trouble he gave me."

"Well, I suppose I could be wrong about Garbarini and Gonnella," I conceded. "But if they were looking to murder me, they had all afternoon to slit my throat or knock me on the head—and they didn't. Unless something happened I don't know about, they had no reason to change their minds."

"The police raid might be reason enough," said Mr. Clemens. "But I reckon if they'd wanted you dead, they'd have killed you before they left the place. Instead, they left you with a fair chance to get out on your own. If they were caught by surprise, they might not have had the chance to get back to you. Still, I don't like their setting the place on fire."

"And I still don't know for certain it was they who did it," I responded. "In any case, I'm safe home, and there's an end to our alliance with the anarchists. I doubt they'll be able to fulfill their own part of the bargain, in any case, with the police hot on their trails."

"You mean looking for clues to the murder?" said Mr. Clemens. "Well, I don't know how much we'd have gotten out of them, anyhow. Maybe their contacts in the underworld are as good as they say, but they may not be so willing to pass on what they've learned. If the professional crooks learned that the anarchists were informing on them, they'd shut them out in a minute. I wasn't much counting on their help, anyway."

"Ah, so your offer to write an article defending them was never serious," I said. This somewhat relieved me; I thought it rash for a visitor in a foreign country to take up the pen in support of an outlawed political sect. And in any case, whatever my personal opinion of my chess opponents, their politics seemed the pinnacle of lunacy to me.

"Oh, I was dead serious," my employer said, his eyebrows raised. "I'm still going to write it. As a matter of fact, I've got a first draft already done—I started it while I was at their place, and finished when I got back here."

My mouth fell open in amazement. "Are you pulling my leg again?" I said. There was nothing in his expression to indicate a humorous intention, but I knew that my employer had long practice at telling the most absurd lies with a straight face. "Their central tenet is to abolish government, and anyone can recognize the folly of that. Besides, their long record of assassinations and bombings gives the lie to their peace-loving rhetoric. What can you possibly say in their favor?"

"Not so much in their favor as against the government's," said Mr. Clemens quite placidly. "It's bad enough that Italy's gone and given themselves a king, and all the other claptrap of royalty. But now they're doing their level best to adopt all the worst traits of the older monarchies, right up to sending their army to seize colonies in Africa and enslave the natives. At least the anarchists and Socialists are willing to call it by its right name, which is theft and murder. That's why the government is sending the cops to suppress them. And if they're not being allowed to tell the truth, then somebody else has got to do it. It might as well be me."

"And what if they decide to suppress you?" I asked. "*Capitano* Rosalia seems a pleasant enough fellow, but I'm sure he can be as ruthless as anyone when it's to his advantage—or when he's given direct orders to do so. I suspect that his rescuing me at the jail this evening was a charade, and I don't like to think what might have happened if he'd decided I needed to be taught a lesson."

Mr. Clemens raised his chin. "I know the dangers, Wentworth," he said. "Myself, I'm willing to take my chances. But old Francis Bacon was right as rain—no man with a wife and family can take on a corrupt government without thinking about what could happen to them. I'm not going to leave Livy and the girls exposed to danger. Before I publish anything that could cause trouble for them, I'll make sure they're good and safe in some country where the government doesn't owe Italy any favors. For that matter, if you're worried about your own safety, I'll send you away, too. It's one thing to take that kind of risk myself, but I'm not so arrogant as to subject somebody else to it without his consent."

"I'll stick with you, sir," I said, even though I'd seen enough in the Italian jail to know what I might be facing if the authorities decided to use me as a lever to put pressure on my employer.

"I figured you'd say that, Wentworth," said Mr. Clemens. He walked over and put his hand on my shoulder. "That's one of the things I like about you—you aren't afraid to stand up to a bully. But I don't want you to be reckless about it, either. If you find yourself in hot enough water that you want to change your mind, I'll understand—hell, maybe you'll make me change my own mind, if I'm being enough of a fool. Don't think you have to jump in front of a bullet, just because you said you'd stick with me."

"I appreciate your saying that, Mr. Clemens," I said, looking him in the face. "But I've got a job to do—and not just for you. Whoever killed Miss Fleetwood is still at large, and I mean to do whatever I can to track that murderer down and see that he pays the penalty for his crime. If that means exposing myself to personal danger, it's a small price to pay."

"I can't say I'm sorry you feel that way," said Mr. Clemens, giving my shoulder a squeeze. "But I think we're going to need more than courage to solve this puzzle. We've been going over the same ground again and again, and getting nowhere. Let's sleep on it, and see if we can come up with some fresh ideas in the morning. Today has been way too various for my taste, and I reckon you've had more than your share of fun, too."

"I wouldn't put it in quite those words, sir," I said, standing up. "But I'm not about to contradict you, either." I returned his smile, and then we drained our drinks and went upstairs to our beds.

I slept like a log, despite my midnight dose of coffee and brandy; the brandy must have trumped the coffee, or perhaps I was just so tired the coffee made no difference. Still, I was up by eight o'clock, and when I came downstairs to the breakfast table, I found Mr. Clemens there before me. His plate—the well-cleaned bone of a beefsteak and several rinds of toast still on it—was shoved to one side, and his coffee cup sat half-full next to his elbow. He was writing. "Good morning, Wentworth!" he said, looking up as I came in. "Have the cook get you some breakfast, and then come help me figure this out."

I went through the swinging door into the kitchen and found *Agente* Maggio sitting on a stool by the stove, a thin book in his hands. He looked at me over his spectacles as I came in and said, "*Ciao, Signore* Wentworth. Is good to see you back at home."

"What on earth are you doing here?" I said, somewhat heatedly. "Haven't you done enough by sending the police with guns and torches to harass me? I'm surprised Mr. Clemens let you in the door."

"It was *Signora* Clemens let me in," said Maggio equably. He put the book down on the counter next to him, and stood up. "But I don't send the police after you, yesterday, because I don't know where you are."

"I don't believe that," I said. "The police came in firing their guns, set the place on fire, and took me to the station like a common criminal. Then your captain very conveniently showed up, just in time to prevent their interrogator from whipping me. I'm sure it was done on purpose, to frighten me into talking to the police. This isn't the way you treat an American citizen."

"I don't know how the *capitano* finds out where you are, because I don't tell him," said Maggio, shrugging. "When I leave the cafe, I come right back here, and stay until after dark. You ask *Signorina* Clara—she talk to me a long time. She speaks very good Italian. *Signore* Clemens comes home to eat, and I come back to the kitchen to wait until night, when I go home. You ask the cook—he can tell you I was here."

I was taken aback by the *carabiniere's* answers—if he was not telling the truth, he was a much smoother liar than I had given him credit for. But I thought I saw a loophole in his story. "If you came right back here, how did the police know where I was staying? You must have followed me there, or told somebody else to follow me."

"I don't know what place you went to," said *Agente* Maggio insisted. "But stop a minute—don't you think the *guardia* know where these people have their meetings? They watch them all the time, not just yesterday. They don't need me to tell them where you are."

I thought a moment and said, "You must have known I was going off with Garbarini, though. If your captain considers him and his group so dangerous, why *didn't* you inform him of where you thought I was going?"

Maggio smiled. "I have my own mind," he said. "Giovanni Garbarini looks me in the eye when he comes in the cafe, and I stare back at him, very serious. But he acts like he doesn't worry—and he *would* worry if he's the one that kills the *signorina*. He knows my face. So I decide to watch what happens. Then he gives you that piece of paper; I think it must be a message from your *padrone*, and so I let you go with him. I come back here, and when *Signore* Clemens comes home, I think everything is good. Nothing to tell *Capitano* Rosalia."

Now I *was* surprised. "Nothing to tell? You were in the same room with a main suspect in a murder case and let him walk away without finding out where he was going. Can't you get into trouble for keeping that kind of information from your superiors—especially if something happens?"

Maggio shrugged. "But nothing happens, see? You come home all right, so nothing to worry about."

"If you don't count my nearly getting burned to death," I said. "Are you sure you didn't tell somebody that I had gone off to meet Garbarini?"

Now the *carabiniere* put his finger to his lips and leaned forward. "I tell you a secret," he said. "I don't think Giovanni Garbarini is the killer we want. The *capitano* has orders to blame this murder on the anarchists. But he doesn't give *me* those orders, and so I just try to find the real killer. If I make a mistake, maybe it gets me in trouble. But I think is better to find the real killer than to make the anarchists look bad. So I take that chance."

I wasn't certain whether to believe Maggio or not, but as I had no way to refute his explanation, I decided provisionally to accept it. "Very well," I said. "It sounds as if you're telling the truth. Now, if you'll excuse me, I need to talk to the cook."

I was ravenous, and so I ordered up a huge breakfast, with toast, eggs, several rashers of bacon, and plenty of coffee to wash it down. I took my coffee cup and was headed toward the dining room when I realized Maggio might be able to help us. "Excuse me again," I said. "Mr. Clemens and I are going to talk about the murder. Why don't you get a cup of coffee, and come into the dining room and join us?"

"You want me, I join you," said Maggio, putting down his book and taking off his glasses. He filled up a coffee cup and followed me through the door. Mr. Clemens raised an eyebrow as the *carabiniere* followed me into the room, but said nothing.

Maggio and I sat down and I turned to Mr. Clemens. "It seems to me we've reached the end of our own resources," I said. "I don't think we can count on any help from Garbarini and his friends, and most of Stephens's crowd isn't talking to me. *Agente* Maggio knows the city better than either of us, and he's in the business of catching criminals. Let's find out if he can help us get out of our impasse."

"That's fine with me," said Mr. Clemens. "But how about you, Maggio? Do you believe the captain's story about the anarchists killing the girl? I recall you said a few harsh words about the radicals when we first talked about them."

Maggio shrugged. "I said what I believe," he responded, then took a sip of his coffee. "They think they can solve the people's troubles by making the government go away. All right, we all know the government makes us pay big taxes so the big officials can live like rich men, and do stupid things with our money. But if the government goes away, who's left to feed the hungry ones or build railroads or factories or hospitals? Who's stopping bad men from doing whatever they want? So I think those anarchists don't know what the people need, or how to help with the real troubles we have in Italy."

"Or the real troubles anywhere else," said Mr. Clemens, nodding. He leaned forward across the dining room table and peered at the *carabiniere*, then said, "I reckon we agree on most of that. Most reformers I've known have had trouble getting their feet to touch the ground. But you still haven't said whether you think the anarchists stole the painting and murdered that girl."

"I don't think they steal the painting, because nobody asks *Signore* Stephens for money to bring it back," he said.

"Couldn't they get the money by selling it?" I asked.

"Sure, but it's slower and they got to find somebody who wants a Raphael bad enough he doesn't care if it's stolen," said Maggio. "It don't hurt to ask Stephens for money, because if he says No, they still got the painting."

"I see problems with that, but let it go for now," said Mr. Clemens. "What about the girl?"

"If they don't steal the painting, why do they need to kill the girl?" said Maggio, with the air of someone proving a geometrical proposition. "Giovanni Garbarini isn't the kind of man who kills her, then looks a police in the eye without showing he is feeling guilty. He is the—how you say in English?—*idealista*, but not the *fanatico*."

"That rings true, from what I saw of him, and of Gonnella, too," said Mr. Clemens. "All right, then—if not them, who? Where do we start off?"

Agente Maggio turned his eyes toward me for a moment, then cleared his throat and said, "Usually, when someone is killed, the killer is somebody they know before. Not always, but most of the time."

"By that, do you mean that I'm still a suspect?" I asked. My fists involuntarily clenched. "If you're willing to exonerate Garbarini so quickly, why are you still considering me a suspect? Why, I was . . ." *Practically in love with her,* I almost said before stopping myself. Of course, love was one of the prime motives for murder. Everybody knew that.

"I know Garbarini five, six years," said Maggio. "You, I know less than a week. Is a big difference." He paused a moment, looked away from me, and added, "I hope we find out you didn't do it. I think you are innocent the more I know you, but I am not the judge. Even the judges don't decide before they get all the evidence."

"I appreciate your fair-mindedness," I said, with only a touch of sarcasm. I might have gone on in a similar satiric vein, except that the cook emerged from the kitchen just then, bringing my breakfast. I took its arrival as an opportunity to let the subject drop. And, in fact, I had little to say for the next few minutes, shoveling bacon, eggs, and warm Italian bread—with plenty of melting butter—into my mouth.

Mr. Clemens took up the slack. "Okay, Maggio," he said. "I'll grant that for the sake of completeness that my secretary has to be a suspect. But he wasn't the only person the young lady knew in Florence—not by any means. Who else is on that list? Could you make a good case for any of them being the murderer—or the art thief, which may amount to the same thing?"

Maggio leaned forward. "First of all, the husband of her sister—*Signore* Stephens—he would be a suspect. They live in the same house, so they would disagree sometimes, argue with each other. And Stephens, he also has a good chance to steal the Raphael—or to send somebody to do it, while everyone eats the meal together. If a man everybody knows comes to take away something in a house, they all think it is permitted."

"What makes you think he'd steal his own painting?" asked my employer. "Stephens claimed he already had a buyer lined up. He doesn't seem like a man who'd throw away ready money."

"It is a puzzle," agreed Maggio. "And it does not explain why the frame of the painting is by Piazza Donatello, in the artists' quarter, or why the *signorina* is there with it."

My employer rubbed his chin, then said, "Wentworth, you'll pardon me if I ask this, but I need another opinion on a question that's got to be asked. Maggio, do you think the young lady could have stolen the painting herself? Could she have tried to sell it to the wrong person, and ended up being killed to keep from giving her a share of the loot?"

Despite a mouthful of bread and butter, I was about to register a protest. Maggio forestalled me by saying without hesitation, "I don't think so." He took a sip of his coffee and continued: "*Capitano* Rosalia and I, we know all the art dealers in Firenze—the good ones and the bad ones. Even the good ones will sometimes make a few extra lira by doing something not so honest. We don't catch everything, and we don't punish everything we catch—is the way of life here, *capisce*?"

"It's the way of life everywhere," said Mr. Clemens. "Why, I've even heard of that kind of thing in America."

"Just so," said the *carabiniere*, spreading his hands apart. "Everyone is stealing, and we can't punish it all. But if someone is killing, that is a much worse thing, and everybody knows it. We will make life bad for all the dealers if we think one of them kills somebody. So if one of them does it and the others find out, maybe they tell us who it is. That way, only the killer gets in trouble."

"It's a great system in theory," said Mr. Clemens. "I'm not sure I'd put a lot of faith in it, though. Especially with a pretty young girl dead, and the police looking for scapegoats instead of trying to find the real killer. But let's assume you're right. Who else do you consider a serious suspect?"

"I think all the people at Stephens's party have to be suspected," said Maggio. "Maybe how they stole the painting is, somebody goes out from the dining room while people are eating, and hides the painting someplace they can get it after they leave. They bribe the butler, or some other servant, not to tell. Then when they leave, they get the painting and go to meet a dealer to help sell it. The *signorina*, maybe she sees them and follows them, surprises them. Then the thief is afraid she will expose them, and kills her."

"That suggests some planning in advance," said Mr. Clemens. "Otherwise, they wouldn't have a middleman all ready to meet them—at midnight in a cemetery, for God's sake. It's an idea straight out of bad fiction. Not that I haven't used that kind of business myself, of course."

I pushed aside my breakfast dishes, and said, "They didn't have to plan it that far in advance. It could be done by telephone. Of course, it depends on both parties having a phone available. I don't know if Stephens has one in his home . . ."

"He does not," said *Agente* Maggio. "We Italians, we invent the telephone, but we do not have so many in our houses."

"Oh, really!" I interrupted. "Everyone knows the telephone was invented in America, by Alexander Graham Bell."

"Who was Scotch, if I remember right," said Mr. Clemens. "But Maggio's not just blowing smoke. There *was* an Italian—what was his name, Maggio?"

"Antonio Meucci," said Maggio, holding his chin up. "He invents the telephone before 1860, but the Americans steal it from him."

"Yes, that's the name," said my employer. "There were a couple of others who contested Bell's patent, too, maybe with good reason. So the case ain't as clear-cut as you think, Wentworth. But that's off the point. With no phone in Stephens's house for somebody to make spur-of-the-moment plans, it looks as if the thief was someone who knew Stephens was going to show the Raphael in his house."

"That's everyone at the party, and half the crowd at Diabelli's," I said. "And who knows how many others? He bragged about it enough."

"But the others he bragged to weren't at the party," said Mr. Clemens. "Or—wait a minute. Maybe they *were* at the party. Did Stephens hire any outside help, waiters or cooks or somebody, or did he just use his regular household staff?"

"I don't know," I admitted, and shot a quizzical glance at Maggio.

"He brings in some people," said Maggio. "The *capitano* had me question them—a cook's helper, two waiters, some musicians. None of them are suspects."

As he was speaking, Elsa, the German maid, stuck her head through the door and said, "*Bitte, Herr Clemens, hier kommt ein Mann Sie zu sehen.*"

"Somebody to see me? Damnation, who is it?" said my employer, pushing back his chair.

"*Kenne ihn nicht,*" said the maid, with a flounce, and she turned and left.

"I guess she don't know," said Mr. Clemens. With a shrug, he followed her. Whoever it was waited in the entry hall, just outside the dining room. So when he spoke to my employer, every word was audible from where I sat.

"*Signore* Mark Twain, I hear you search for the old master paintings," said a baritone voice with an Italian accent. My ears must have perked up like a horse's when I heard that, and I could see Maggio's eyes widen as he realized what the man had said.

"Well, it depends on what you've got," said Mr. Clemens. "I like some better than others, you know. I'm not going to hang just any old master over the fireplace."

As quietly as possible, I stood up and tiptoed over to the doorway so as to hear better. *Agente* Maggio did the same, and soon we were both leaning forward, trying our best to eavesdrop on the conversation.

"Someone tells me you want to buy a Raphael," said the man. The voice wasn't familiar, but I didn't dare stick my head out far enough to see him, on the chance I might be seen myself.

"Sure, I'm in the market for that," said Mr. Clemens. "Do you have the goods? I can talk pie in the sky anytime I want, but I'd rather talk turkey."

My employer's figure of speech must have exceeded the other man's grasp of English, for he said, "Turkey? You don't have to go to Turkey—the Raphael is here in Firenze. If you want, you can see it today."

"Well, that would suit me fine," said Mr. Clemens. "When can you bring it here?"

"No, no, is impossible," said the man—quickly, and very firmly. "You come with me, I take you where you can see it."

"Well, I reckon I can get away," drawled my employer, slowing down. "But I'll have to bring along my secretary, Cabot. He's my art expert, and I won't buy as much as a ten-cent chromo without him approving it."

Again the man said, "Is impossible," but before he could say another syllable Mr. Clemens cut him off.

"If that's impossible, then you'll have to find another buyer," he said. "I've got money to spend on the real thing, and I'm ready to move if I see something I like. But if you won't let me bring my man along, you can go whistle."

"*Signore* Mark Twain, the owner of this painting wishes to keep its location a secret," said the man. "We must go in a closed carriage, so that you cannot find the way back there by yourself. And my carriage holds no more than two."

"What, is that the whole problem?" said Mr. Clemens. "I can solve that. Your driver can take my carriage—it'll hold the three of us easy—and you can close the blinds if you're so particular about secrecy. That way, I can bring Cabot, and your seller can keep his secret. When we've seen your picture, he can bring us back home and then take your carriage home again. But I'll warn you, if he mistreats my horses, it'll cost you. So, are we in business, or are you going to think up more reasons not to take my money?"

The other speaker hesitated a moment, muttering. As I strained to hear, Maggio tapped me on the shoulder, and when I turned to look at him he was grinning. I understood; we'd been beating our heads against the wall trying to figure out who'd stolen the painting, and now they'd strolled up to our door. I nodded at him, smiling myself, and then I heard the man in the other room say to my employer, "Oh, very well. I will trust your groom to take care of my horse while we are gone, if you will trust my driver with yours. Make your carriage ready."

"Good enough," said Mr. Clemens. "Cabot," he called out loudly, "will you come out here? We're going to go look at a painting."

I counted to twenty, to make it seem as if I had come from a greater distance than I had, then went out into the entry hall. To my surprise, the man standing beside my employer was one I had seen before—in Cafe Diabelli, no less. I didn't know his name, but perhaps it would come to me. And when it did, a lot of questions would be answered.

And until then, I had to put on my best imitation of an art expert, to look at what I hoped would be the Raphael stolen from Frank Stephens's house—and possibly to confront both the thief and the man who had murdered Virginia Fleetwood.

⌐ 22

Our guide introduced himself as Lorenzo, with no surname. Lorenzo was a tall, blond, northern Italian who smoked cigarettes one after the other. He wore a suit of expensive cut and material over a brightly colored shirt, and his expression seemed constantly on the verge of breaking into an outright leer. Too many things about him hit a false note; I didn't relish going off with him to view a stolen painting—the theft of which had been the occasion of a murder. For all we knew, Lorenzo himself was the murderer.

I tried to catch my employer's eye, hoping to speak to him in private to warn him. But Mr. Clemens ignored my efforts to pull him aside. Instead, he let Lorenzo talk, which the fellow seemed perfectly willing to do, babbling on about his connections to various people of importance, most of whose names meant nothing to me. No doubt Mr. Clemens hoped Lorenzo would let slip some clue by which we could trace him, but he said nothing I could make use of. Nor could I remember where in Diabelli's I had seen him— he was not a chess player, nor one of Stephens's associates. Could he be among Volponi's hangers-on? I didn't think so—he would undoubtedly have dropped Volponi's name, if he could claim any connection.

I tried to break away and speak to *Agente* Maggio; possibly he could follow us surreptitiously and discover our destination. But Maggio kept out of view, no doubt worried that Lorenzo would recognize him; and when I finally made some excuse to leave the entry hall for a moment, I could not find him. Perhaps he had already made plans to follow us without my prompting.

After a little while, the groom sent word that the carriage was ready, and we went out to the courtyard to go on our mysterious errand. I climbed up next to my employer, while Lorenzo gave his driver a few instructions in rapid Italian, which I couldn't follow. Then he settled into the seat across from us, and pulled the curtains shut. He lit a cigarette and said, "Now, *signori*, be comfortable—it will not be a long drive. I am sorry you cannot view the scenery, but it is a gray day after all."

"Yes, it is," said Mr. Clemens. He rubbed his chin and said, "I assume we're going to the artists' quarter, near Piazza Donatello." The jouncing of the carriage's springs made it clear that we had moved out of the courtyard onto the road.

"That could be, *signore*," said Lorenzo, grimacing behind the hand holding his cigarette. "But where we go is not important—your purpose is to see the painting. Does it matter whether it is at Piazza Donatello, or in Sicily, as long as you like it and can take it home with you?"

"It better not be in Sicily," said my employer, with a frown. "I've already gone off on one snipe hunt that kept me overnight. Livy won't forgive me another quite so soon."

"Ah, the *signoras*," said Lorenzo, leering more than usual. Then his face turned more serious, and he said, "I am a free man, and I would not change that. A man needs to make his own decisions, without someone to tell him always he is wrong or foolish. My sister Angela—don't mistake me, I love her like a sister—but she makes her poor man almost a prisoner. I could not live like that, I tell you."

"I didn't think I could, either, until I met the right woman," said Mr. Clemens, shrugging. "When you do, you find out you can give up a lot of so-called freedom if you get something that's worth more. Considering what I was doing with my freedom, it was a pretty easy trade."

Met the right woman. The phrase jerked my thoughts back to the topic I couldn't escape: Virginia Fleetwood. For a while, I had thought she *was* the right woman for me—had even considered giving up my work with Mr. Clemens to share my life with her. Despite our falling-out after I rejected Stephens's offer to become part of his business, I thought we still might have found some way to make a common enterprise of our lives. Now that was impossible . . .

Between the dim light inside the carriage, and the rhythmic motion of the wheels, I found myself in a sort of reverie, preoccupied with what might have been, and how I might have prevented Virginia's death. And so, while I was vaguely aware of the conversation between my employer and our guide, I was caught by surprise when the carriage door opened and I realized we had stopped. "Come on, Wentworth, we're here," said my employer. "Let's go see if this painting's what it's cracked up to be."

I alighted from the carriage, and had just enough time to notice my surroundings—a cobble-paved courtyard enclosed by an ancient-looking wall of brownish stone, over which the top of a pine tree loomed against the gray sky—before Lorenzo hustled us through a battered wooden door. Inside, the smell of tomatoes and olive oil greeted us as we went quickly through a kitchen where an ample-bosomed woman with gray hair done up in a bun stirred the contents of a black iron pot. She ignored us.

Lorenzo led us through a short, dimly illuminated corridor lined with cupboard doors, past a wider door through which I saw a dining room with a pair of large oil portraits hanging over the mantelpiece on the wall opposite: a young man and a woman in modern dress. One of the portraits caught my eye as we swept past. If the subject was who it seemed to be at first glance, I now knew where Lorenzo had brought us. But before I could stop to examine the painting, Lorenzo turned and said, "Come quick, *signore*."

We followed him to a small dark room where the curtains were pulled. After a moment's fumbling, he lit the gas, and I saw that we were in a storage room, with a number of unframed canvases in vertical slots in a kind of open cabinet—I had seen a similar arrangement at Battista's shop. *An art dealer's or collector's home, then*, I thought. That was no surprise, considering what our business here was.

Mr. Clemens took in the room at a glance, nodded, and said, "Where's the Raphael?"

"Ah, I like a customer who comes to the point," said Lorenzo. He stepped over to an easel in the center of the room. "Here!" he said, and pulled away the cloth covering it.

I gasped. There was the portrait of a beautiful blonde with laughing eyes, in the costume of a late-Renaissance contessa. The frame was missing, but I had no doubt this was the very painting that had disappeared from Frank Stephens's home.

"Not bad," said Mr. Clemens. "I like that face, and those colors. Take a look at it, Wentworth—tell me if you think it's the real thing."

"It is the real thing, have no doubt," said Lorenzo, smirking, as I stepped forward to examine the painting. Of course, my expertise was largely imaginary. I knew something of art, from visits to museums in America and on this first trip to Europe, but that left a great deal for me still to learn. Presumably if I had taken the job with Stephens, he would have trained me in the fine points of connoisseurship, but for now I was left to my own resources. I stared at the brushwork, not quite certain how to evaluate it.

"It looks genuine enough," I said, turning to Lorenzo. "I could judge better in natural light." I pointed at the gas fixture, then at the curtained window. Of course, I had never seen the painting in any other kind of light, so opening the curtains would tell me nothing about it, but the question seemed reasonable. Besides, I thought a glimpse of the neighbors' houses (or whatever lay outside the window) might provide some clue to our whereabouts.

"I am afraid we cannot grant that request," said Lorenzo, with a peremptory gesture. He turned to my employer. "*Signore* Mark Twain, when you went to Piazza Donatello inquiring about a Raphael for sale, you were thinking about this very painting, no? Perhaps you can understand why my principal is not so anxious for people to know that he has it to sell—especially not the meddling neighbors, who are curious about everything and do not know how to keep their mouths shut. But now you have seen the painting. Are you buying it or not?"

"You haven't told me the price yet," said my employer. He leaned forward and looked again at the painting. "It looks pretty good, I'll admit. But I don't claim to know a lot about painting; that's Cabot's job. I just know what I like. Maybe I can afford to like this one, and maybe I can't."

"An authentic Raphael is not for sale every day," said Lorenzo, rubbing his hands together and grimacing. "If you wish it, there will be no bargaining. My principal will not part with this for less than two hundred thousand lira."

My employer frowned, then turned to me. "What's that in dollars, Wentworth?"

I did a quick mental calculation. "Forty thousand dollars, sir." Even that figure was astronomical, as far as I was concerned. If forty thousand dollars was the going price for an old master, perhaps I had made a mistake in turning down Frank Stephens's job offer.

"That's an awful lot of money for something to put up on the wall," said Mr. Clemens, peering at the canvas. "I'd be better off buying a few hundred good chromos and papering the walls with 'em."

Lorenzo pulled himself up straight. "*Signore*, I must remind you: My principal will hear no bargaining over the price. If you are not interested in this painting, there is no shortage of serious collectors in Firenze."

"I'm not arguing over the price so much as trying to

determine the quality of the goods," said Mr. Clemens. "You swear up and down it's the real thing, but you bring us here in a closed carriage, and you won't let Wentworth have a look at it in honest daylight. What conclusion am I supposed to draw from that?"

"Draw what conclusions you will," said Lorenzo, picking up the cloth cover he had removed from the painting. He began to drape it over the canvas and turned to look at us, saying, "If you are not going to buy, I do not think we need to waste any more of our time today."

"Not so fast, I haven't ruled anything out," said Mr. Clemens, stepping forward and raising his hands. "But I'm not used to pulling forty thousand bucks out of my hat. Can you give me a couple of days to get my hands on the money?"

Lorenzo stopped with the cover partway over the canvas and looked at Mr. Clemens. "I cannot promise the painting will still be available by then," he said. "My principal has no reason to prefer your money to anyone else's. He is quite firm about getting his price, and as quickly as possible. If someone else offers the full price . . ."

"What if I could give him a down payment?" said Mr. Clemens, interrupting. "I can raise ten thousand bucks by tonight, and bring you the rest by Saturday."

"*Signore* Twain, we don't do business that way," said Lorenzo, with a patronizing chuckle. "We have something you want—not so? If you want it badly enough, then you will meet our terms. If you do not like our terms, there are others who will buy it."

"Damn it, I can raise the money if you'll give me forty-eight hours," said Mr. Clemens, slamming a fist into his palm. "I may even be able to get it by tomorrow afternoon. I'm talking about American money—gold dollars, not the funny stuff they use around here. Do you want to do business or not?"

"I will convey your offer to my principal," said Lorenzo haughtily. "If it is acceptable to him, I will let you know. But do not delay, *Signore* Twain. If someone else appears with money in his hand, he will take the painting away with him. And now, if you do not mind, we will convey you and *Signore* Cabot to your home again."

Lorenzo rode back to Villa Viviani with us, no doubt to ensure that we would not attempt to peek out of the carriage windows to learn where we had been. Perhaps because my employer had not opened his pocketbook and dealt out forty thousand dollars, our guide was relatively subdued on the ride home—at least, in comparison with the ride out. Even so, he and Mr. Clemens managed to find enough subjects for conversation to keep the silences from becoming uncomfortable. For myself, I had plenty to think about.

At last, our carriage entered the courtyard at Villa Viviani again, and we sent Lorenzo and his driver on their way in his own carriage. And, despite his earlier protestations of not being able to wait for Mr. Clemens, Lorenzo promised to get back in touch the next day to see if we had managed to raise the money. And then, with a wink and a smirk, he hopped back into his carriage and drove off.

Mr. Clemens and I stood side by side, hands on hips, and watched it go. Then, before I could say anything, he turned to me and said, "So, it looks as if we've hooked our fish—how are we going to haul him in?"

"The money ought to bring him back," I said. "You aren't really going to raise forty thousand dollars, are you?"

"Not hardly," he said, wincing as if I'd suggested a visit to the dentist. "If I could get that kind of money overnight, I'd spend it on something more important than paintings of pretty Italian girls—like paying a few creditors. I hope our friend Lorenzo doesn't learn my real financial situation, or he's likely to slip the hook on us."

"Oh, I think I know where to find him," I said smugly. "Or at least, I know where to find the Raphael, assuming they don't sell it before the police get there."

"Aha, so you've been playing Sherlock," said Mr. Clemens, grinning. "Well, come on inside and let me in on your discovery. I'm about ready for a drink. See if you can find Maggio, too—maybe he can help us decide what to do next."

I followed him into the front entrance, where we quietly

closed the door and peered around. Maggio wasn't in sight, but the butler appeared—for once, at least, alert to our arrival. "Is *Agente* Maggio here?" asked Mr. Clemens.

"No, *signore*, he left right after you did," said the butler. That was good news, I thought; perhaps he had trailed us, after all. I congratulated myself that I would be able to surprise him with word that I had already learned where we had gone.

My employer shrugged. "Never a cop around when you really need them," he said. "Well, when he gets back, send him up to my office. We need his brains in this business, too."

Upstairs in the office, Mr. Clemens went over to the mantelpiece where a whisky bottle sat, and poured a couple of fingers into a glass. He handed it to me, then poured himself a similar dose. We raised our glasses, took a sip, and then he turned to me and said, "Well, Battista got his claws into that painting quicker than I thought he would. I wonder if he stole it himself, or if he's just fencing it for the real thieves?"

I was thunderstruck. "How did you know it was Battista's house we were in?" Of course, it was the same conclusion I had come to myself. It had been the little artist's portrait I had seen through the open dining-room door—a second glance on the way out had been sufficient to confirm my initial speculation as to the subject's identity.

My employer shrugged. "It wasn't too hard, if you know how to add two and two together. I calculated that it took just about as long as when we'd driven with Maggio into that part of town, which is where a lot of the art dealers live, anyway. And from the quick look we got of the back entrance, I saw we were in town, not out in the country. The house obviously belonged to a successful dealer, and that points to Battista, as well."

"Very good deduction," I said. "Still, most of that is true of any of the dealers at Piazza Donatello, not just Battista. What convinced you that it was his house we were in?"

"Oh, he was the one dealer who recognized me when I was asking about buying a Raphael, and Lorenzo *did* know my name—so it made sense he was Battista's agent. But I think what clinched it was when I saw Battista's name on a label attached to one of the paintings in that cabinet," said Mr. Clemens, with an impish grin. "I thought that was a pretty good indication. What clues did you pick up?"

It was lucky for him, right that instant, that I still had two fingers of good Scotch whisky in my glass, or I would undoubtedly have flung it at his head.

"All right, Battista has the stolen painting," I said, after I had regained my equanimity. As I had plenty of reason to know, it was difficult to stay angry with Mr. Clemens for very long. "What should our course of action be?"

Mr. Clemens smoothed his mustache, thinking. "A good question," he said. "It depends on whether or not we think he's the killer, and I don't know what to think about that."

"Of course he's the killer," I said vehemently. "The frame of that painting was found next to Virginia's body; the robbery and the killing must be connected."

Mr. Clemens shook his head. "Maybe, but that doesn't mean Battista did it, or even that he knew about it when he got the painting. He could be fencing it for somebody else, remember?"

"Nonetheless, he's an accessory to the crime," I said bitterly. Now that I knew Battista was selling the painting, I was impatient to see him brought to justice. "I don't see why we don't just tell *Agente* Maggio or *Capitano* Rosalia, and let the police do their job."

"That would be the easy thing to do, wouldn't it?" said Mr. Clemens, staring at the scotch in his glass. He was silent for a long moment, swirling the amber liquid.

Just then, there was a knock on the door, and it opened to reveal the butler. "*Signore* Wentworth, a man is here to see you."

"Who is it?" asked my employer. He looked first at the butler, then at me.

"I'm not expecting anyone," I said, rising to my feet.

"He doesn't give his name, but he says to give you this," said the butler. He handed me a small carved wooden ob-

ject; I looked at it and then held it up for Mr. Clemens to
see. It was a knight from a chess set.

"Oh-ho, that's a different story," he said, rubbing his
hands together. "Bring the man on up, and don't let anybody else see him."

A few moments later, the butler ushered in Giovanni
Garbarini, wearing a winter coat and muffler, and holding
a large floppy hat in his hand. Garbarini's eyes grew wide
as they took in the office and its large shelf full of books.
Mr. Clemens indicated a chair next to me, and the chess-
playing anarchist took a seat. "Like a drink of whisky?"
said my employer. "Or I can get you wine, if you'd rather."

"No, *grazie, Signore* Clemens," said Garbarini, unbut-
toning his coat. "I come to bring you some news, to show
we keep our side of the bargain. But I should not stay long,
with the *polizia* watching this house."

"And you want your wits about you when you leave,"
said Mr. Clemens. "Unlike the other night, if I can believe
my secretary's story about what went on. Tell me—who
set the place on fire?"

"It was not my party that did it," said Garbarini. "We
had removed all our documents, so there was nothing left
to hide. Besides, the place belongs to one of our friends.
Why would we do something to hurt him? We might need
his help again, and now he will be less willing to give it."

"Besides, you'd get damn-all help from me if you burned
up Wentworth," said Mr. Clemens, peering closely at the
man sitting opposite him.

"We were trying to escape," said Garbarini, lifting his
chin. Then he turned to look at me. "*Signore* Wentworth,
we don't know the police are to be shooting, and we don't
know they come with fire. If we know this, we wouldn't
have left you there. I am glad you were not hurt."

"I was pretty certain you didn't set the fire," I said. "For
one thing, I couldn't imagine you leaving behind your chess
set if you knew the place was going to burn down. Which
reminds me—you'll want this back." I handed him the
carved wooden knight he'd sent up as a calling card.

"Ah, *grazie*," he said, smiling. He put the chessman in

his coat pocket, then said, "Is hard to play without all the pieces. But I come to give you news. Just this morning, I and some friends are eating, and a man comes who says he knows of a Raphael painting for sale. From what he says, the one who sells the painting wants to sell it fast. I think this is the stolen painting you look for."

I said, "That's all very good, but . . ."

Mr. Clemens held up his hand and gave me a meaningful look, and I fell silent. "Yes, that's good," he said. "Do you know the seller's name, or where the painting is?"

"He didn't say the seller's name, no," said Garbarini, with a shrug. He held out a hand, palm up, and explained, "People who trade in these things, they don't like to give names. Names make it too easy for *polizia* to find them."

"I understand that," said Mr. Clemens, leaning his chin on the back of his hand. "Still, the man you talked to must have given people some way to get in touch with the seller, if they wanted to buy the painting."

"*Si*, that is what I come to tell you," said Garbarini, with a grin. "A man who wants to see the painting must go to a certain cafe near the Uffizi, and look for an artist with a paint box, who sits on the terrace outside . . ."

I sat up straight in my chair. "Wait a minute," I said. "That's Cafe Diabelli!" That reminded me that I had seen Lorenzo at the cafe, although I didn't remember him with a paint box. He didn't dress like most of the artists I had seen . . .

"Cafe Diabelli, that is what I thought when he said it," Garbarini said, nodding. "Is not wise for me to go there, with the *guardia* looking for me. But if you go there and find this person, I think you find the stolen painting—and maybe you find the man who kills the poor American *signorina*, too."

"We'll look into that," said Mr. Clemens. "This is good work, Giovanni. To tell the truth, I was worried you might not want to help us—considering that your hideout got raided just after I left."

Garbarini nodded again. "Some of the brothers thought maybe you tell the *guardia*, but Bruno and I tell them it is

not so. You wouldn't leave Wentworth to be burned up,
any more than I leave my chess game. We have plenty
enemies, we don't need to go look for more."

"I know how that feels," said Mr. Clemens. "But for
some reason, I keep making more enemies, anyhow. I
reckon I'll have a few good ones before we're done with
this business." He took a sip of his whisky, then looked up
and added, "Assuming we all live to see how it comes out,
that is."

Garbarini didn't seem to find this the least bit amusing;
and I must say, neither did I. But before either of us could
respond, there was a knock at the door. Mr. Clemens signaled to me to answer it. I opened it a crack, and saw the
butler standing there. "Excuse, *signore*," he said. "*Capitano*
Rosalia is here and wishes to see *Signore* Clemens at once.
Shall I bring him up here, or will you meet him downstairs?"

~ 23

When he heard the butler's announcement of who had come to visit, Mr. Clemens stood up. "*Capitano* Rosalia, eh?" he said, glancing in Garbarine's direction. "I reckon I'll meet him downstairs." He began moving toward the door.

Garbarini quickly said, "*Signore* Clemens, I know you are worried that the captain finds me here. But if there is some good hiding place I can hear you talk with him, I want to listen. Perhaps I will learn something."

Mr. Clemens nodded and signaled for the butler to wait. "Sure, I reckon I owe you that much," he said to Garbarini. He looked around the room, presumably for somewhere for Garbarini to eavesdrop on the police, but there was nowhere a person could easily be concealed. He frowned and said, "Damn, where can we hide you?"

"That will not be necessary, my friend," came a voice from the doorway. We all turned to see *Capitano* Rosalia standing there, both hands braced against the doorway. Behind him I could see *Agente* Maggio, and peering over their shoulders, the flustered-looking butler.

"What the hell do you think you're doing?" said Mr.

Clemens, his voice an angry bark. "Nobody invited you upstairs."

"This is not your America," said the captain of *carabinieri*, stepping into the office. "Our police are not bound by the same rules, and that is a good thing in my opinion. But *Signore* Garbarini has nothing to fear from me today. He will walk away from here as free as he came—I promise him this." He lifted up a hand as if swearing an oath.

"What?" Mr. Clemens and I said it almost in unison, while Garbarini stared at the policeman in utter disbelief.

"It is true," said *Capitano* Rosalia. "Garbarini, you may leave at this very moment if you so desire, although I think it might be to everyone's advantage if you stay for a few minutes."

"I don't understand," said Garbarini, with a suspicious frown. "What you want from me?"

"The same thing *Signore* Clemens wants," said *Capitano* Rosalia, waving his hand to indicate my employer. "Information to help us find the man who stole the painting and killed the young woman. You came here to talk about that, no?"

"If that is all you want, you are welcome to it," said Garbarini, shrugging. He repeated the story he had told us about the man with the paint box at Diabelli's.

"Ah, that is interesting, but we are one step ahead of you," said Rosalia, with a satisfied smile. "This is what I come to tell *Signore* Clemens. We have recovered the stolen painting!"

"Recovered the painting?" echoed Mr. Clemens. He stared a moment, then said, "Wonderful! Sit down and tell us all about it. Would you like something to drink?"

"I think not, today; I have many things to attend to before evening," said the captain, sliding into the chair my employer had indicated. "But it is very simple. An informant brought us word of a man offering stolen art for sale, late last night. This is our advantage over any private party, *Signore* Clemens—we have a network of sources that no single person could match. After checking that the information was reliable, we sent out a team first thing this morning and recovered the painting—although the thieves managed to escape us."

"First thing this morning?" Mr. Clemens raised his brows and cast a quick look in my direction; I shrugged. In that instant he must have decided not to tell the captain about our own discovery—for it seemed impossible that this could be the same painting we had seen. "That's very interesting," my employer continued smoothly. "What part of town did you say this was in?"

The captain raised his own brows in return. "I did not say, but since you ask, it was in the Oltrarno—not very far from where *Signore* Stephens lives. In fact, Maggio and I took the painting directly back to him so that he could verify that it was the one stolen from him."

"I see," said Mr. Clemens. "Well, it's a shame you didn't catch the thief while you were at it."

"We search for him," said *Capitano* Rosalia. "Perhaps Garbarini's information will be useful in that regard—although looking for an artist with a paint box at Diabelli's is like looking for a priest near il duomo—there will be no shortage. Still, we will send an agent to visit the place and see what he can discover."

"A good idea," said Mr. Clemens. "I reckon Stephens is glad to have his picture back, but you can bet your hat he'll be even gladder to see the murderer caught."

"Yes, one would think so," said Rosalia, wrinkling his brow. "Indeed, he did not appear quite as happy to have the painting back as I would have expected. No doubt you are right that he awaits the capture of the murderer."

"Well, he's got lots of paintings, but he only had one sister-in-law," said Mr. Clemens.

"That is correct," said the captain. "Alas, we cannot return the young lady as easily as we did the painting."

"All the more reason to put all your efforts into catching the murderer," said Mr. Clemens, standing up. "And now, Captain, unless you have other questions for me . . . ?"

"I think not," said the captain, standing in turn. "As I say, we have a busy day ahead of us. We will let you know our progress in finding the killer, and my thanks for your help so far. *Signore* Garbarini, my thanks for your help, as well. Perhaps you and I can become allies, after all." He bowed to us, and took his leave as Garbarini watched him, openmouthed.

But *Agente* Maggio did not leave. Instead, after following his superior downstairs, he came back to the office and leaned on the doorjamb, staring directly at my employer. "*Signore* Clemens, we need to talk," he said.

"I reckon *so!*" said Mr. Clemens, standing up. "Come on in and set down. I tell you, I was sitting there wondering whether you were going to pull the rug out from under me while we were talking to your captain. Why didn't you tell him what we did this morning?"

"I don't know what to tell him," said Maggio, taking the chair next to Garbarini. "He sends for me right after you go away, so I don't get to learn what you learn from Lorenzo—and since you don't tell the *capitano*, I figure you don't want him to know it, so I keep quiet. But now I think you better tell me, and I can decide what *Capitano* Rosalia needs to know."

Mr. Clemens raised his eyebrows. "I'll be damned," he said. "Well, if we're working together, we need to play straight with each other. Here's what we saw . . ." He gave a circumstantial account of our trip with Lorenzo, his offer to sell us the stolen Raphael, and our belief that these events had taken place in the home of Luigi Battista, the art dealer.

"That story is very interesting," said Maggio, rubbing his chin. He had listened in silence as Mr. Clemens spoke, his eyes following my employer as he paced across the room while telling the story. "But with my own eyes I saw the Raphael that was recovered, and I heard *Signore* Stephens say it was the one that was stolen. Now I have to say, somebody is not telling the truth, and I don't know who it is."

" 'Tain't me," said Mr. Clemens. "We saw that Raphael the night it was stolen, and Lorenzo showed us the same painting today—I'll eat my hat if it wasn't the same. But if Rosalia recovered it early this morning, it couldn't have been at Battista's place when we saw it."

My jaw dropped. "There must be more than one Raphael," I said. "That seems impossible, but . . ."

Mr. Clemens came to a halt and spun around to face us. "Not impossible if there's some dirty dealing going on," he said. "What does it mean if there *are* two Raphaels?"

"Two?" asked Garbarini. "I think it may be three!"

"Then some of them are fakes," I said. "But the original painting hasn't been stolen long enough for even Battista to paint a convincing copy, has it?"

Agente Maggio slapped his hand on the desk. "Here is what I think," he said. "The false Raphaels could have been painted before the real one was stolen."

"I don't follow you," I said. "How could that happen?"

But Mr. Clemens let out a low whistle. "Maggio's on the right track," he said. "Maybe the old count Stephens bought it from had a copy or two made before he sold it— to remember his ancestors by, maybe. Or Stephens could have asked one of his artist buddies to do a copy of it, so he'd have a record for insurance purposes."

"Yes, I seem to remember his saying something like that right after it was stolen," I said, thinking back to the morning when the theft had been discovered. "Eddie Freeman had been doing the copy, I think, and Stephens was going to show it to the police to help them identify the original."

"I see what the trick is," said Garbarini, who had been following the talk with interest. "When the true painting is stolen, the one who has the copy offers to sell it, pretending to have the original. Is very clever, and the buyer does not ask hard questions, thinking he buys the stolen goods."

"Yes, that's the kind of thing I was thinking of," said Mr. Clemens. "So, the question is, who's got the original? Is it the one Stephens got back, or the one we saw at Battista's?"

"Battista is a known forger, so his must be the counterfeit," I said. "Besides, Stephens wouldn't be fooled by a copy of a painting he owned."

"You wouldn't think so," said Mr. Clemens. "Hmm—

I'm still not sure we've got all the angles figured. How long *does* it take somebody like Battista to run off a good copy? It's more than just a couple days' work, isn't it?"

"I'd think so," I said. "I'm no painter, though. We need to ask an expert about that."

Mr. Clemens clapped his hands together so abruptly that I jumped at the noise. "That's the ticket, Wentworth! Let's invite Battista over here to tell us about fakes—and drop a broad hint just which fake it is we're talking about. We'll get our answer straight from the horse's mouth—and look him in the eye while he's giving it. I reckon I'll know whether he's telling us the truth or not."

"That's all very good," I said. "But what's to keep Battista from declining the invitation? Or from refusing to answer our questions, once we get him here?"

Mr. Clemens had an answer for that. "I reckon the way to get him here is to send somebody he can't ignore to deliver the invitation," he said. "Somebody big, with a uniform on." He looked over at *Agente* Maggio, who was sitting quietly. "How about it, Maggio—can you help us out?"

Maggio nodded. "I do it," he said slowly. "You want me to bring him back with me, or just give the message?"

But before Mr. Clemens could answer, Garbarini frowned and shook his head. "You send the *carabiniere*, Battista runs away instead of coming to see you. Is what he would do if he thinks he is caught. Better you don't talk about police until he is here and can't get away."

That sounded logical to me. "I think I should be the one to go," I said. "I'll tell him we want his expert opinion before we spend our money—I think I can play the part well enough to lure him in. He'll think we're ready to buy the painting, and try to convince us that he's selling the real thing. Once he gets here, then we can bring out *Agente* Maggio if we think it'll make him talk."

Mr. Clemens slapped his hand on his thigh, and said, "I'll be damned, you two chess players are a move ahead of me. That makes a hell of a lot more sense than my idea.

Sure, that's the way we'll do it—give him a few yards of rope, and see if he hangs himself."

Garbarini made a face. "If he is to be hanged, he will have to do it himself. We have done away with that in Italy. In that, at least, we are a civilized country."

"I've seen one hanging, of a rotten scoundrel who deserved to die if anyone ever did," said Mr. Clemens soberly. "And if I could abolish hanging forever, I would. But there are times—whoever strangled that poor girl . . ." His voice trailed off, and he shook his head grimly.

Garbarini muttered something under his breath, but raised no overt objection, so I leaped in and turned the talk back to the previous subject. "Good, I'll go deliver the invitation."

"For tonight, after dinner, let's say," said Mr. Clemens. "And *Agente* Maggio, I hope you can be here to play your part in this little show."

"I will be here," said Maggio. "The captain told me to stay, in fact, until he is certain he has captured the murderer." He turned to me with an apologetic gesture. "*Signore* Wentworth, I am afraid he still thinks you might be the one who kills her."

"As long as *you* don't think so," I said. "I promise you, I'll be the happiest man in Florence once the real murderer is discovered and punished."

"All the more reason to get cracking, then," said Mr. Clemens. "Head on over and see if you can lure Battista into our parlor. The sooner we can start asking him questions, the sooner I think we'll get to the bottom of this."

24

Giovanni Garbarini was also headed back into the city, so we walked over to the *tramvia* station together. The footpath followed the crest of a hill that gave us a fine view of Florence to the west. There were a few purple clouds around the sun, but the sky above the city had cleared up, and I thought we should have a clear day tomorrow. Perhaps it would be a bit warmer, as well—there was still a trace of winter in the air.

For a while, we trudged along and surveyed the scenery, but it seemed awkward to walk together in silence, and I said, "I hope you and Gonnella escaped from the police raid without any hurt."

"None except to have the headquarters burned down," he said. He kept his hands in his pockets; I had noticed that he had no gloves. "We can replace the things we lost. It will cost the man who owns the building much money to rebuild it, though, and to replace his printing press. That is why the *polizia* did it, of course. He is a good friend of our movement, and they want people to think it is not safe to befriend us. I hope it will not change his heart, but it cannot be easy for him."

"I don't understand your police," I said. "On the one

hand, they do something like that. But on the other, *Capitano* Rosalia comes all the way out to Settignano to tell us about finding the stolen Raphael."

"Perhaps it is a trick," said Garbarini, raising an eyebrow. "Maybe the *capitano* tells us they find the painting so he can see how we act. If so, I think we disappointed him. What makes me curious is, the *capitano* was not surprised at the news I told *him*—from which he might learn there are two Raphaels for sale in Firenze. If we can guess that, why can't he? Or does he already know it and pretend not to?"

"That is a very interesting point," I said. We had reached the *tramvia* stop by now, and I could see the cars approaching a short distance away. It was perhaps twenty minutes before the next scheduled tram, and I thought this must be the previous one, arriving late. In all my time in Italy, I had never seen a public conveyance arrive anywhere on schedule. I turned to Garbarini and said, "After I talk to Battista, perhaps I'll go to Diabelli's and see if the other fellow is there. I suppose he might have been arrested by now, though."

"If he learned that the police had seized the stolen painting, he would leave the cafe before the *carabinieri* came for him," said Garbarini. "I don't think this is a good day to be selling stolen art in Firenze."

"You're right," I said, and then the tram arrived in the station, and the half-dozen other passengers waiting for rides pushed forward to board. Garbarini and I joined them and soon we were on our way. Once aboard the noisy tram it was hard to talk, and so we said little until I left the car at Piazza Beccaria, a short walk from my destination. Then Garbarini clapped me on the shoulder and said, "We play chess again, my friend!"

"Yes," I said. "And the next time, I'm going to win." I stepped off the tram and waved to him as it pulled away. When it was gone, I walked across the tracks and followed Via Principale Eugenio north to Piazza Donatello.

•   •   •

When I entered Battista's shop I was met not by the little artist, but by an imposing woman—tall, with long hair and striking features, and dressed in a wild costume—something like what I imagined a gypsy dancer might wear. "I have come to see *Signore* Battista," I said. "Is he here today?"

"Luigi not here today," she said in a husky voice. "I am Angela—you want to buy something, I can sell you. What you want to see?"

"Actually, my business with *Signore* Battista was personal," I said. "Do you know when he will be back?"

"He goes into the city, there all day," she said. "You want to leave message, I tell him."

I had no idea whether or not this woman knew of the conspiracy to sell the stolen painting, and thus I was reluctant to relay my message through her. But I said, "Tell him that Mark Twain would appreciate a visit from him this evening, to discuss a business matter. We are most anxious to see him—here is the address." I gave her Mr. Clemens's card.

"I don't know when he gets home," she said again, taking the card and putting it on the counter. Then she put her fists on her hips and looked at me for a moment, sizing me up. After a moment, she nodded and said, "If you go looking for him, try Cafe Diabelli—maybe he still there. Is near Uffizi, on Via—"

"Ah, thank you very much," I said. "I know the place quite well. I will look for him there." And I turned and left the shop.

I found myself whistling as I walked back toward the tramway stop, to ride the rest of the way into Florence. Now I was certain I knew the answer to one question that had been puzzling us. It must be Battista himself who was at Diabelli's, hawking the counterfeit Raphael.

I wondered if Stephens would be there. After a moment's thought I decided it would be better if he weren't. At least, I wouldn't have to decide whether to tell him what Battista was doing right under his nose. I'd had my share of moral dilemmas the last few days, and I was not in the mood for still another.

Diabelli's was crowded when I entered. Volponi was reading aloud from a dog-eared manuscript, with extravagant gestures; Pietro and his minions were darting between tables, bringing food and drink to their patrons; the odors of coffee, pipe tobacco, and good food filled the air. In one corner, somebody was strumming softly on a guitar. And at the tables against the back wall, there were three chess games in progress, and a handful of spectators awaiting their turns. Just walking through the door was enough to give me a jolt of energy, as if someone had connected me to an electrical wire. Coming into the place on a brisk spring day, I remembered why I had liked Diabelli's so much when I first saw it. I had been afraid it might remind me too much of Virginia, but to my surprise I found that I was glad to be back.

I was tempted to play a game of chess, just to see if my marathon session with the cafe's two uncrowned champions had done anything to improve my game. But my mission for Mr. Clemens came first. I looked around the room for Battista—or for his clandestine agent, Lorenzo—but saw neither one. Perhaps I would find my quarry out on the terrace, where many of the artists were wont to congregate around Stephens's table. I pushed through the doors and stepped outside.

As I had expected, there was a good-sized group around the tables usually occupied by Frank Stephens, although he was not present this afternoon—no surprise, so soon after Virginia's funeral. Nor was Battista among those present, much to my disappointment. Nonetheless, there were plenty of familiar faces. Eddie Freeman and Heinrich Muller were there, engaged in animated discussion over some pencil drawings that lay on the table. Penelope Atwater and Jonathan Wilson sat side by side, drinking wine and sharing a plate of roasted peppers and anchovies. At a nearby table Sarah Woods sat tête-à-tête with a young Italian violinist she had introduced to the group—Basile was his name, if

I remembered correctly. Somewhat to my relief, Bob Danvers was also among the missing. I should be able to approach the group without encountering the overt hostility he had displayed toward me recently.

"That face just isn't right," I heard Freeman say. "There's something about the expression—nobody'd ever draw a face that impertinent-looking in the quatrocento . . ."

"You are wrong," said Muller, shaking his finger at the bigger man. "A Saint John of Fra Angelico with the identical expression I will show you in the Boboli palace. Because it is old, it does not mean it is without life . . ."

"Good afternoon," I said, stepping up to the table and addressing myself to Jonathan Wilson, who seemed to be playing the role of host in Stephens's absence. "Do you mind if I join you?"

"Certainly not," said Wilson amiably. "Good to see you, Cabot. Pull up a chair, we've got some wine—I'll have Pietro fetch you a glass."

"Thanks," I said, taking a chair from a nearby table and sitting down across from him. I was inwardly relieved that Wilson, at least, was ready to welcome me back into the group. I didn't know how many of them shared Bob Danvers' belief that I was responsible for what had happened to Virginia. "I can't stay long," I said, "but I guess I'll have a drink before I head home. It's been a busy day, and likely to stay so through the evening."

"It's been busy all around," said Wilson, leaning forward with a confidential air. "Did you hear the news?"

"What news?" I said. "I've been so tied up in Mr. Clemens's business, I've barely had time to draw a breath before now."

"The police have found that Raphael," he said, with the air of a man playing a trump card. "They took it to Stephen's place just before noon, for him to verify that it was the stolen one. I can't wait for him to come here and tell us the story."

"That's wonderful news!" I said, trying my best to appear surprised. "Did the police catch the thief?"

"I hear the fellow got away," said Wilson. "As best I understand it, they'd gotten word that it was being offered for sale by somebody down in the Oltrarno—curiously enough, not that far from where it was stolen. They broke into the place this morning, but the seller made his escape by a back door."

"A shame," I said. "Odds are the thief is the one who murdered Virginia, as well. I wish they'd caught him."

"Well, there's no way to know if this man was the thief," said Wilson. "More likely it's just a middleman, selling the painting and giving the thief a share of the price. That's the usual routine with stolen goods, I understand."

"It makes sense," I said. "Well, now that Stephens has it back, you'll have another chance to buy it."

"Perhaps," said Wilson. He took a sip of his wine, then sighed. "Until the piece is authenticated, I'm not certain I'd pay what Stephens was asking."

"Authenticated?" I asked. Without knowing it, Wilson had hit on the exact question Mr. Clemens and I had been pondering. "Why, is there some doubt about it now?"

Wilson grunted. "Enough to make me think twice about laying out the money, anyhow. The man the police say was selling it is a known forger of old masters. So there's a chance this is a copy, not the original. Although I can't see how somebody could turn out a decent copy on such short notice. At least, not one good enough to fool Frank Stephens."

"Ah, I understand your caution," I said. Just then, Pietro passed the table and Wilson signaled to him. The waiter nodded, and soon returned with a glass for me. I filled it from the bottle on the table, then said to Wilson, "Thanks for the wine. By the way, I wonder if you've seen Luigi Battista today. I was by his shop looking for him, and the woman in charge said he might be here."

"Ah, that would be Angela," said Heinrich Muller, chuckling. "I don't know what Battista sees in her—she has a temper like a mad hornet. Did she sting you, my friend?"

"No, she was moderately civil to me," I said. "But that's neither here nor there. Has Battista been here?"

"Not today," said Wilson. He took one of the roasted

peppers on his fork, lifted it halfway to his mouth, then looked at me with a curious frown and said, "If he comes in, I'll tell him you're looking for him, though. What do you want with that old forger, anyhow?"

"Mr. Clemens is thinking about investing in a painting, and he's got the same worry you do, whether it's genuine," I said. I took a sip of my wine, then twiddled the stem of the glass in my hand before continuing: "He likes to get his opinions from the horse's mouth, and since Battista is a leading, ah, *copyist* of old masters, he thought he'd ask him to examine the piece for him."

"Set a thief to catch a thief," said Penelope Atwater briskly. "It's a good theory, but you'd best be careful the thief you're setting doesn't rob you himself."

"Aye, there's the rub," said Wilson, chuckling. "Old Luigi pretends to be honest, but you need to watch him like a hawk. What sort of painting is Clemens buying, anyway? From the way he talked at Stephens's party, I didn't take him to be the sort of chap that'd be in the market for art."

"Well, there's a first time for everything," I said. I took another sip of wine—it was excellent, as usual—and went on. "In fact, it was the Raphaels at Frank Stephens's party that piqued Mr. Clemens's interest. He was rather taken by the one that was stolen, in fact."

"Well, if the Raphael turns out genuine, I hope he won't start bidding against me," said Wilson.

"Perhaps he will," I said. "I can't always predict what he'll do once he gets an idea into his head."

"That must make it . . . *amusing* to work for him," said Wilson, with another chuckle. "But he wouldn't be the first man I've gone head-to-head with for a painting I like. If he wants that Raphael, he'd best be ready to open his purse strings—I'll promise him that, no two ways about it."

Eddie Freeman leaned his elbows on the table and said, "If you fellows are so determined to spend your money on art, why don't you give it to somebody who needs it? Right here you've got an artist who can paint you anything you've a mind to see. I'll set up my easel and start right in on it, for half of what you'd pay for something from one of those rascals who's dead and in his grave three hundred years."

I laughed. "I think Mr. Clemens would agree with you," I said. "But, speaking as someone who's already on his payroll, I think he'd want you to set a more reasonable price."

"Reasonable?" Eddie scoffed. I could tell now that he'd had his share to drink; his voice was slurred and his eyes didn't seem to focus very well. "I can do anything the old masters could do—I've studied them all. Ask Frank when he gets back—I can do Botticelli, Titian, Leonardo—the only difference between my stuff and theirs is that mine is better. Why should you buy an old painting with fading colors and chipping paint when you can get a bright new one? Ninety-nine people out of a hundred couldn't see any difference between them if you stuck their noses in the wet paint."

"Well, that's a blamed good question, Eddie," said Wilson. "You've got a good eye and a good hand, from what I've seen. But it isn't the ninety-nine who set the prices; it's the one percent, and one percent of that, who insist on the real thing and can afford to pay what it's worth."

Eddie reached—somewhat unsteadily—for his wineglass, and knocked back the contents. Then he leaned forward again and pointed at Wilson. "The one percent of one percent aren't as smart as they think," he said. "Luigi Battista's been selling fakes for years." He turned to me. "Don't put too much faith in old Luigi—he'd sell his mother's eyeteeth for hard cash. He'd as soon trick you as walk across the street."

"Maybe he is a trickster," I said. I tossed back my own glass of wine and stood up. "But perhaps Mr. Clemens can keep him honest. In any case, if he comes by here, please give him my message. He's welcome at Villa Viviani this evening. And let him know that time is of the essence, will you, Wilson?"

"I'll tell him if I see him," said Wilson.

Penelope Atwater tossed her head. "If you can't find him, I'm sure you could get one of us to look at the painting," she said. "Jonathan is an excellent judge, and I fancy I've a rather good eye, if I say so myself. Or perhaps Eddie or Heinrich would be willing to do it—they're both experienced copyists, you know."

"Best not ask Wilson," said Muller. "If he thinks it's real, he'll tell you it is false and snatch it for himself!" Everyone laughed, although Wilson's face turned red and his laughter seemed forced.

"Thank you for the suggestion," I said. "I'll pass it on to Mr. Clemens—but I think he's already made up his mind to use Battista."

"If you let Battista in the house, watch out he doesn't steal the silver," jeered Eddie Freeman. There was another round of laughter, but I was on my way out, and saw nothing to be gained in responding to Freeman's gibes.

Back at Villa Viviani, I reported my apparent lack of success to Mr. Clemens. He nodded and said, "Well, we didn't give him much notice. Maybe he'll get the message, and if he does, maybe he'll come. Or maybe not—these Italians don't worship punctuality the way we Yankees do. It must be the hot weather—people are the same way down South, back in America. All we can do is wait and see if he shows up, I guess."

I stood looking out the window at the courtyard—empty, this time of day. "Yes, I suppose there's always the chance he had a previous engagement, too. We can't expect everyone to drop all their appointments just because we want to see them."

Mr. Clemens grimaced. "Hell, that's true even in America. For me, it's truer now than it used to be, since I lost my money. I used to think people were interested in me for myself—for my talk, for my ideas, for my accomplishments. But when I didn't have the money to set a fancy table with seven courses and the best champagne, a lot of my friends—not all of them, mind you, but some I expected better of—discovered previous engagements when I asked them over! It's a mighty humbling experience, Wentworth.

Lord, how it'll open a man's eyes. Carnegie and Rockefeller ought to try it."

"Perhaps you should write them a letter proposing the experiment," I said. I drummed my fingers on the windowpane, then turned to look at him. "You're beginning to sound like an anarchist yourself, you know?" I said. "Have you been working on that article you promised them?"

"Pretty near finished it," he said, leaning back in his chair and stretching. "I don't expect they'll like everything I say, but I didn't promise them that. They'll like most of it, and they ought to have known beforehand what kind of horse they were buying."

"I suspect that as long as the byline reads 'Mark Twain,' and it isn't an outright attack on them, they'll consider it an asset," I said. "They can't have won many respectable supporters."

"Oh, they have their share," said Mr. Clemens. "There's a ready market for almost any kind of political nonsense, if you wrap it up pretty enough. I hear tell old Leo Tolstoy has been promoting some mighty strange ideas lately, for example. And he's more or less sensible, compared to some of his countrymen. But that's no more than you'd expect, given the government they've got to live under."

"I suppose so," I said. I sat down on the broad windowsill and continued. "The more I see of other countries, the gladder I am to be an American."

"We don't do everything right, but we do have a few important things figured out," he agreed. Then he threw a glance toward the clock over the mantelpiece, and said, "But it's almost time for supper. Let's go join Livy and the girls."

At the dinner table, all the Clemens daughters wanted to talk about was the discovery of the painting—and the puzzling appearance of a second copy of it. Little Jean could barely contain herself when she learned that we had invited Battista to visit us. "Is he the murderer?" she demanded, nearly jumping out of her chair. "Can we see him when he comes?"

"Certainly not!" said Mrs. Clemens. "Besides, the man might not even come tonight."

"That's right," said my employer, helping himself to a warm roll. "But I don't see any reason not to let the girls see Battista when he comes, Livy. If I act as if I trust him—bring him to meet the family and do all the normal things I'd do for somebody visiting my home—then he's likely to talk more openly when we do get down to business. I doubt we're in any danger from him."

Mrs. Clemens's face turned hard and she shook her head to signify her opposition. "Miss Fleetwood was perhaps twenty-five—not very much older than Susy is. And there is a very good possibility that Mr. Battista was the one who murdered Miss Fleetwood. Or have you abandoned that theory, Youth?"

Mr. Clemens picked up his wineglass and leaned back in his chair. "If you'd seen Battista, you might have your doubts about him being the murderer. He's a little banty rooster of a fellow. He'd have a tough job overpowering a healthy young woman, in my opinion. Of course it's not impossible—but it's not the way I'd see him murdering somebody. With a dagger, maybe, or with a pistol . . ."

"What a subject for dinner conversation!" said Mrs. Clemens, throwing up her hands. "We never had suspected murderers coming to the house in Hartford, or in Elmira, I'm glad to say."

My employer got an impish grin. "Now, Livy, I shouldn't have to remind you that Wentworth here has been a suspected murderer at least twice since I've met him, and he comes from one of the best families in New England. Why, he's even been arrested twice. Watch what you say, or you'll hurt his feelings."

All three Clemens girls began to giggle, and I opened my mouth to protest—it hardly mattered what I said, since I knew Mr. Clemens would take it as pretext for another impertinent remark. I knew, by now, not to take his gibes seriously—they meant that he considered me one of his inner circle, and therefore a proper subject for wit. But before I could object to having two false arrests held against me, the door burst open and in came *Agente* Maggio. He was breathing heavily, as if he'd been running, but his face was white as a sheet.

"*Signora* Clemens, I ask your pardon for interruption," he said. "*Signori*, come with me—I have very bad news."

Mr. Clemens stood up at once, exclaiming, "What the devil? Excuse us, Livy, but we'd better see what this policeman wants." His wife nodded her assent—obviously distressed at the interruption—and I arose to follow them.

As we hurried out the dining room door, I heard little Jean's voice behind us saying, "Can I come?" and her mother's sharp hiss of admonition. Then we were in the hallway, and Mr. Clemens stopped and said, "All right, Maggio, what's the trouble?"

"Very bad trouble," said Maggio. "Luigi Battista is outside, not far from here. He is dead."

"Dead!" Mr. Clemens and I said the world practically in unison. Then Mr. Clemens asked, "How?"

The *carabiniere*'s face was distraught. "*Signore* Clemens, the body looks to me as if he was strangled."

"Strangled," I said in a half whisper, and Maggio nodded. The murderer had come to our own neighborhood, obviously with the purpose of silencing Battista.

"Well, let's get a light, and go see what we can do," said Mr. Clemens, and he pointed toward the door.

"*Si*," said Maggio, and they strode together toward the front door of the villa. Almost as if I were sleepwalking, I followed them out into the chilly evening air.

25 ⌒

Luigi Battista's body lay in a pool of shadows just off the footpath, within a hundred yards of the front door of Villa Viviani. Standing over the body holding a lantern, I saw no sign of blood nor wounds, but it was clear that Battista's death had not been peaceful. The bulging eyes and protruding tongue were ample proof of that. Maggio knelt beside the body, and began to go through the dead man's pockets.

"Should you disturb the body before it's been looked at by the police?" I asked, remembering the care with which Scotland Yard's detectives had examined the room where a man had been murdered, a few months ago during our stay in England.

Maggio paused in his search and looked up. "I am the police," he reminded me. "This man has been dead only a short while. I want to find any clues quickly. Maybe then we catch the one who killed him before he kills again."

"Kills again?" said Mr. Clemens. "I reckon he already has killed again—the same person who strangled that Fleetwood girl did this, didn't he?"

"Is a good bet," said Maggio, looking up solemnly. Returning his attention to the corpse, he emptied the pockets methodically. He found a handful of coins, a small folding knife, a box of matches, a crooked Italian cheroot—and in the right coat pocket, a rectangle of cardboard. I knew even before he held it up to me what it would be. In the lantern's beam I could see Mr. Clemens's printed name. It was the card I had left with the woman at his shop. I took it and handed it to my employer.

"If we didn't already know it, there's the proof he was coming to see me," said my employer. He looked at me, then at Maggio, and asked, "Anybody who doesn't think he was killed to keep him from talking to us?"

"In any case, it was no robbery," said Maggio, holding up the coins he had taken from the pocket. The lantern light picked up the gleam of gold.

"Not necessarily. The killer could have heard you coming and skipped off before he had a chance to go through the pockets," said Mr. Clemens.

"That is possible," admitted Maggio, "but it is not the way most bandits work. Easier to get money by showing a pistol or a knife than to kill a man with your bare hands."

"Granted," said Mr. Clemens. He stood turning the card over and over in his hands, as if to see whether there was anything written on it besides his name and address. Then he stopped and looked at Maggio. His frown was visible even in the dim light from the lantern. "How did you happen to find the body, so soon after he was killed? Did you see or hear anything?"

Maggio stood and looked down at Mr. Clemens. "I know what you mean," he said—rather calmly, I thought, considering that Mr. Clemens had just implied that Maggio might have done more than merely discover the body. "Here is what happened. As you know, I go home to change clothes and eat with my wife. I come back on the *tramvia*, just a little while ago, and many passengers get off here. It already starts to be dark, so I can't see other people in the crowd. But one woman, she falls down getting off the car, and I stop to help her. Her husband is right there, but her ankle is twisted, and I help him get her to their house, a little ways off—so it takes me ten, maybe fifteen minutes before I start up the road to your place."

"Very convenient," said Mr. Clemens. "I suppose this man and his wife will remember you?"

"He will, yes," said *Agente* Maggio, still calm. "They live not far from the *tramvia* stop. He is a barber, very well known in this neighborhood. Enrico Russo is his name."

"OK, I suppose we can check up on the story if we need to," said Mr. Clemens. "What happened next?"

Maggio shrugged. "I come up the hill toward your place, and as I come around that corner"—he pointed back down the hill—"I hear a noise to the side. I can just see some man run away, and somebody lying here. I shout to tell the man to stop, but he keeps running. I stop to look if I can help this one, but I can see he is dead—and I recognize who it is. By then, the other man is gone—I search for a minute, but don't find him. Then I come up to the villa, and the rest you know."

"Yes, I guess I do," said Mr. Clemens. He shook his head. "I just wish Battista had lived long enough for me to ask him a few questions about that damned painting. He might have given us the key to the whole damned case. But now we'll never know."

Agente Maggio cocked an eyebrow. For a long moment he said nothing. Then he said, "I am sure that Luigi Battista would also wish he had lived long enough for you to ask him a few questions—and perhaps even longer."

Satisfied that he could learn no more from his examination of Battista's body, *Agente* Maggio asked me to help him carry it up to Villa Viviani. Mr. Clemens carried the lantern, and without too much effort, Maggio and I lifted the little artist's lifeless body by the shoulders and legs and took it up to the courtyard.

At first we were going to take the body in the house, but Mr. Clemens demurred. "Livy and the girls don't need to see this lying on the sofa," he said. Maggio and I agreed, so instead we took it into the gardener's toolshed, and placed it on the floor. Then, after bolting the door to the shed, Mr. Clemens and I went inside the house while *Agente* Maggio went back down the hill to send word to his headquarters.

Mrs. Clemens met us at the entrance. "What is wrong, Youth?" she asked, an anxious look on her face.

"Luigi Battista has been murdered," he said. "He was on his way to see me—his card was in my pocket. It looks as if he was killed to keep him from talking to us." He stated the facts bluntly; this was no time for joking.

"That is terrible," said Mrs. Clemens. Then, cocking her head to one side, she said, "I'll keep the girls in the parlor, so you can discuss this without their interruptions."

"Let's go to my office," said Mr. Clemens, looking at me. Then he turned to his wife and said, "It'll be a little while before Maggio gets back, and you can send him there when he does."

Upstairs, Mr. Clemens poured us both a bumper of whisky to steady our nerves, then looked at me and said, "All right, who knew Battista might be coming here?"

I took a drink—it burned my throat, but it might help me get a grip on myself after moving the body. "A lot of people," I said, after a moment's thought. "That woman at his shop—the card in his pocket was the one I'd given her. Maggio. Garbarini. The people at Stephens's table in Diabelli's—Wilson, Mrs. Atwater, Freeman, Muller, Miss Woods . . . anybody they talked to after I left . . ." The list was depressingly long. I began to wish I hadn't told quite so many people at the cafe about my employer wanting to see Battista.

"I don't think we need to worry about Miss Woods or Penelope Atwater," said Mr. Clemens, standing behind his desk. "And probably not the woman at Battista's shop, either. When a woman kills someone, it's almost never by choking them to death."

"Can we eliminate Maggio, too?" I asked.

Mr. Clemens paced a few steps before answering. "His story about the woman falling will probably hold up, but he might still have helped her home, then caught up with Battista and killed him. It seems odd that he was on the same tram as the victim and didn't know it. Hmm—if somebody else killed Battista, odds are he was on the same tram, too."

"Not necessarily," I pointed out. "Someone might have come out here as soon as they learned we wanted to talk to Battista, and waited for him."

"True," said Mr. Clemens. He took another sip of his whisky, then sighed. "Let's step back a bit. Whoever it was, they had to have some reason for killing him. If we can figure that out, maybe we can figure out the rest."

"He was killed to keep him from telling us something," I said. "That seems obvious. If we can discover what that was, it should tell us the murderer's identity."

"Well, we were going to ask about the stolen painting—and that other copy of it," said Mr. Clemens, sitting on the edge of his desk. "That painting must be behind the killing—behind both killings, if we can just figure out the connection."

"That seems logical," I said. I stared into space for a moment, trying to think, then continued: "The timing of Virginia's death suggests that she witnessed the theft of the painting from Stephens's."

"That makes sense," said Mr. Clemens. "But how did the thief get her to go with him out to that graveyard? Did she accompany him under duress or voluntarily?"

That seemed obvious to me. "Voluntarily, of course—he had no weapon, so he couldn't have frightened her into silence."

Mr. Clemens slammed his fist into his other palm. "Then the killer was somebody she knew and trusted," he said. Then he frowned. "That doesn't narrow the field much—most of the men at Stephens's party fit that description, wouldn't you say?"

"Yes, I suppose so," I said dejectedly. "That's the problem here—we have too many suspects, none of whom seem to have any more motive than the others."

"Well, let's try this angle," said Mr. Clemens. He stood up and began to pace, picking his way between the piles of books on the office floor. "Let's assume that both killings were meant to cover up some kind of monkey business with

he painting. Who do you think stands to gain the most
rom that?"

"That's hard to say," I said. "Mr. Stephens loses the most
rom the painting's being stolen, and I guess the thief gains
he most."

"Hmmm . . ." Mr. Clemens rubbed his chin. "If I take
money out of my pants pocket and put it in my jacket
pocket, am I ahead or behind?"

"Excuse me?" I said. "I don't follow you."

My employer returned to his desk and picked up his
glass. It was empty, and he gave it an annoyed stare before
continuing. "It don't matter," he said. "I've got an idea how
things might have happened. But I need to verify a couple
of hunches before I can connect all the loose ends. That
means talking to a couple of people who might have a stake
in making the truth known. I want you to go get one of
them, and Maggio, when he gets back, may be able to find
he other one for me."

"Certainly," I said. "Who are these mysterious witnesses?"

Mr. Clemens picked up the whisky decanter and refilled
his glass. "One's the woman in Battista's shop—she may
be the last person who talked to him before he was killed."
He sipped his drink, then went on. "I want you to go get
her. You may have some trouble convincing her to come
with you, but if you show her my card again, maybe it'll
work. One thing—unless she already knows, don't tell her
Battista's dead."

"I'd best go now, in that case," I said, standing up. "Even
now, I may have missed her. Odds are she won't be at the
shop this late."

"Go to Battista's home," said Mr. Clemens. "They'll
know where to send for her."

As it turned out, there was no need to send for the
woman—Angela, I remembered her name was. It was she
who answered the door at Battista's home. "*Signora* Angela?" I asked.

"*Si*," she said, not opening the door far enough to let me

inside, had I wanted to enter. "You come looking for Luigi again? I give him your message already. He tells me he is going to see *Signore* Mark Twain." I could almost see her thinking, *Did he lie to me and go somewhere else?* I decided right then that she knew nothing of what had happened to Battista.

"He came there, yes," I said, more or less accurately. I took out one of Mr. Clemens's cards and showed it to her. "But now we need to talk to you, too. Can you come to *Signore* Twain's house with me?"

"What you need to see me for?" she asked, peering suspiciously at me—and at the carriage I had come in. "Why don't Luigi come for me? Is he in trouble?"

"Oh, no," I said—somewhat less accurately than before, but perhaps still not an outright lie. "He's at Mr. Twain's house, and he can't leave just now. I work for Mr. Twain, and he asked me to come bring you."

Angela stared hard at me, then nodded. "You don't try to trick me, or you don't like what happens to you," she said, in a tone that left no doubt that she meant every syllable—or that she was capable of backing up the unspecified threat. "I come with you. You wait here—I get ready, then we go." She shut the door and left me standing outside. I stood there long enough to begin worrying whether she might have left the house by the back entrance—but after an interval she appeared, wearing a huge shawl over her elaborately dressed hair. I helped her into the carriage, then took the seat opposite her, and the driver gee'd up his horses.

We rode in silence out to Settignano, and I was just as happy; if I had any further conversation with her, I was likely to reveal something of the circumstances she would find at the end of our journey, or to make it clear that I was hiding something important from her. It was apparent that Angela's attachment to Battista was more than just as an employee. I did not want to be the one from whom she heard the news of his death.

•   •   •

I ushered Angela through the front door of Villa Viviani, only to find *Capitano* Rosalia sitting in the parlor. He was not in a good mood—especially when he saw the lady I was escorting. But he bowed to us, and spoke briefly to her in Italian. Then he turned to my employer and said, "*Signore* Clemens, I have asked this lady to wait while we talk. Can we go to your office?"

"Sure," said Mr. Clemens. "Wentworth, have the butler bring the lady some refreshments while she waits."

"A stiff drink of brandy would be appropriate," said the captain, and he turned and stalked off in the direction of the office. Mr. Clemens looked at me with a raised eyebrow, and I nodded and rang for the butler. After telling him to bring Angela her choice of refreshment, I hurried upstairs to join the captain and my employer.

There, I found the captain in the midst of delivering a full-scale scolding. "*Signore* Clemens," he said, shaking his outstretched finger no more than two inches in front of my employer's nose, "I am the policeman here, not you. It is not for you to call and question witnesses in an important crime. It is not for you to send my officers all over the city on your personal business."

Mr. Clemens was not about to be intimidated. He puffed up his chest and said, "I know the difference between my personal business and my public obligations, Captain. Unlike a lot of people, I take the latter pretty seriously. I asked *Agente* Maggio to bring back a witness who may help us solve these two murders once and for all. It's a good thing you're here—you'll have a chance to hear him firsthand, instead of waiting for a report from Maggio."

Rosalia leaned forward, putting his face closer to my employer's. "We should be interrogating this witness in the police station, not in a private home."

"With a bunch of overfed bruisers on hand to make sure he cooperates?" Mr. Clemens scoffed. He opened a drawer of his desk and brought out one of his pipes. He looked into the bowl, as if checking whether it needed cleaning, then looked up at Rosalia and said, "The man hasn't done anything to deserve that. I was worried that sending a cop to fetch him would scare him—but I had to send Wentworth to fetch that woman, so Maggio was all I had left."

"That woman." *Capitano* Rosalia stood up straight and put his hand over his eyes. "One of us is going to have to tell *that woman* that Battista is dead. She is not going to take that news at all well. It would have been much better to tell her such bad news in her own home." He looked behind him, as if to make sure she had not crept upstairs to listen, then turned to me and asked, in a soft voice, "Did you happen to notice whether or not she is carrying a knife?"

"Why, no," I said. "It never occurred to me . . ."

"You Americans!" said the captain. "I suppose it never occurred to you that she might become violent at the news her man has been murdered. Are your women so tame?"

Mr. Clemens answered before I could open my mouth. I suspect he saved me from expressing myself more bluntly than is wise when speaking to a police officer. "Look here, Rosalia, we could insult each other all day long, and it'd get us no place either of us want to be. I asked this woman to come here because she might be the last person who talked to Battista before he was killed. So it's a good thing you're here—you'll be able to talk to her while the details are still sharp in her mind. And I'll have a chance to talk to her, too—I reckon I'm doing as much to solve this case as you are. Did you know Battista was peddling a copy of that stolen Raphael?"

"What?" Captain Rosalia's mouth fell open. Then his eyes narrowed, and he said, "Why didn't you tell me so when you learned of it? It is a crime to conceal evidence from the police, you know."

"Is that so?" Mr. Clemens raised his eyebrows. "I've just told you about it, so where's the crime? Besides, we've got bigger fish to fry. Do you want to catch whoever killed Battista—who, I suspect, is the same person who killed that Miss Fleetwood?"

"Of course I do," said Rosalia, leaning over the desk. "Do you know who it is? I demand that you tell me at once."

"I can't tell you something I don't know," said Mr. Clemens, staring the looming *carabinieri* captain directly in the eye. "But I can help you find out, if you'll listen to my suggestions instead of demanding things nobody's got to give you. Can we do business in a civil manner, or not?"

Rosalia straightened up and looked down at my employer. "And what is your price for doing business with me? The lion's share of credit for solving a crime? Making the police look like fools and amateurs?"

"Hell no," said Mr. Clemens, so sharply that the captain fell back a pace. "I don't give a rat's ass for the credit. I just want to see that everybody responsible for the death of that girl—and of Battista, too—gets his full punishment. If you'd gone right to work and caught the killer the day after the murder, I'd have applauded and gone back to work. But you were more interested in using it as an excuse to go after the anarchists, until you realized that horse wouldn't pull the plow. If you hadn't wasted time on that pack of nonsense, Battista might still be alive."

Capitano Rosalia snorted. "If you want to blame someone for Battista's death, *Signore* Clemens, I suggest you look closer to home. If you hadn't stuck your nose into a delicate police investigation—"

My employer flung his pipe down on the desk. "Why, you—"

I could see that Mr. Clemens was ready to work himself up to a volcanic outburst, and I realized that was my cue to step forward. I raised my hands and said, "Gentlemen, aren't we forgetting our purpose here? While you argue, there's a murderer running loose. And unless you've forgotten, there's a woman waiting downstairs—no doubt getting more worried by the minute. We need to tell her of Battista's fate, and to learn what she knows about the circumstances that led to his death. Are we going to snipe at each other, or shall we pull together to catch the monster who's snuffed out two lives?"

I found myself with both men looking at me in amazement. After a long moment in which I began to worry that I had overstepped myself, they both began to nod. At last,

Mr. Clemens broke the silence. "Jesus, Wentworth, you've got more sense than either of us. Captain, my apologies—let's put this squabbling behind us and get down to our business."

Capitano Rosalia bowed. "*Signore* Clemens, I agree. And *Signore* Cabot, I thank you for reminding us of our duty. Let us go fulfill it without further distractions."

They strode out the doorway side by side, leaving me standing openmouthed. After a moment, I followed them downstairs.

❦ 26

It seemed strange to be returning—yet again—to Cafe Diabelli. But everything had begun here, and so in a sense it was the logical place to end it. After pausing in the main room to place our witnesses for later retrieval, Mr. Clemens and I strode through the doors to the terrace. There sat Frank Stephens with his coterie of hangers-on, with a couple of bottles of wine open on the table and laughter in the air.

It had occurred to me as we were riding in from Villa Viviani that we might arrive to find half our suspects missing, perhaps even out of town—after all, the police raid that had netted the stolen Raphael must by now be common knowledge. The parties to the conspiracy might already have taken flight. Then there would be no way to spring the trap. But luck was with us—or perhaps the conspirators were so arrogant that they thought, even now, that they could escape the consequences.

Frank Stephens was the first to notice us. "Clemens!" he said, waving and beckoning. "What a pleasure to see you here! Come on over, join us—have a glass of wine." I noticed that he did not include me in the invitation.

Mr. Clemens and I stepped forward. "I appreciate the offer," my employer said, "but I reckon I'll pass on the wine so you can't claim I've abused your hospitality. You aren't going to be so pleased to see me after you learn what I'm here for."

"What the devil are you talking about?" asked Stephens, still smiling. He picked up the bottle and a glass. "Come on—it isn't everyone who gets the chance to buy a drink for Mark Twain, and I don't mean to let it get past me."

Mr. Clemens strode over toward the table, stopping far enough back so he could take in the entire crowd in a glance. "I'm not here to cadge a drink from you. I'm here to expose a murderer—the man who killed Virginia Fleetwood. So put down the bottle, Stephens. I wouldn't want you to drop it and spill all that wine after you hear what I'm about to say."

"Clemens, this is in poor taste," said Stephens, turning red and rising to his feet. "I'm surprised you'd think it amusing to suggest that I or one of my friends murdered my wife's sister. No wonder your career has gone bust."

Mr. Clemens waved a hand. "Sit down, Stephens, I haven't accused you yet—although I'm pretty sure you bear a share of responsibility for Virginia Fleetwood's death. I don't know what the law will do, but your friends have a right to know the story—the ones that weren't in on the plot, that is."

"Plot?" Penelope Atwater lifted an elegant eyebrow. "Your imagination has come a long way since *Tom Sawyer*, but it's not any more mature."

"I'll consider that a compliment," said Mr. Clemens. "But I want to finish my business and be gone—it leaves a bad taste in my mouth to bandy words with killers and thieves. What put me on the right track was figuring out that you stole that missing Raphael yourself—and why you did it."

"Be serious, man," said Jonathan Wilson exasperatedly. "The theft was reported to the police instantly. The whole art world knows of it by now—there are telegraphs, you know. The thieves would have the devil's time getting rid of it."

Stephens laughed. "Yes, are you sure you don't work for the insurance people, Clemens? That's the kind of nonsense I'd expect from them. Why, before I got the Raphael back, they were hinting that they wouldn't cover my loss because I didn't have it properly guarded. What should I have done, had a squad of Pinkerton men search my dinner guests?"

There were snickers from several of those at the table. But my employer shrugged and said, "My sympathies would be with you, there—if you weren't trying to run a fraud."

"That's twice you've accused me of that," said Stephens, his face darkening. He put both hands on the table and leaned forward. "See here, I've been dealing in art, here in Florence and back in the States, for fifteen years, and there's not a man alive who'll say he got the worst of a deal with me."

"He's right, Clemens," said Jonathan Wilson. "Frank's reputation is rock-solid; there are hundreds of collectors who'll vouch for him. If all there is to this business is your word against his, you're not going to make any headway."

"Point taken, Wilson," said Mr. Clemens. "As long as it's just my word against Stephens's, I might as well go home and write my books. But in fact, I do have backing for what I say. Wentworth, would you like to bring in the lady?"

"The lady? What nonsense is this, now?" Penelope Atwater raised her head and peered around like some watchful bird, but I was already on my way to fulfill Mr. Clemens's instruction.

I found Angela where we had left her, at a table in the front room of Diabelli's, drinking a glass of red wine. She looked up as I approached, and I said, "We're ready for you, *signora*."

She drained her glass and stood. "Good," she said. "I wait long enough for this." I made a motion to indicate that she should lead the way, and together we went out to the terrace.

Penelope Atwater was staring at us intently as we entered. As she saw the woman I was escorting, her nostrils contracted and she tossed her head and exclaimed, "Really! Have you taken to consulting Gypsies, Mr. Clemens?"

Angela said something in Italian, a single staccato word I didn't understand. But Penelope Atwater did. She turned crimson, opened her mouth to say something, and evidently thought better of it. She lifted her chin as if raising it above a rising tide, and proceeded to act as if Angela were invisible.

Mr. Clemens raised an eyebrow, but upon seeing Mrs. Atwater's response, he decided to let the unspoken remain unspoken. Instead he said, "Allow me to introduce Angela Battista; some of you know her, I believe."

"Oh, yes, I know her," said Eddie Freeman. "Luigi Battista's wife, isn't she? Or perhaps not the wife—I don't know if they were ever married."

"Are you a priest, that it is your business?" snapped Angela, her eyes flashing. I thought she was about to say more, but Mr. Clemens put his hand on her elbow and she turned to look at him instead.

"Don't let him bother you," he said quietly. "If you start trading insults with this crowd, you'll never get to the end of it. Just tell them what you told me last night, and that'll be enough."

"I will tell what I saw, and what I know," said Angela. She turned to face the group at the table. "Luigi, he is dead, and I come here to pay back the one who kills him."

There was general surprise at this revelation—the news of Battista's death had not been made public before this. Of course, one person here knew it—the one who had killed him. Mr. Clemens held up his hands and said, "Hold on, you'll find out everything soon enough. Now, let the lady tell her story. Miss Angela—you were saying?"

Angela put her hands on her hips and looked at her audience. "So," she said. "It was how long ago?—three, four months, back before the winter comes. Luigi tells me a man asks him to paint a Raphael. Not a copy, but a new Raphael."

"Paint a new Raphael?" Sarah Woods laughed. "Impossible! The imposture would be obvious to any trained eye."

"I wish it were so simple," said Jonathan Wilson, with a sigh. "I have told you this before, dear Sarah. Poor Raphael would have had to do nothing but paint, every day of his life, to produce even half the paintings he is credited with nowadays. There are three men I know of in Florence who can paint a Raphael good enough to deceive all but the most experienced eye."

"And Luigi was finest of them all," said Angela, with obvious pride.

"Yes, he was," said Wilson, nodding gravely. "I fear the world lost a very talented artist when he decided that forgery paid better than honest work."

"I know Battista's work," said Stephens matter-of-factly. "Everyone in the city knows it. I employed him on several occasions myself."

"Yes, so I understand," said Mr. Clemens.

"I know what you're getting at, and I deny it," said Stephens. He shook his forefinger in the air. "It's standard practice to make copies of masterworks, so if the original is lost, we can still get a hint of the artist's vision. Not to mention the training in technique that students get by doing the work. It's been done since painting was invented."

"You leave out the main reason it's always been done," said Mr. Clemens. "To make bushels of money, by selling the copy to some gullible buyer—and that's what you were going to do here, once word got out that the original was stolen."

"I deny that," said Stephens, glowering. "Yes, Battista could have produced a convincing Raphael pastiche, although I doubt he could have fooled anyone with my experience. His real forte was Botticelli, who's easier to fake. There's more to it than the layman supposes. Besides, you can't link me to this alleged forgery—*Signora* Angela, I was sorry to hear that Luigi had died. But do me the favor of answering one question: Did he ever say I was the man who asked him to paint this Raphael?"

"*Ciao, Signore* Stephens," the woman said, bowing her

head slightly. "No, Luigi did not tell me who asked him to paint the Raphael. He did not even say whether the man was *inglese* or Italian."

Jonathan Wilson fanned himself with his hat, although the season was not yet warm—except perhaps by British standards. He looked at Mr. Clemens and said, "There's a hole in your argument, old man. And here's another. Only a fool would buy a painting at that price without knowing its provenance and authenticity," he said. "That's the first rule of collecting: Be sure of what you're getting, because the market is full of counterfeits."

"Except the rules change when you think you're buying a stolen painting," said my employer. "Any reputable expert will turn you in if he sees the piece is stolen. And any expert who doesn't care where the piece came from is corruptible—and therefore untrustworthy. So you can't really be sure of what you're getting. That's what you were banking on, Stephens."

"That's pure fiction, Clemens," said Stephens, with a smirk. "Not bad, but then, that's your stock in trade, isn't it? Don't try to sell *Capitano* Rosalia that story, though; he has a level head on his shoulders."

Mr. Clemens nodded. "Mostly he does, when he's not following politicians' orders. Once we convinced him that the radicals didn't steal the painting—a silly theory, but his bosses were peddling it, so he had to take it at face value—he looked at what had really happened that night. You'd told everybody that the painting was missing, but the only thing that had left the house was the frame it had been in. You had it dropped off in the cemetery to convince everybody the painting had gone with it. You hadn't counted on your sister-in-law catching your accomplice in the act—and certainly not on his luring her out to the cemetery with him."

Stephens picked up his glass and took a swig of Chianti before answering. "My accomplice?" he said, the smirk back on his lips. "Who is this accomplice, and why would I be going through all this hugger-mugger, to begin with?"

"I've already answered that last question," said Mr.

Clemens. "For piles of money. The point of the swindle is that you can sell three or four copies of the same painting—maybe even more. Since the customers think they're buying stolen goods, they won't compare notes. And since you sell all the copies through middlemen, nobody can pin it on you if they ever do realize they've been swindled."

"You have an answer for everything," said Stephens, still with a sneer on his lips. "Remind me again: Who was this accomplice of mine? Battista? Even Angela says she didn't hear Luigi mention my name."

"A very weak point in your argument," said Mrs. Atwater, who had recovered her composure. "How do you know it wasn't some other Raphael he was hired to forge—assuming that woman didn't concoct the entire scheme out of whole cloth?"

"Battista was killed to keep him from talking to me," said Mr. Clemens. "That's a pretty good sign that there was substance to his allegations."

"You keep dodging the issue," said Stephens, waving his glass, which was now empty. "Even if this ridiculous plot is real, you haven't shown that I'm connected with it. What's your evidence, Clemens? What's your evidence? Not even an Italian court will convict a man on no evidence."

Mr. Clemens leaned his chin on his closed fist. "For a start, the police are holding two copies of that Raphael—make that at least two, they might have found some more by now—that were being offered for sale, both touted as the original. And that's not counting the one they returned to you. You're the only one who had the chance to get copies made."

"What do you mean?" said Stephens indignantly. "I barely had the painting two weeks before my party. Not even Battista could turn out a finished copy that fast, let alone two."

"You've missed a wrinkle, Clemens," said Jonathan Wilson, his eyes gleaming. "I'll wager that old *don* out in the hills ordered up those counterfeit Raphaels, from Battista or whomever else—and he had all the time in the world to get them made. Ten guineas says he took the best one and sold it to Stephens, then arranged to have it stolen back so he could sell all the copies as originals. I think Frank's a victim of this hoax, not the perpetrator."

"On the face of it, that's plausible," said Mr. Clemens. "But Rosalia's going to have his experts evaluate that so-called original again. If it's a fake—and I'll bet *you* ten guineas it is—Stephens's whole story falls apart. Odds are he knew it was a fake all along."

"That painting is genuine," said Stephens, with considerable vehemence. But his face was pale.

"Maybe it is," said Mr. Clemens, shaking a finger. "But Angela says Battista had a whole stable of artists to turn out counterfeits for him. The stuff that wasn't up to scratch, he sold in that shop of his—honestly labeled as fakes. But the best work was near impossible to tell from the originals, and a lot of it got sold as if it were."

"I'd credit that," said Wilson. "Why, I've seen old masters in museums that I'm morally certain came out of his studio. Work good enough to fool even you, Frank."

"So Rosalia tells me," said Mr. Clemens. "What do you want to bet that the work Battista considered too good to sell as pastiches or copies ended up in Stephens's hands—sold as original old masters?"

"I have never in my life sold a fake," roared Stephens, his face now red. "Anyone who claims otherwise is a liar, and I'll tell him so to his face."

Bob Danvers lurched to his feet. I could tell that he'd taken on a fair amount of drink—pretty much his usual condition any time after luncheon. "Damn it, Clemens, Frank's taken good care of me while I've been over here. I won't sit here and listen to a washed-up clown slang him. You back down from what you say, or I'll shut you up."

"Show him, Bob," said Eddie Freeman, reaching up to push his friend forward. He had a crooked grin on his face. I stared at him with disgust; any real friend would have done his best to calm Danvers down instead of inciting him.

Danvers slouched forward, a menacing expression on his

face. "I'll shut you up," he repeated, his reddened eyes fixed on my employer.

"Danvers, I'd stop right there if I were you," I said, moving forward to interpose myself between him and Mr. Clemens. I didn't want to fight him again; I was sick of fighting. On the other hand, I wasn't about to let him attack my employer.

To my relief, Stephens put his hand on Danvers' shoulder. "Come on, Bob," he said in a quiet voice. "I appreciate your sticking up for me, but fighting Clemens isn't going to help. Come on, old fellow, let it go."

"Oh, hell, I suppose you're right," said Danvers. Then he turned to Mr. Clemens. "You watch what you say, though, mister. I'm a reasonable fellow, but I won't hear any more against Frank. You hear me?"

"If you don't want to hear it, put your fingers in your ears," said my employer. "I'm here to tell you all: Frank Stephens may not have killed that girl himself, but her death is the direct result of what he did do: offer handfuls of money to a starving artist. It's no surprise if a fellow who's been living on beans goes a little crazy when he sees real money—and when he's threatened with losing it all."

Stephens drew himself erect. "This is ridiculous," he said. "I don't know what you're referring to."

Mr. Clemens sighed. "Too bad. I thought you'd want to salvage some dignity instead of letting me expose you in front of all your friends. All right, this is how I figure it happened.

"After dinner, but before most people had left the party, your confederate left the room on some excuse, took the painting off the wall and went down to your study to take it out of the frame. But Virginia Fleetwood was still in the library, where she'd been talking to Cabot. She saw your confederate go by, carrying the painting. That aroused her curiosity. She followed him and watched him remove it from the frame, and then she asked him what he was doing."

"Nonsense," said Stephens. He'd sat back down and was fidgeting with his wineglass. "There was a house full of people there to notice the painting was gone. Why would he do it then?"

"That didn't make sense until I realized what you were doing," said my employer. He pointed the pipe stem at Stephens and said, "The reason for having it disappear while there were people still there was to have witnesses to the so-called theft. Everybody saw it before dinner, now it's gone—it must have been stolen! And you've got a dozen people ready to blab about the theft, to get the word out to those collectors who'd consider buying something they knew was stolen. That way there'd be a ready market when the crooked dealers came around offering a Raphael for sale."

"What a wonderful scheme!" said Stephens, his voice oozing sarcasm. "It's a shame to have to point out that, even if the plot had taken place, it could all have been done without my knowledge. Who was this confederate Virginia saw taking the painting? I suppose you're going to tell us that he was the one who strangled her—and Luigi Battista, as well."

"Yes, there's the real question," said Penelope Atwater. "Who is the mysterious killer?"

"Not so mysterious," said Mr. Clemens. "In fact he's sitting here right now. Right there!" He pointed and every head turned to look.

Every head except one, that is. That person scratched his head and said, "I thought you'd gone off the tracks before, but this is just plain crazy. I've got the same question Frank's been asking. Where's your evidence?"

"Waiting in the other room," said Mr. Clemens. He turned to me. "Wentworth, I reckon it's time to bring in the clincher."

"Clincher? What do you mean?" asked Frank Stephens, but I was already on my way out of the room.

$\approx$ 27

When I returned to the terrace, every eye turned to look at me. To most of them, the stout little man I was escorting would have been a total stranger. But to one of them, his face was quite well known. "Why, that's Emilio, my driver!" said Jonathan Wilson.

"*Ciao, Signore* Wilson," said Emilio. He shot a crooked grin at his employer; then, perhaps remembering for what serious purpose he had been summoned, his face turned grave again.

"What is this fellow supposed to know about art?" said Wilson, puzzlement plain on his face. "I doubt he could tell a Raphael from an El Greco—the fellow can barely read and write."

"Emilio didn't come to talk about the painting," said Mr. Clemens. "I wouldn't give a rap about it myself, if that poor girl hadn't been murdered on account of it. That's what Emilio is here to tell us about—the murder."

"You don't mean to tell us that he witnessed it," said Stephens. He was toying with his empty glass, looking as if he wanted it refilled; but the bottle was empty, and there was no waiter in sight. "If he did, why has he waited so long to come forward?"

"Let's just let the fellow tell his story," said Mr. Clemens. "You'll get your chance to pick holes in it when he's done." He turned to the driver and said, "Emilio, can you tell us what you did last Saturday night?"

"*Si, signore*," said the driver, his eyes gleaming. "I drive *Signore* Wilson to the banquet of *Signore* Ste-*fans*, at his house in the Oltrarno."

"What did you do after you left Wilson at the banquet?"

"Is a place not far away where all the *cocchieri* gather, to talk and smoke, drink the *vino*, maybe play the cards," said Emilio. "I go there to wait."

"Did you know the other drivers who were there that night?" Mr. Clemens asked.

"No, is not the part of town I go to before," said Emilio. "I come to Firenze from Fiesole just a little while ago, get good job with *Signore* Wilson."

"That's right," said Wilson. "Emilio's been with me less than a month. My old driver, Mario, quit me right after the start of the year. It took me a good while to replace him."

Mr. Clemens nodded. "Did you stay with the other drivers all night?" he asked, turning to Emilio again.

Emilio shrugged, spreading his hands apart. "I stay most of the night, but I don't know nobody, and I don't got money to play cards. So late at night, a message come that somebody wants a ride from *Signore* Ste-*fan*'s place out to Piazza Donatello. I think that isn't so far—I can go there and be back before *Signore* Wilson needs me. I already know when he goes to visit friends, he stays very late— always the last to leave. So I decide to take the person who wants a ride. Is extra money, *capisce*?"

"Yes, of course," said Mr. Clemens. "And who was the person who needed the ride?"

"Was two people," said Emilio. "An English *signore* and *signorina* . . ."

"English or American?" asked Penelope Atwater sharply. "It's important that we know exactly."

"Who can tell?" The driver's expression was pure bafflement. "The *signorina* speaks the good Italian, but the man, he speaks only the English. He gives me the orders, and if I don't understand right away, he talks louder."

"Well, sometimes it works," said Mr. Clemens, undoubt-edly aware of his own inadequacies with that language. "But tell me—do you see either the man or the woman here?"

Emilio looked around the group, then said, "I don't see the *signorina*. But that is the man, sitting right there." And he pointed straight at Eddie Freeman.

"That's a damned lie," said Eddie Freeman. "I mean, he must be mistaken. Why would I be going out to that part of town at midnight, anyhow?"

Mr. Clemens walked over to Freeman and stood next to him. He leaned down to look him in the eyes and said, "You were leaving a picture frame—the frame you'd taken off the Raphael forgery—in the graveyard to make us think it had been stolen and fenced to one of the art dealers at Piazza Donatello. Of course you didn't go out there with the actual painting in that weather—you couldn't risk dam-aging it, since Stephens needed it to fetch the same price as a real Raphael."

"That's absurd," said Freeman. "If I was doing what you say, why would I haul Ginny along to be a witness? What even makes you think it was her that was with me? It could have been anyone from the party."

Mr. Clemens spread out the fingers of his left hand and began to touch them with his right index finger, as if count-ing. "It couldn't have been my wife, because she'd come home with me. It couldn't have been Mrs. Stephens, be-cause she stayed home with her husband. It couldn't have been Penelope Atwater or Sarah Woods, because they're sitting right here and Emilio didn't identify them as the woman who went with you. Besides, they had their own driver. The only other English or American woman at the party was Virginia Fleetwood."

Freeman's jaw worked for a moment, then he repeated, "The driver's lying, then. I've already told you I didn't go out there that night. I don't even know anybody in that part of town."

"If he says that, he lies," said Angela, who'd been staring

more and more intently at Eddie Freeman ever since the driver pointed him out. "I see him plenty in Luigi's shop, bringing paintings to sell. Luigi helps him—tells him where to get old canvas, gives him special paint that makes a painting look old—new paints, they look too bright. Luigi hires many painters who can copy old things, and this man is one of them."

"You were making copies of that phony Raphael, weren't you?" Mr. Clemens put his finger under Freeman's nose and raised his voice. "When Virginia Fleetwood caught you taking the painting out of its frame, you were afraid she was going to expose your scheme. You'd lose all the money you expected to get for painting fakes, and you were desperate for the money. So you lied to her, maybe told her you were playing some kind of prank on Stephens, and lured her out to that graveyard. Then you sent the driver away and killed her to keep her from talking. When you heard Wentworth say that I was going to consult Battista about forgeries, you killed him, too—because his word could put you behind bars. You're the murderer, Eddie Freeman."

"That's another lie!" shouted Bob Danvers, leaping to his feet. I'd been watching for this, and I quickly stepped forward to intercept him. His face was distorted with rage, and I had no doubt that he meant to harm my employer.

Help came from an unexpected quarter. "Sit down, Mr. Danvers," snapped Penelope Atwater. "You really are becoming tiresome. I'm afraid Mr. Clemens is tiresome, as well, but I'm beginning to wonder if he might not have truth on his side." Openmouthed, Danvers took a step back, then shook his head and slumped back into his seat. Relieved, I turned my attention back to Mr. Clemens.

"I do have truth on my side, ma'am," said my employer, bowing to her. "I don't accuse people of murder without some good evidence to back up what I say."

"Your allegations are disturbing," said Mrs. Atwater, lifting her chin to look at him. "I am not yet convinced that Mr. Freeman is a murderer, although you have given us rather damning evidence of his part in the art fraud—which

I think may be as you say it is. But it is a long step from there to cold-blooded murder."

"Yes, it is," said my employer. "But it's a short step from copying old masters to selling the copies as originals. And another short one to pretending to steal one and then selling five or six copies of *it*. Every step is short, but one step leads to another—until you've got so much at stake, the next step doesn't seem so terrible. But it's still murder."

"I didn't do it, Clemens," said Eddie Freeman, holding up his hands as if to protect himself. "I didn't do a single one of the things you're talking about."

"You're forgetting the proof, Eddie," said Mr. Clemens. "It looks pretty bad for you—you've got the motive, you had the opportunity, and the method is no stretch of the imagination—you must outweigh both the victims by fifty pounds or more. Poor Battista never had a chance once you got your hands around his neck . . ."

What Eddie Freeman would have answered to this, we never found out. For Angela, who had been following the exchange with a deepening frown, suddenly cried out, "You! You murder Luigi! I kill you!"

Big as he was—I suspect any football coach in America would have been glad to have him show up at practice— Eddie was not prepared to have a large, fierce-looking Italian woman scream at him, then lunge at him with mayhem in her eyes and her hands held out to grab him. He stood up and backed away from her, but the terrace wall was in his way. At that precise moment, Angela snatched up a knife from the table. "I kill you!" she screamed again.

That was too much for Freeman. He turned and leapt over the wall and began to run away.

Mr. Clemens shouted, "Get him, Wentworth!" but I was already in pursuit. I dodged around Bob Danvers, who stood openmouthed by his chair, to vault over the wall like a hurdler. Half a dozen running strides and I was breathing down Freeman's neck. He must have heard my footsteps, for he turned his head to look back, and I saw his face, a mask of sheer panic. That glance backward was his undoing; his foot landed wrong on a cobble, and he fell heavily.

I pounced on him like a cat, with my knee across his chest, to make sure he didn't get up. From behind I heard another scream from Angela. That must have unnerved him at last. "Don't let her kill me," he babbled. "I didn't have any choice—I would have gone to the gallows if Luigi talked. I didn't have any choice."

I put my hand on his throat, and leaned closer. "They don't hang murderers in Italy," I growled. "But if they did, by God, I'd spring the trap myself."

"That's enough, Wentworth," I heard Mr. Clemens say behind me. There were others standing around me, too—I was vaguely aware that some of them were in police uniform, as they gathered around the fallen fugitive.

But I was only interested in the face in front of me. "You don't deserve to live, Freeman," I said again, my fist poised over his face.

"He didn't give me any choice," he whined again. Then a hand fell on my shoulder and someone pulled me away from him. It is just as well—I have no idea what I might have done.

"**F**reeman has confessed, and Stephens has begun to admit to his part of things," said *Capitano* Rosalia. "It was a much bigger plan than what we first saw." The captain and *Agente* Maggio were sitting with us in my employer's office, with coffee, brandy, and sweet cakes. Rosalia had granted us this final meeting to let us know the outcome of the murder case my employer had done so much to solve. Now Freeman and Stephens, Heinrich Muller, Lorenzo—who was Angela's brother, as he had told us—and two or three others I knew only as names, were in police custody. Bob Danvers, surprisingly, was still free. Stephens had considered him too unreliable to include in the plot. The arrested men would be charged with fraud and as accessories to the two murders Freeman had committed.

"I think Battista would have confessed, if he'd lived to talk to us," said Mr. Clemens. "After the girl died, I think he began to have second thoughts."

"Yes, Luigi Battista is a sad lesson," said the captain, nodding. He stirred a lump of sugar into his coffee, sipped it, then continued: "He had the talent and the inspiration to be a fine painter, in my opinion—his original work, it is good. I have seen it. Yet nobody buys original art by an Italian who has the bad taste not to be dead for two or three hundred years. And so, to make some money, Luigi began to paint the false old masters, selling them honestly as copies in his shop."

"They looked pretty good to me, though I admit I'm no expert," said Mr. Clemens. "But you say, when he started getting really good at copying, he stopped being so honest."

The captain nodded vigorously. "Yes, there were many paintings he sold through intermediaries, as genuine old masters, for much money. Still not quite enough for him, though. If it had been enough, he might not have entered into Stephens's plot."

"Is always the mistake to become too greedy," said *Agente* Maggio, leaning forward. "We see it always from the criminals—it is why we catch so many."

"I am glad they did not get to the next part of their plan," said *Capitano* Rosalia. He made a motion as if counting on his fingers. "First they would make three or four very good copies of a masterpiece in a museum. Then they would steal the piece from the museum and sell the copies—and the buyers would ask no questions, thinking they were getting the stolen originals. If we had not found two identical 'stolen' Raphaels—and then more—they might have made a great deal of money."

"I think they would have gotten away with it, too," I said. "Except that Eddie Freeman was so nervous about the plan being exposed that he was ready to murder to keep it a secret." I still found it hard to think of him without becoming angry.

"Yes, he was the weak link in the chain," said Rosalia. "Stephens was paying him only a tiny amount until they could sell the paintings, and he was heavily in debt. So he was dependent on the scheme succeeding. So when *Signorina* Fleetwood discovered him as he was removing the false Raphael from its frame, he thought all his work would be for nothing."

"And as a consequence, he threw three lives away," said Mr. Clemens, shaking his head. He took a puff on his pipe and continued: "Better that he'd let the plot fail, done his stint in prison, and had the chance to go on to a career in art. Now he's likely never to see anything but the inside of a dark cell."

"What penalty will Stephens pay?" I asked. "As the architect of the scheme, he ought to bear the main responsibility for Eddie's murders."

"It will depend on whether the judges hold him responsible for the death of the young woman," said *Capitano* Rosalia. "It is plain to me that she and Battista would still be alive except for his plot—but a judge may not agree with me. I think it will count against him when he is judged for his other crimes, perhaps not heavily enough, but he will not soon be a free man, either."

"That'll have to do," said Mr. Clemens. "That, plus the weight of guilt for what he did—which ought to torture him the rest of his days. Beyond that, it's out of our hands."

Maggio nodded soberly. "Yes, it is out of our hands."

I thought of the lively young woman whose remains now rested in a cemetery thousands of miles from her native land, years before she should have died—Virginia, a woman I had been ready to consider for my life's companion. I remembered walking about Florence with her, excitedly pointing out the sights to one another, chattering and laughing—sometimes about nothing at all except our own enjoyment. She was gone forever, and I would be hard-pressed ever to see her like that again.

A man had died, too—someone I had not known as well, one who had not been entirely without fault, but who among us is without fault? He left behind his mourners, as well.

At that moment, I thought there was no punishment great enough for Frank Stephens, who had set in motion the train of events that left these two people dead. But Mr. Clemens and *Agente* Maggio were right. It was out of our hands, and no power on earth could bring back the dead.

I sighed. "We must rely on the justice of another world, then," I said. "What the law can do here is but a fraction of what these murderers deserve."

"God forbid that any of us get what we deserve," said Mr. Clemens. I supposed there was some point to that, but for the moment I did not appreciate it. It would be a long time before I was ready to see past what I had lost.

I sipped my coffee and stared out the window, into the cold, bright sunshine of a city that, to my injured senses, felt like nothing more than a lovely, inhumanly perfect tomb.